Concrete

By

Conrad Jones

PROLOGUE

San Francisco

The drive across the golden gate bridge to the giant redwoods at Muir Woods had been exhilarating. He slowed the motor home to a crawl to glance across the bay at Alcatraz Island. Across the bay, the pepper pot shape of Coit Tower looked like a chess piece from that distance. The bay wind buffeted the side of the RV threatening to blow it across into the next lane of oncoming traffic. Below the bridge, thick clouds of mist rolled in on the breeze making it impossible to see the water below.

It had been easy to blend in with the other visitors to the city. Hunting them had been simple. Immensely exciting but simple. The tenderloin area of the city, on nob hill, thus known because it was where the dark underbelly of life was situated, was a predator's paradise. It was saturated with prostitution, porn, and pills. Finding and trapping his prey was easy. The hunt for his victims was over. He had his prizes and now he relished the thought of their pain.

It had been a long time since he had enjoyed the look of terror in a captive's eyes. He yearned for the tears that flowed freely down their cheeks, the sobbing, the pleading, the coppery smell of their blood. Their fear drove him to a state of excited insanity.

His journey through the woods took a little over two hours. The sun was sinking and the shadows beneath the tree canopy deepened. He'd parked in a secluded area away from the most popular tourist sites and lowered the blinds in the driver's cab. As he stepped into the living area of the huge camper, he could sense their fear. The smell of their bodies drifted to him, sweat, perfume and despair. Few would ever know that despair had an odour, but he had been so close to human agony so many times, that its smell was like an old friend.

He walked to the table near the sleeping area and listened to their breathing. Short shallow gasps, in and out, in and out. He smiled as he ran his fingers over his tools. The feel of the cool metal and the glint of steel in the lantern light heightened his ecstasy and increased their despair. Sweet despair. The faces of his victims drifted through his mind, fear and pleading in their eyes. They were always more distressed when they watched him working on the other victim. Always. It didn't matter what nationality they were; American or English, Dutch or German, French, or Spanish, male or female, young or old, their reaction to watching another suffering was always the same. He made them watch the other suffer and bleed, thrash and tremble beneath the agony of his implements. It reduced them to quivering mutes.

It was the realisation that their time under the tools was close that distressed them most. Knowing that their turn was just minutes away and that it was totally inevitable was too much for some of them. Many lost consciousness as their brains shut down to escape the madness before them. Of course, he would wake them, and they would suffer the same horrors that they'd witnessed happening to the other victim and then he would allow them to rest and recover for a while. Sometimes he had to tend to their wounds to keep them alive longer. They would live until he was ready.

He closed his eyes and listened to their muffled sobbing. They had seen his tools and their imaginations would be running wild. The anticipation of the pain that would come would cause them more mental distress than the blades ever could. They couldn't close their eyes or turn their heads away as he worked on the other. He made sure of that. They had to watch. That was the integral point of the game. The anticipation of their suffering was all that mattered to him now. Beautiful pain. Human emotion at its most intense.

When he was done with them and their life force was extinguished, he would take the long road back across the bridge and out through Bakersfield. He would continue for a few hundred miles or so and then head east into the Mojave Desert. There he could stop each night and dispose of the bodies a little at a time, spreading the evidence widely across the desolate sun parched soil where the animals and insects would complete their disposal. Then he would take his twisted memories and head through San Bernardino leaving the RV in Los Angeles before flying home.

His fingertips touched the serrated edge of a small bone saw and lingered there. A smile crept across his lips. He picked it up and then studied the women. If they could have closed their eyes, they would have. Tears trickled from the corners of their eyes leaving trails of black mascara on their cheeks. He watched their chests rise and fall, their bodies racked by sobs. Sheer horror was etched on their faces. 'now, my darlings, whose turn is it to go first this time?'

CHAPTER 1

Jayne Windsor frowned as she watched her friend making a fool of herself again. Every time they went out together it was the same routine and each time Jayne would swear that she wouldn't go out with her again. The problem was that she didn't have many friends, in fact she had one. Despite all her promises to herself, whenever Jackie called and suggested going dancing, she folded and agreed. If she didn't go out with Jackie, then she wouldn't go out at all. Her work colleagues had shunned her ever since the Barton kid went missing. She felt sorry for his family, but it wasn't her fault. She had had no choice. Her workmates hadn't had much time for her before the kid vanished but afterwards, she was virtually a pariah. They blamed her. They weren't allowed to say anything but then they didn't have to. She could hear the whispers, sense the disgust, feel the hate that was aimed at her.

Jackie was the only true friend that she had. Sad but true. Despite what had happened, they'd remained friends. They had been through a lot together but every time they went out, she knew what would happen before it happened. Jayne would drive because she didn't like the way alcohol made her feel and Jackie would be smashed before she got into the car. Within an hour of being in the club, she would have her tongue down the throat of whoever would buy her a cocktail and Jayne would be left fending off the advances of the losers that no one else wanted to talk to.

As she watched Jackie gyrating about on the dance floor, the fact that the evening had gone exactly as she had predicted came as no surprise. Tonight's selection of drunks desperately trying to pull had been particularly cringeworthy. She had batted away a succession of dribbling idiots, some of them so inebriated that they circled the dance floor continuously, pint pot in hand only to return ten minutes later for a second attempt. Then a third and fourth and so on. If she had had a gun, there would be at least three dead bodies already.

The club was a dive. She had to be careful that her shoes didn't stick to the carpet. The smell of stale ale permeated the air and she knew that her clothes would stink the next day despite not touching a drop of alcohol herself. The only upsides to the dump were the music and that it was close to the car park. Jayne liked the DJ and she wanted to dance but not with any of the idiots who were loitering around the dance floor. It was like a cattle market. Drunken men stood around the periphery of the dance floor watching the women dance, sizing them up, stalking them, looking for the intoxicated ones who would be easier prey to drag home to their lairs. Jayne hated the whole seedy charade. A leery smile, a few vodka cocktails, a greasy kebab in the taxi, casual sex, and the embarrassing walk of shame home in the morning. She couldn't understand why some women did it, regretted it and then looked forward to repeating the entire process again the next week. It wasn't her thing. She wanted a bit more from an evening out. She wanted a bit more from life full stop.

'Your friend seems to be having a good time,' a deep voice said from behind her. Jayne sighed and turned to look at the speaker, ready to rebuff his approach with a suitably cutting remark but when she looked at him, her breath stuck in her throat. 'There's nothing worse than watching your friend getting off with someone while you're left alone with an empty glass is there?'

'No.' Jayne smiled. She felt her pulse quicken. 'Nothing worse,' she stammered. The power of intelligent speech had deserted her.

'I can fix that very easily.'

'Pardon?' Jayne asked confused.

'The empty glass,' he pointed to her hand.

'Sorry. I don't understand?' she asked feeling very silly.

'I can fix the empty glass problem.' He laughed. 'I can have it refilled quite quickly.'

'Oh!' She blushed. 'I see. I'm sorry but I didn't realise what you meant.'

'No need to apologise.' He smiled. 'Can I buy you a drink?'

'No thanks,' Jayne said. She habitually refused drinks from strangers although she had never found it quite as difficult before as she did this time. 'I'm driving,' she added as an excuse. 'I'm only on diet Coke anyway but thanks.' He looked slightly offended. The smile disappeared from his face for a moment, but it was still in his eyes. Maybe she hadn't put him off completely. It had been months since anyone half as good looking as him had approached her. On second thoughts it was years. If she blew him out, she would kick herself for months.

'I'm going to have one anyway,' he said holding up his empty glass. The smile returned. 'I'm designated driver tonight too so I'm sipping diet Coke while my friend is dancing like my dad.' He pointed to the dance floor where Jackie was attached to a man's face. 'Well, when I say 'dancing' I mean that in the loosest sense of the word.' They laughed and Jayne felt him touch her arm. She felt electricity run through her. 'Your friend looks like she's sucking the air from his lungs!'

'Oh don't,' Jayne grimaced. 'She's so embarrassing.'

'So is he.' He shrugged and held up his glass. 'Sure, I can't tempt you?'

'Go on then.' She smiled coyly.

'It doesn't mean we have to get married or anything.' He smiled as he turned to walk towards the bar. His eyes held hers for a moment.

'You wouldn't have to drag me to the church,' Jayne muttered under her breath as she watched him walk away. She felt her knees going weak and her skin tingling. He was the type of man she could sleep with and introduce to her mother. The two things rarely went hand in hand. No doubt about it.

She turned back to the dance floor to watch Jackie gyrating around her latest catch. The term 'twerking' popped into her head for some reason. She wasn't sure why. Jackie was more likely to knock over a table of drinks by shaking her arse than she was to sweep a guy off his feet. She had a pretty face and plenty of cleavage but if she ever asked Jayne, 'does my bum look big in this' then the honest answer would be, 'yes, it looks massive,' so she was never honest. Sometimes lying was the best option, especially where Jackie was concerned. Not that she felt bad about lying to her, Jackie was the biggest liar to walk the planet. This time, her lies had dug them both into a deep hole. One she wasn't sure that they would get out of.

A lone male dressed in skinny jeans and a striped shirt spotted her looking at the dance floor. His quaffed hair would have been okay on the lead singer of a boy band, but he was ten years too old and ten kilos too heavy. Jayne had several categories for men and she instantly placed this one in the 'knobhead' group. A sickly grin crossed his lips as he staggered towards her. Jayne held up her hand like a traffic warden stopping an approaching vehicle. It didn't deter him.

'Do you want to dance?'

'No.'

'Can I buy you a drink?'

'No.'

'I suppose a bonk is out of the question?'

'Get lost!'

'I was joking!'

'Go away.'

'Come on. You look bored on your own there,' he slurred. 'Have a little dance with me.'

'You can hardly speak never mind dance. Go away.'

'Don't worry about me, darling,' he slurred again, 'beer has never affected my performance.' He winked but the drink made it look more like he had a bad twitch.

'Go away.'

'Come on you'll enjoy it.'

'Go away.'

'Have you ever done any modelling?' He grinned like a snake. 'I'm a photographer you know?'

'You're making me want to heave.' Jayne shook her head and sighed. 'Go away!'

'The lady said go away,' her knight in shining armour said returning from the bar. 'So, I suggest you piss off before you get hurt.' The man thought about challenging him but then he thought better of it. He turned and staggered across the dance floor in search of easier prey. 'I don't think he wants to dance anymore,' he said handing Jayne her drink with a smile. 'Have you done any modelling?'

'Shut up!' She laughed. 'Don't you start with the corny chat up lines.'

'You have to give it to him though,' he joked, 'he tried hard.'

'Too hard!'

'You could be a model though.'

'I don't think so but thank you.'

'You're welcome.'

'My hero,' she said sarcastically. She clinked his glass and sipped the Coke. 'You haven't told me your name.'

'Mike.' He smiled. 'And you are?'

'Jayne with a 'y'.'

'Nice to meet you, Jayne with a 'y'.' They touched glasses again and she gulped the cold liquid down. The sporadic waves of dry ice had made her throat dry. 'What do you do, Jayne?'

'Oh, I don't normally tell people that.' She giggled. 'It puts people off.' She saw his smile disappear again. The mask slipped for a second. His eyes narrowed and for a second, he wasn't as attractive. She didn't want to lose his interest. 'You first and then I'll tell you what I do,' she relented.

'Okay then. I'm a student.' He grinned. His eyes smiled again, and she melted under his gaze.

'A student?' She laughed.

'Yes. I'm a student.'

'A mature student.' She frowned and shook her head. 'You must be thirty something?'

'Cheeky!' He tilted his head. 'I'm a medical student now.' He left the sentence unfinished.

'What do you mean, 'now'?'

'I was a police officer for four years, but I had an urge to become a doctor, so I quit and went back to school.' He shrugged as if it was nothing unusual to leave one career and jump into another.

'Wow, you gave up the force,' Jayne said impressed. She touched his glass with hers again and drank her Coke thirstily. 'Good for you!'

'Thank you. It was a tough decision, but it was what I wanted to do.'

'I'm very impressed and that makes it much easier for me to tell you what I do.' She smiled. As they chatted, his eyes flashed in the strobe lights. She felt dreamy. She felt like she had known him forever. She felt safe. Although she felt a bit tired too. Tired and weak. It was getting late and it had been a long week. A cloud of dry ice engulfed them, and the strobe made real time seem much slower.

'Easier for you how?' He frowned. 'I'm not sure I follow.'

'To tell you what I do,' she said. Her mouth felt a little odd. Her lips felt numb. 'I don't normally tell,' she explained. 'Did I tell you that it puts people off?' she raised her eyebrows in question and noticed that they were struggling to move as normal. Her forehead felt awkward. *I wonder if that's what Botox feels like?* she thought. Then she forgot the debate which was going on in her mind immediately. In fact, she forgot what she was thinking completely. 'Sorry, what was I saying?'

'You mentioned something about it putting me off, but I wouldn't worry about putting me off.' He smiled. He put his hand on her arm, 'Come on let's dance.' Before she could speak, he had guided her to a spot not far away from where Jackie was dancing. The music drifted from one track to another, mingling into one deafening tune. At one point, Jackie had gyrated over to her and whispered something about a Porsche and a jet-ski, giggling like a schoolgirl, and then she gyrated away just as fast as she had appeared. Jayne wasn't the best dancer in the world but tonight she couldn't keep her feet moving in time with the music at all. Mike held her hand, which reassured her somewhat. She could feel sweat trickling down her back. She had never perspired that much. The more she danced, the faster her blood pumped through her veins and the worse she felt. Another cloud of dry ice swallowed her, and she closed her eyes. She wanted to sleep. The image of the Barton kid drifted into her mind. He was handcuffed and begging for help. A car crash victim from the month before flashed into her head, his brains dribbling down the windscreen. She felt sick and closed her eyes again to make the image disappear. When she opened them, the image was gone. The music seemed to warp from one genre to another, some she liked and some she hated but her legs would only maintain one beat. Left, right, left, right, left, right. 'Rhythm is a Dancer' boomed out. Her favourite tune but rhythm had deserted her. She felt like her heels were filled with concrete.

Time merged with the music. She was trapped inside a bubble looking out. Everything else was outside her bubble in a different dimension. The strobe flickered faster and the world became a time lapse movie.

Mike watched her intently. He looked concerned. His concern made her uneasy. Why was he concerned? He took her arm and she felt that she had floated back to the spot where they'd been standing earlier. Her throat was dry. She picked up her empty glass and Mike replaced it with a fresh one. You don't accept drinks from strangers, Jayne. Don't you tell young girls that every day? Don't you?

'You were telling me about your job?' Mike said in her ear.

Has he asked me that already? Maybe he hadn't heard her. She tried to maintain control of her speech. 'I don't usually tell people because it puts them off,' she mumbled. She felt that she was repeating herself. 'Have I said that already?' Her tongue felt alien in her mouth. Mike laughed and nodded his head patronisingly. Had she said that already or not? She questioned herself in her mind. 'I don't normally tell people, but I think I'll tell you.' She nodded thoughtfully.

'Oh, I see, well I'm very flattered.' He smiled. He seemed to be studying her as they spoke. That wasn't odd for a doctor though was it, studying people? 'Don't keep me in suspense. What do you do?'

'JLS,' she said pointing to the dance floor. She was confused because she was sure Labyrinth had been booming out a second ago. She noticed that Jackie had gone. Was she lost in the fog of dry ice? Probably at the bar or in the toilet. She needed the toilet, but her feet felt rooted to the sticky carpet. Sticky like congealing blood. Sticky like grey matter on glass.

'You like JLS?'

'What?'

'You were telling me what you do for a living, then you mentioned JLS,' he said confused. She listened to the music. The track was something completely different. Jackie still wasn't dancing. If she had gone outside with that guy, then she would never go out with her again. 'Are you okay?' he added.

'I was gutted when they split up,' Jayne mumbled. She could hear her own voice, but it sounded different. The revellers on the dance floor were thinning out. In fact, nearly everyone had gone. 'They split up.'

'Really?' He nodded. He was still smiling but he looked concerned. At least she thought it was concern. 'You were telling me what you do?'

'I'm a police officer too,' she mumbled. 'Just like you are. Were, I mean.' She felt tired. 'Well, I'm a Special Constable. At least for now anyway.' The smile disappeared from his face again. This time it had gone from his eyes too. She felt drunk which was impossible. She sniffed the empty Coke glass, but it had no odour. Could he have put vodka in her drink? He said he was a police officer for a while, hadn't he? Yes, he had. Had he drugged her? Get a grip, Jayne, he was a police officer and now he's a medical student.

'Which force were you with?' she asked. A lucid moment made her feel much better. She was just tired. Her voice seemed to echo around the club as she spoke. Echo around the club or your head? 'Cheshire?'

'Merseyside.' He smiled.

'Oh wow.' She smiled. 'Me too. What station where you at?' she asked in a whisper. At least she thought she'd asked him that. He didn't seem to have heard her. She felt herself gliding across the dance floor. Her feet were moving without direction from her brain. She didn't have any input into her movements. 'Rhythm is a Dancer' was playing again but no one was dancing anymore. The dance floor was empty, and all the people were drifting towards the doors. Bouncers the size of grizzly bears stood around snarling at anyone who moved too slowly or still had a drink in their hand. Jayne was floating, being taken by an invisible current in a direction that she didn't want to go. She had to get a grip. Something wasn't right. She felt drunk. Chunks of time had simply disappeared. She felt that she was watching proceedings from behind glass. She wanted to bang on it and shout for help, but she was mute. 'Zombie, zombie, zombie nation'. The tune rattled in her ears.

Suddenly, she knew in her mind that she had been drugged. She turned to shout for help. Help. Help. Help. Her mind shouted but her voice didn't work. She looked around and the world was dark. The club was gone. The people were gone. It was dark and she felt a sensation of motion. The vibration of an engine. There was a radio playing music. JLS? Or was that in the club? She couldn't remember. Dull yellow light illuminated her mind at regular intervals. Darkness, yellow light, darkness, yellow light, darkness, yellow light. It reminded her of something from her childhood, red lorry, yellow lorry, red lorry, yellow lorry. She could never get the tongue twister right. What was she thinking before that? Where was she? Yellow light, darkness, yellow light, darkness, yellow light, darkness. Open your eyes, Jayne, or bad things are going to happen. She begged and pleaded with her brain. Work you bastard. Please work. Fight the drug, please fight it.

Jayne felt her eyelids twitch and then they opened to nothing more than slits. Streetlights raced by. Trees, houses, taxis, a big green bus. Yellow light, darkness, yellow light, darkness, yellow light, darkness. Her neck wouldn't bear the weight of her head. She tried to look around and her head lolled uselessly as if she was a scarecrow with no sticks attached or a marionette with the head string cut. Cut. Cut. She didn't want to be cut. She pushed the word from her mind, but it kept coming back. The Barton kid sneered at her through the glass, wide eyed, tongue lolling from his black lips. Go away! She screamed in her head. She slammed a door closed in her mind and he was gone but she knew he was waiting on the other side eager to come back. Her eyes focused again. The stereo was like the one in her car. It was the same brand but in the wrong position. The steering wheel had a BMW logo on it just like hers. So did the gear stick. The driver had sunglasses on the dashboard. They were just like hers. They were next to some loose change and a packet of Polo mints. Jayne did that with her change too. And she kept Polo mints there but on the other side. Her car was the same. Same radio, same logo, same sunglasses, same Polo mints. The car smelled familiar. Except something was different. She looked again. It was her car, but the perspective was from the passenger seat. She was sitting in the passenger seat of her car. How had she got there? Who was driving? Her chin was resting on her chest. She strained to see the driver's face and as she focused, she felt a sob trapped in her chest. She felt hot stinging tears run from her eyes, tickling her skin as they rolled down her cheeks.

His head was bald. Huge tufts of white hair stuck out from above his ears. Like a mad professor. The nose was hooked, and the eyes were sunken but unnaturally so. The mouth was fixed into an evil grin. She recognised the face from somewhere. Somewhere from her childhood and it frightened her. It wasn't real. It was a rubber mask. It had frightened her as a little girl and it still frightened her.

'You're awake?' he rasped but the mouth didn't move. It was rubber. Just like the mask he was wearing. Why would you wear a mask? 'That's good. We're nearly at your place.' Jayne wanted to scream until her lungs burst but nothing happened. A tiny sob escaped her lips. 'Have you got the back-door keys?' the voice asked. He seemed to be looking in the rear-view mirror. She hoped that he was worried about being followed. Worried about the police. She sensed someone moving behind her, but she couldn't be sure. *My house keys are on the car keys*, she thought. She was frightened and confused. Darkness clawed at her, threatening to drag her down into unconsciousness. There would be no escaping danger there, no rest, no peace. She could sense evil nearby. It was an inky black pit. She didn't want to go down there. *Please, God help me*, she thought, but he didn't.

CHAPTER 2

Detective Annie Jones shivered as she climbed out of her Audi. The wind was blowing through the trees, which bordered the garden of a three-bedroom detached house. Oak, ash and elm stood strong against the gusts although their golden leaves were starting to fall forming piles of rotting foliage against the kerb stones and the walls of the house. The well-manicured lawn was dotted with shifting spots of gold. Each time the wind blew, the patterns changed shape. Each gust made her good eye water blurring her vision. Her eye patch had been causing a skin irritation lately and she had reluctantly started using a prosthetic, which she hated. It left her feeling vulnerable and naked. Her patch gave her comfort somehow. A physical covering up of the terrible injury she had sustained at the hands of a murder suspect four years prior. A lapse of concentration, and a biro in the hands of the wrong person became a weapon. Her eye was destroyed, and her face was changed in a moment. The memory was as sharp as if it had happened yesterday. She still couldn't leave a pen on a desk.

The wind whistled through the branches once more chilling her exposed skin. It hinted at the cold winter months ahead. She had tied her dark bob into a ponytail to combat the wind and her decision to opt for faded jeans and Ugg boots was the right one. She pulled her quilted jacket tightly to her neck and wiped a tear from her good eye as she looked towards the house.

Detective Sergeant Jim Stirling loomed in the doorway of the house, his huge frame almost filling the double-glazed porch. Annie could tell from the colour and condition of the white window frames and the sheen on the new roof tiles that the house had been built in the last few years. Uniformed officers were making a cordon with yellow crime scene tape and a small gathering of neighbouring residents were comforting an elderly woman. She was well dressed and visibly distraught. A female Family Liaison Officer was questioning her and making notes. It was a far too familiar scene.

'Here we go again,' Annie said to herself as she locked the car and walked towards the path. Jim Stirling waved and walked to meet her.

'Bad one, guv,' he growled and shook his head. He sounded like he had gravel in his throat. Annie had seen career criminals turn white at the sound of the big sergeant's voice.

'They're all bad, aren't they?' she smiled thinly. Another gust of wind whistled through the branches, rustling the dying leaves, and whispering secrets that only the trees knew. Stirling handed her a small jar of eucalyptus gel in answer to her question. Obviously, the victim was already ripe. 'I see,' Annie said applying a smear of the gel beneath her nostrils. 'Do we know who the victim is?'

Stirling nodded and pointed towards the grieving woman. 'The victim's cleaner found her and called her mother. Luckily, we got here before her mother did and stopped her going in,' he grimaced. 'There's no way a mother should see her daughter like that.' He sighed. 'She's one of ours, guv. She's a Special Constable from the Halewood station. Somebody went to town on her.' He shrugged and stood aside as they reached the porch. A CSI handed them forensic suits and plastic overshoes. Annie removed her jacket and climbed into the suit. Jim Stirling struggled into his and turned towards Annie. 'There's no sign of forced entry,' he said looking at the mortice locks on the door. He pointed to the wall, 'the alarm was reset by whoever left her here. All the doors and windows are secure. The cleaner had to use her set of keys to get in and she had to turn the alarm off. She thought her employer had gone away without telling her at first but then the smell hit her.'

Annie looked around the hallway. She was pleased to see wood laminate covered the floor along the hallway and that it continued up the stairs; it was always a decent medium for recovering shoe prints and hair samples. 'Let's have a look at her first,' Annie said peering into the living room. It looked like a set from Ikea, bright and airy but unlived in. She headed for the stairs and climbed them slowly. The stench of decomposition grew stronger with each step. That was normal but there was something else in the air. Something that didn't belong there. It was subtle but it was there. She paused to speak to her sergeant. 'Can you smell petrol?'

'All I can smell is the victim.' Stirling stopped and sniffed the air. 'My sense of smell isn't great.' His crooked nose looked like he had been smacked in the face with a spade. Annie had asked him a dozen times how he had broken his nose, but he always shrugged it off saying, 'You should see the other guy.' The thought of what the other guy would look like made her shudder. 'Now you mention it, I can smell something. It's definitely a fuel of some type.'

The smell of petrol made Annie think. 'Whose is the car on the driveway?'

'Her mother's,' Stirling answered. 'We know the victim had a vehicle, a BMW 3-series. It's missing. Traffic have been informed.'

'Good.' The landing was L-shaped with three bedrooms and a bathroom off it. Pine framed photographs hung on the magnolia walls. Annie had the feeling that the victim had left the builders' neutral décor untouched, adding only pictures and photographs as her own stamp on her new home. 'This is a nice house,' Annie commented, 'expensive too.' They reached the main bedroom and Annie instinctively took a deep breath before stepping through the door. The scene which faced her was in stark contrast to the rest of the house. It went from organised to carnage in one step. Kathy Brooks was engrossed with directing her camera man, but she noticed Annie and held up her hand in greeting.

'Meet our victim.' She gestured to the bloody form on the bed. 'The house belongs to Jayne Windsor. I think this is her.' She nodded towards the body. 'Or what is left of her.' She sighed. 'I need five minutes to tie up the initial scene photos. As you can see, there is plenty to photograph.' She smiled thinly and began walking the cameraman through an array of angles which she needed to be recorded. 'There's a strong smell of petrol coming from somewhere and it's bothering me that's why I haven't got the full team in here.'

'Have you called the fire brigade?'

'They're on the way.' She smiled nervously. 'I thought it was better to be safe than sorry.'

'It's faint downstairs but it's definitely stronger here,' Annie said. She remained near the doorway; Stirling towered behind her. Both remained silent while they analysed their own first impressions of what might have happened.

The victim was face up on the bed. Annie could only tell that by the position of the feet, which were pointing at the ceiling. The face was gone, replaced by a bloody maw surrounded by blond hair, which made the police hat on her head look ridiculous. Her arms were positioned straight out on each side in the shape of a crucifix. There were no fingers or thumbs attached to the hands. None that she could see anyway. The position of the body was staged, that much was obvious. Oddly the police uniform she wore, seemed undamaged and unstained. It didn't belong in the scene. Blood splatter arced up both sides of the wall above the headboard, reaching the ceiling. Between the arcs of blood, a pentagram had been daubed. Mirrored wardrobes, the glass smeared with bloody handprints, covered one wall; the gory reflection added to the horror of the vista.

'First impressions?' Annie said.

'My first impressions were the same as yours,' Kathy said inspecting something on the bedside table. It looked like a glass of some kind. 'But my impressions are not the same now and they're changing by the minute. Give me a few more minutes and I'll be with you.' Annie turned to Stirling and he shrugged. There was little to no point in arguing. Kathy Brooks was the best CSI around and if she was still digesting the evidence then there was nothing to gain by crowding her.

'We'll look around the other bedrooms, okay?' Annie gestured to Stirling that they should move along the hall.

'We haven't been in them yet. Don't touch anything!' Kathy called after them. Annie looked at her, eyebrows raised, annoyed by the comment. 'Sorry.' Kathy shrugged and blushed. 'All is not what it seems here. Trust me.'

Annie nodded and accepted the half-baked apology although she was intrigued by Kathy's concern. 'I'll see if I can find where that smell is coming from. We don't want the firemen slowing us up if it's nothing to worry about.'

'Thanks.' Kathy nodded.

Annie grimaced and walked out of the room. 'She seems a little spooked,' she said quietly.

'She's a scientist,' Stirling grumbled. 'They're always spooked about something. It's part of their icy charm.' His black leather jacket creaked as he moved. The smell of leather reminded Annie of her teenage years riding horses. She had loved the smell of the tack-room and it evoked happy memories of a time when death was something that happened on TV.

Annie smiled and walked into the second bedroom. The curtains were closed, and the quilt was ruffled. Someone had slept in the room recently but there was nothing obviously untoward. The third bedroom was a box room with a single bed in it and little space for anything else. The mattress was covered with a quilted protector but unmade.

'The curtains are closed in here too,' Stirling pointed out. 'Bit odd. Closed by the killer do you think?'

'I'll forgo having any opinion for now,' Annie said walking into the bathroom. She looked around and the practiced senses she possessed began to prickle. 'Look here,' she said. Stirling stood in the doorway and watched. 'No toilet roll, no towels. No woman worth her salt leaves an empty toilet roll on the holder.'

'That's a man thing,' Stirling agreed. 'I had a bad experience once; I had to use my socks, now I keep my spare rolls within arm's reach of the toilet.'

'Too much information.'

'Sorry, guv.'

'There are some images I don't need to imagine, thanks.'

'Only saying,' he said sulkily. 'It is a bloke thing.'

Annie grinned sarcastically. 'Do we know if she had a boyfriend?'

'Single, guv. One of the sergeants from Halewood implied that she might be on the other bus.'

'Of course, she was.' Annie frowned. 'Female constable who doesn't shag everything at her station?' she shook her head and tutted. 'She must be 'on the other bus'.'

'His words not mine.'

'I know that,' Annie said.

'He also said that she wasn't very popular.' Annie looked at him waiting for him to expand. 'Something to do with the Barton case. Remember that?'

'Of course, I do.' Annie frowned. 'What did he say?'

'Nothing detailed. He couldn't get off the phone quick enough to be honest.' He shrugged. 'I'll look into it later. It might be worth a trip to Halewood.'

'Okay,' Annie said thoughtfully. 'Ask one of the CSI to start in here and tell them to look for the dirty laundry.' She noticed a circle on the tiles next to the toilet. Something had been removed from there. Annie guessed it was a pedal bin. Whoever had killed the victim had been very precise in cleaning up. That much was obvious. They were organised and had spent a long time in the house. That displayed a cool confidence which only an intelligent killer could possess. 'Have uniform do a sweep of the tree line and all the bins in the street before it starts raining again.'

'Guv.' Stirling grunted and headed towards the stairs. 'The smell is stronger here, guv,' he said on the landing. Annie looked around, sniffing but couldn't see anything obvious that explained the fumes.

'I'm ready for you, Annie,' Kathy's voice called from the master bedroom distracting her. Annie took a last look around and noted other obvious items missing. Bleach, soap, shower gel, shampoo, toothpaste, and conditioner. Minimum requirements for a young woman's bathroom. Had the killer taken them? Her toothbrush was lonely on the basin, accompanied only by a tub of cold cream and bactericidal hand wash, which was on the windowsill. A loofah mitt hung from the shower hose. The chrome drain trap sparkled as if it had been cleaned recently. Annie thought that any killer that thorough wouldn't leave any clues behind for free. In hindsight, she couldn't have been more wrong.

CHAPTER 3

Tod Harris woke up feeling guilty although the feeling wasn't as intense as it had been days before. The day after it had happened, he was panic stricken. He had expected the police to kick his door in and drag him off to jail at any minute. The urge to run was overwhelming. Despite all the planning and promises, he couldn't sit and wait. He had to go before he drove himself insane. Within an hour of waking up, he was on a train heading south to Birmingham and from there he had taken a cab to the airport. His budget ticket to Alicante had cost him less than he expected, having said that, he would have paid ten times the amount to escape the fear of being caught. He'd had a three hour wait for his flight, which he spent pretending to read a newspaper while keeping an eye out for approaching police officers. Paranoid wasn't a strong enough word to describe his state of mind. He waited until the boarding gate was empty and double checked that there were no detectives waiting for him before approaching the stewards with his passport and boarding card. He had only relaxed when the aircraft had left the runway.

On arrival, he took a bus from Alicante and found an apartment at the third time of trying in the busy resort of Benidorm. Tod had calmed down somewhat since then. His head felt fuzzy as the previous night's alcohol clung to his nervous system. The sun was blazing through the balcony doors making it impossible to sleep any longer. Despite drinking himself into a stupor the night before, he'd spent hours in a nightmare filled daze somewhere between sleep and consciousness. There was no escape. The images that haunted his dreams remained with him through his waking hours. He couldn't outrun them.

There was no explanation for his actions, certainly no excuses. Once the intense wave of lust that drove him had waned, all that was left was guilt and remorse. What he had done made him feel physically sick. He had crossed a line from which he couldn't return. If they caught him, not only would he go down for a long time, his family and friends would be horrified and devastated. They would be destroyed. He couldn't bring himself to think of what effect it would have on the health of his elderly mother. Her beloved son a monster? It was inconceivable.

He climbed out of bed and looked out across the balcony. The view of the sea was obscured by a forest of towering hotels but the pool area and the narrow streets beyond were pleasant enough to look at. The 'Old Town' of Benidorm was quiet in comparison to newer parts of the resort a mile or so away, which were plagued with stag and hen parties, yet it was busy enough for him to remain anonymous. The beer was cheap, the tapas bars were excellent, and he could spend all day on his sunbed by the pool scouring the British newspapers for information. So far so good. Whatever was going on at home, he didn't appear to be a known fugitive just yet. Maybe they would never link him to any crime. Maybe pigs would fly over the Spanish resort too.

Tod walked into the bathroom and tried to make himself feel human again. The man in the mirror didn't look as bad as he felt. His skin was already tanning, and his dark brown hair looked neat and well groomed. He showered and shaved and then pulled on a pair of black Nike shorts and a matching vest before gathering his wallet and sunglasses and heading down to the lobby. He had placed his mobile in the room safe the moment he arrived, and he was determined to leave it there too. Switching it on would be like waving a big flag saying 'I'm over here. Come and get me.' Although the urge to turn it on was overpowering, he couldn't. He valued his liberty too much to take any risks. Once everything had blown over, he could go back to his normal life. It would take time, but he had plenty of that.

He opened the door and looked up and down the corridor. He thought about armed police officers hiding in doorways waiting for him to leave his room. It was ridiculous yet it was a real fear. Taking a deep breath, he stepped out and closed the door with a click. He twisted the handle to check that it was locked. It was. Relax, he told himself. You're on a long holiday, nothing more, nothing less. He placed his forehead against the wood, and it felt cool and refreshing. A full English breakfast, some orange juice, and a few laps of the pool would sort him out. He turned and headed for the lift. There was never a car waiting. The hotel was sixteen floors high and as the summer months disappeared, families were replaced by a tide of British pensioners. They wouldn't or couldn't walk up the stairs unless they absolutely had to. He was convinced that if the hotel caught fire, hundreds of nearly dead people would sprint down the stairs like a herd of aging Olympians without giving their arthritis a second thought but on any normal day they were crammed into the lifts from dawn to dusk.

He pressed the call button and waited nervously. He could hear the cables rattling in the shaft although it gave him no indication of how long it would be before a car empty enough for him to squeeze into arrived. On the first night, he had waited fifteen minutes before a car with room in it came. It was almost comical. The lift doors opened four times to reveal a car full of wrinklies staring at him with inane grins on their faces, barely an inch between them. The third time that the doors opened, he was positive that the same geriatrics were just cruising up and down for fun. They all looked alike, blue rinses and grey comb-overs. He had taken to using the stairs since but today his hangover had stolen his energy. As he pondered walking, the bell dinged. The doors opened to reveal an empty car. Relieved, he stepped in and pressed the button for the ground floor.

The reception area was dull, cramped, and full of shadows. Tod peered around before stepping out of the lift. There were three armchairs on either side of the reception desk, each had a sleeping pensioner on them but apart from that, there was no one around. He put on his shades and walked confidently across the marble tiles heading for the revolving doors which led out onto the streets of the Old Town. The warmth of the sun was still bearable. It was early and that side of the hotel was in the shade in the morning. An hour later, the sun would be so intense that he wouldn't be able to move far away from the pool unless he chose to sit inside in the air-conditioned recreational areas of the hotel. That would mean watching the other residents enjoying their daily activities, waltzing, playing bridge, bingo, sleeping, and dribbling. He couldn't bring himself to do that, even as an observer. He would stay on his sunbed and use the pool to regulate his temperature but first, he needed some food and the newspapers. The newspapers were important. Vital to keeping his sanity. Well, almost.

It was a short walk across the town hall park to the cobbled lanes of the Old Town. Local school children were rattling down the paths on their skateboards, the smell of fresh cut grass was in the air. Flowers every colour of the rainbow were still in bloom and their fragrance drifted on the warm breeze. At the far side of the park, he crossed on a zebra, which the local drivers ignored. He was convinced that the Spanish were taught to speed up wherever there was a marked crossing especially if a pasty-faced tourist was on it. He bought twenty Marlboro from a tobacconist shop that he had found on his first day and then went next door to buy the British papers. *The Mirror*, *The Mail*, and *The Express*. They would keep him going most of the day. He barely glanced at the front pages as he paid for them; his focus was on the smell of bacon, which was drifting from the café next door. He weaved his way between a myriad of Day-Glo rubber rings that hung from the ceiling and an assortment of inflated killer whales, dolphins, and crocodiles before stepping over a basket full of bucket and spade sets to get to an empty table. He was pleased that his favourite table was free. He had sat there every morning since his arrival and being a creature of habit, he had become attached to it.

'Back again?' a Scottish accent asked with a chuckle. The man had served him every day so far. His name was Gordon and he and his partner, Gordon owned the café. Gordon and Gordon were a gay couple, who had emigrated to the sunshine a few years before. They made much of the fact that were the 'Gay Gordons', which they explained at length was a Scottish country dance group in the nineteenth century. They were like a comedy double-act. 'I'm Gordon,' one would say, 'and I'm Gordon too,' the other would add with a chuckle. 'We must be doing something right with the food or is it my charming personality that brings you back?'

'Definitely the bacon,' Tod quipped.

'You can go off people quickly you know!'

'Don't make me go and eat egg McMuffins.'

'Heaven forbid,' Gordon frowned and stuck his index finger down his throat. 'I wouldn't wish that on anyone.' He smiled and patted Tod on the back. The other Gordon watched his partner flirting with undisguised distaste all over his face. 'Are you having your usual?'

'Yes please.'

'Coming up!' Gordon paused and frowned again. 'Now why don't you have a bit of square sausage too?' he asked coyly. 'It's a Scottish delicacy.'

'Is it extra?'

'Of course.' He giggled. 'We have a pool to maintain you know.'

'Okay, square sausage it is.'

'Juice or tea or both?'

'Is that extra too?'

'Of course!'

'Both.'

Tod couldn't help but smile as Gordon walked away with a strange wiggle of his hips. If anyone could make a success of a café bar in the sunshine, it was them. One Gordon was an amazing waiter, the second a great cook. He sat back and lit a cigarette, allowing the sun to warm his face. Gordon placed a pot of tea and a glass of juice next to him and he gulped the orange down in one swallow. Unfolding the papers, he scanned the headlines. A sex scandal on Big Brother, financial instability in the stock markets and Muslim against Muslim in the Middle East. Nothing new there. He slurped his tea and speed read the main stories. It wasn't until he got to page two of *The Mirror* that the blood in his veins turned to ice. Suddenly he wasn't as hungry as he thought.

CHAPTER 4

Kathy brooks had her hands on her hips, and she was biting her bottom lip thoughtfully. Her auburn hair was tied tightly into a bun where it couldn't cross contaminate the scene. Her photographer stepped aside to let Annie into the room. The air was rank with the stench of decay. Kathy acknowledged her with a nod and began her summary into a voice activated recorder, which she used to recount the details when she came to type up her reports. She smiled thinly at Annie without looking up from her deliberations. Jim Stirling stepped into the room and gave a thumbs-up signal. He folded his arms and waited for Kathy to begin.

'Friday morning, second of October. We are at the home of one Jayne Windsor. In the main bedroom we have the body of a young female, age twenty-five to thirty-five. There is deep bruising and lacerations to the wrists and ankles indicating that she struggled violently against metal restraints. The pattern of the scarring indicates the killer probably used handcuffs.' She took a breath. 'She has massive facial trauma. The mandible or lower jawbone has been removed as have the ears, teeth, and facial skin tissue. The nasal bones, orbital surfaces, glabella, and frontal bones have been shattered. Blunt force trauma with a heavy object.' She turned to Annie for the first time. 'All the phalanges or fingers and thumbs have been severed with a sharp two-sided implement like rongeurs or bone scissors and removed from the scene. The body appears to have been redressed in a police officer's uniform and posed into the shape of a crucifix post-mortem. I need to take a good look at the garments to continue my assessment. There is something unusual about them.' She turned to Annie and raised her eyebrows in question.

Annie nodded and stepped to one side of the double bed, while Kathy went to the opposite side. They bent lower and looked closely beneath the limbs. Kathy glanced at Annie and frowned. 'Can you see what I can see?'

'I think so.' Annie nodded and pulled gently at the material which covered the extended left arm. The material came away easily. 'The tunic and trousers have been cut in half and placed over the body.'

'Then the killer has tucked the material underneath the body to give the impression of her being dressed,' Kathy added. 'Can you give us a hand here please, Graham, and bag the uniform as we remove it.' The photographer stepped forward as they lifted the material from the corpse. 'Jesus Christ!' Kathy hissed.

'What the hell?' Stirling whispered beneath his breath. He had seen some sights in his time but this one took his breath away.

Annie inhaled sharply and looked at Kathy confused. At first, she thought the victim had been wearing a strangely patterned body-stocking but as she focused on the details it became clear. 'What the hell is that?' the photographer bagged up the clothes and then snapped dozens of shots from all angles. Stirling took a step closer and stared at the intricate scabbed carvings.

Kathy was visibly shaken, and she swallowed hard to compose herself before continuing. 'On removal of the uniform we can see that some form of ancient text, may be Greek or Hebrew in origin, has been scratched into the skin from the wrists to the neck and down to the ankles, covering the entire body. At first glance there are several thousand words carved into the victim with a very fine implement. There appears to be huge tranches of text 'written' on the body.' Kathy paused and pointed to a bedside table next to Annie. Annie turned to look at it. There was a glass tumbler placed on it and a thin bloodstained handle protruded from it. 'On the bedside table we found a tumbler which contains liquid and blood. The liquid has an odour of antiseptic. Placed into the tumbler is a dental implement called a skin hook. First impressions are that the skin hook was used to 'carve' words into the victim's skin.'

Annie stood up and stepped back from the bed. She blew out a lung full of tainted air reluctant to breathe it in anymore. 'Tell me she was dead when he did this.'

A brief shake of Kathy's head indicated the opposite. 'No, she was alive through all this.' She sighed and pointed to the deep welts which cut into her wrists. 'She fought hard to get free. This would have taken days to complete,' she said shaking her head in disbelief. 'When was she last seen alive?'

'Saturday night,' Stirling answered. 'She worked an early shift and told a colleague that she was going out that night with a friend. A neighbour said she saw her leaving about seven o'clock. She said that she was dressed to go out for the night. We're still trying to trace where she went to and who with.'

'Her sergeant didn't miss her at work?' Annie frowned.

'She called in sick, guv.'

'What?'

'She wasn't due back on shift until Tuesday lunchtime. They have a sick call logged on Monday night saying she had food poisoning.' Stirling shrugged. 'Unfortunately, there is no record of who made the call. Could she have been dead already?'

'Between rigor, lividity, and her decomp, I would say she's been dead for less than seventy-two hours.'

'So, she was alive Monday night when the call was made.'

'Which gives the killer at least three days alone with her?'

'At least. The severe bruising here on her thighs indicates repeated sexual assaults.' She pointed to a dark patch on the bed. 'We could have a break here. I've swabbed some seminal fluid from the bed but apart from that, I can't be more specific until I get her back to the lab.'

'He left fluids?' Annie frowned. 'That's odd. The place has been cleaned down. Are you sure it's seminal?'

'I think I can safely say so but…' She shrugged and turned to her CSI.

'I know,' Annie said. 'You can't say until you get her to the lab?'

Kathy nodded. 'Let's get her to the lab.' The CSI nodded and walked out of the room to fetch assistance and a body-bag. 'I really need to pick this room apart with my team, Annie.' She lowered her voice. 'I'm not a happy bunny.'

'What are you thinking?'

'The entire scene except for the pentagram on the wall has been wiped.' She looked around. 'But the killer left the skin hook and fluids for us to find. I'm not feeling right about any of this. The carpet looks spotless, yet the mattress is saturated with blood. Take off your glove and touch the carpet.'

Annie hesitated and then knelt to feel the fibres of the carpet. She removed a glove and touched it. 'It's damp,' she said looking at Stirling. He frowned and knelt to follow suit. She smelled her finger and frowned. 'Bleach?'

'That's what I think but watch this.' She sprayed Luminol onto a square of carpet and then took an ultraviolet torch from her belt and pointed at the carpet where Annie was crouched. 'It's everywhere.'

Annie's jaw dropped to her chest. She stood up quickly almost staggering backwards. She looked at Kathy wide eyed with shock. 'Oh my God!' The light revealed detailed writing on the fibres.

'That script is the same as on the body,' Stirling mused. 'Daubed onto the carpet in blood and then scrubbed clean?'

'Exactly,' Kathy agreed.

'That would take time.' Annie shook her head. 'This guy had no fear of being here for days. I want every inch of this photographed, Kathy,' Annie said. 'Do you think this is part of a ritual?'

'The pentangle?' Stirling pointed to the bloody symbol. 'A sacrifice of some kind?'

'I hate that word.' Kathy shrugged. 'All the signs are pointing at a ritual murder but on the other hand has it been left to appear that way for our benefit?'

'I don't know but I would have to say that the killer has left exactly what he wants us to find. He's trying to make a point.'

'Until we can identify this script, I can't tell what its relevance is.' Kathy shrugged. 'There are no other obvious signs of a genuine ritual. I mean why clean the carpet but leave that on the wall?' she pointed at the blackened mess that was once the victim's face. 'this could indeed be part of a ritual however,' she raised her index finger, 'the killer has taken everything that we'd need to make a positive identification of the victim. If it is a 'sacrifice' why try to hide the identity of the victim. It wouldn't matter, would it?'

Stirling stepped closer to the victim. 'Face, teeth, fingerprints, jewellery, what about distinctive markings?' He walked towards the door. 'I'll ask the mother if Jayne had any tattoos or birthmarks.'

'Do that and ask her what size feet she has,' Annie agreed. 'Do you think he's taken more than you have already listed?' Annie grimaced. 'There's not enough personal stuff in here, Kathy.' Annie pointed out. She walked toward the mirrored wardrobe and caught sight of her reflection. In her mind, her prosthetic eye screamed out from her face, 'false eye, false eye, false eye, false eye!' it was unnoticeable until her good eye moved. Despite the gore around the room it looked too sparse, void of personal belongings to be inhabited by a young woman. Annie was convinced that things were missing.

Kathy nodded her head in agreement. 'I noticed that. The bathroom too, yes?'

'Yes,' Annie said. She walked to the window and looked outside. A television crew from the BBC was setting up across the road and a gaggle of newspaper reporters were hovering at the edge of the cordon. The neighbours were still gathered in a huddle to her left. Some of the women were visibly upset. A box of tissues was being handed around. One man stood back from the group and his appearance drew Annie's attention to him. He had his hood pulled over his head, but his face was visible. Annie frowned when a smile crossed his lips.

'Any sign of the fire brigade yet?' Kathy disturbed her thoughts. 'I really want to get my team up here.'

Annie turned from the window and shook her head. When she looked back the solitary man had gone. 'once we get cleaned up in here, we can ask the cleaner and her mother what is missing.' She could hear heavy footsteps climbing the stairs. Stirling ducked through the doorframe. His brow was furrowed with deep lines. 'what did she say?'

'She said Jayne has size six feet and a flower tattoo on her left foot, middle toe.' They all looked at the victim's foot and then looked at each other.

CHAPTER 5

Dale Reeves scanned the street beyond the police cordon and pointed to the spot where the crowd was gathered. 'Put the blues on and move that lot back,' he ordered the engine driver. 'Dave, come with me and we'll see what the score is. Chris, when the other engines arrive, I want one to the left of the driveway and the other in front of us. Set up as if this place is lit up.'

The sirens screamed and the gathering moved back. Uniformed police officers cleared the area so that they could bring the tender safely to a stop. 'Quick in and out, boys. We're making the place safe and then we're gone,' Dale said as he opened the door and jumped down onto the pavement. 'Where's the DI?' he asked a young constable, who looked confused by their arrival. Dale had met a thousand baby faced coppers during his career. As Dale neared retirement age, they seemed to be getting younger every day.

'She's inside.' The officer pointed to the house and lifted the tape so that he could duck underneath. Dale nodded a silent thank you and clomped across the lawn towards the front door. Dave Cooper jogged to keep up with the taller man. They reached the house and screwed up their noses as the smell of decomposition met them.

'Something's gone off,' Dave mumbled adjusting his helmet.

Dale smiled grimly and scanned the hallway. 'DI Jones?' he shouted. He heard muffled voices coming from the upper floor and headed for the stairs. 'DI Jones?' he repeated. As he climbed, he noticed the distinct whiff of petrol. 'Can you smell that?'

'Petrol somewhere.' Dave nodded. Annie appeared at the top of the stairs joined by Kathy and Stirling. They all looked irritated by the presence of the firemen.

'I'm DI Jones,' Annie said. Dale thought she was an attractive woman at first glance although there was something funny about her eyes. He tried hard not to stare at the jagged scar that ran down her face. 'We have a murder investigation going on but there's a smell of petrol coming from somewhere. It seems to be stronger here on the landing than anywhere else.' She frowned. 'I want the place made safe so that we can get the forensic teams in.'

'Have you searched the bedrooms yet?' Dale asked with a sigh. He looked around the narrow landing; his black skin already had a sheen of sweat glistening on it. His heavy safety clothing and his age combining to make the simplest of jobs an effort.

'We've had a brief look around but there's nothing obvious, hence we called you.'

Dale shrugged his wide shoulders and scratched at his greying beard. 'I'm going to need you all to leave while we check the place over,' he said with a toothy smile. 'You know the drill. We'll be as quick as we can and then we'll be out of your hair.' He shrugged in apology.

Annie puffed up her cheeks and blew out a deep breath. 'Kathy, we need to get out for five minutes.' She nodded to Stirling and he stepped back to allow Kathy to go down the stairs first. 'Please don't go in this bedroom unless you absolutely must,' she said firmly. 'This is a complicated crime scene and we don't need half a dozen pairs of size elevens stomping all over it, please.'

'Heaven forbid,' Dale smiled. 'I'll do a quick check of the other rooms; get the steps off the wagon, Dave,' he said briskly.

'Don't move anything,' Kathy shouted up the stairs as she reluctantly left the house.

'Don't stomp on anything and don't move anything,' he muttered to himself and shook his head. 'I'm a fireman not Dynamo the magician. Levitation isn't one of my many skills.' Dale watched them leave before walking to the bathroom. Although the fumes still permeated the air, they were thinner there. 'Follow your nose, Dale,' he whispered as he walked into the second bedroom. He kneeled and peered under the bed. Nothing but dust and hair. It always fascinated him how much hair a female shed and where the hair ended up. He doubted very much if the occupier spent much time under the bed in her spare room, yet there were strands everywhere. Standing, he sniffed the air again and opened a narrow wardrobe. Shoes, some coats, and a suitcase. Dale used his index finger and thumb to pick up the case by the handle. It lifted easily. Empty.

'I thought you'd be in the underwear drawer by now,' Dave's voice boomed, making him jump. He balanced a set of metal stepladders against the wall and grinned. 'What next?'

'Check the small box room,' Dale said moodily. He had a lot of time for his number two but sometimes his incessant sarcasm grated on his nerves. Dale walked to the main bedroom where the stench of death was the strongest. He peered around the door and instantly wished that he hadn't. 'Jesus Christ,' he hissed. He tried to peel his eyes from the butchered woman but even when he did, the image was still etched into his brain. He was tempted to open the mirrored wardrobes, but a hunch told him not to bother. There was no doubt that the odour was stronger on the landing. He looked at the hatch in the ceiling and walked beneath it.

'Nothing in there,' Dave said disappointedly. He shifted his squat frame to look upwards at the ceiling. 'I'm thinking it's coming from the attic, are you?'

'That's why I asked for the steps, Einstein.'

'Sorry for thinking at all, Sherlock.' Dave grabbed the ladders and opened them underneath the hatch. 'Safety first,' he said holding them steady. 'After you!'

Dale shook his head and smiled. He held each side and climbed the first two steps inspecting the hatch lid and frame closely. Two hook-and-eye fastenings were fitted to hold it closed but one of them was hanging loose. The frame was painted with white gloss and dirty smudges marked the wood near the hook. Fingerprints. They were impossible to see from below. He had no idea when they'd been made but his instincts told him they were recent. They also sent alarm bells ringing in his head. 'I don't like this one bit,' he said quietly. The expression on Dave's face changed immediately. He knew when Dale had a hunch, it was usually correct. 'The smell is much stronger up here.'

'Do you want the hoses in?' Dave asked concerned.

'Not yet,' Dale said staring at the corners of the hatch. He reached up and pressed a finger against the fastened hook and pushed it from the eye. It rattled as it fell loose. He pressed the fingers and thumbs of both hands against the lid and pushed gently. It didn't move an inch. He looked down at Dave and grimaced. 'Feels like there's something on top of it.'

'It's your call,' Dave said seriously. 'We don't know what we're dealing with until we move that hatch.'

Dale bared his teeth and pushed a little harder. The hatch moved up from the lip and air rushed out from the attic. It was so thick with petrol fumes that Dale could almost taste it. 'No doubt it's up here.' He paused to think.

'No one keeps petrol in the attic.' Dave shook his head. 'Could be a model train enthusiast I suppose.' He tried to lighten the atmosphere.

'Nah,' Dale humoured him. He took a deep breath. 'Trains run on diesel.'

'I was joking.'

'So was I.' Dale tensed. 'Now shut up while I concentrate.' He pushed again opening an inch-wide gap between the lid and the frame. Squinting into the blackness, he tried to let his eyes become accustomed to the dark. He stared intently at the edges, studying each of the four sides of the rectangular opening. The weight on the hatch shifted and something fell over with a dull thud. Dale froze and listened. Metal on wood, then a rolling sound like a ball bearing. It came to a stop with a metallic click. In the darkness to his right, Dale saw a green light come on and he dropped the hatch back into place and jumped from ladder, landing with a thump. 'Run!'

Dave looked stunned for a second and Dale grabbed him by the arm and dragged him towards the stairs. The metal ladders clattered to the floor as they hurtled across the landing and sprinted down the stairs in a whirlwind of arms and legs.

CHAPTER 6

The investigation team huddled in a circle at the side of the house, sheltering from the wind. 'There was no tattoo,' Kathy folded her arms and tutted. 'And her feet are nowhere near a size six; four at the most.'

'That isn't Jayne Windsor,' Annie said turning to Stirling. 'So, where is she?'

'Well, there's no way the killer brought a victim back to this house without knowing full well that the owner wouldn't be a problem.' He shrugged. 'Jayne Windsor is either dead or she's being held somewhere else.'

'Let's look at it another way.' Kathy shrugged. 'She could be complicit.'

Annie frowned but looked around at the growing Press crowd and thought about the possibility for a second. 'All her personal things are gone. Her toiletries, her car, what about her clothes?' she paused. 'Did you look in the wardrobes?'

Kathy shook her head. She shivered against the wind and a shower of leaves whirled around their feet. 'I was waiting to process the body first and for you to arrive. I thought it was premature to start checking around.' She stopped in her tracks as muffled shouts came from the house. They moved quickly to the front path, alarmed and confused. They heard heavy boots thundering down the stairs and then the firemen appeared at the bottom, panicked expressions on their faces. A yellow helmet bounced down the stairs behind them and clattered off the banister rail before rolling down the hallway. Dale reeves was waving his arms around. He stumbled to one knee and his colleague gripped him beneath the armpit and dragged him through the front door and into the porch. 'Get back!' Dale shouted as they spilled out onto the path. Their momentum carried them away from the house and onto the grass. 'Get everyone back!'

Annie felt Stirling pulling them backwards like they were ragdolls. Time seemed to slow down to a standstill. She was about to turn and bite his head off when the bedroom windows exploded outwards. Thousands of tiny shards whistled past her. Tongues of orange flame reached out beyond the eaves, blistering the guttering and an audible whoosh sucked the oxygen from the air. Thick black smoke and embers climbed skywards, and the fire crackled loudly as it began to devour the house.

'Move back!' the firemen screamed at the top of their voices. They sprinted past Annie like 100m finalists. Her reactions seemed painfully slow as she turned to run. Kathy was five metres in front of her, Stirling five metres behind. It took time to get his bulk moving at speed. As they reached the cordon, the fire reached a new intensity. She turned to look as the flames roared upwards. The heat was unbearable even at that distance and she raised her arm to shield her face.

'Tell me that Graham took all the evidence bags out with him,' Annie said panting. Kathy nodded, her mouth open gasping for air. She was about to speak again when an explosion rocked the building. Roof tiles were launched high into the air, leaving a ragged hole ten metres across. Annie was reminded of a volcano erupting. The chimney stack teetered and then collapsed into the hole with a thunderous crash to be replaced by a tower of flickering orange flames. Broken tiles, splinters of roof beams and nuggets of concrete began to fall from the smoky sky showering the onlookers with a deadly hailstorm.

CHAPTER 7

Tod Harris stared at the lead story on page two of the mirror. His hands were shaking worse than before. He could hardly hold his tea to his lips without spilling it. The more he read, the worse he felt. There had been times over the last few days when he thought that he might get away with it. Lying on his sunbed, floating in the crystal-clear pool or drinking ice-cold beer and listening to music in the busy bars had all given him a false sense of security. He had felt that he could stay there forever, untouchable, invisible, and safe from arrest but the newspaper article had shattered his illusions into smithereens.

'Here you go, handsome,' Gordon placed an oval shaped plate in front of him. It looked like a heart attack on a dish. 'And here's some toast,' he said leaving a rack of golden triangles. 'If you eat all that up, you're a pig!' He chuckled. He noticed the pallor of Tod's face and stopped smiling. 'You look like you've seen a ghost, are you okay?' He frowned and leaned toward him. 'Are you feeling okay?'

Tod looked up from the paper with a blank expression on his face. His eyes seemed glassy and unfocused. 'I'm sorry,' he mumbled. 'What did you say?' He looked around and saw that some of the other diners were staring at him. That was all he needed. Tourists staring at his face. A face that would be splashed all over the newspapers when they realised what he had done. It might take a day, or it might take a week, but they would remember his face and when his mugshot was all over the Press, they would remember him from their holidays. He tried to pull himself together.

'You look terrible,' Gordon said kindly. 'Too much to drink last night?'

'Yes, I'm sure that's all it is.' Tod tried a smile, but it turned into a sneer. He sat back and put the newspaper down next to his plate. 'This looks good!' he commented a little too enthusiastically. 'This would get a rhino back on its feet. It's just what I need.'

'Do you want another orange juice?' Gordon smiled again. 'The vitamin C will do you good and it's on the house.' He held up his hand to stop any arguments. 'To hell with the boat, another juice please, Gordon,' he shouted inside. 'This wee man needs some energy inside him. Tuck in and I'll bring your juice.'

Tod smiled thinly and picked up his knife and fork. His appetite had vanished, but he didn't want to draw attention to himself. He put the knife down and reached for the ketchup, zigzagging the red sauce across his eggs. He took a triangle of toast from a stainless-steel rack and dipped into a bright yellow yolk. It popped and ran across his sausages. He took a bite and closed his eyes and wondered what the hell had happened that night. How could things have gotten so out of hand?

CHAPTER 8

'The victim didn't have a tattoo on her toe, Mrs Windsor,' Annie said calmly. She was sat in her car watching the fire brigade trying to get the inferno under control. The old lady had a gauze pad pressed to her head where a piece of debris had fallen from the sky and cut her scalp. A bloodstain the shape of Africa had seeped through. Ambulances were en route but Annie needed some answers before they arrived and began to take the injured away. 'And her feet were much smaller than a size six.'

Mrs Windsor's eyes widened, and she shook her head. Tears stained her cheeks and a look of confusion set in. 'I don't understand,' she spoke quietly. 'I gave the police officer a picture from my purse. Was she that badly hurt that you couldn't identify the body from the photo?' Her voice was almost a whisper. Annie detected a privileged background in her accent. That might explain how a single woman could afford a new three-bedroom house on a Special Constable's wage.

'Photographs can be deceiving,' Annie lied. 'That's why we always ask for distinguishing marks, tattoos and the like.'

'I'm not stupid, Inspector.' Deep lines creased her face when she frowned. 'It would be much simpler to use the photograph unless her face was so disfigured that it made it useless.'

Annie sighed and felt a little embarrassed, 'I know you're not stupid. I can't talk about the details. The long and short of it is that the victim didn't have the tattoo that you described on her toe.'

'Are you telling me that Jayne is not dead?' Her thin lips quivered as she spoke.

'No,' Annie said frankly. 'I'm not telling you that at all but the victim in the bedroom was not Jayne.'

'Of course, you can't say much more can you?' As she spoke, her hand touched her face, wrinkled by age and coloured with dark liver spots. She was a pretty woman for her years. There were deep lines at the corners of her eyes, but her cheeks were smooth. Only her hands gave away clues to her age. Annie put her closer to sixty-five than fifty. 'I don't understand, Inspector.' She jumped visibly as the roof of the house collapsed in on itself. A deep rumble echoed across the street. Embers, smoke, and steam spiralled skyward. 'She could be in there couldn't she?' Another tear broke free and rolled down her face. 'Buried beneath all that rubble.'

Annie looked at the notes that the liaison officer had made. 'Listen, Elsbeth,' she said. 'May I call you that?'

'Beth.' She sniffed. 'Everyone calls me Beth.'

'Okay, Beth. The facts are that the body we found didn't have a tattoo and her feet were too small to be Jayne's,' Annie explained. 'The other thing to consider is that her car is missing. Can you think of any reason why it wouldn't be parked on the drive?'

Beth thought about her comments and shook her head. 'She didn't drink so she never left it anywhere else.'

'Then the chances of her being in there,' Annie looked at the smouldering shell, 'are very slim. We didn't have a lot of time in there, but a preliminary search was done by the responding officers. There was no sign of another victim.'

'I'm not sure that's a good thing, Inspector,' Beth smiled thinly. Her eyes had intelligence behind them. 'Whoever killed that poor woman probably took Jayne with them.' She watched Annie's face for a reaction. 'At least that's what I would be thinking if I was in your position. She could be lying dead somewhere while we're sat here discussing her, couldn't she?'

Annie nodded and sighed. 'She could be, but we don't know that for a fact. A neighbour saw her going out on Saturday night. Who did Jayne socialise with?'

'Jayne didn't have many friends,' Beth said staring at what was left of her daughter's home. 'Might be my fault that she was awkward around people.'

'How so?'

'I had her very late in life you see,' she explained. 'I'd turned forty. Her father died when she was a baby, heart attack, and I wrapped her in cotton wool. I was a little overprotective.' A tear formed and spilled from her left eye. She wiped it away with the back of her hand and took a deep breath. 'Do you have children?'

'No.' Annie smiled. 'They're not conducive with being a DI.' In her head she added 'and now that I'm a one-eyed freak, I'm hardly likely to have much choice in the matter.' But she didn't say it aloud.

'Yes, that must be difficult to get a balance.' Her voice drifted off as if she was in deep thought. A tear escaped and rolled down her cheek. 'Don't leave it too late like I did. Every woman should have a child, it makes them complete.'

Annie didn't agree. Some of the mothers that she encountered daily should never have been allowed to breed. It wasn't a debate that she needed to get into. She didn't want to lose her just yet. 'You were telling me who her friends were?'

'Pardon?'

'Her friends?'

'Oh yes.' Beth snapped back to reality. 'Please forgive me. A senior moment that's all.'

'You have suffered a nasty shock, Beth but it would really help me if you could tell me their names.'

Beth nodded and smiled but it was a sad smile. 'That won't be a very long list, Inspector. As I said, she didn't have many friends at all.' She wiped another tear away. 'Her best friend is, was, oh dear,' she sobbed. There was a long pause as she closed her eyes and composed herself. 'Jackie Webb. She lives in a flat near Sefton Park. She told me that they were going out to town on Saturday night.' Her eyes widened and she looked at Annie in the eyes. 'Do you think that might be Jackie in there?'

Annie swerved the question. 'Do you have an address and a number for her?'

'Yes,' Beth stammered. 'I have her business card here. A few years back she set herself up as a mobile beauty therapist, doing permanent mascara, lip liners, and the like.' She fumbled in her handbag, which Annie noticed was a hand stitched designer Vuitton. 'Here it is.'

'Was she blond?'

'Yes, most of the time. She had a jet-black phase, but it didn't last long,' she half smiled. 'Was the victim blond?'

Annie didn't want to answer that question. Luckily the sound of ambulance sirens arriving rescued her. 'I'll need to talk to you again soon but for now, we need to get you to hospital and get that head wound stitched.'

'Do you think Jayne's alive?' she asked quietly. 'I mean in your mind; do you believe there's any hope?'

'There's always hope, Beth.'

'Not always, we both know that.' Beth seemed to shrink in on herself. She looked frail, shattered, and vulnerable. 'This is a violent world that we live in. Sometimes there is no hope at all.' She touched Annie's hand. 'Find her for me, Inspector. I want my daughter home.' She swallowed hard. 'Even if she is,' she couldn't bring herself to say the word, 'you know what I mean?'

'Yes.' Annie nodded. 'I know what you mean. I'll do my best,' Annie squeezed her hand and opened the door, desperate to escape the woman's grief. She climbed out of the Audi and took a deep gulp of smoke tainted air before walking over to Stirling who was talking to a CSI. He saw her approaching and broke off from his conversation. 'Anything?' Annie asked.

'Nothing yet, they're still searching the neighbouring gardens, bins etc.' He shrugged. 'Early days yet, guv. Did you get anything from the mother?'

'I got the name, address, and phone number of Jayne's best friend, Jackie Webb. She said that Jackie is who Jayne had planned to go out with. Apparently, she's a blond.'

'Oh dear.'

'Oh, dear indeed. Get uniform to her house just to check. She works for herself and she's mobile so if her vehicle is parked up and there's no answer, we've found our victim.'

'You said she was mobile, mobile what?' Stirling frowned.

'Beautician apparently.'

'In which case if she is missing, she'll have a lot of disappointed customers leaving angry messages on her phone,' he said. 'I'll get her phone records and check her inbox. It could speed things up.'

'Good thinking,' Annie looked around as they spoke. 'Where's Kathy?'

'She's gone back to the lab to get started on what they'd bagged.' Stirling pointed to the growing group of Press reporters. 'Are we going public to see if we can trace where they went on Saturday night?'

Annie bit her bottom lip and watched the group. Some were chatting, some squabbling. The BBC camera crew were jostling for the best position to film the fire. 'Last resort,' she decided. 'Let's get pictures of them both distributed around the city centre. Two girls out on a Saturday night, they'll have been wherever still has a dance floor. That should narrow it down to a few hundred places.' She said sarcastically. They were looking for a needle in a pile of needles. 'I want a team of four working on the script that was on the body. Put Watkin's team on it. Graham took a lot of pictures of it. Have him send over everything he has and tell Watkin that I want to know what it is and what it says and tell him that I want to know today. In the meantime, let's hope Kathy finds something.'

CHAPTER 9

Constable Bowers brought his vehicle to a halt outside a new apartment block, which overlooked Sefton Park. Ornate railings separated the manicured lawns from the road and the entire plot was surrounded by well-established trees. Bowers recalled that a school once stood on the spot. Developers had built sixty flats on it, which netted them millions. 'How the other half live.' He sighed. He checked his notes for the apartment number and grumbled to himself about how many years he would have to save just to raise a deposit to buy a flat in a property like that. Feeling aggrieved at being sent on such a tedious errand, he opened the door and climbed out.

He glanced over at the park; acres of lawns ran gently down to the boating lake. A tractor purred in the distance, trimming the grass and clearing fallen leaves. The cool breeze that ruffled his greying hair had deterred all but the most determined walkers from enjoying the greenery. Bowers walked through the gates and checked the parking bays. According to control, a woman called Jackie Webb owned apartment number four and had a Mercedes SLK registered to her name. Most of the parking bays were empty but number four had a vehicle in it. There was a German made vehicle there, but it wasn't a Mercedes. It was a 3-series BMW.

Bowers thought about calling it in but decided not to. He needed to be sure of the details before he made a report. He turned towards the apartments and walked along a stone path to where the ground floor flats were. The numbers went up in twos; Jackie Webb's being the second door along the path. The front window was bowed, Georgian style with lots of small square panes. Some of the panes were dimpled. His view inside was blocked by heavy curtains that were closed. He tapped his knuckles on the window and listened for movement inside. Nothing.

Bowers moved to the front door and peered through the bevelled glass. It was a pointless exercise. The image was so distorted that he couldn't glean any information from it. He had a blurred impression of the hallway and nothing more. His orders were to knock on the door and check out the car parking bays. They had specifically ordered him not to touch the letter box or try to enter the property. He had heard about the explosion across town and reading between the lines, it was obvious that there was a connection. He rapped on the door with his knuckles and waited. Nothing.

'Seven, five, five,' he called into his coms. The radio crackled and buzzed.

'Go ahead, seven, five, five.'

'No reply at number four Sefton Heights but there is a 3-series BMW parked in the owner's bay.'

'Roger that,' the voice replied. 'I'll relay it to the DI. Standby.'

'Roger,' he said distracted. A black Ford sped into the car park, tyres squealing as it screeched to a halt. The driver, a casually dressed middle-aged woman with blond hair opened the door and walked quickly towards him, her face a picture of fear and concern.

'This is my daughter's flat,' she said breathlessly. 'Jackie Webb is my daughter. I have a key.' She tried to pass by him. 'I need to get in to see if she is all right.'

'I can't let you in there, Mrs Webb?' Bowers put his arm across her path. 'Are you Mrs Webb?'

'Yes, I am,' she snapped. 'What do you mean I can't go in?' she gasped. She pushed against him. 'I have to get in there. Jackie may be injured!'

'Please calm down, Mrs Webb.' Bowers held firm. 'Now what makes you think that Jackie is injured?'

She tried to step around him, her face flushed red with frustration. 'Move you idiot!' she shouted. 'Jayne's mother called me, and someone has been hurt. I have to get in there now!'

Bowers grabbed her by the arms and shook her gently to gain her attention. 'Mrs Webb!' he growled. 'I cannot let you into that property until we know that it is safe.' He shook her gently again. 'Do you understand me?'

Mrs Webb tensed and then seemed to flop into his arms. Bowers had to grab her under the armpits to hold her weight. Her legs had turned to jelly. 'Jackie could be hurt,' she whined. 'Please!'

'Calm down,' Bowers said soothingly. He walked her backwards away from the front door. 'Now what makes you think that she's been injured?'

'My friend called me,' she sobbed. 'Jayne Windsor's mother. She said that there's been a murder,' she rambled. 'Jackie was with her daughter and I haven't heard from her this week. I have to get inside.'

'Do you normally hear from her every day,' Bowers asked.

'No,' she stammered. 'Not every day but she was with Jayne Windsor. Something terrible has happened.'

The name meant nothing to officer Bowers. His orders had been specific but had little in the way of details attached. He guided Mrs Webb further from the apartments; reluctantly but she didn't resist. 'Seven, five, five,' he kept one eye on the distraught woman as he spoke.

'Go ahead.'

'I have Mrs Webb here,' he tempered his voice so as not to panic her further. 'She has keys to number four Sefton Heights and is keen to go inside to look for her daughter.' He paused. 'She seems to think that she might be injured.'

'Negative, seven, five, five,' control replied. 'The DI is en route with support vehicles. She specified that no one is to attempt entry under any circumstances. ETA fifteen minutes.'

'Roger that.' Bowers raised his eyebrows and shook his head. 'You heard that, Mrs Webb. I'm afraid we'll have to wait until the detective in charge of the case arrives. I'm sorry but I can't allow you near the apartment.'

Mrs Webb huffed and squeezed her hands together, childlike. 'This is ridiculous!' she turned and stormed off towards her Ford. Bowers watched her suspiciously. Frightened people could be unpredictable but frightened parents were different again. They would do anything to protect their children even if it meant putting themselves in grave danger. 'I'll be filing a complaint.' She turned and wagged her finger at him. 'I'll sue if anything happens to Jackie.' She looked panicked and confused. She wiped her sweaty palms on her jeans and check shirt and stomped her feet in anger. Bowers felt for her. He had children himself. Teenagers. He spent all day working with the scum of the earth, which made it very difficult not to worry whenever they were out of his sight. Mrs Webb looked around, desperate for the detectives to arrive so that she could try to find her daughter. When her eyes fell on the access road, which led to the rear of the apartments, she jumped into the driver's seat and slammed the door. Bowers followed her gaze and realised what she intended to do. As she started the engine and the vehicle lurched forward, he swore under his breath and sprinted along the path.

CHAPTER 10

'We can rule out ancient Greek, Hebrew, and Sumerian,' DS Watkin said excitedly. If there was anyone geeky enough to enjoy tracing an ancient script and identifying it, he was the man. 'I would recognise them at a glance.' The three other officers in his team looked at each other and rolled their eyes skyward. They called him Google as it seemed there was no limit to his knowledge. Or so he claimed. 'I could spot them a mile away.'

'Of course, you would,' Gwen said sarcastically. She had worked alongside him for two years and understood his enthusiasm for the task at hand. She often told him that he should have been a forensic investigator. 'Why don't we google 'ancient text' and eliminate them in alphabetical order?' The others nodded in agreement. 'Surely it will speed things up.'

'No need to.' Watkin shrugged as he typed commands onto his keyboard. 'most ancient scripts are runic in their origins, but this is definitely not runic. That negates much of what you'll find on the net. I'm guessing these are biblical texts carved into the victim.' he mused as he scanned the screen with his tongue between his teeth. His thick lenses and chubby face gave him a schoolboy appearance. 'I've seen this before and I'm certain it's a type of Cyrillic.'

'Put your tongue back in your mouth,' Gwen teased him. 'It makes you look simple.'

'Using this word here as a template, it matches with Glagolitic!' He sat back and folded his arms proudly, ignoring her jibe. 'I knew it. Some schools of thought in the old Eastern Block call it the 'witches' language' because there are many dark books of spells and the like written in it.'

'Spells?'

Gwen folded her arms and nodded in agreement. 'They used it in case the books fell into the wrong hands.' She shrugged. 'So that the uneducated couldn't use the content unwisely.'

'They also use it in case the authorities found them. Practicing witches were burned at the stake.'

'They found a pentagram at the scene, didn't they?'

'Let's not jump to conclusions just yet.' Google looked at their faces and grinned. They didn't look as excited by his discovery as they should. 'What are you waiting for?' He pointed to their computer screens. 'Google Glagolitic and pull up the alphabet. Take a photograph each and get on with translating the script. We can have this done by tonight!' He grinned again.

Gwen blew air from her cheeks and whistled. 'Oh goodie,' she mumbled. 'Let's see what our latest psycho has to say shall we. I'll take a five-pound bet that it's gobbledygook.'

'Oh no, you're very wrong,' Watkin said sternly. 'Anyone who can learn this script and uses it to this extent, has something very important to say but he wants the reader to work very hard to decipher his words. I'll take your five-pound bet that it's gobbledygook.' He leaned over the desk and held out his hand. Gwen shook his hand and scoffed. A second later, Google was scribbling letters onto a pad.

'It's probably the lyrics to an Eminem album,' she muttered. She picked up a crime scene image of the victim and immediately felt a pang of guilt for making light of the text. It was after all, carved into her flesh. 'Whatever it says' —she looked at the others '—let's hope it helps us to find this sick bastard.'

'Amen,' Google said. His team looked surprised. He smiled and shook his head. 'Amen! It's the first word on her left collarbone. I knew there would be something biblical!'

'Of course, you did.' Gwen smiled, hiding the urge to poke him in the eye with her finger.

CHAPTER 11

PC Bowers sprinted as fast as his expanding waistline and arthritic knees would allow him to. He had been pulled off the frontline years ago and was coasting towards his retirement taking statements for insurance companies following burglaries or car thefts. He hadn't had a partner for twelve months. Nowadays all he needed was a pen and a notepad. After just a few strides, his breath was coming in rasping bursts. His joints and connective tissues were straining under the unaccustomed pressure.

The Webb woman was determined to enter her daughter's apartment and the chances were that, she would make it to the back door before he did. He heard the engine of her vehicle racing in low gear. It accelerated quickly putting distance between them. It roared out of view behind the apartment block, the tyres screeched as she turned the corner into the rear car park. He heard the gravel crunch beneath the wheels as it skidded to a halt. She was already at the rear of the flat. Bowers reached the end of the front path and turned the corner at full pelt. His feet slipped from beneath him and he hit the floor hard, taking his full weight on his elbows. Gravel ripped his uniform and tore the skin; friction burned his flesh. The impact knocked the wind from his lungs. 'I'm too old for this shit,' he moaned.

Sirens wailed in the distance. He took a moment to compose himself and to get his breath back. The thought of being on the receiving end of a ticking off from his superiors was top of mind. All he had to do was keep an empty apartment secure. He couldn't be outwitted by an aging housewife. The thought spurred him on. He would be the laughingstock of the station if his orders were thwarted by a middle-aged woman. He pushed himself to his hands and knees like a sprinter in the blocks and then ran towards the rear. As he reached the next corner, he heard the Ford stop, the door opening, and then her footsteps on the gravel. He slowed as he turned right, his bruises reminding him of the result of losing his footing again.

His momentum carried him onto the path and straight into a blue wheelie-bin. He tumbled head over heels, his weight knocking the bin sideways, scattering bottles and cans across the car park. He fell, palms splayed, and knees grazed onto the concrete. 'For fuck's sake!' he hissed as he scrambled to his feet. He kicked the wheelie-bin in anger and shouted after the woman. 'Mrs Webb!'

The rear gardens were separated by high Waney Lap panels and concrete posts. A series of wooden gates gave access to each ground floor plot. Jackie Webb had secured her gate with a mortice lock that could be opened from either side, offering her visitors the option to enter from the rear providing they had a key.

'Mrs Webb,' he shouted breathlessly. She was fumbling with a set of keys, trying to open the gate. She looked up and saw him thundering around the corner towards her. 'Mrs Webb!' he called again.

She dropped the keys and scrambled on the floor to pick them up. He was fifty yards from her. She looked panicked as she sorted through the bunch. There were three keys that could fit a mortice. Her fingers trembled as she slipped the first into the lock, twisting it until it grated against metal. She tried twisting it further, but it wouldn't budge. He was forty yards away; his mouth was moving but she couldn't hear the words. Jackie was inside and she was hurt. She knew that she was in terrible danger, hurt, frightened, and alone. Her instincts told her that something terrible had happened. The second key rattled against the lock and then slid in. It turned a quarter then stopped. The policeman was closing the gap quickly. She picked the third one from the bunch and pushed it home, twisting it with sweaty hands, the lock clicked open.

'Mrs Webb!'

Twenty yards. His voice made her actions more urgent. She turned the handle and pushed open the gate, running through it as fast as she could. She slammed it closed, forcing her back against the panels to stop him entering. She scrambled to get the key into the lock. Bowers crashed into the other side of the gate; his weight almost splintered the wood. She locked the mortice as he turned the handle and rattled the gate in its frame. 'Mrs Webb, you cannot enter the property!' he crashed into it again with little effect. The gate wouldn't hold for long. She breathed a sigh of relief and walked quickly towards the back door. The gate rattled again as Bowers put his shoulder against it. 'Mrs Webb!' The frame creaked and the wood splintered slightly but it held firm.

PC Bowers looked up and contemplated climbing over the fence but dismissed the idea quickly. His arms were no longer strong enough to pull his body weight up and he doubted that the flimsy Waney Lap panels would support him. He could end up breaking his spine. 'Mrs Webb!' he shouted again in desperation rattling the handle with all his might. Looking through the cracks between the panels, he could see her putting a key into the back door. 'Mrs Webb, please listen to me,' Bowers lowered his voice in one final attempt to stop her. 'You're putting yourself and your daughter in danger if you enter the building.'

Mrs Webb stopped for a second and looked back to where he was stood. Her face looked confused but determined. She shook her head dismissing his pleas and searched for the key to the back door. Bowers began battering the gate with renewed vigour, driving her into a fluster. The lock was a Yale. She sifted through the bunch, one key at a time until she found one with the correct brand etched onto it. The gate cracked and she heard wood splintering.

She slipped the key into the lock and turned it, but it wouldn't open. 'Shit, shit, shit!' she whispered under her breath. She pictured her daughter's kitchen in her mind. The back door was half glazed, fixed with a Yale lock at the centre. The image of sliding bolts, top and bottom appeared in her mind. 'Shit!' she sobbed. 'Jackie!' she shouted and banged on the glass. 'Jackie!' her name turned into a wail. A panel gave way beneath Bower's force and clattered onto the garden path. He reached through the gap, searching for the handle. It reminded Mrs Webb of cinema posters advertising *The Shining*. Jack Nicolson's manic face replaced the policeman's for a moment, despite being in her own horror story now. She looked around for inspiration and saw a stone flowerpot near the wall, its contents long since withered. They had bought it at a car boot sale in the spring. She could hear Jackie complaining about its weight as they walked back to the car. The thought forced tears from her eyes. Her fingers gripped the edge and she felt a fingernail split. Ignoring the pain, she swung the pot upwards in an arc. The impact shattered the pane and shards of glass exploded across the kitchen. Long daggers of glass remained fixed to the frame making it impossible for her to reach inside to free the bolts without ripping her flesh. 'Mrs Webb!' The sound of another panel cracking made her intensify her efforts as she swung a second time, and a third and fourth smashing the remaining pieces of glass from the door. The glass tinkled across the tiled floor and she reached down to undo the bottom bolt.

'Jackie!' she shouted as she fumbled with the bolt, her fingers only just reaching it. It lifted and she slid it open, trapping her index finger between the bar and the fastening. She yelped in pain and put it in her mouth instinctively and then looked at the injury. A blood blister was rising quickly. She felt desperation taking a hold of her senses. 'Jackie, it's Mum!' Her greeting was met only by silence and the pounding of her blood in her ears. The gate gave way beneath the relentless battering from the police officer's shoulder, wood cracked and splintered, and the remaining panels clattered along the path. She turned to see him climbing through the gap only to catch his sleeve on an exposed nail. It gave her precious seconds.

'Mrs Webb,' his voice had reached full volume now, anger and exertion tinged his words. 'Do not enter that house or I will arrest you!'

The garbled threat meant nothing to her. She reached up and grasped the top bolt with her fingers. The blood blister burst, and she whimpered in pain but struggled to slide it open regardless. It slotted home with a clunk and she turned the Yale key with her other hand using her weight to open the door. 'Jackie!' she shouted as she stumbled into the kitchen. The silence inside was deafening. 'Jackie!' She felt broken glass crunching beneath her feet as she ran towards the door, which led to the hallway. 'Jackie!' She turned the handle and pulled it open, her vision now blurred with tears. 'Jackie!'

'Mrs Webb!' Bowers was entering the kitchen door. He reached out to grab her, his fingers touching her clothes briefly. 'Stop right there!'

Mrs Webb bolted into the hallway and glanced into the bathroom. Her mouth fell open loosely and her features changed to an expression of anguish. The sink was covered with dark stains. It looked like blood. Dried black blood. Jackie's blood? Her legs turned to jelly. The taps were covered in it and the mirror was smeared with finger marks. Blood. Jackie's blood? 'No, no, no,' she whispered. She couldn't think straight. There were words on the mirror, but they didn't register; all the information flashed through her mind in an instant. Where was Jackie? She grabbed at the wall for support, her knees weakened by the sight of blood. Her daughter's blood? 'Oh, God no,' she gasped as she looked into the living room. Bloody handprints smeared the walls, the door, and the frame, long finger marks as if someone had been dragged bleeding along the hallway, desperately trying to claw at the walls for grip. 'Jackie!' she screamed as she reached the bedroom door. 'Jackie?' she said in a whimper. 'Jackie?' Her knees buckled and she flopped to the floor like a pilgrim at prayer. 'Jackie?' Her chest heaved, and her voice cracked with pain. 'Oh, no, please no.' She sobbed. 'Jackie, Jackie, Jackie.' Her words just a whisper in the silence.

Bowers reached her, a panting sweaty heap. His face was purple with anger and exhaustion. 'Mrs Webb,' he started to say. As he took in the scene in the bedroom his voice trailed off and his breathing stopped in his chest. He felt the half-digested contents of his stomach rising in his throat and he gagged as it erupted from his mouth and splattered onto the carpet.

CHAPTER 12

'Even though they've given the all clear, I'm not in the slightest bit happy,' Annie said as she stepped into the kitchen at Sefton Heights. Broken glass cracked beneath her tan leather boots. 'Did the Bomb Squad say they're checking the BMW?' she said to Stirling, who was a few steps behind her.

'They're on it now, guv. Underneath it and inside are clear but they want to check the engine just in case.' He grunted. 'We didn't recover the keys, so they broke into it instead of waiting for a spare remote to be programmed at a dealership in the city. They're letting residents back into their apartments so they must be sure there are no devices.'

Annie nodded silently and looked around. The kitchen was tidy; all the appliances were new and expensive. A single cup stood on the draining board. She opened the fridge with a gloved hand and studied the empty shelves. One egg remained in a half dozen box on the top shelf. An inch of semi-skimmed which according to the use by date, was a week old stood in the door. 'Looks like she dined out a lot,' Annie said to herself. The image of the jawless corpse at the first scene entered her mind. She shuddered and walked towards the hallway. Stirling filled the bathroom doorway with his bulk. He turned as she approached and grimaced. Annie looked inside and shook her head. It was the opposite of the previous scene. Blood stained the enamel sink and the stainless-steel fixtures. There had been no detailed clean up here. The mirror was smeared with congealed blood and the words, 'when you look in the mirror, what looks back at you?' were written on the glass.

'What indeed?' Annie answered the question, wondering what the animal that had written it saw when he looked in the mirror. She avoided looking at her own reflection. She hated the false eye with a passion. The jagged scar beneath it had faded significantly and her surgeon had recommended a concealing foundation used by burn victims, which all but hid it completely but she still couldn't bring herself to linger in front of her reflection.

'Is this all for shock value or is our killer a real loon?' Stirling growled. 'I never was good at riddles.'

They glanced into the living room. It was a wide space with real wood flooring and a huge flat screen plasma mounted on the wall. Three White leather settees and two recliners seemed lost in the room. 'Mobile beauticians must be raking it in these days,' Annie raised her eyebrows. Stirling grunted in agreement. Blood stained both arms of a reclining armchair as if someone had sat for a while resting or watching television. The black stains stood in stark contrast against the leather. The thought of the killer relaxing before, during, or after such an evil act worried Annie to her core. He was ice cold, detracted from reality with no empathy for the victims. They were hunting the most dangerous type of killer that one could encounter.

As they approached the bedroom the air grew thick with decay. Not as bad as the first scene but still stomach churning. She could smell fresh vomit mingled with the decomposition. Although hardened to seeing murder victims in situ, the sight that met them was enough to make her take a sharp intake of breath.

'Mrs Webb saw this?' Annie raised her eyebrows and looked at Stirling. 'Jesus.'

Stirling frowned and nodded. 'According to PC Bowers she did, although she hasn't spoken a word since. The paramedics sedated her and took her to the Royal. Bowers threw up,' he added pointing to a pool of sick. 'Don't step in it.'

'Same killer?' Annie asked no one in particular as she stepped over the gooey puddle. She stepped inside and analysed the carnage. The victim lay dressed in a basque, stockings, and suspenders, her skin striped by hundreds of narrow cuts and slashes. Her head had been severed and placed on the dressing table facing the mirror. The same words, 'when you look in the mirror, what looks back at you?' were smeared on the glass in blood. 'See the make-up,' Annie pointed at the severed head. She walked to the dressing table and studied it closely. 'That's been put on her by a man. Clumsily.' She paused. 'She looks like a clown.' She scanned the body and saw ink on her toe.

Stirling stared at her foot. 'The flower tattoo,' he said looking at Annie. 'This is Jayne Windsor.'

'Yes,' Annie agreed. 'We have to assume that it is. Our killer is playing a game with us and I for one, am not enjoying it one bit.' She tossed ideas around in her mind, but nothing made sense. 'Jackie Webb was killed in Jayne Windsor's house and dressed in her uniform.' She shrugged. 'Jayne Windsor is here, tortured to death, beheaded, and dressed in lingerie?'

'Could be his fantasies,' Stirling offered. 'Cop's uniform, stockings, and suspenders, makes sense?'

'Nothing makes sense here but thanks for putting the male perspective on it.'

'Just thinking aloud.'

'Best not to sometimes.'

'Sorry, guv,' Stirling sounded wounded.

'Don't be. You are probably right.'

Stirling looked confused. He walked around the bed and looked at the corpse. 'I think she was dressed post-mortem just like the first victim. There's not enough blood on the basque for it to have been worn when he removed her head.'

'Just like the first scene,' Annie agreed. 'The killer dressed them after he had finished with them.'

'In which case it's not a sexual fantasy. It's a message.'

'Yes, but what is the sicko trying to say?'

'God knows.'

'God was never here,' Annie said. She stepped closer to the severed head and studied it further. 'Her eyelids have been glued open.'

'He wanted her to watch something.' Stirling shrugged. 'Do you think he made her watch what he did to Jackie Webb?'

'Probably.' She noticed a purple triangle that protruded from the lips. 'There is something in her mouth,' she said reaching for a pair of tweezers. She took her phone from her pocket and snapped three pictures of the lips before pulling at the triangle with the tweezers. Once an inch was revealed, she stopped, leaving the evidence in place for the CSI team to analyse. 'It's a twenty-pound note.'

'He's degrading the victim.' Stirling frowned. 'Money in the mouth, the lingerie, removing the head?'

'We are looking for one sick puppy,' Annie agreed. She turned from the dressing table and looked closely at the body. Deep bruising encircled the wrists and ankles. The indentations had broken the skin in places. Her nails were neatly painted with a natural pink varnish, the tips split and caked with blood. 'I hope this belongs to our killer.' Annie commented on it. 'And this,' she gestured to sticky residue on the quilt between her thighs. There was deep purple bruising to her legs above the suspenders. The main injuries visible were the long shallow cuts that ran parallel across her skin. 'How long would it take to slice the skin so finely like this?' she asked studying the arms and legs.

'Hours, maybe days.'

'It's been done using a razor blade or a carpet knife?' She shook her head. 'The cuts are so fine it couldn't be anything else. What a way to die.'

'Doesn't warrant thinking about,' Stirling mumbled. He looked at the walls and ceiling. 'There are no satanic markings daubed anywhere, no ancient text similar to the first scene.'

'The level of violence is similar, yet the details are different.'

A tallboy stood next to the base of the bed. The top drawer was slightly open. He stepped across the room and opened the drawer an inch wider. 'I'm guessing the killer used underwear from here to dress her,' he said nodding towards the drawer. 'This is full of similar stuff,' he said,' he said poking at the silk, satin, and lace with a gloved finger. 'Bloody hell!' he recoiled.

'What?' Annie asked in a concerned tone.

'That thing is massive!'

'What is?'

'A big pink monstrosity.' He shook his head. 'Surely it's a novelty toy?' he paused. 'I mean surely you couldn't, well you know what I mean. You would do yourself an injury with that.'

Annie raised her eyebrows and looked in the drawer. She puffed out her cheeks and sighed. 'Each to their own, Sergeant.' His embarrassment was mildly amusing under the circumstances.

'All the same,' he huffed. 'That could be classed as an offensive weapon. Maybe she hadn't dated for a while.'

'I hope you're not jumping to conclusions, Sergeant,' Kathy Brooks said from the doorway. 'And I hope you're not trampling on my evidence.'

Annie sighed and pointed to the severed head. 'We've had a preliminary look around. There's a twenty-pound note in her mouth. I pulled it an inch to see what it was, no more than that. It's still in place. We haven't touched anything else.'

'I can't moan about that considering our last victim is nothing but ashes,' Kathy said smiling thinly. 'I'm tempted to move her immediately,' she shuddered. 'There's no smell of petrol here, which is reassuring. This looks slightly more disorganised don't you think?'

'He hasn't taken as much care cleaning up, but I'm convinced what he has left behind belongs to the victim, not himself. He's playing games.'

'Agreed.' Kathy nodded. She looked impatient. 'I've sent everything from the first scene for analysis as a priority. If we can get to work quickly here, then we can run comparisons on whatever we find,' she said matter-of-factly. 'I'll get started. Unless you need more time here?'

'Crack on,' Annie smiled sarcastically. She gestured to Stirling that they should leave. 'We've got plenty to be getting on with although I'm not a hundred per cent sure where the starting line is on this one.'

'Thanks, Annie.' Kathy smiled. 'As soon as I have anything, I'll call you.'

The detectives left the bedroom and headed down the hallway. Annie was relieved to be away from the cloying smell. She held her breath until she reached the back door only releasing it when she was a few metres clear of the kitchen. White suited figures filed in as they left, nodding mumbled greetings. Their eyes were filled with a mixture of anticipation and dread. She felt slightly amused as they walked through the shattered gate. A vision of an overweight constable battering his way through it sprang into her mind. A fit police officer would have been over the fence in a heartbeat. It was a tiny drop of dark humour in an inky black ocean of despair. What the mother suffered trying to gain access to her daughter's house was beyond understanding. Annie felt sick inside.

'Where are we with her phone messages?' Annie asked sifting through an ever-growing list of priorities.

'I'm hoping there's a printout on my desk when we get back, guv.'

'Okay. For now, we must assume that the first victim is Jackie Webb, and the phone messages will hopefully confirm that, agreed?'

'Agreed.'

'I don't think this a random slaying, agreed?'

'Agreed.'

'More importantly, I don't think the sick bastard is going to stop there, agreed?'

'Agreed.'

'See how Google's team is getting on with the text translation and get a handle on the phone records. I'll take a look at the BMW and meet you at the station.'

'Guv.' Stirling closed his leather jacket against the breeze and ambled off to his car. Annie guessed that it had taken a full cow hide to make the back of his coat. She ducked beneath the crime scene tape and approached the Army Logistics officer, who had supervised the search of the flat and the BMW.

He smiled as she approached. 'Inspector,' he greeted her. 'The car is safe.' He gestured towards the vehicle. A man dressed in a bomb suit, which made him look like he was related to a rhinoceros, raised a gloved thumb. 'There is blood and hair in the boot. I'm sure your forensic team will have plenty to play with.'

'Good,' Annie replied. 'We need a few breaks on this one. Have you got anything from the first scene that could help me?'

His chest seemed to swell beneath his protective vest as he thought about her question. His boots were polished to a mirror finish, his greying hair cropped close to his scalp. 'I've spoken to the fireman who lifted the hatch to the attic and from what he said, I can tell you that your killer is an accomplished incendiary bomb maker.' Annie raised her eyebrows and waited for him to elaborate. 'He said he heard a metallic 'click' and something rolling before a light came on in the loft.'

'Which means what exactly?'

'Your killer probably made an electric circuit of some kind and then used a metal ball bearing as the trigger.'

'Can you explain that to me?'

'He balanced a metal ball on something, then when the hatch was lifted, it moved it. Once it was dislodged from its seat, it rolled down a tube or a pipe where it lodged between two electric contacts completing the circuit.'

'Switching on the light?'

'The light could have been part of a simple cooking appliance, which heated up quickly igniting the fuel.'

Annie frowned, 'Cooking appliance?'

'Yes.' He shrugged. 'A hotplate or even a heating element like the ones campers use to make a cup of hot water.'

'The ones which look like a coil?'

'Exactly. If the element was inserted into a sealed container of petrol, the ball bearing makes the circuit, the element is switched on, reaches a high temperature in seconds and whoosh.' He clapped his hands together making Annie jump. 'Simple yet very clever and a method widely available on the Internet.'

'Would you say he was ex-military?'

'Possibly but it's not a given. A military mind may have opted to make an explosive device rather than an incendiary. Your killer basically started a fire. With a little practice, anyone with half a brain could have rigged that up.' He smiled. 'Having said that, it might be beyond some of the squaddies I've met in my time, but most would manage it.' He laughed at his private joke. Annie was too deep in thought to catch it. 'As soon as we've sorted through the remnants of the device, I can tell you more.' He nodded his head. 'Good luck with catching him, Inspector.'

Annie smiled in thanks and watched him walk away, his movement regimented. He began to dismantle the bomb suit that his officer was wearing, unfastening the back and detaching the sleeves. The wind blew harder causing her good eye to weep. She wiped a tear from the corner and blinked to clear her vision. There was a chill creeping into the air; winter was well on the way. She sighed and walked towards her car thinking hard about what she had heard. Her killer had spent time researching, planning and testing his incendiary device. The simplicity of its construction was frightening. She ruled out the military connection for now. Why make an explosive when petrol is freely available and simple to ignite? If they did find more victims and she was sure that they would, their investigation would be threatened by the possible presence of booby-traps. Killing the victims wasn't enough. He wanted to interact with the investigators. Was he trying to injure and maim those who came to investigate the deaths or was he simply destroying evidence? Annie shivered and hoped that it was the latter.

CHAPTER 13

Jim Stirling drove to Canning Place on the banks of the River Mersey, with all four windows down as far as they would go but he couldn't shift the smell of the dead women from his airways. He had witnessed some gruesome crime scenes, murders, suicides, and road accidents but the images of today's victims would stick with him for a long time. The level of depravity showed that the killer had hatred so powerful that most normal functioning human beings couldn't comprehend it. Inflicting pain was ultimately as important as their death. Yet their death was still not enough to satiate his desires. The dressing up and the dismemberment were post-mortem abuse inflicted by a twisted individual. Dealing with that was difficult. When he thought about the suffering that had been inflicted upon the women over an extended period, he felt anger burning in the pit of his stomach. How many times did they beg him to stop, plead for their lives or beg him to speed up their deaths? He was a special kind of evil.

Stirling thought of his own family, his new wife and child and how fragile they were. Indeed, how fragile life itself is. One thing was for sure, he would kill to protect them, die to save their lives and crawl over razor wire to keep them from harm. All that said, they could be taken from him in an instant. Illness, a terrible accident, or a random act of violence and they could be parted forever. He could never know when or how they would be parted from each other and it didn't do to dwell on that one surety, death. They would part someday, and nothing could stop that. Life is short and sometimes tragic, he mused. All he could do was take down the criminals that operated in the city. Every killer they locked up was one less threat to his loved ones. The man who had slain Jayne Windsor and Jackie Webb was right at the top of his hit list.

He used his pass to access the secure car park at the rear of the concrete fortress. He checked his rear mirror and noticed two armoured riot vans had pulled in behind him before the ram-proof gates slid closed. There were fifty or more vehicles in the compound, a mixture of private and police owned. He drove his Volvo as close to the entrance as he could and pulled the vehicle to a halt. He turned the engine off and sucked the sea air deep into his lungs. The riot vans parked near him as he opened the door and climbed out. Shutting the door, he walked towards the station's rear entrance.

'Windows are open, Empty Head!' a voice shouted from behind him. A team of uniformed officers dressed in body armour were disembarking from the van closest to him. One of the men took off his protective helmet and visor to reveal a black balaclava. Stirling recognised his eyes, but he didn't have a clue what he was shouting about. 'You have left the windows down!' he shouted removing his balaclava.

Stirling recognised him as his ex-colleague from ten years earlier, called Lee. He looked at his car and grinned. 'I'm on a different planet at the moment.' He laughed. His friend walked around the vehicle and they shook hands. 'We're on a wet one. Double murder we think.'

'You think?' Lee scoffed. His perfect teeth looked unnaturally bright against his Asian skin. 'Which bit are you unsure about, that there are two victims or whether they were murdered? You should redo the detective exams.'

'Funny,' Stirling said sarcastically. 'You've done the 'smart-arse' course recently?'

'Failed it.'

'That figures.'

'I heard about the explosion,' Lee stopped joking. 'Was it a bomb?'

'Incendiary, as far as we can tell.' Stirling shrugged. 'There was a strong smell of petrol coming from the loft. The firemen lifted the access hatch and boom!'

'And all your evidence went up in smoke?'

'Apart from the photographs and some bits and pieces that had already been removed, we lost the lot.' He shook his head and changed the subject. 'What's with all the armour?'

'Drugs raid in the Everton Valley.' Lee shrugged and grinned. 'Crappy job to be honest. When I got my papers telling me that I'd been posted to the Forced Entry Unit, it was like getting an arrow through the neck and finding a tax bill attached to it. Still I'll take that over your gig right now. Listen, I'll have to go but if you fancy a few beers after work one night, let me know.'

'I will.'

'You won't.' Lee grinned. 'You're under the thumb.'

'I will,' Stirling insisted. He lowered his voice. 'Do you still work with that sergeant from the Halewood station?'

'Woody?'

'That's him.'

'I don't see him every day. We're on opposite shifts. He's on the nightshift this month, why?'

'I need some inside info on a Special who was stationed there.'

'Why the interest?'

'She's one of our vics.'

54

'Nightmare.'

'Keep it to yourself for now.'

'Of course, got a name?'

'Jayne Windsor but it has to be hush hush.'

'Leave it with me. I'll message you later.' He hugged the big detective and jogged off to catch-up with his team. 'See you later, Empty Head, and don't forget to close your windows; there's a lot of criminals around!'

'Smart arse,' Stirling grunted as he opened the door and put the keys back in the ignition to close the windows. That done, he headed for the lift.

The doors opened on the fifth floor, which was the home of the Major Investigation Team. The sound of chatter greeted him; some voices were on the telephones and some in conversation with other officers. He could see that Google's team were busy at their desks and decided to leave them to it for now. Getting involved in an in-depth conversation with Google was the last thing that he needed. Google would take thirty minutes to say what others could say in ten.

The coffee station looked to be fully functional and stocked up with a fresh brew, which made a pleasant change. He walked over to it and filled a mug with the steaming liquid, debating whether to add three sugars or stick to his diet and use sweeteners. The diet lost. He needed the calories. Today would be a long day.

'Those phone records that you asked for are on your desk, Sarge.'

'Cheers,' he said with a thumbs-up. Putting the mug down, he struggled out of his leather jacket and hung it on the back of his chair. There was a stack of brown manila files on his desk and he sifted through them as he sat heavily in his swivel chair. Preliminaries from forensics, which basically listed everything that needed testing. Until the results came back, it was of little to no use, so he put them to one side. Beneath them was the record of Jackie Webb's mobile phone account, calls, text messages, and the PIN code to access her voicemail. He glanced over the first page and took a slurp of coffee. There were some landline calls and some mobile numbers. All the calls were incoming, but the majority were from withheld numbers. That didn't seem too odd for a mobile beautician. The numbers wouldn't tell them much until they could be traced. He took another sip, slouched back in his chair, and turned the page.

His eyes widened when he read the first text message and almost choked on his coffee when he read the second. The text messages ranged from suggestive to pornographic. They were enquiries about the services that she provided but not the type that he was expecting. She hadn't replied to a single text. He'd worked enough cases to know that prostitutes didn't communicate via text message. Her business card had said 'beauty therapy' but Stirling had serious doubts about the type of therapy that she was offering. He sat and read two pages of smut before he decided to skip straight to the voicemail.

'You look flushed,' Annie's voice disturbed his thoughts. 'What's up?' she pointed to his half-filled coffee cup. 'Do you want that topping up, I could murder one?' she frowned at her pun. 'Wrong choice of words, do you want another?'

'Yes please, guv.' He put the receiver down and waited for her to return. She placed his cup on the desk and then took the seat adjacent to him, sliding her coat off as she settled into the chair. He noticed that her scar reddened and became more obvious when her skin was exposed to the wind. Her false eye was the elephant in the room whenever they were alone together. They had never really discussed the attack by Richard Tibbs. He had often wanted to tell her that she was still an attractive woman despite her scars, but he didn't want her to take it the wrong way. They had a good working relationship and he wanted to keep things that way. She smiled and rubbed her hands together and breathed onto them.

'It's gone cold out there now,' she said. 'So, what has got you so hot and bothered?' He felt her gaze on him, studying his expression, which always made him feel uncomfortable. Sometimes he thought that she could read his mind. 'Come on spill the beans.'

'Have a peek at them,' Stirling said handing over the text messages. 'I think Jackie Webb was offering more than a manicure.' Annie glanced over two pages, raised her eyebrows, and nodded in agreement. 'I was just dialling her voicemail when you walked in.'

'Dial away,' Annie said reading on through the records. 'It certainly appears that she received more enquiries about the price of a blow job than a blow-dry. It would explain how she could afford that apartment.'

Stirling dialled her voicemail box and punched in the code to access her messages and then sat back and listened. 'They're running latest message first,' he informed Annie. He listened for a few moments. 'The first three are the same guy asking if she is coming or not. He doesn't sound very happy.' Annie flicked through the pages of messages as he listened. Her face blushed at some of them. 'Two abusive calls from another bloke calling himself, John. He wants to know why she's wasting his f-ing time and he won't be using her again.' He frowned. 'And he called back to tell her that she had a fat arse anyway, apparently.'

'Oh dear,' Annie said sipping her coffee. 'At least she'll never have to hear that.'

'Two more calls asking why she didn't turn up for their appointments.'

'Men?'

'Yes.'

'I'm guessing that they weren't booked in for a conditioning treatment.'

'We'll need to track all these callers down,' he said growing more convinced that his hunch was right. 'Not a single female voice or mention of waxing or nail extensions. Obviously, Jackie Webb has gone off the grid so we can assume our first victim is her and that she was a call girl.'

'Hmm, I wonder if she kept it from her best friend because she was a Special Constable or if she knew?' Annie thought out loud. 'Or maybe she did know and Jayne Windsor just didn't tell her mother what her friend did for a living.'

'Maybe.' Stirling agreed. 'Her card clearly states that she's a beautician. Having said that, if you were in that game what else would you have on your business card?'

'The mind boggles.'

'This changes things.' Stirling frowned. 'They could have been a client.'

'Could be. It was planned out too well for it to be random.' Annie looked at the messages again. 'My money is on a client.' She nodded.

'If not, did the killer know she was on the game?'

Annie tapped the desk with her index finger. 'Have you spoken to Google yet?' She looked over her shoulder to where the teams were busy analysing the crime scene photographs.

'Not yet,' Stirling said with his phone trapped between his left ear and his shoulder. He was marking the number of callers on a pad as he listened. 'I thought I'd leave that to you.' He grinned. 'I wanted to get this out of the way before I got distracted with riddles.' He shrugged. 'I've never been good at riddles.'

'So you said.' Annie frowned. 'I'll go and see where we are at.' She looked at her coat and decided that it could stay there. It had her purse and car keys in the pocket, but it was also surrounded by thirty detectives. Her mobile was another matter and she picked it up as she headed to where Google and his team were working. As she approached, the officers stopped what they were doing. 'How is it going?'

'Well this is very exciting,' Google picked up several pieces of paper and held them up as if they were trophies. 'We started by ruling out the more popular ancient scripts, Hebrew, Greek, Samerian,' Google began his thesis. 'I knew it was a type of Cyrillic but not the most popular text used. It's different.'

Annie held up her hand and grimaced. 'Stop, stop,' she said loudly. 'Listen, Google,' she joked. 'Please don't think that you have to detail exactly how you've arrived at every conclusion.' His three team members grinned widely. He didn't look offended by the use of his nickname. He deemed it a compliment about his intellectual prowess. 'All I need to know is why the killer used it and what it says.'

'Sorry, guv,' he took off his glasses and wiped them on his tie. 'Firstly, it's a script called Glagolitic. In the days when it was used, it was sometimes called the 'witches' language'.' He paused. Annie's expression told him that she wasn't in the mood to be spoon fed the findings crumb by crumb. Although he wanted to go into as much detail as he could muster, he thought that a summary would be better for his career. 'It became popular in about eight hundred, along with other Old Church Slavic languages but Glagolitic was also used to record spells and ceremonies so that prying eyes couldn't decipher them. Bearing in mind that for centuries before it became widely used, there was paranoia about witches, which led to the burning of hundreds of women, you can see why some would seek a text which couldn't be translated if their writings were discovered. It was a method of hiding information.' He shrugged matter-of-factly as if what he was saying was obvious.

'Slavic?' Annie raised her eyebrows.

'Yes, it's part of the old 'Eastern Block'.'

'I know where Slavic refers to, Google!' Annie sighed, slightly annoyed.

'Of course, you do, guv. Sorry.' He blushed and carried on nervously. 'It was used in parts of Russia, Ukraine, Serbia, and even some of the Mongolian tribes used it.'

'Okay,' Annie said slowly digesting his words. 'Why carve that specific script into our victim?'

'You'll have to ask the killer that,' he said putting his spectacles on the end of his nose. 'At first, I thought it was linked to a satanic ritual because of the pentangle daubed on the wall but the more we translate, the less likely that is.'

'Go on,' Annie said intrigued.

'Get this,' Google said excitedly. "We are each our own Devil, and we make this world our own hell, amen."

'The bible?' Annie guessed.

'Oscar Wilde.'

'Oscar Wilde?'

'Not what you were expecting, I know but when put it together with the other stuff, we have a theme and some numbers that don't make any sense yet.'

'Numbers?'

'Yes, although I can't see anything that they relate to yet.'

'Do you know what he's trying to say?'

'On its own, it means nothing to me,' he held up his finger, 'but listen to this, 'As evil as the Devil and twice as pretty.' He looked over his glasses. 'He's berating women.' He paused. "The Devil became a serpent and tempted Adam; his male descendants are still tempted by snakes this day. They will tempt you and then destroy your world." He shrugged. 'He's quoting text relating to women being the root of evil.'

'Who said that?'

'No idea but he's got a point.' Google added. Annie raised her eyebrows in mock offence. Google was oblivious and continued. 'Then we have the numbers 3-71-73.'

'That means nothing to me.'

'Nor me, guv.'

'I'm assuming he means 'women' when he refers to snakes?' Annie asked.

'He seems to think of them as one and the same. I don't think he's paying homage to an evil entity. In fact, quite the opposite.' He picked up another sheet of paper. 'On her chest it says, 'The finest skill the Devil has, is to make us believe that he is male and there is only one of him. In truth there are millions of them everywhere we look.' Followed by 4-76-77.' He shrugged. 'Can you see where I'm going with this?'

'It's as clear as mud.'

'Sorry.' Google reached for another pad. "If there is a God, he'll spit in your face. He will take your deal with the Devil, the whore of Babylon and he'll let you burn."

'Oscar Wilde said that?' Annie frowned.

'That wasn't him.' Google shook his head. 'Not as far as I know but he may have,' he added flatly. The others exchanged amused glances and raised their eyes to the ceiling. 'That is followed by 37-68-75. The numbers don't fit any obvious sequence so we're leaving them to work on later. We're trying to pinpoint where all the quotes are taken from, but we haven't found all the sources yet.'

'I'm still not sure that I can see a message here,' Annie grimaced. 'Is it just the ramblings of a lunatic?'

He pointed to another line. "The world ceases to believe in God yet it still believes in evil. And so it should for 'you' are proof that the Devil acts through you. Then 6-71-72." He took his glasses off again and looked for her reaction. 'Do you see?'

'He's obsessed with Devil worship?'

'He is obsessed by evil, not the devil.' He shook his head. 'He is not worshiping the Devil, he's denouncing him. But everything he is saying is written as if it's aimed at the victim personally. It's accusing 'her' of being evil. In his mind, women are evil personified.'

'You're sure?'

'The more I read, the more certain that I am.' He nodded. "The Devil pulls the strings that make you dance, you are entertained by loathsome things that they do.' I think 'they' in this case, are females.' He shrugged. 'I can't see anything but accusations of collusion with evil rather than admiration of it.'

'So, you think it's personal,' Annie asked thoughtfully. 'I mean is it aimed at her specifically?'

He shook his head and turned a page searching for something. "While men desire women, women will never be at a loss and the Devil will stand beside them for desire is his bait." He sighed. 'Some of it's aimed at 'women' in general so I can't be sure that it's aimed at your victim specifically. It is written by someone who has little respect for women. I would go so far as to say he hates them.'

'The crime scenes would back that up.' Annie nodded. Her new-found knowledge that Jackie Webb was a prostitute slotted right in with the evidence carved into her flesh but until forensics made a positive identification, she couldn't share that. 'What he did to them shows that he hated our two victims for sure.'

'Hates them or blames them?' Gwen joined the conversation. She pushed her ginger hair from her forehead as she spoke. 'I'm sensing blame in the text. Accusations and blame.' She picked up a piece of A4. "Bring food to a dog and watch it wiggle and dance. Buy a gift for a woman and watch her do the same. When the food is eaten and the gift tarnished by time, both may bite your empty hand and then dance and wiggle for another. Such are the attributes of women and dogs and Satan himself." She paused and scoffed. 'This is from a satanic website although it could have been written by my ex-husband.'

'And a couple of my ex-boyfriends,' a sergeant called Sue Carrol agreed with a smile. 'Can you round them all up as suspects and arrest them?'

'No problem,' Gwen laughed. 'Just the bitter and twisted ones?'

'You had better take a bus then,' Google said clumsily. Annie and Gwen looked at each other open-mouthed and almost offended. 'No offence.' He looked from one to the other. 'According to my missus, all ex-boyfriends are bitter and twisted.'

'You rescued yourself there.' Gwen frowned. Google looked confused. 'You were nearly in so much shit then.'

'What did I say?' he said frowning.

'Forget it.' Gwen sighed. He had no sense of social skills. She shook her head and turned back to Annie. 'I agree with Google that the killer is accusing the victim. I think he daubed the pentangle on the wall to tell us that Jackie Webb was a demon to him.' She shrugged. 'Maybe using the 'witches' script' is his way of telling us that she was 'evil'. This is not a satanic murder, guv, although it's ritual in my opinion. Our killer has a warped sense of good and evil.'

'You said that the language was Slavic. Are we looking for someone from that region?'

'Not necessarily.' Google shrugged. 'This language is used by religious academics, historians, and orthodox Catholics across the world. There's no knowing.'

Annie held her chin between finger and thumb and nodded. 'Good work,' she said to the team. 'I want everything you can translate and your theories as soon as possible okay.'

'Guv.'

She was about to turn and leave when the mirrors at the second scene sprang to mind. 'Have you come across anything that says, 'when you look in the mirror, what looks back at you?" the team had blank faces. 'It was written in blood on the mirrors at the second scene.'

'No, guv but we'll keep a look out for it.' Gwen said returning to her screen. 'Despite the amount of text here, he hasn't repeated himself once so it could be somewhere that we haven't reached yet.'

'Good work.' Annie felt pleased with the results so far. The translation of the script had opened a window into the mind of the killer. He was angry with a woman or women plural. She thought back to Tibbs, the man who had gouged out her eye with his solicitor's pen. He had anger issues and when they spilled over, he took her face and her confidence forever. Her life would never be the same, but she had lived to tell the tale. Jayne Windsor and Jackie Webb had not. Were they his first victims? She doubted it. Had he targeted them for something that they'd done or just because they were female? Annie didn't really care what the answer to the question was. Either way he was a violent killer. Working out his motive would simply help her to catch him.

'Guv,' Stirling shouted her from his desk. 'Traffic have found footage of the BMW in the city centre on Saturday night.'

'Where?' Annie asked excitedly. The department went silent. All ears were listening to the breakthrough.

'They have it pulling in and parking on the multistorey on Mount Pleasant at nine o'clock.'

'What about leaving?'

'Nothing yet.' He shook his head. 'They're working on the footage from later on that night.'

'We need that urgently,' Annie felt butterflies in her stomach. 'We could have the killer returning to the BMW with them.' She bit her bottom lip and walked to the bank of screens to her right. She looked at a digital map of the city centre and found Mount Pleasant.

'Alert uniform to concentrate their efforts on the nightclubs closest to the car park first. Have the pictures of the two women been sent out?'

'Yes, guv.'

'Good,' she said trying to keep a calm exterior. 'We need to know where they went and who they went back to that car park with.' She took a deep breath, 'I've got a good feeling about this,' she said in almost a whisper. 'Get yourself down there and make sure that uniform don't mess this up,' she said to Stirling.

'I'm on my way, guv,' he said already rising. 'I'll ring as soon as I have the footage.'

'Do you mind if I tag along?' Alec appeared from his office. 'You can bring me up to speed on the way.'

'No problem, guv,' Stirling said looking to Annie for permission. Annie grimaced and shook her head.

'I need a word, guv.' She wagged her finger at Alec. 'You go,' she said to Stirling. 'I need to run something by you, guv. Can we use your office?' Alec frowned. He liked taking the opportunity to accompany his detectives every now and again. Feeling a little deflated, he smiled and nodded. If Annie Jones had an issue that she wasn't prepared to discuss in front of the team, then it was of vital importance.

CHAPTER 14

Stirling parked his vehicle on the fourth floor of Mount Pleasant multistorey car park and walked down one floor to the security office. The stairwell smelled of urine masked with a hint of bleach. Black blobs of discarded chewing gum decorated the landings and graffiti covered the walls to head height. The office was situated at the rear corner of the structure, overlooking the grey Portland Stone built Adelphi Hotel, which was on the opposite side of the road. As he turned the corner, he saw what he was looking for. A pay station machine flanked one side of a reinforced plastic window and an overweight pensioner in a blue uniform sat behind the screen. There was an expression of sheer boredom on his face. He looked up as the big detective approached and spoke through the communication vents in the screen.

'Bugger me, if it isn't Big Jim Stirling!'

'Hello, Harry,' Stirling smiled. He noticed how old and worn out the man looked. It had been five years since he had last seen him, but he had aged fifteen at least. Whisky had changed the shape and colour of his dimpled nose. 'Is this what happens to us coppers in retirement?'

'Beats fishing or sitting at home with the wife and it keeps me in beer money,' he joked. 'Your lads are in the back office looking through CCTV footage. Come around to the side door.'

Stirling walked around the pay machine and waited for him to open the door. 'Fascist Bastards' had been scratched into the paint beneath a plaque which identified it as the 'Security' office. The fact that the door could be vandalised undetected was testament to how observant the security team was. He thought back to a time when Harry Thompson, or 'Tomo' as he was known, was a well-respected sergeant. The lock rattled and the door opened. 'Come in, Jim,' he said stepping back. 'Through the door there.' His watery eyes smiled as he spoke. 'Good to see you again.'

Stirling nodded and squeezed through the door, shaking his outstretched hand. He could feel Harry's bones near the surface of his skin. 'You too.' The office smelled of booze and sweat. He walked into the back office where two uniformed officers were sitting in front of a screen. The images were whizzing along on fast forward. 'How are we doing?' he asked making them jump in surprise.

'Sarge,' one of them said standing up. 'We're putting anything relevant onto my tablet for now.'

'Is it connected to their system?'

'No, Sarge.' He shook his head and blushed. 'The car park owners have said that you can take the disk when we're done. I'm photographing the screen for now.'

'Clever, well done. Sit down,' Stirling gestured to his chair. 'How long have you been staring at that?'

'Five hours.'

'It's not why you joined the force is it?'

'Not really, Sarge,' he chuckled. 'But if it helps us catch the bad guys, it's all good.'

'It is. Show me the image of them leaving the car.'

The young officer flicked the screen and brought up a blurred image of the women exiting the vehicle. Although the picture wasn't clear, he could identify the vehicle and Jayne and Jackie. 'That is them. Have you got the women returning to the BMW?'

The officers shook their heads in unison. Stirling reckoned their combined ages would still not add up to his own. 'Not yet but we've got this.' He pulled up an image on his tablet. Stirling squinted and frowned. The image was from the interior of the car park focused on a row of parking bays. Only a few vehicles could be seen. He thought he was missing the point as there was nothing obvious to see. 'Look there across the road.' The young officer pointed to two women, who were standing next to the Adelphi Hotel. 'There's a bar and a nightclub under the hotel.' He grinned, 'Flatfoot Sam's. The camera moves at that point, so we don't see them going in, but I bet they did.'

'Why?' Stirling frowned.

'Women get free entry on a Saturday night.'

'Good man,' Stirling smiled. 'Has anyone been over there to speak to them yet?'

'No, Sarge. We've only just found it. One of us could go now.'

'No need,' Stirling said turning for the door. 'You're doing a great job there. I'll go there myself. Find me those women going back to the BMW!' He added as an afterthought. He stepped into the front office where Harry Thompson was tilting a slug of whisky into a mug of coffee. 'I hope that's not whisky.'

'It is and I don't care who you tell!'

'If you make those two a brew without the alcohol, I'll pretend that I never saw a thing.'

'Deal. Are you going already?'

'I'm going across the road,' Stirling said reaching for the door handle. 'Do you know any of the doormen over there?'

'Flatfoot Sam's?' a wry smile crossed his lips. 'Speak to Coco. Colin Cousins, he's the head doorman there.'

'Is it one of your haunts?'

'No chance,' Harry scowled, 'I can't afford their prices. He chucks me a few quid every month to keep a parking bay reserved for him and his bouncers. Saves them from walking up to the top floors when they've finished work late at night.'

Stirling smiled and opened the door. Harry had always been open to persuasion. There were rumours towards the end of his career, but Stirling didn't judge him one way or the other. The man had given thirty-five years of his life to the force. If he had applied a little pressure here and there, so what. He headed for the stairwell, which led him out onto Brownlow Hill. From the pavement, The Adelphi Hotel was a grey monolith, recessed balconies and Roman columns gave it a look of grandeur. The traffic was light as he crossed the road and walked towards a flashing neon sign, which pointed to steps that went down beneath the hotel. He looked around. The nightclub was well hidden from the main road, almost anonymous beneath the grandiose building. It was the perfect spot to acquire a victim. The clubs further into the centre were mostly on pedestrian areas where thousands of revellers packed the streets every weekend.

At the bottom of the steps, he looked up at the car park, but the view of the lower floors was blocked by the slope. The car park cameras couldn't pick up the front door of the club. As he reached the entrance, the smell of stale beer hit him. A wall mounted ashtray overflowed with cigarette stumps and a single patio umbrella was the only shelter offered to smokers. The sound of a 60s band drifted to him, but he couldn't think of their name. When he opened the door, the volume of the music became ear splitting. He winced and stepped into the gloomy venue. To his left, a group of elderly men stopped talking, turning to look at the stranger as he entered. Stirling scowled and they turned back to their chatter. He wondered why hardened drinkers of their age would choose such a noisy venue to frequent, until he noticed a Day-Glo banner advertising a happy hour. It ran from 10 a.m. until 5 p.m. 'Happy seven hours?' he shook his head in disbelief and headed to the bar.

'Hi, what can I get you?' the barman appeared from behind a large pillar. Stirling looked along the mirror backed bar, which ran in an L shape for at least thirty metres. He guessed that there were more than a hundred optics above the mirrors. The bar itself was interspersed by thick support pillars every ten metres or so. The club was built in the building's foundations. A dance floor the size of a tennis court spread into the gloom at the far end of the club. He counted six CCTV cameras at a glance. Whether they were all working or not was another matter. The place looked run down and rough around the edges. 'All draught beer is a pound until five o'clock.'

'I want to speak to the manager please,' Stirling said flashing his ID. The elderly barman nodded silently and picked up a telephone, which was fixed to the pillar. He ran his fingers through his white hair and tutted in annoyance. His manner was nonchalant, and he eyed Stirling with suspicion.

'A bloke claiming to be Old Bill wants to talk to the manager,' he rolled his eyes at the reply. 'How the hell would I know what he wants?' he snapped and hung up. 'She'll be on her way down if she can get off her fat arse for five minutes,' he bitched. 'I was due my break four hours ago.' He rolled his eyes. 'Four hours! She takes the piss. The lazy cow.' One of the elderly drinkers approached the bar and stood within earshot. 'Oh, here we go. What do you want, nosey old goat,' he grumbled to Stirling as if he was an old friend?

'Hey,' the old man scolded. 'We pay your wages. Less of you lip, sunshine!'

'Bloody coffin dodgers,' the barman said from the corner of his mouth. He poured a pint of dark ale and put it in front of the old man. The old man scowled and counted out a handful of coins, handing them to the disgruntled barman. 'None of them leave a tip. It's not like they'll be taking it with them, is it?'

'What did you say?' the old drinker stuttered. Loose skin hung from his chin making him look turkey like. Brown liver spots speckled his bald scalp and his thin lips quivered as he spoke.

'I said, I wouldn't buy a Christmas tree if I was you,' the barman winked at Stirling. 'Might be a waste of money, you old git.'

Stirling heard a door open at the end of the bar and walked towards it, glad to be away from the whining barman. A barrel shaped woman in her fifties waddled in. The expression on her round face told him that she wasn't overjoyed at being disturbed. He took out his ID again and held it up as she approached. 'I'm DS Stirling from the Major Investigation Team. I'm investigating a double murder.' Her face softened; anger replaced by concern. Her severe bob cut made her face look rounder than it was and dyed black, it exaggerated how pale her skin was. 'I have reason to believe that the victims were in your club last Saturday night.'

'There would have been over seven hundred punters through here on Saturday,' she grimaced, 'we're licensed for three hundred before you ask but by the time people come and go to other clubs that's about the right number.'

'Do all those cameras work?'

'Yes.'

'I'll need your disks from Saturday night,' Stirling said flatly. 'And I'll need to speak to your door staff.'

'My head door supervisor is right over there,' she gestured to a booth behind them. Stirling hadn't noticed it before as it was hidden from view by one of the many pillars. A man with a sullen expression sat pouring over a stack of papers. His head was shaved, and the exposed flesh of his arms was covered in tattoos. Stirling reckoned him to be in his late forties. 'He can give you what you need. Coco,' she called out. 'Help this detective out will you, I've got work to do.' She turned and walked away without another word. The doorman stood up and stretched his arms above his head. His upper body was pumped up with nandrolone. Stirling could spot steroid-built muscle a mile away.

'Detective.' He offered his hand with an unexpected smile. 'Colin Cousins, head doorman. Everyone calls me Coco.' Close up, Stirling realised that he was mixed race and that would account for his nickname. His voice was deep and calm, and his accent was local but well educated. 'How can I help you?'

'I'm investigating a double murder. We have reason to believe that our victims came to town last Saturday night,' he paused and pointed to the car park across the road. 'We know that they parked their car over there, but we need to know where they went to and who they went home with.' He shrugged. 'The surveillance tapes from the multistorey show the women standing at the top of the steps here. I need to look at your footage from that night.'

'A lot of people come in here on a Saturday,' Coco said in a concerned tone. 'But we have a lot of regulars. Have you got a photograph?'

'Yes, sorry,' Stirling mumbled, taken aback by the man's polite cooperation, which was rare among doormen in the city centre. He took two pictures from his inside pocket and handed them to him. 'They went out frequently together, usually just the two of them.'

Coco looked at the pictures and raised his eyebrows, 'She's dead?' he shook his head. 'She was a nice lady.'

'You recognise them?' Stirling asked surprised.

'This one I know,' he held up the picture of Jackie Webb. 'I recognise the other one vaguely, but I've never spoken to her. They have been in here a few times. I'm pretty sure that they were in here on Saturday, but I couldn't be certain. The CCTV will tell you for definite.'

'How do you know Jackie Web?'

'I wouldn't say that I know her. I know her face. Some of my doormen know her better,' Coco frowned. 'She was a bit of a player.'

'We think that she may have been an escort.'

'She was,' Coco said matter-of-factly. 'No doubt about it. When she was out in the club, there was no funny business, but she did tout some of my men on the odd occasion. She often gave her card out.'

'Mobile beautician?'

'Yes, that's the one.'

'That's how you're sure she was an escort?'

'Yes. Some of the lads enquired about her services but she was high end. Way too expensive for my lot!'

'Can you remember if she left here with anyone on Saturday?'

'She would spend all night flirting, but I've never seen her leave here with a man, Detective.' He shrugged. 'Her friend on the other hand, was totally different. I don't recall her ever flirting with anyone.'

'Did you see them leave on Saturday?'

Coco thought about it for a second and then shook his head. 'I'm sure that I didn't see them leave. There were a couple of stag and hen parties in if I remember rightly. I spent most of the night by the DJ box.' He shook his head. 'Without knowing what time they left I'm speculating. Let's go and look at the CCTV, shall we?' He turned and walked across the dance floor towards the DJ box. They skirted around it to a door, which was marked as 'private'. Coco took out a bunch of keys and opened the door, stepping aside to allow Stirling in first. The lights were tripped by a sensor as they walked in. 'Impressive, isn't it?' he said watching the expression on the detective's face.

'It certainly is.' Stirling nodded. A bank of nine screens showed images from all around the club. 'Everywhere but the toilets is covered?'

'I wish.' Coco sighed. 'The cameras are remote and swivel through ninety degrees, but these bloody pillars give me a headache.' He pointed to three of the screens. 'We had a major problem with cocaine dealers when I took over the door. It was mainly because the doormen were on the take. I sacked the lot of them, hired good men and got rid of the dealers. Don't get me wrong, we still have an issue with it but we're realistic enough to know that we'll never be rid of it completely. I position men in the blind spots, that's the best we can do.'

'It looks like a good set-up to me.'

'The club belongs to the hotel and it's part of a big chain. Anything bad happens in here is bad for business.' Coco nodded and typed his password into the keyboard. He typed the relevant date in, and the screens flickered, and the images changed. The screens showed the club on Saturday night when it was at full capacity. 'What time do you think they were outside?'

'Half past nine-ish.' The images flashed by nine o'clock, ten and eleven before they caught a glimpse of the women. 'There!' Stirling said excitedly. 'Right by the edge of the dance floor. They were here.'

'Okay, let's see who they talk to,' Coco said zooming in on the women. They were approached several times, chatted to a few other women but nothing important happened for a while. 'Here, Jackie goes dancing with this guy here.' He focused in on his face. 'I'll print a picture of his face for you.'

'Thanks. Do you recognise him?'

'No. Sorry.' Coco grimaced. 'What's the other woman called?'

'Jayne.'

'Jayne is the wallflower left watching her friend dancing.' The images whizzed by and showed nothing except Jackie Web gyrating around a dark-haired male. Jayne was approached a few times but rebutted any advances quickly. All apart from one.

'Wait there,' Stirling said. 'Stop that there.'

'Got it,' Coco slowed the tape down and zoomed in again. Jayne was chatting happily with a tall dark male. 'By the look on her face she was interested in him.'

'He goes off to the bar there. Can we follow him?'

Coco flicked to another camera. 'We lose him here. He's behind the pillar there. We can't see what he orders from the bar but he's walking back to Jayne here,' he paused as they watched him handing Jayne a glass, 'That is a clear shot of his face.' He turned and grinned at Stirling. He clicked on print screen and a laser-jet whirred into life. Stirling picked up the photographs and nodded. The images were good enough to circulate.

'Do you know this guy?'

'No.'

'They don't look like they came together, do they?'

'There's been no interaction between them.' Coco slowed the image again. Jayne and Jackie spoke briefly on the dance floor, but the men didn't even acknowledge one another. 'I don't think the men know each other. Now if we fast forward, we can see if they leave with them.'

The footage showed the women dancing and chatting to their suitors. From the sequence of events, Stirling saw Jayne take three glasses of a dark liquid from the man. Each one seemed to make her shoulders stoop as if it was sucking the energy from her limbs. 'Does she look like she's having a good time?' Stirling frowned. Stop the tape there. 'Look at her face.'

'She looks totally spaced out,' Coco agreed. 'Her head looks too heavy for her neck.'

'She was driving.'

'So, she was drunk.' Coco shrugged. 'Lots of people still drink and drive.'

'She was a Special Constable.'

'You're kidding me?'

'No.'

'In which case, she was spiked.'

'That's what I'm thinking.' Stirling nodded. 'Run it and let's see if she leaves with him.' The images flickered on, covering about forty minutes before Jackie could be seen staggering across the dance floor to the Ladies. Ten minutes later, Jayne Windsor heads for the exit, escorted by the mystery male. He appeared to be holding her up by the elbow. Her face was a picture of confusion. 'There she goes. That's all I need. You've been a great help. Can you burn this onto another disk for me?'

Coco shook his head and frowned. 'No, sorry but you can take the originals.' He hit the eject button and two disks slid out of the system. 'Take them and I hope they help you to catch whoever killed them. Do me a favour and hang the bastard, will you.'

'If only I could,' Stirling said taking the disks, 'Thanks again for the help.' He shook Coco's hand and headed across the club. He looked at the photographs again and studied the faces. 'We're coming for you,' he muttered to himself. Something told him that the uniformed officers at the multistorey would have images of one of the men getting into Jayne Windsor's car with them.

CHAPTER 15

Tod Harris stepped out of the hotel into the muggy evening air. The sun was on the wane, but its heat remained long after the yellow orb had begun to melt into the sea on the horizon. He crossed the Parc de L' Aguera, sticking to the paths that would take him past the skateboarders. Their daredevil antics fascinated him and were worth the detour. They made it look so easy. It reminded him of a time not so long ago when he would go to Southport with his friends on long summer days where they would cruise along the pier on their skateboards looking for girls. It was harmless teenage fun back then. It was natural. Hunting for women was natural for males. It was a carnal instinct. Brute force had been replaced by civilised conversation, aesthetics, and aftershave. Women now had the choice to say no. That's where it all went wrong. They used their sexuality when it suited them. Men were subjected to a barrage of beauty day and night from the Press and television, but the message was clear, look but don't dare touch. Tod didn't see things quite that way. He lit a cigarette and watched the boarders doing their tricks for a while. It took his mind off the newspaper reports that he had read. His first reaction had been fear, pure panic but now he had taken time to mull over the facts, he wasn't as concerned. The police were working in the dark and there was no way that they could connect things to him. Hopefully the reported fire would have destroyed any evidence. Hopefully.

He felt hungry and decided to leave the boarders to their own devices. He walked along a curved path that took him to the narrow lanes of the Old Town. He could see the last glimmer of the sun on the sea and a warm breeze tickled his skin. The lanes were bustling with tourists and locals alike. The tourists were shopping and bar hopping, enjoying the myriad of tapas available, while the locals soaked up the atmosphere on the way home from work with espressos and cognac watching the people go by. Tod wanted to eat. He wanted to eat, drink, and find a woman. His self-imposed abstinence had come to an end. His fear was dissipating and being replaced by the carnal urges that had gotten him into this mess in the first place. He couldn't control his sexuality, who could?

As he moved through the crowds, the aroma of food cooking was mixed with the occasional waft of perfume and he wasn't sure which was the most provocative. He took a left off the main artery onto Pintor Lazano and felt the relief of leaving the crowds behind. He wandered around the evocative cobbled streets for a while, browsing in shop windows admiring the leather and silver craft shops and the females who were attracted to them. He could see a blue domed church at the top of the hill surrounded by whitewashed houses. It was a tiny piece of authentic Spain nestled between forests of tower blocks to the east and west. It was an easy place to lose himself and pretend that nothing had happened. His hunger took control once more. A neon sign advertising San Miguel lager blinked and as he neared it, the aroma of garlic drifted from the bar. He smiled to himself and headed for one of the empty tables outside. The waiter was at his table in a second, placing an ashtray and a beer mat in front of him.

'San Miguel please,' Tod said as he settled.

'Large?'

'Si.'

The tables around him were full. He heard Spanish, French, and Italian being spoken. Four young English women were sat adjacent to him, giggling and laughing. From the volume of their conversation, he guessed that they'd been drinking most of the day. A mixture of cigarettes and perfume drifted from them on the breeze and he inhaled deeply. He could almost taste them. The lane was quiet, only a few families were ambling along it. An elderly couple linked arms and studied the bar's menu. They decided against eating there. Tod watched the husband shaking his head, put off by the group of rowdy English women and they wandered up the lane towards the busier streets, pausing to window shop at a small silversmith a few buildings away. A lone male stopped and stood next to them. He was a local, short and had a wiry build. Although he was looking at the jewellery, he was also eyeing the woman's handbag. He looked around to see if anyone was watching him. Tod locked eyes with him for a second before the waiter returned blocking his view.

'Tapas!' the waiter announced his arrival. He placed an oval plate with a selection of savoury smelling tasters on to the table in front of him and put his lager onto the beer mat. 'Enjoy!' Tod grinned and picked up a small black pudding. He bit it in half and swallowed it and then washed it down with a mouth full of ice-cold beer. The waiter returned his smile and moved on to the next table. When he stepped aside, Tod noticed that the lone male had taken a seat at a table opposite him. It was almost impossible not to look directly at him and every time he did, the man was staring back but would look away immediately. He wasn't sure why, but the man's presence made him feel uneasy. Very uneasy indeed.

CHAPTER 16

Detective Superintendent Alec Ramsay put the phone down and sighed. He hated dealing with the government. Junior ministers tended to be overzealous, under informed, and tenaciously interfering. The Major Investigation Team were handpicked detectives. They were the cream of the force and more than equipped to run the investigation into the murders and resulting explosion. The problem with an explosion is that everyone automatically assumes that an extremist cell is to blame. MI5 talk to Special Branch, they talk to the local police hierarchy and report back to Westminster. Westminster automatically assume that the local force is run by incompetents and cover their backsides by pestering the most senior officers involved in the case at source. They always tried to bypass the Secret Service to get to the information first. It was all about point scoring. Junior Ministers climbed the ladder quickly if they had the ability to capture information by whatever means necessary. However, bullying a senior police officer wasn't easy especially one hardened by working in the inner cities for decades. Alec had told Donald Roebothan to go forth and multiply in the politest way that he could without putting his pension in jeopardy. There was absolutely no suspicion of terrorism at all. None. Alec had suggested that whoever had informed him that they hadn't ruled it out was an idiot and a liar and they certainly hadn't spoken to himself or DI Annie Jones. It would relieve the pressure momentarily, but it would return with a vengeance if the team didn't make progress quickly. Very quickly.

He stood up, looked out of the window and exhaled slowly, calming himself. The view of the Albert Docks and the huge Ferris wheel always made him feel better. The waters of the River Mersey looked like liquid metal today, reflecting the grey clouds above. A majestic cruise ship was docked at the Pier Head begging the question how something so big could float. Its modern curves set it in stark contrast to the historic riverside buildings. Alec felt his karma restored and turned to head for the MIT section. He could hear the noise from their offices long before he reached them. The tension in the atmosphere was almost electric like the moments before a thunder storm begins. He opened the door and paused, allowing the ambiance to wash over him. The excitement of an investigation was something that never lessened no matter how many he had been involved in. It had been enough to keep him focused on the job for over twenty years at the expense of his marriage to his departed wife. Her death had opened his eyes to how much he had neglected her, but it was too late to put things right. She had had a knack of making him feel guilty when she was alive, and she was still doing it from the grave except now it was far more intense, and it didn't ease when he arrived home. In the dark hours their empty house seemed to echo with her voice. Her essence was gone from their home leaving it void of life. It had been void of love for years but when Gail was alive, it still felt like home. Now it was an empty shell. Bricks and mortar, nothing more. It had no soul. He tried to shift her from his thoughts whenever he stepped inside.

The DI was addressing the troops using a bank of screens to display various images related to their case. She caught sight of him and paused, 'Guv.' She nodded.

'Please carry on where you left off,' he said apologetically.

'How did the call from London go?' she asked.

'If idiots could fly, Westminster would be an airport!' a ripple of laughter spread through the room. 'Please, carry on.'

'This is the CCTV footage from the nightclub,' she said pointing to a screen. 'Jayne Windsor can be seen leaving with this man.' Annie held up a photocopy of the suspect, which Coco had printed off. A female detective handed Alec a copy. He studied the face but didn't recognise the man.

'She looks out of it,' Stirling said, 'but she doesn't drink. He's almost dragging her along there. The head doorman informed me that Jayne and Jackie were regulars at the club and that he has never seen Jayne leave with a man.'

'Rohypnol?' Alec asked.

Stirling nodded. 'We think so, guv.'

'Here is the footage of her being bundled into her car,' Annie continued. 'The same man puts her into the front seat of her BMW and then he returns to the stairwell and returns with Jackie Web. We can only assume that she left the club via one of the fire exits earlier in the evening as there is no record of her leaving through the front door. He throws her into the back of the car and then drives it out of the car park. CCTV footage from a wine bar further up Brownlow Hill, shows the vehicle stopping outside but we can't see what happens.'

'So, he drugged both women before taking them in the BMW?' Alec asked. 'Isn't it more likely that he had an accomplice? Was Jackie with anyone in the club?'

'She was with this guy,' Stirling pointed to another screen. 'She danced with him most of the evening but at this point here,' he paused and pointed to a still from the CCTV, 'our suspect returns from the bar with three drinks. He could have spiked both women on his own. Jackie Web is last filmed walking into the toilets, but we never see her coming out. She may have left the club another way, felt ill and returned to the car park. We have the other man leaving via the front entrance alone.'

'Maybe she passed out on the stairwell?' Alec nodded.

'Maybe the suspect got lucky.'

'Or maybe it was planned,' Alec wasn't convinced. 'You have to keep your minds open to an accomplice.'

'Realistically, yes, although we can't assume that there was one at this stage,' Annie said thoughtfully. 'My problem with the entire case is the incendiary that he rigged up.' Nodding heads around the room agreed with her. 'Did he set that incendiary device to kill or maim the responding officers?'

'Good question. Did he?' Alec shrugged. His forehead wrinkled. Deep lines creased his skin. 'Or did he set it to destroy evidence? He knew that at some stage the attic would be searched but how could he know exactly who would lift that hatch?'

'Fact is that he couldn't know but I think the whole scene was set to confuse the investigation. He murders the women in each other's home and makes the identification of the first victim difficult enough for us to assume that it was Jayne. Her mother was devastated when the body was found in her daughter's house, then she finds out that it might not be her daughter only to be devastated a second time when we discover the second body.'

'So, is he trying to cause as much emotional turmoil for the families or is it for our benefit?' Alec asked.

'The text carved into Jackie Webb is personal,' Google pitched in. 'Maybe causing the families distress is part of his game.'

'Game?' Alec thought it was an odd description.

'Yes, game.' Google blushed. He removed his glasses and wiped them on his tie. 'He has planned this in meticulous detail. The Rohypnol, the car, the empty houses, the use of the text,' Google rubbed his eyes, 'there's no way that he could have become fluent enough in Glagolitic to create all this,' he said holding up a crime scene photo. 'He must have had reference material with him.'

'He could have had a tablet or simply used his mobile,' Annie said.

'Agreed.' Google nodded. 'But the planning involved is meticulous. Switching the victims to confuse us, the booby-trap, everything about it has been designed to taunt both us and the families.' He cleared his throat nervously. 'That's just my opinion, obviously.'

'Why go to so much trouble though?' Alec asked. 'Isn't it just as likely that the killer went looking for a victim with the Rohypnol in his pocket, stumbles across Jayne Windsor and then runs with the situation improvising along the way?' the room was silent as the scenarios were analysed mentally by each detective. 'Once he realised the victims had an empty house, he indulged himself.'

'Why take Jayne to Jackie's apartment unless it was part of a complex plan?' Google countered.

'Time,' Alec replied ruffling his sandy hair, 'he had finished with the first victim and wanted to spend time with the second victim. The longer he stayed at the first crime scene the more likely it was that someone would call at the house.' He smiled thinly, 'he sets the incendiary to confuse the respondents giving him more time with the second victim. It could simply be a case of making the most of the opportunity. Don't get me wrong, he is one sick bastard but be careful that you don't gift him with a level of cunning which might not be there.' Alec walked to the window and looked outside. 'There are too many variables that could have gone wrong on the night. Even the most detailed plan could have gone tits-up that night. I mean, what if Jayne Windsor had decided not to go out at all? She was the driver. That would have left Jackie Webb stranded at home.' He shrugged. 'Would she have gone out alone?'

Google looked wounded, 'I concede that there are many possible answers to this conundrum, but my gut tells me that our killer is too smart to be an opportunist.' He paused. 'I'll grant you that it may be random but,' he nervously cleaned his glasses again even though they were spotless, 'the incendiary wasn't constructed on a whim. It was designed and built to be triggered by moving the loft hatch. He had to have bought the individual components and experimented with them before even contemplating the murders. That couldn't possibly be random.'

'It was a simple device.' Alec shrugged. 'How long would it have taken you to put together if you had to?'

Google tilted his head and smiled nervously. 'Twenty minutes or so if I had the components to hand.'

'I think you could do it in ten,' Alec pointed his finger at him. 'Let's assume that he intended to use the device to destroy the evidence at a crime scene at some point in his future. It would fit into a suitcase and could have been primed and ready to use for months, couldn't it?'

'It could have been, guv,' Stirling tried to take the focus from Google. He was too smart for his own good sometimes. 'We have found instructions for several similar devices on the net. I'm with you that we need to keep an open mind as to the motive. Catching the bastard is all that counts.'

'Agreed,' Annie said relieved that the debate was smothered. 'The facts are that we have a perfect mugshot of the suspect. We have their whereabouts on the evening in question and CSI is testing DNA from both scenes. It is a matter of time before we identify him. I was going to ask for your input at this juncture, guv.'

'How can I help?'

'I want to go national with this mugshot.'

'National?'

'Yes.' She paused and looked at Stirling.

He nodded in agreement. 'We want to broadcast his mugshot and share the MO with the other divisions.'

'There's no way this is his first time, guv.' Annie flicked images from the first crime scene. Alec nodded as a picture of the Cyrillic script etched into pale skin appeared. 'He has done this before. I think we should cast the net widely and see what we catch.'

'I agree,' Alec said rubbing his hands together. 'I'll set up a Press conference for first thing in the morning. I'm owed a few favours. It might be time to cash them in.'

'Thanks, guv.' She turned to the room. 'In the meantime, I want everything that we can find on the victims especially Jackie Webb. I want motive.' Heads nodded as the room went back to work. 'Jim, find out what you can on Jayne Windsor. It might be worth a trip to Halewood station. Speak to her DI in person but tread carefully.'

CHAPTER 17

Tod Harris wolfed three plates of tapas and only stopped eating when he could smell garlic on his own breath. The tables around him emptied as diners finished eating and then moved off onto different bars. He swilled four beers with his meal and felt relaxed if not a little bloated. The noisy English women made to leave; their language was spiralling towards the gutter. Louder and coarser. When the waiter arrived to take their payment, one of them grabbed his crotch, much to the amusement of the others. Their hysterical cackling laughter drew withering looks from the remaining diners and passersby, but they were oblivious. Tod laughed to himself as the red-faced waiter scurried back inside the bar.

Their chairs scraped on the cobbles as they stood to leave. A brunette staggered backwards and clattered into a nearby table. Luckily it was empty. She shrieked loudly and blushed. She turned and looked at Tod, giggling like a schoolgirl, shrugged her shoulders and staggered off. The lone male appeared from inside the bar. Tod hadn't noticed him leaving the table that he was sitting at. There was something shifty about the man, something about the way his eyes darted around. Tod returned his attention to the English women. He studied them as they teetered on their heels and headed down the lane. Any one of them would be an easy lay with or without Rohypnol. Wine or vodka would do the trick. They were up for it anyway although only one of them really interested him. She was curvy and her blond hair was made longer and thicker by extensions. Her black Lycra dress hugged her in the right places. His imagination played images of her in his mind, moaning, writhing, sweating, urging him to go faster, harder but then the images darkened to sobbing, screaming, struggling against him and then there was blood. Why did his thoughts always have to turn dark? He felt his stomach tightening as he watched her. It dawned on him that he might be staring at the woman a little too hard. Looking, staring, leering.

He looked away quickly and blushed. He caught the lone male studying him. As soon as their eyes met, the man dropped his gaze. An elderly couple on the far table caught his eye too. They were whispering and looking in his direction. He turned to look behind him and saw that one of the English women had tripped and fallen. Were they looking at her or him? Was it guilt that made him feel that they were staring at him or was it just natural? Was paranoia natural? It is when you were on the run. It had to be. The women screeched with laughter and dragged their friend to her feet before staggering on their way once more.

When his attention returned to bar, he noticed that the elderly couple were attempting to pay but the old man couldn't find his wallet. He checked and rechecked his pockets half a dozen times without joy. His wife sat tight lipped shaking her head embarrassed by her husband's forgetfulness. She tutted and rolled her eyes skyward before taking her purse from her handbag and handing the waiter enough money to cover the bill. They stood and walked slowly past his table arm in arm. The old man was mumbling about how certain he was that he had brought his wallet out and the old woman was equally as convinced that he couldn't remember his own name some days.

Tod caught the waiter's attention and slipped three ten Euro notes onto the table. That would cover the bill and leave a decent tip. He glanced at the lone male and walked across the cobbles in the direction that the women had taken. A cool breeze touched his skin. The scent of perfume carried to him. Armani, D&G, Diesel, and Chanel mingled. He knew his perfumes; that was for sure. He prided himself on being able to identify a fragrance although that particular talent didn't always impress the ladies. They were suspicious by nature. Identifying the brand of their perfume provoked images of previous female conquests in their warped minds. They were all warped. All of them. Black Widows spinning their webs to ensnare the male of the species. They were nest builders, pretending to be 'just having fun' but, they were all looking for that elusive man. The one that they deemed could be a potential partner for life. They were as much predators as men were but, in their case, they were playing for keeps. Venus fly traps offering the sweetness they had within, then once you liked the taste, snap! The trap was closed, the ring was on their finger, a mortgage acquired, the nursery was decorated, and welcome to the rest of your life spent at the bequest of her demands. Her aspirations were now yours to achieve, her dreams yours to deliver. They pretended to be complex delicate creatures, but Tod understood the simple reality. He knew the truth and they couldn't fool him.

The women had reached a crossroads and chose to turn right, heading down towards the promenade where the lively bars were situated. They were linked arm around shoulder like a line of chorus girls, forming a rolling roadblock that locals and other tourists had to manoeuvre around. The blond was on the far right of the line. His thoughts turned to a wildlife documentary where hunting lionesses would stalk the prey at the edge of the herd. The thought tickled him. He imagined the faces of startled onlookers as he pounced on her and brought her down in the street. He would be locked away in a padded cell but then maybe that's where he belonged.

The lane was busier as he neared the junction. The crowds were thickening but he could still see the women a hundred metres ahead of him. They had stopped outside a bar deciding whether to go in. A tout was chatting to them, more than likely offering free shots to entice them in. A child cried out and he stumbled.

'Watch where you're going, idiot!' A woman with a London accent snarled at him. Her daughter clutched at her foot and began to cry.

'My toes!' she moaned.

'I'm so sorry,' Tod said genuinely. 'I didn't see her down there.'

'Sorry?' the mother shouted. 'Are you blind?'

'I'm really sorry.'

'What's going on?' a deep voice growled. Tod turned to see a big male approaching. He was fat, tattooed, and his head was shaved, and he looked angry.

'This clumsy idiot stamped on our Madonna's toes,' the mother goaded him.

Madonna? Tod thought. What chance does a child have when it's named after a pop star or a footballer? 'I'm very sorry, Madonna,' he said to the whining child through gritted teeth.

'You will be!' the father approached with a scowl on his face. He squared up to Tod, his nose an inch away from his face. 'You need to watch where you're going!'

Tod thought about head-butting him but the last thing that he wanted now was attention. Violent behaviour was taken very seriously in the Spanish resorts. It would be a huge mistake to become embroiled in a fight in the middle of the street. 'I'm very sorry,' he stepped back and held up his hands. He reached into his pocket for a note, 'here, get yourself an ice cream,' he handed the note to the little girl. She snatched it without any hesitation. He turned to walk away and bumped into an elderly couple. The man looked shocked and swore in a language that Tod didn't understand. 'I'm very sorry,' Tod said turning away quickly. He stepped aside to circumvent the crowd and felt a hard shove in the hip. It came from behind. Turning, he looked around, but the crowd had closed on whoever had pushed him. He was surrounded by strangers. He took a deep breath and tried to put some space between himself and the family and instinctively put his hand to his hip where he had felt the contact. His wallet was gone.

'Shit!' he shouted looking around frantically. The crowd parted for a second and he caught sight of the lone male from the restaurant darting through the tourists with practiced ease. He watched him twist and turn, sidestepping and ducking. He used the tourists as camouflage slipping between them to remain undetected. The old man had lost his wallet at the bar and now Tod's had gone too. It had all his debit cards and cash in it. It had to be him that had stolen them.

'Stop there, you thieving little bastard!' Tod shouted at the top of his voice. The entire street froze for a millisecond as people tried to pinpoint who was shouting and who was a thief. The thief stopped for a second and looked over his shoulder. Their eyes met again. Tod used the moment to his advantage and ran towards him. 'Give me my wallet back, you little twat!' he sprinted towards him, the tourists parted like the Red Sea. He closed the distance quickly, but the thief regained his composure and ran back down the lane towards the bar that they'd come from.

The thief was quick. Very quick indeed. Much faster than Tod. He sprinted as fast as his legs would allow him to, but the thief was making a metre for every metre they covered. Tod regretted shouting at the man. He should have followed him in silence and then cornered him. The cobblestones made running at pace difficult. They were uneven and worn smooth and Tod feared slipping. At the pace he was running, if he fell then he would either break his wrists or smash his face in.

The bar went by in a blur of lights and he could feel his lungs beginning to burn with exertion. His thigh muscles were screaming at him to stop, lactic acid was coursing through the muscle cells tightening the fibres and slowing him down. Lager sloshed around in his belly, threatening to come back up and choke him and he burped an acidic mixture of garlic and beer, which stung his gullet. The thief was pulling further away, his arms and legs pumped like pistons. Tod heaved air into his lungs and ran faster. The effort was unsustainable but losing his bank cards wasn't an option. He had to catch him.

The thief skidded on the cobbles and changed direction. He found his footing and turned right into a narrow lane and Tod lost sight of him for a few seconds. He counted in his head, one, two, three, four, five, six, and then he took the turn himself. The pickpocket was running hard without slowing. Tod felt his heart sink when he saw the gradient of the lane. The cobbles climbed steeply for a few hundred metres to some wide stone steps, which led to the street above, but he couldn't see what was beyond the hill. He wasn't sure if he would make it. His legs were like lead as the gradient began to bite. The thief turned to look over his shoulder and the panicked look on his face spurred Tod onwards. He was tiring.

Adrenalin pumped through his veins as he steeled himself to conquer the incline. His thighs were on fire as he concentrated on putting one foot in front of the other. Blood pounded in his ears blocking out all other sounds except the rasping of his breath. It felt like running through wet concrete. His mind wanted his body to run faster, but his body couldn't deliver. The pickpocket was feeling the pain too as he neared the steps. He stopped for a second and grabbed at the iron handrail that split the steps in half. His chest heaved and he bent double and retched. He stole a quick glance at Tod, who was closing the gap and then bolted up the steps taking them two at a time.

Tod counted the seconds in his mind, one, two, three, four, and he was at the bottom of the steps. He was gaining ground now, but his body was shutting down. He was panting like a dog; sweat soaked his clothes and stung his eyes. The muscles in his legs were exhausted and his knees and ankles sent bolts of pain to his brain every time his feet impacted with the cobbles. The thief was nearing the brow of the hill as Tod launched himself up the steps.

When he reached the top, he could hear the thief's footsteps pounding the cobbles, but he couldn't see him. He looked left down a long sloping road, but it was empty. To his right was a whitewashed church illuminated by spotlights. Tourists milled around taking photographs. Panic gripped him. He couldn't see which way the thief had run. Suddenly he heard a clatter and a muffled cry. Directly opposite him was a narrow alleyway between the buildings. He hadn't seen it at first because the lighting was poor. It was pitch-black in the alley but there was no doubt that the noise had come from that direction.

Tod took a deep breath and burst across the road. He entered the inky blackness of the alley without hesitation. The street lighting hardly penetrated the darkness and within a few strides, he was running blind. He knew that he would have to slow down or risk running into a hidden obstacle. Another clatter up ahead brought him to a sudden stop. He tried to slow his breathing so that he could listen. Another muffled cry and a scrambling sound. Then the sound of feet running again. 'Shit!' Tod wheezed as he took off in pursuit at a jog. He couldn't risk running any faster. A fall here could leave him badly hurt.

His eyes began to adjust to the darkness and deep shadows leapt out at him as he ran. He stepped over an upturned bin and saw refuse scattered. Tod figured it was the cause of the clatter that he had heard. He stared hard into the night as he ran along the narrowing alleyway. There was barely room between the walls to stand without twisting his shoulders at a slight angle. Dark rectangles spotted the walls on either side; it registered that they were doors that gave access to backyards or gardens. The shuffling sound ahead gave him hope. He was close to the thief. Too close to give up. He took a deep breath and his lungs felt like they would explode. His thighs felt like they were pumped full of caustic. They burned and ached like never before. Sweat poured down his face in salty stinging rivulets. The exertion was crippling him. He blanked the fatigue and maintained a steady pace until the shadows in front of him became an impregnable wall. He reached out and touched cold wet rock. Moss and lichen clung to the near vertical surface. Looking up, the wall loomed above him bowing out to block out the stars. 'Shit!' he cursed again. The rocky outcrop formed a dead end.

He was sure it must be part of the promontory, which separated the Old Town from the harbour. Looking back down the alley, a yellow oblong was his only view of the entrance and he hadn't seen any obvious ways out of the alley. Either he had passed by an open doorway in the darkness or the thief had gone over a wall into one of the gardens. He kicked the rock face in anger and sighed loudly. Had the pickpocket tripped over the bin or used it to scale the wall? If he had climbed into the maze of backyards, he was gone.

He listened in the darkness. Blood pulsed through his veins. Thud, thud, thud. His breath rasped, sounding deafening in the blackness. Suddenly, he heard a clumping sound, then another, running footsteps behind him! Tod turned and saw a figure silhouetted against the light from the entrance, running in the opposite direction. He must have passed inches from him in the darkness. Had he crouched down behind a bin or ducked into a doorway? It didn't matter. He cursed and sprinted after him more determined than ever to catch him.

The fleeting figure was running with a lurching gait. He was hurt. Tod figured that his left leg was injured, maybe twisted in the stumble or maybe he had torn a muscle. He couldn't care less. The sight of him limping spurred him on despite the burning in his chest. There was no more than fifty metres between them, and he was gaining fast. The pickpocket staggered into the wall, stumbled, and fell. Tod felt a surge of energy and anger as he neared him. He was thrashing about on the ground, trying to scramble to his feet. A second later, he was up and running once more but now he was bent double, his hands out in front of him. His limp was more pronounced, and Tod could hear him moaning as he stumbled on, bouncing from one side to the other. He was a wounded animal desperately trying to escape an approaching predator. He careered on zigzagging along the narrow alley. Only his survival instinct kept him from collapsing. They were ten metres from the entrance and the yellow street lights cast a dull glow on them. The thief was listing to one side as he ran. Both hands seemed to be clutching his side. He stole a frightened glance over his shoulder, only to see his pursuer closing fast. His injured leg buckled, and he cried out as he stumbled and fell again, landing heavily face down on the cobbles.

Tod was on him in a second. He grabbed him by the arm and turned him roughly onto his back. The man's face was a mask of pain, his mouth hung open and spittle covered his chin. His eyes were wide, staring and filled with fear. His hands clutched at his side. Tod looked down and saw the handle of a knife protruding from his abdomen just above his belt. It was buried to the hilt and blood covered his hands and wrists. A dark stain had formed across his jumper and was spreading down his jeans.

'You fell on your own knife, did you?' Tod panted. He assumed the man had lured him into a dead-end alleyway to stab him. 'That serves you right, you prick!' he reached into his jacket pockets searching for his wallet. Blood saturated the material and soaked his skin in seconds. Its slippery warmth and coppery smell excited him. 'Where is my wallet?' the thief didn't speak but he moaned in reply. Tod patted his trousers and felt a rectangular lump.

Reaching inside, he felt his wallet. He pulled it out roughly and thumbed through the cards and banknotes to make sure it was all intact. 'I hope it was worth it, idiot!'

'Dios mio!' the thief panted. His expression was twisted in agony. He stared at the protruding handle in disbelief. 'Dios mio!'

Tod put his wallet away and thought for a moment. Should he help the man, call for an ambulance or leave him to his own devices? His options were limited. Getting involved with the police wasn't desirable despite the fact that he hadn't broken any laws in Spain on this trip. He looked at his blood-soaked hands and considered how he would look if someone saw him. He was standing over a bleeding male with a knife buried in his guts, his hands covered in blood. That would take a lot of explaining even if he could speak the lingo. He tried to wipe as much of it off as he could using the thief's trousers as a towel and then turned and headed for the entrance of the alleyway.

'Ayudame!' the thief whispered hoarsely. 'Por favor, ayudame.'

'I have no idea what you're saying,' Tod said over his shoulder, 'but fuck you very much!' As he reached the road, he pushed his hands deep into his pockets and peered down the hill. It was clear. He looked up the road towards the church. The square was busy with tourists. He could see a large group huddled before the huge arched doors, staring up at the bell tower. A woman at the centre of the group was addressing them and pointing skywards. Tod guessed that it was a guided tour of the Old Town and there were too many eyes for him to blend in without someone spotting the blood on his clothes. He would have to go back the way he came, across the road, down the steps, and hope that the lanes were so busy that no one would notice him.

He checked down the hill once more and froze when he saw the green and white markings of the Guardia Civil. The patrol car was turning the corner at the bottom of the hill and climbing slowly towards him at a crawl. He could see the silhouettes of two officers sitting in the front of the vehicle and a third man in the rear. The headlights picked him out immediately. It was too late to slip back into the alley without looking suspicious. Running would be pointless and his legs were still like lead. He put his head down avoiding eye contact and stood at the edge of the pavement as if he was waiting to cross the road. The police car slowed to a stop. He recognised the man in the back seat instantly. He was talking to the police officers and pointing at Tod.

The window rolled down. 'Estas bien, senor?'

Tod shrugged his shoulders and grinned nervously. 'I'm sorry but I don't speak Spanish.'

The officer frowned and spoke to the man in the rear of the car. They exchanged words and he turned back to Tod. His English was good even though it was tinted with his accent. 'This man said that you were at his restaurant earlier and then he saw you running after a local pickpocket?'

Tod thought about lying. He could show them his wallet and tell them that the thief had dropped it during the chase, but his hands were bloodstained. He couldn't take his hands out of his pockets without raising suspicion. Droplets of sweat ran down his temples. He shifted his weight awkwardly. The officer in the passenger seat opened his door and climbed out. He eyed Tod with suspicion. The driver stared at him intently. 'Have you been robbed or not, Sinor?'

'I was but I found my wallet,' Tod tried to smile, 'the thief must have tossed it away. I'm fine but thank you for your concern.' He heard shuffling and sensed danger before he could identify where it was. He felt a sharp thud between his shoulder blades and a dull pain. His chest tightened and his breath was trapped in his lungs. Warm blood trickled down his back. He felt his knees buckle and fold as he collapsed onto the cobbles. He watched bemused as both policemen drew their weapons and aimed in his direction. They were shouting a warning that he couldn't comprehend. The pain in his back intensified and somewhere in his confusion he thought he had been stabbed. He wriggled and writhed trying to reach for the offending blade, but it was out of his reach. The policemen approached nearer, becoming louder and more threatening. A shot was fired, and a cry echoed off the houses. He heard a body hit the floor with a thud close to him. A face that he recognised stared at him through glassy eyes. The life seemed to fade from them as he watched. A trickle of dark blood ran from the corner of his blue lips. The pickpocket was dead and in a strange way, he felt saddened by that. Surely a life was worth more than a few hundred Euros. He suddenly felt cold, colder than he had ever been. Reality slipped away as unconsciousness descended on him and the world went dark.

CHAPTER 18

Jim Stirling drove across the city towards an area on the edge of the metropolis called Halewood. It was an area that he was familiar with. Once, a sprawling maze of rundown social housing estates prone to high levels of crime and sporadic rioting, it had reinvented itself in the 90s as a desirable suburb but some of the black spots remained. The police station hadn't moved with the times and still had the appearance of a large factory unit protected by galvanised wire grills. The walls surrounding the vehicle lot to the rear were topped with revolving metal spikes. It was built to resist civil unrest but now decades after it was built, it was a blot on the leafy suburban landscape. As he approached, his mobile rang. He pressed the answer button on the steering wheel, 'DS Stirling.'

'Are you there yet?' Annie asked.

'I'm pulling in now, guv.'

'Just to let you know,' Annie sounded excited. 'Alec has wangled a slot on Crimewatch tonight. That should give us a name. You might want to mention it if you meet any resistance.'

'Excellent news,' Stirling said as he steered out of the traffic. 'Nothing like the spotlight to loosen tongues. Thanks for that, guv.'

'No problem, see you later,' Annie hung up.

'Good old Alec,' Stirling mumbled to himself as he parked in a visitor bay at the front of the building. He climbed out, locked the doors, and walked into the reception area.

The vinyl floor had lost its sheen years ago and a black tide mark clung to the skirting boards, the result of sporadic mopping with dirty water. Two teenage girls dressed in velour tracksuits sat next to their prams. They stopped chewing for a second when Stirling walked in, exchanged knowing glances that he was a copper and then continued their summations of the X-Factor. Stirling showed his ID to the uniformed officer that manned the desk from behind a thick sheet of reinforced Perspex. His age and the stripes on his sleeve denoted many years service. Although they were both sergeant rank, the gulf between uniformed officers and detectives was vast and bred resentment. 'DS Stirling from MIT,' he said through the perforations, which made the reception desk look like a giant hamster box. 'I'm here to see DI Haig.'

'Take a seat and I'll let him know that you're here,' the sergeant grumbled with disinterest. Stirling figured the grey-haired officer was serving the last months of his career doing something that he hated. The lines etched into his face told the story of years of disappointment at never making it out of the uniformed ranks. Too many mistakes made at the wrong time, too many poor decisions made in front of the wrong senior officers and each one had left a crease in his flesh. As time ticked by, his enthusiasm had dissipated, and the decades had gone by in a heartbeat. Stirling had seen it all before.

'How long have you been stationed here?' Stirling asked, ignoring the offer to sit. The officer eyed him with distain as he picked up the phone and informed the DI that he had a visitor.

'Twenty years.' He rolled his eyes.

Stirling whistled in admiration. 'How long on the job in total?'

'Twenty-five,' he said proudly. 'I worked the city centre for five years before they transferred me here, been here ever since.' He smiled thinly and relaxed a little. 'I'm retiring in six weeks. Twenty-five years, you don't get that for murder in this country, eh!'

'Not often enough,' Stirling agreed. 'That's twenty-five years of knowledge we're losing. I bet you know more about what goes on here than anyone upstairs does.' Stirling laughed gruffly.

'You know how it is.' He winked slyly, 'the suits upstairs wouldn't know a crook if one stabbed him up the arse.' He paused and cocked his head to one side. 'What brings MIT over here anyway?'

'Fishing trip really,' Stirling tapped the end of his nose. 'Can't say too much.'

'I'll put a pound to a penny,' he wagged a wrinkled finger, 'that's a hundred to one to a young pup like you,' he lowered his voice to a whisper, 'that it's to do with that Special Constable, Windsor, isn't it?' He folded his arms and winked. 'Am I right?'

'Put it this way.' Stirling leaned closer to the Perspex. 'I wouldn't shake hands on your bet!'

A conjoining door opened behind Stirling and he turned to see a tall black man dressed in a dark blue suit. He held a thick manila file under one arm. 'You must be DS Stirling,' he said with a smile, 'I hope Arthur isn't giving you his solution to the county's drug problems?' his smile faded as he looked at the uniformed officer. 'Executing people in front of the Town Hall steps will never be allowed.' Arthur scowled in response and went back to his paperwork. 'I'm DI Haig,' he said offering a handshake.

Stirling stepped forward and shook his hand. 'Jim Stirling, guv, nice to meet you.'

'We'll use the interview room, shall we?' he pointed to a door at the side of the reception desk and used his pass-key to open it. 'I'm assuming that you need background on Jayne Windsor?' he said offering Stirling a chair. 'Terrible business. We're all deeply shocked by her death. Have you made any progress in arresting her killer?'

'We have recovered DNA and we have an image of the man that she was seen leaving a nightclub with, we're going public on Crimewatch tonight,' Stirling kept it brief but had dropped in the television coverage early. The worried expression on Haig's face told him that it had the desired effect. 'Obviously we're waiting for results and it's very early days yet. I can't say too much, guv.'

'Crimewatch, bloody hell you've done very well there!'

'They've squeezed us into the program at short notice. The DS pulled some strings.'

'Alec is a good copper. Sounds like you'll have the animal in custody pretty soon.' He smiled again although Stirling sensed something behind the smile and offered no more information. After a few seconds of baited silence, the DI spoke. 'I've pulled her paperwork for you to take with you,' he said in a serious tone. 'And we've emailed her electronic files across to your DI. How else can I help you?' he asked sliding the file across the table.

'I won't bullshit you, guv.' Stirling shrugged his huge shoulders, 'but when we were trying to identify Jayne Windsor, I contacted her sergeant and I was given the impression that she wasn't very popular with her colleagues. He couldn't get off the phone quick enough.'

DI Haig puffed up his cheeks and then blew out the air slowly. He looked Stirling in the eyes and shook his head. 'Station gossip, Sergeant. You've been in the job a long time, you know how these things work.' He shrugged. 'No one likes Special Constables to begin with, 'plastics' they call them here.' His smile reappeared. 'Everything is in that file for you to read. I wish I could give you the details of a cover-up that would help you catch the bastard that killed her but there simply isn't one.'

'This case will come under intense scrutiny.' Stirling shrugged again. 'There's rarely any smoke without a fire, guv.' He persisted. 'Once the television appeal goes out, all the rumours and gossip will resurface. Something started the rumours. We'd be interested to know what it was so that we can deflect them.'

The DI grimaced and thought about his next words carefully. He paused and folded his arms. 'You heard about the Barton case about four years ago?'

'I know as much as I've been told, and I've heard some of the gossip but I don't know all the details.' Stirling said frankly. 'The devil is in the details, right?' Stirling sat forward and grinned. 'I heard that someone dropped the ball and the killer walked?'

'Killer?' Haig tilted his head. 'We never recovered his body.' The DI looked mildly offended and shook his head. 'We arrested the uncle, Peter Barton, for the boy's murder but we never recovered the boy's body. Everyone on the case had him nailed as the killer from day one. He had this long mad grey curly hair going on like an aging hippie. On paper, he was the ideal candidate for 'Uncle Pervert' but he was an ex-copper. Did you know that?'

'No, I didn't,' Stirling said surprised. 'That was never mentioned in the news.'

'There was a lot of detail withheld because we didn't have a body.'

'That must have hampered the investigation?'

'It did. He was always one step ahead of the investigation. He knew what we'd do before we did it. Add to that the fact that all the evidence was circumstantial and we we're struggling.'

'What did you have on him?'

Haig sighed. 'We had suggestive text messages sent from Barton on the boy's phone and inappropriate images of the boy on Barton's Blackberry.'

'Surely that's evidence of abuse?'

'Not enough. They weren't pornographic images or sexual text messages. They just weren't right. We found DNA in the boot of his car but it was degraded so it was only a partial match, but it was compelling evidence nonetheless. On top of that he had no one to corroborate his alibi for the night of the disappearance. It took the jury four days to deliberate but they came back with a guilty verdict anyway. He got life.'

'Sounds like you had enough to keep him inside so what went wrong?'

The DI looked down at the desk and shrugged. 'Before the appeal hearing the defence presented new evidence.'

'What new evidence?'

'An alibi. They argued that when the boy was taken, Barton was at a music festival being held at Sefton Park. During the original trial, no one could corroborate his story but when they submitted their appeal they had new evidence that he had had a conversation with a stallholder and a Special Constable about the time that the boy went missing.'

'Jayne Windsor gave him an alibi?'

'No,' the DI shook his head, 'the stallholder did, and she testified that Windsor was there. Jayne Windsor couldn't remember talking to him, but.' He shrugged, 'she wasn't a hundred per cent sure that she hadn't either. The abduction was twenty miles away from the festival so if he was there then there was no way that he could have taken the boy. The judge ruled that no jury could convict beyond a reasonable doubt and because the DNA evidence wasn't conclusive on its own, he overturned the verdict to save the cost of another trial. Barton walked from prison and a lot of people here blamed Windsor.'

'And the alibi?'

'Solid. The stallholder was there over the two-day event. She had the booking confirmation from the organisers, hundreds of customers backed up with receipts and she had a debit card receipt from a purchase that Jayne Windsor made herself around the time the kid was abducted.' He sat back and folded his arms. 'Faced with all that, we had no reason to question it.'

'But if Jayne Windsor had testified that she had never seen or spoken to Barton, he would still be inside?'

'Exactly, we'll never know if the appeal jury would have upheld the verdict without the alibi but with it, the case was dead in the water. The Barton family are very popular around here. Their son played for the local football team… the father runs the local scout troop. Pillars of the community. He was a good kid and Barton's release sent ripples through the area.'

Stirling mulled over the information and decided that it shed little light on their case. There was plenty of reason for her colleagues to lose respect for her but no motive for murder. 'That would explain her sergeant's attitude when I enquired about her absence.'

'Indeed,' the DI stood and held out his hand. 'If there's anything else that I can do to help, please call me directly.'

Stirling followed his lead and shook his hand. 'Thanks for your time, guv.'

He felt a sense of disappointment as he walked to his car although he wasn't surprised that there was no sinister plot to uncover. Rumours often circulated in the police force and were rarely based on substance. Jayne Windsor had apparently screwed up her career by 'telling the truth'. She simply couldn't be one hundred per cent certain that she had spoken to Peter Barton and she wasn't prepared to testify under oath that she 'definitely' hadn't spoken to him. Some would have to admire her principles, but others wouldn't think twice about twisting the truth slightly to keep a killer behind bars.

He started the engine and reversed out of the parking bay. As he looked over his shoulder through the rear window, he noticed the desk sergeant walking towards him. He had a thick padded jacket over his uniform and Stirling guessed he had finished his shift. He tapped on the passenger window and bent down to peer inside. Stirling pressed the button to lower the glass.

'Any chance of a lift?'

'Jump in, Arthur.' Stirling said instinctively brushing the material of the passenger seat. He leaned over and picked up three empty coffee cups, dumping them in the back. 'Excuse the mess but I wasn't expecting visitors.'

Arthur climbed in and winced in pain as he shuffled into the seat. 'My hips are knackered. Age is a terrible thing,' he moaned.

'The alternative to getting old is worse than a bit of arthritis,' Stirling grunted. 'Count your blessings!'

'I'm allowed to moan at my age,' he said,' he said putting his seat belt on.

'Not in my car. If you want to moan, get on the bus.'

'Charming.'

Stirling knew the old sergeant wanted more than a lift, but he put the car into gear and steered into the light traffic without a word. He had no idea where he wanted to go but headed towards the city anyway.

'I live near Calderstones Park,' Arthur said matter-of-factly. 'It's on your way back into town.'

'No problem.'

'How did your meeting with DI 'vague' go?'

The play on the DI's name didn't go unnoticed. Stirling smiled to himself. 'He was very helpful to be honest.'

'I bet he was,' Arthur scoffed. 'He wouldn't know his arse from his elbow. He's on a fast-track, you know. Another token ethnic in my opinion.' He turned to Stirling. 'Have you forgotten the Toxteth riots?'

'That was in the 80s, Arthur.'

'It wasn't that long ago when you put it in context.'

'You're a dinosaur, Arthur. That kind of prejudice doesn't go down well anymore,' Stirling grumbled. 'It's probably why you're riding a desk.' Arthur's face reddened. Stirling couldn't tell if it was anger or embarrassment and he didn't care either way. Fast tracking detectives had never been popular especially with officers who were still in uniform. Fast tracking women or officers from an ethnic background allowed the bigots to feel that their failure to progress was somebody else's fault. He had no time for their poisonous rhetoric and no sympathy for their plight.

'Oh, I know why I'm on desk duty.' Arthur laughed sourly. 'You're right. I'm a dinosaur but that doesn't make me a bad copper. I'll be glad when I'm out of it. The job has gone to pot. We've got kids running around with their magnifying glasses playing at detectives while the real experienced coppers are drowning in paperwork to stop criminals from suing us. We know who the bad guys are, but we can't do anything about it nowadays. We can't have a crap without filling in a risk assessment form.'

'It's called progress, Arthur,' Stirling yawned and opened the window a few inches. 'In your day we just arrested anyone who fit the bill and bullied them into a confession and if we locked up the wrong guy, who cared because they were bad ones anyway!'

'We had respect from the public back then. Not anymore. School kids nowadays have no respect and no fear for authority. It's no wonder society is going down the toilet.'

'Just because we can't beat confessions out of people or give a schoolboy a good hiding for stealing from the local shop doesn't mean we're failing. The force is more efficient now and we do things by the book.' Stirling shook his head and looked across at the aging sergeant. 'Are you going to whine all the way home or are you going to tell me what it is you have to say?'

'I wish I had got the bus.'

'So do I.' Stirling looked along the pavement and spotted a bus stop. 'I can drop you here if you would rather?'

'Yes, pull over. There's a bad atmosphere in this car.' Stirling sighed and indicated left, sliding the vehicle into the stop. Arthur undid his seat belt and looked directly at Stirling. 'What did the DI tell you about the Barton case?'

Stirling took a deep breath and debated what to tell him. 'He told me that Jayne Windsor couldn't testify categorically that she hadn't spoken to Peter Barton and that allowed him to walk.'

'They brushed it all under the carpet the first time around in my opinion.' He sat back and gloated. 'There's nothing more damaging than a youngster dying on your patch, if you know what I mean. The quicker it goes away, the better.'

'What are you trying to say, Arthur?' Stirling said irritably. 'Spit it out.'

There was a twinkle in Arthur's watery eyes. 'I've been following the news on your case closely.' He smiled and tapped his nose. 'Unlike DI Vague. I told you he doesn't know his arse from his elbow.'

'I'm lost.' Stirling sighed. He could see a double-decker bus approaching in his rear-view mirror. 'There's a bus coming, put your belt back on.' He put the car into first and moved out of the way. 'I might have a detective's badge, Arthur but I'm not a bloody psychic.' A car beeped its horn as he pushed into the traffic. Stirling responded with the middle finger of his right hand. The other driver caught a glimpse of the size of him and sped by without responding. 'You're going to have to spell it out for me.'

'Peter Barton had an alibi which Jayne Windsor couldn't confirm or deny, right?'

'Right.' Stirling shrugged.

'Drop me off here,' Arthur said suddenly. Stirling shook his head angrily and pulled the car over to the curb. 'Like I said earlier, I've been following the news ever since I heard Jayne Windsor was the victim.' He opened the door and struggled out as fast as his aching joints would allow. He leaned back into the vehicle and pointed to the manila file that was on the back seat. 'Take a good look at that file, Detective.' He winked. 'Take a look at who the stallholder was.' He slammed the door with more force than was necessary and walked away back towards the bus stop. Stirling turned to grab the file but another burst of horns from frustrated drivers told him that he was blocking the traffic. He swore beneath his breath and drove on towards the city. The file would have wait until he got back to the station.

CHAPTER 19

Annie looked around the MIT office. Half the desks were occupied with detectives that were prepped and ready to receive calls from the public when the Crimewatch appeal went live. The other half were empty as her detectives were out following leads and interviewing witnesses from both scenes. When Jim Stirling stepped out of the lift holding up a manila file, she knew that he had found something.

'There's a man with something to say,' Alec interrupted her thoughts.

'I was thinking the same myself,' Annie agreed. 'It's not often you see him smiling. He's usually dark and moody.' She joked.

Alec grinned. 'When you're built like a house, you can be as dark and moody as you like.'

'What has got you so excited?' Annie asked as he approached.

'I think we should go into your office,' Stirling said red faced. Alec led the way and they went into Annie's office. Stirling shrugged off his leather jacket and hung it on the back of a chair and placed the file on the seat. Alec stood by the window and watched as the street lights below began to twinkle into life. Dusk was turning to night and thousands of yellow bulbs joined forces to stop darkness from swallowing the city. 'You're going to love this.' Stirling tapped the file.

Alec and Annie exchanged amused glances and waited expectantly. 'Who did you meet with?' Alec asked. The lines on his forehead furrowed.

'A DI by the name of Haig,' he said sitting down opposite Annie. 'Although one of the sergeants calls him DI Vague.'

'I hope you haven't been upsetting the natives,' Annie commented.

'No more than usual,' Stirling grunted. 'The DI was very helpful to be fair. He gave me her paperwork and he has emailed her digital files to you, guv.' He nodded at Annie.

Annie frowned and immediately grabbed her computer mouse. She clicked it a few times and nodded. 'Yes, he has.'

'I asked him why Jayne Windsor's sergeant had been so abrupt when I enquired about her absence. He explained about what happened with the Barton case a few years back. You remember that don't you?'

Alec grimaced and looked at Annie. 'We nearly had to pick that up at one point.' Alec rubbed his hands together as he spoke.

'Why didn't we get it?' Annie frowned.

'We were up to our necks in sand on Crosby Beach.' Alec shrugged. 'It happened during our investigation into The Butcher. The chief didn't want us taking on anything else at the time.' Annie seemed to hold her breath for a moment. Alec watched her, conscious that she would be thinking about the horrific moment in the investigation when everything changed for her. A second of complacency and she lost her eye. He carried on. 'The case was floundering, and they never recovered a body. The Crown Prosecution Service were very reluctant to proceed until they found DNA in the suspect, Peter Barton's car.'

'That's the one,' Stirling agreed cautiously. He sensed Annie's discomfort too. 'Did you know that he was an ex-copper?'

'No.' Alec frowned.

'DI Haig said that he was.' Stirling shrugged. 'The case fell to bits at the appeal hearing and Peter Barton took a walk.'

Alec nodded thoughtfully. There had been so many cases over the years. Some took him longer to recall but he never forgot the details, especially when children were involved. 'It was only a partial DNA sample, right?'

'Correct but that wasn't the main issue,' Stirling held up a finger. 'At the appeal hearing, the defence came up with an alibi.'

'As they do,' Annie said sarcastically. She seemed to have settled her nerves. 'Where did they pull that from?'

'Barton claimed that he was at Sefton Park music festival and that he had had a conversation with one of the stallholders and a Special Constable at the time of the abduction.'

'How did they miss that the first time around?' Annie asked incredulously. 'An alibi from a Special would be gold dust for the defence. Was it overlooked?'

'No, I don't think so. I think it might have been buried.' Stirling lowered his voice, 'And this is where it gets interesting,' he paused, 'Jayne Windsor couldn't confirm or deny his story. She couldn't remember talking to him, but she couldn't definitively say that she hadn't either. She was in uniform on the day and the crowds were drinking. Hundreds of people stopped to talk to our officers, taking pictures on their phones or just engaging in general drunken banter but the stallholder testified under oath that Jayne had been there when Barton was there.'

'Bloody hell,' Annie mumbled. 'So, she couldn't deny seeing him and gave the judge a 'reasonable doubt' issue?'

'Exactly.' Stirling nodded. 'Windsor bought some items from the stall with her debit card at the time the stallholder claimed that Barton was at the stall.'

'You can see why the judge threw it out,' Alec said. 'I can see where the resentment towards her came from but it's not enough for a motive unless one of the Barton family wanted revenge for Barton walking.'

'Not the way she was killed. Annie shook her head, 'our killer is not an angry relative, he's a monster.'

'I was at the same point as you are until I was leaving the station.' Stirling grinned. 'The desk sergeant was waiting for me outside.' Alec and Annie exchanged confused glances. 'He asked me for a lift home and then started ranting about how crap the brass is. He has been following the case in the news because Jayne Winsor was a victim. When he got out of the car, he told me to take a look at who gave the alibi.'

'The stallholder?' Alec frowned.

'Who was it?' Annie asked.

'The stallholder was booked on to the festival selling 'cruelty free' make-up and 'fair trade' cosmetics, moisturisers, and massage oils to promote her beautician business. Her name was Jackie Webb,' Stirling closed the file and put it onto Annie's desk with a thump.

CHAPTER 20

'Who is working on the financials?' Alec asked.

'Becky,' Annie replied. She stood up and walked to the door, opened it, and called across the office. 'Becky, can you come in here for a moment please and bring whatever you have on the financials?' All eyes turned to her in anticipation. It was obvious that something was breaking. Becky Sebastian unplugged her laptop and grabbed a pile of papers. She was six months into her new position and still a little nervous in front of senior officers. She blushed as she rushed across the office. Some of the male detectives swapped appreciative glances as she passed them. Her long black hair almost reached the waistband of her faded jeans. 'Come in and take a seat,' Annie said smiling.

Stirling stood up to make room at the desk and Alec nodded hello. 'What have you found on our victims so far,' he asked smiling. The wrinkles around his eyes deepened. His smile had a disarming quality, which endeared his officers to him. 'Anything interesting?'

Becky nodded enthusiastically and opened her laptop. She sifted through her papers and picked out the three sheets that she needed. 'I was about to come and ask your opinion on something that I've found.'

'What is it?' Annie asked, taking her seat opposite.

'I went back two years and found nothing out of the ordinary. Both women have mortgages, and the usual direct debits for utility bills and the like going from their current accounts monthly, gas, electric, water, council tax, and mobile phones. Everything is paid like clockwork.' She looked up and smiled nervously. 'They both have a number of credit cards which are well within their limits.' She shrugged and picked up a sheet of paper. 'That is where the similarities end. Jayne Windsor has her salary paid in monthly and everything that goes through her account is done electronically. However, all Jackie Webb's income is paid in by cash deposits with no pattern to it. There are sporadic amounts paid in randomly throughout the month.'

'We would expect to see that from a self-employed 'beautician',' Stirling commented.

'Everything looks normal on the face of it,' Becky agreed.

'Except what?' Alec prompted.

'Well, they do okay financially, and there's no excessive spending, but their mortgage payments looked too low to me.' She looked around at her superiors and smiled nervously. 'I know how much I pay each month for my flat.' She shrugged and blushed again. 'They both have relatively new properties, but their mortgage payments are below five hundred pounds a month.'

Alec frowned and looked at Annie. 'That would be unusual if it applied to one of them. The fact that both are in that fortunate position is not a coincidence.'

'If it is, I need to know who they bank with,' Annie agreed. 'Can you see why their repayments are so low, Becky?'

Becky nodded and reached for another sheet of paper. 'They purchased their properties eight months apart and both paid substantial deposits against the loans.'

'That could be a coincidence,' Stirling said. 'They're both from reasonably wealthy backgrounds.'

'Ah, but neither deposits were paid from their bank accounts.' Becky countered. 'I can't see where the money came from without getting a warrant for the mortgage providers' records.'

'So, if the families financed them, it could be nothing?' Annie said deflated.

Becky bit her bottom lip and shrugged. 'I thought about that,' she said sheepishly, 'so I spoke to both of the mothers to clarify the situation.' Alec smiled at Annie impressed by the young detective's initiative. 'Neither of them contributed to their daughter's mortgage down payments.'

'Excellent work, Becky. When did they purchase their properties?' Alec asked.

'Three years ago,' Becky said blushing. 'That's why I didn't see it straight away. I should have gone further back initially.'

'You've done well,' Annie said. 'Let's get that warrant sorted.'

'Yes, guv!' Becky said excitedly. She stood up and gathered her paperwork.

'While you're on the telephone to the court,' Alec added, 'get a warrant for the financials of Peter Barton too. I have a feeling they'll be connected.'

'Peter Barton?' Becky looked confused.

'I'll explain who he is and bring the team up to speed.' Stirling nodded to Alec.

'I want everything they have on the Barton case,' Alec added. 'I want to know exactly what they had on him and I want to know where he was a copper and why they kept it under wraps.'

'Yes, guv. Do you want me to bring him in?'

'Let's not rush this. If he once served, he'll be anticipating us making the connection.' Annie shook her head and looked at Alec. She pushed her hair behind her ear and frowned. 'He could have escalated from killing Simon Barton and turned his attention to the women who gave him an alibi, I suppose?'

'Tying up loose ends?'

'The man who took them from the nightclub is not Peter Barton,' Alec aired his thoughts, 'but that doesn't mean that he's not involved.'

'There is the Eastern European connection to the script carved into Jackie Webb,' Stirling interrupted. 'Google said that it's where it was used the most.'

'I don't remember any emphasis being put on him being an immigrant at the time,' Alec said. 'If I remember rightly, his surname came from his real father and he was brought up by a stepfather.'

'Do we wait to see what the Crimewatch pitch gives us or do we bring him anyway?' Annie mused. She put her finger to the corner of her damaged eye. The scar tissue felt raised to the touch. 'If he sees it, he might run.'

'If he hasn't already,' Stirling added. He checked his watch and looked at Alec. 'Haig said that he was always one step ahead of the investigation. How long till it goes out, guv?'

Alec looked at his own watch instinctively. 'Less than an hour. Do we know where he is?' The detectives looked at each other blankly.

'He wasn't even on our radar until Jim uncovered this connection.' Annie shrugged.

'Okay,' Alec said running his fingers through his sandy hair. 'It will be a stretch but let's get everything we can on Barton first. If we can pinpoint his whereabouts, lift him. Let's see if he has an alibi. In the meantime, Becky, get onto the courts and sort out the warrants that we need.'

'Yes, guv.'

Stirling and Becky moved with purpose. Alec couldn't help but notice the physical contrast between them, beauty and the beast. The door clicked closed. 'How long on the forensic results?'

'Kathy has prioritised the secretions,' Annie said checking her emails just in case. 'Nothing yet but she said we'd have them later tonight or early tomorrow. The sooner the better.' She sighed. 'We've got so many angles to come at this from that I'm not sure what direction to focus on.'

'Rationalise it,' Alec said. 'From my perspective, we have two ritualistic murders. The killer took his time to swap the victims' homes and identities, which tells me he had prior knowledge of who they were and what they did for a living. The women have a possible connection to a murder four years ago and they both had a mystery benefactor shortly after the main suspect walked.' He paused. 'Unless the forensic evidence tells us differently, my money is on Peter Barton. Fumbling about in the dark is a waste of resources and energy and until we have concrete evidence from Kathy's team, we focus on the links that we know exist.'

Annie stood up and stretched her back. She caught her reflection in the window. The darkness outside had turned the glass into a mirror. Scar, scar, scar, her mind shouted at her. She walked over and closed the blinds to block the image. 'That makes sense.' He blushed.' She smiled thinly and didn't finish her sentence.

'But?'

'But what about the other details that the killer left for us to fall over?' Alec had a confused expression on his face as she spoke. 'The script on the body, the pentagram, the incendiary device, the words that he daubed on the mirrors and the money in Jayne Windsor's mouth. I get the feeling that some, if not all of that, was for our benefit. I just can't see where it all fits.'

Alec smiled and nodded his head. He walked over and squeezed her shoulder before heading for the door. 'Did you ever make a model airplane when you were a kid?'

Annie frowned and shrugged. 'I was more of a Barbie girl to be honest, but my dad made a few with my younger brother.' She looked sad for a moment. 'They would spend hours painting them before they glued them together.'

'Exactly.' Alec grinned and the dimple on his chin deepened. 'Your dad did things properly. I on the other hand, would always have a handful of pieces left when I'd finished. I didn't see the point in fiddling about with the bits that no one could see so I didn't use them let alone paint them. I wanted my airplane to look like an airplane within ten minutes of me taking it out of the box.'

'Is there some deep and meaningful lesson to be learned from this?' Annie said with a puzzled expression.

'My point is that when they were finished, no one could tell that all the pieces weren't put together perfectly. My airplane looked just like the picture on the box. No one could tell that not all the pieces were in place.' He opened the door. 'I need to get to the Press room.'

'Guv,' Annie called after him.

'What?' Alec poked his head around the doorframe.

'You had a set of instructions to follow, didn't you?'

'Yes.' He grinned. 'Good point.'

Annie smiled as he closed the door and she thought about which pieces she could leave out. She decided very quickly that despite Alec's reminiscence she didn't want to have any bits left over. She wanted all the questions answered.

CHAPTER 21

The MIT office was unusually silent. Annie had never heard it so quiet. The calm before the storm, maybe. She was perched on the end of a desk staring at the bank of screens, waiting for Alec to appear. Every pair of eyes in the room were transfixed on the Crimewatch presenter, who was introducing him. Alec had wangled a thirty second slot into an already packed program. Detective teams from across the land were desperate to get their cases featured on the monthly broadcast and the waiting list was endless. Annie wasn't sure how he had managed it and she didn't care. The fact that their investigation involved the death of a serving police officer, a female, made it an extraordinary case. It was an especially brutal double murder, which had obviously persuaded the producers to find thirty seconds somewhere. The introduction was detailed and brief. Liverpool's MIT were looking for 'this' man in connection with the brutal slaying of a serving police officer and her friend. Annie was pleased at how much detail Alec crammed into his half a minute and their suspect's photograph was displayed through the entire piece. When the camera switched back to the presenter, the team applauded. Annie smiled and a knot of excited anticipation tightened in her guts. It was a feeling that only her work gave her. Nothing outside the world of tracking dangerous criminals came close to it.

'He looks even more like that pesky chef on the television than he does in real life, guv!'

'Except he doesn't say 'fuck' as much, guv.'

'I'll be sure to pass on your comments.' Annie laughed. She was about to comment on the piece when a phone began to ring. A detective picked up the handset with the speed of a gunfighter at the OK Corral. Then a second, third, and a fourth joined a cacophony of ringtones. It was like turning on a tap. Information from the public began pouring in. The floodgates had opened. Crimewatch had the morbid ability to fascinate the public and millions tuned in every month in the hope that a face that they knew would appear. It transformed the Union into a nation of wannabe informers. Within a minute of the appeal, the phone lines were jammed.

Annie walked around the desks listening to one-way conversations. She looked at the notes that were being scribbled down onto notebooks and entered into computers. Most of the calls were coming from in and around the city. A small percentage were crackpots claiming to be the killer. One man was adamant that he hadn't just killed their victims; he was also responsible for releasing the Ebola virus into Africa via a popular brand of energy drink. Such calls were cut short and the details kept to pass onto the uniformed division at a later stage.

The callers would get a severe warning but not much more. Annie thought that it would be more productive to have hoax callers sectioned for a while. The experience might dissuade them from doing it again.

The office was filled with hushed chatter and the atmosphere was palpable. Annie saw several names being offered as their suspect. She noted a few in her mind but one name in particular was given more than a dozen times by different callers. Tod Harris.

'We need to look at this guy, Tod Harris,' Annie said to Stirling. 'See what we've got on him. Let's hope he's in the system.'

Stirling tapped the keys on his laptop and the screen began to scroll through the police database. A photo of Tod Harris in a custody suite popped up within seconds. Although years younger, the arrest photo was undoubtedly that of Tod Harris. Stirling looked over his shoulder at Annie and nodded. 'Are you reading this?'

'Well well.' Annie smiled. 'It looks like Tod has been working his way up from date rape to murder. He's been at it for years. He has a sexual assault charge on a relative when he was thirteen. As an adult, assault, sexual assault, and a rape conviction that didn't stick.'

'All the victims claim that he drugged them,' Stirling growled. 'We've got an address in Halewood. Coincidence?'

'I don't like coincidences.'

'Me neither.'

'Becky!' Annie called across the office.

'Yes, guv.'

'Have you got an address for Peter Barton yet?'

'Yes, guv,' she lifted a pad. 'He lives on the Oak Tree estate, Halewood.'

'That's about four miles from where Harris lives. Another coincidence,' Stirling raised his eyebrows.

'We need a warrant for Tod Harris too, Becky,' Annie called. 'Send the details to her computer.' Stirling tapped on the keys again.

'Sent.'

'Got it. I'm on it, guv.' Becky nodded. 'Judge Ryland is happy to sign off whatever we need.'

'Send his details over to the forensic lab,' Annie added, 'Kathy can run his DNA against the samples. She'll be pleased that he is in the system.'

'Hold on, guv,' Google shouted from his desk. He was compiling the computerised data as it was being entered in by the detectives on the telephones. 'We might have a problem.'

He frowned and tapped at his keyboard. 'We've got three recent sightings of Tod Harris. All of them this week.' He frowned again and kept typing. 'You're not going to like this.'

'Give us a clue, Google.' Annie rolled her eyes. She could feel her heartbeat racing. Alec stepped out of the lift and clapped his hands together, happy to see that every telephone was in use. He looked expectantly at Annie. She nodded and smiled. 'We've got a name, guv.'

'Do we know him?'

'Oh yes,' Stirling said pointing at his screen. Alec leaned over and squinted to read the records. He whistled as he digested the details.

'Google?' Annie asked impatiently. 'What have we got?'

'Six callers all giving the same location, guv.'

'Which is?'

'Benidorm.'

'Benidorm?'

'Spain, guv.'

'I know where Benidorm is.'

'Of course, you do.' Google blushed. 'Sorry, guv.' He typed furiously, oblivious of the smirks around him. 'The last sighting was yesterday around the Old Town.'

'Okay,' Annie pressed her palms together beneath her chin. She closed her eyes for a second. 'Find out which flight he took out there and where he is staying. Run his credit cards and contact the local police. We need them to hold him until we can get out there and drag him back. Can you sort authorisation for us to travel, guv?'

Alec frowned as he thought about the situation. 'No problem. Should be simple enough to track him down and the Spanish won't want to obstruct the removal of a scumbag like Harris.'

'What about Barton, guv?' Stirling asked. 'What do you want us to do about him?'

'There was nothing in your television pitch that would make him think that we've connected him to the victims yet but I think that his own sense of self-preservation will make him join up the dots,' Annie said. 'What do you think, guv?'

'The link between him and our victims may be tenuous, but we can't ignore it and neither will he. I think that he'll be concerned at least,' Alec agreed. 'The women responsible for his release have been murdered. That means that we're going to connect him to them sooner or later whether he was innocent or not.'

'Take an armed unit and a forced entry team,' Annie said cautiously. 'I want him shaking in his shoes when he gets here.'

'You need to take an officer from the Bomb Squad too,' Alec added gravely. 'I don't want any risks taken.' His face darkened. 'If he was involved in the murders, he may have rigged the incendiary device and if he was watching Crimewatch, he'll be expecting us. I don't want any nasty surprises.'

CHAPTER 22

The Barton residence was a detached house situated on the outskirts of Halewood. It was the last house on the row before the road snaked onwards through a green-belt area made up mostly of arable farmland, woodland, and grazing land. It was to all intents and purposes, the border of the city. Stirling watched the front of the house through night vision glasses. A small garden that consisted of two small lawns dissected by a path offered no obstacles to their entry but gifted them no cover either. It was a hundred metres from the pavement to the front door. There were no doors or windows on either of the side elevations of the house. They couldn't see the back of the house at all and the rear garden was shrouded by coniferous trees.

'There's one light on in the downstairs room to the left of the front door,' Stirling noted. 'The rest of the house is in darkness.'

'Thermal imaging is giving one heat signature, which is in the room with the light on.' The Bomb Squad officer added. 'Your suspect is sat in an armchair watching the television.'

'I'll send two men to the rear. As soon as they're in place we'll make entry through the front door.' The Forced Entry Team leader said nonchalantly. 'The quicker we do it, the less chance we have of him rigging the place, right?'

Stirling nodded. 'What do you think, Lieutenant?'

'If he has rigged anything up then we won't know until it's too late.' The Bomb Squad officer smiled. 'He could have sensors on the windows, pressure pads behind the front and rear doors, infrared sensors in the hallways and stairs. If he has, then they'll be battery powered so there's no point in cutting the power. You'll be blown to bits before you cross the welcome mat.'

'That's helpful,' Stirling mumbled. 'Thanks for that.'

'I'm just advising.' The lieutenant shrugged. 'The possibilities are endless but if you were the suspect would you rig your home to blow and then sit in the living room watching the television?' he patted Stirling on the back. 'My advice is to make sure that it's your suspect that's home first. If he is and he doesn't cooperate, smoke him out. Bring him to us. That way there's less risk.'

'That makes sense,' Stirling agreed. 'We'll stick to the same plan, two men at the rear and the rest of us out front. We'll call him out and if he refuses, we'll use the gas as a last resort?'

'I'll get the men in place. We'll be ready to go in five.'

****

Inside the house, Peter Barton was drinking whisky and surfing the Internet. The Crimewatch program had rattled his fragile world. He always watched the news and read the newspapers. His interest had become an obsession. But it only confirmed how much evil there was in the world. He couldn't handle anymore evil. Not another drop. For as long as he could remember, he had wrestled with the evil inside himself. It was a constant war of attrition, but he knew that ultimately it was a battle that he would lose. He would lose because he was weak. His stepfather had told him from as far back as he could remember that he was weak. He was useless and he would never make anything of himself. His abuse was often spat out in his native Ukrainian tongue interspersed with the odd abusive word in English for good measure. The message was usually reinforced with a good hiding from his stepfather's belt. Sometimes the belt was wielded like a whip and other times he would wrap it around his neck and choke him until he passed out. He often woke up bruised and battered lying in his own urine. The leather belt with its heavy metal buckle in the shape of an eagle was now hidden in his box with his other mementos. It was the only thing that he wanted to keep when his stepfather had finally died from cirrhosis, a reminder of the harsh and brutal upbringing he had endured. He left money too, but he didn't want it. The money that he left went to a good cause. He was the only mourner at his funeral and when the vicar had gone, Peter went behind the curtain at the crematorium and pissed on the coffin. It was the best piss he had ever had.

After watching Crimewatch, he knew that the police would come for him. It might not be today, and it might not be tomorrow, but they would come. It was only a matter of time. He couldn't go back to prison. Not for a day. His time incarcerated following Simon's disappearance had been a nightmare. He had loved Simon, no one listened, and no one understood. It wasn't perverted or dirty; he loved him like any uncle would. They made it sound dirty. They twisted everything. He was locked up as a child killer, a paedophile, a pervert, a nonce, and as such, he'd been vilified, beaten, and brutalised by the other inmates. They were the animals, not him. Although he'd been freed at the appeal hearing, he was still guilty in the eyes of those he met. They sneered at his newly discovered alibi and cast aspersions at its validity. There were no bars on his windows, but he was still a prisoner, nonetheless.

He searched online for as much information as he could find. Constantly. He drank and he searched then he drank some more. Tracking them was relentless. There were hundreds of them out there, maybe thousands. He shadowed them incessantly, recording their actions and hunting for new ones to show themselves. They plagued him day and night, but the police did nothing. So many of them stayed under the radar, at liberty, free to do as they pleased but he knew that they were there. The whisky bottle was three-quarters empty and his vision was blurry. He emptied his glass and refilled it, swallowing the burning liquid with a gulp. There were plenty of articles but there wasn't much detail. Not that it mattered. They would come and when they did, he would plead his innocence and they would ignore him just like they had last time. They would look at him like he was dirt and lock him up again. He couldn't go back to jail.

'You'll be back, paedo,' one of his tormentors had hissed when he was leaving jail. 'And when you do, we can have some more fun. Next time they lock you up it will be for good, scumbag.' He heard the threats in his mind over and over. His sleep was haunted by the images of his stepfather beating him and his face would change and morph into those of the inmates. The stench of sweat and urine would overwhelm him, and he would wake up in his own bed soaked to the skin in his own fluids. He couldn't go back to jail. Not for a second.

Peter closed the laptop and tossed it across the room. It clattered underneath his dining table, which had only one chair next to it. It had been nearly five years since he had shared a meal with another human being. Even the animals in jail refused to sit at the same table as him while they ate the slop that the prison kitchens called food. His mother and her sisters had shunned him. All of Simon's relatives were convinced that he had abducted him, molested him, and murdered him. As if he could do that to his beautiful nephew. They were the only family that he had, and they despised him. Five years of persecution and loneliness had taken its toll and the blinding light of scrutiny was always upon him. It was a desolate existence at home but in prison, it was intolerable. He couldn't go back. There was enough whisky to fill the tumbler once more. His hands were shaking as he tipped the contents into his glass. He dropped the empty bottle onto the carpet and took another long glug of the malt. It burned its way down into his stomach and he could feel the alcohol coursing through him, warming, soothing, numbing, wiping away the memories.

Peter put the glass on the arm of his chair and reached down for his Laurona. Although it was nearly a hundred years old and single barrel shotguns were seldom sought after, it would do the job. He stood up on shaky legs and broke the gun. It was loaded. He had checked it at least six times and had unloaded it and reloaded it each time. Evil had taunted him all his life. It had burrowed into his soul and spread through him like cancer. He had sought it out and fought with it and held it at bay for a while, but it always returned, niggling at his brain, making him think things that he shouldn't. He knew that evil was a universal entity, a force that moves between dimensions and now it had focused itself on him once more. The poor women who had helped him escape the hellhole of prison had met evil themselves face to face. Their murder would make the police reopen the files on Simon's disappearance and if they did, they might find something to shatter his alibi and send him back to jail. Once, all he wanted was his freedom. He had begged a God that he didn't believe in to help him escape the brutal beatings, the huge walls, and the barbed wire. Now he had his freedom, but it wasn't what he had envisaged. He was still tortured, still bitterly unhappy, and guilt racked his very core. His search never ended. Evil was the root cause of his pain. The evil inside him was powerful but it couldn't survive in there when he had a 12-bore shotgun. He snapped the gun closed and walked out of the room.

****

'The suspect is on the move!' The lieutenant hissed as Stirling left the van and struggled into his body armour. 'All units standby,' he ordered over the comms. 'If you're going to call him out, now is the time.'

Stirling nodded his agreement and signalled for the armed unit to follow him to the front door. He fiddled with his earpiece as he walked down the path. The lights in the hallway came on illuminating three fan shaped glass panels on the front door. 'Suspect has moved into the hallway,' the comms crackled.

I wonder how he fathomed that... Amazing technology, Stirling thought. Heat signatures were one thing but a light bulb being switched on was equally revealing.

'I know what you're thinking, Detective,' the lieutenant added. 'That was for the benefit of the officers at the rear.'

Stirling chuckled to himself inside, 'take the pole from up your arse, soldier boy,' he thought. The lieutenant and his squad were incredibly brave men. He respected that. But the officers he had met seemed to be cut from the same mould, always concerned about how others perceived them. Especially non-military persons. 'I'm at the front door, standby.'

'Roger that, all units standby.'

Stirling stepped to the left-hand side of the front door and knocked hard with his knuckles. 'Peter Barton, it's the police,' he called loudly. 'We need to speak you!'

Silence.

'Peter Barton.' He knocked harder. The door rattled in its frame.

Silence.

He knocked harder still.

Silence.

'Where is he?' Stirling whispered into the coms.

'He's still in the hallway but nearer the rear of the house.'

Stirling knocked again. The door thudded against the frame.

'Peter Barton!' The lights inside the house went out, plunging the gardens into darkness. 'What happened then?' Stirling growled.

'Barton has turned the power off.'

'Brilliant.'

'I've got more good news,' the lieutenant sounded panicked. 'I've lost his heat signature.'

'Forced Entry Team, green light to go!' Stirling ordered. He moved aside as an armour-clad figure raised a metal battering ram and slammed it against the lock. The wood splintered and cracked, and the door bust open under the first hit.

****

Peter Barton had frozen with fear when he heard the first knock. It was almost a relief when the caller identified himself as the police. Almost. Whatever doubts he had in his mind vanished immediately. He had to do it now. There was no choice now, no options, no way out; he was at the portal to a new existence. He opened the cupboard beneath the stairs and stepped inside. When the second knock resounded through his house, he opened the fuse box and pulled the main switch. The lights went out all over the house and he felt a strange kind of relief spreading over him. All his pain and the constant fear of persecution dissipated in seconds. Everything that transpired from here on in was in his hands. No one could stop it now. He could finally make amends for Simon without anyone judging him. He knew that they would kick the door in any second, but they would be too late.

****

The entry team moved quickly and silently. The hallway carpet was threadbare, and cracks ran across the plastered walls from floor to ceiling. Their gun-lights illuminated a dark wooden staircase to their left and the unoccupied hallway to their right. As they swept the rooms, the second team entered through the rear.

'Kitchen clear!' came over the comms.

'Living room clear!'

'Hallway clear!'

'That's the ground floor swept, Detective.'

'No one climbed the stairs,' the lieutenant added. 'He must be there somewhere.'

Stirling followed the unit inside. It seemed obvious that the only place Barton could have hidden was a cupboard beneath the stairs. One of the entry team had a sensor against the door. He listened intently. The house was silent apart from the sound of men breathing nervously. He shook his head and signalled that they should open the door. Stirling paused to think. Could the door be booby trapped? Of course, it could be, but he doubted it. He nodded for the team to move.

Heckler and Koch MP5s were aimed at the door as it was pulled open. Stirling held up three fingers and counted down, three, two, one, go. The door was thrown open and two officers moved quickly into the cramped space. There were a few seconds of silence then they called, 'clear.' Their tone was both muted and confused. 'It's empty, Sergeant.'

Stirling frowned and walked down the hallway. The smell of must and mothballs tainted the air. The entry team shuffled back to allow the big detective to look inside. The cupboard was no more than a wooden partition that boxed in the space beneath the stairs with a door added for access. The fuse box was mounted on the far wall and Stirling reached inside and switched it on. A bare bulb illuminated the cupboard. There were two cardboard boxes and a Dyson upright vacuum cleaner. A shelf fitted to the wall above his head had a tin of furniture polish and some Brasso on it and two coat hooks were overloaded with winter jackets. Stirling tapped the walls with his knuckles. They were solid brick. He looked at the floor and stamped his foot on a filthy Moroccan rug. It sounded hollow beneath the wooden floorboards. He grabbed the edge of the rug and pulled but it didn't budge an inch.

'It's glued to the floor,' Stirling grumbled. 'There must be a hatch to the cellar in here.'

'There's no cellar on the plans,' the lieutenant informed them over the comms.

'Been there and bought the T-shirt. Plans aren't worth shit.' Stirling stepped out of the cupboard. 'Can you cut that rug off and see what's underneath please.'

An FET officer unsheathed a lethal looking blade from his belt. He knelt and began cutting the dusty material away from the wood. 'There are hinges here,' he panted. 'There is a hatch, but it must be bolted from underneath. Pass me a wrecking iron and I'll force it.' His colleague handed him a metal tool that resembled a crowbar. 'I'll try to wrench the hinges first.'

Stirling froze to the spot when a shotgun blast resounded from beneath them and echoed off the walls of the house.

CHAPTER 23

Tod Harris began to surface from a drug-induced slumber. His memories of the hours before he blacked out were sketchy at best. He remembered eating and drinking and the smell of perfume. Then he remembered running as fast as his legs could carry him, breathlessness, pain in his back, and then the police. The police had arrived. The image of policemen aiming their guns, shots, blood, and then a face with dying eyes. Then nothing. He could hear voices. Muffled voices. Spanish voices. The odour of disinfectant drifted into his consciousness. He felt someone touching his wrist. The pressure on his flesh was almost painful. He heard two voices close by, but he couldn't understand what they were saying. Although he was becoming aware, he was as helpless as a baby. He was breathing, his senses were becoming functional, yet he had no control over his body. Moving was way beyond him yet. He couldn't even open his eyes.

His mind wandered from dreams to a blurred reality. The anaesthetic made him feel warm and safe inside a bubble, but he knew that all wasn't as well as it seemed. He was in hospital, but he wasn't sure why. There was a warm numbness in his back. Had he been punched hard? He remembered the blow. Then he remembered the blood trickling down his skin. Had he been stabbed? Maybe. A knife flashed into his mind, but it was stuck in someone's abdomen. Not his. He was an onlooker. As he focused on the strange sensation from his back, he became aware that the numbness had an edge to it. There were tiny prickles of pain radiating from it. He didn't like that feeling. He didn't want the numbness to fade. He didn't want to know what it was masking. The image of a woman flashed into his mind. Her face was impassive. He was having sex with her for a few enticing seconds then she was gone replaced by newspaper headlines. His blood ran cold. His consciousness reached another level. He was coming around. The prickles of pain became darting bolts of white light in his brain. Breathing was painful. He didn't want to come up out of the warmth. He wanted to stay down in the pleasant oblivion. Fear crept into his mind. Fear of the pain that was intensifying but there was something else. Something that he should fear more than the pain. He had been hiding from something. He was on the run. The sudden realisation shot through him like an electric shock.

His eyes twitched as he tried to open them. They felt glued shut. His mouth was as dry as sandpaper. He couldn't swallow. Panic replaced his feeling of wellbeing spreading through his veins like poison. His eyes opened and the overhead lights hurt. He blinked hard and tried to clear his vision. The surroundings were sterile, white and magnolia. There was a drip hanging from a stainless-steel stand. The tubes ran from two bags of clear liquid into his right hand. He lifted his hand to inspect it. There were no handcuffs fastening him to the bed. It was a relief, but he felt like a tortoise on its back. He wanted to get up but couldn't. His brain screamed at him to move. Get out! Get out! But his arms and legs weren't listening. They were disconnected from his motor neurons.

Tod tried to speak. He desperately needed water. He wasn't sure what he tried to say but it came out as a rasping cry. A woman appeared from his left as if she had been standing over him. She picked up his wrist and touched his forehead.

'Tranquilo! No pasa nada,' she said in a soothing voice. He didn't have a clue what it meant but it sounded nice. Her eyes were deep brown. He could dive into them and get lost. She was beautiful. Her presence soothed his nerves. 'Tranquilo! No pasa nada.' She repeated softly. Tod tried to speak again but could only rasp. 'Beber,' the nurse said putting a glass to his lips. 'Beber.' She smiled. Tod sipped the water and felt it hydrating his mouth and throat. He swallowed a little and nearly choked. He took a deep breath to clear his airways and pain racked his back and chest. The nurse turned at the sound of a male voice. The uniformed figures of four armed police officers loomed into his sight and he couldn't control himself any longer. Tod knew what he had done. He felt his lower lip trembling and then he began to sob like a child.

CHAPTER 24

Stirling climbed down the cellar steps tentatively. The wood creaked beneath his bulk threatening to give in beneath the weight. Three bulkhead lights that were fixed to the walls threw pools of light across the concrete floor leaving the corners draped in dark shadows. The air was dry and dank and tinged with the smell of urine, excrement, and the unmistakable coppery aroma of blood. The body of Peter Barton was slumped in a kneeling position in the centre of the room. His dead hands still clung to a single barrelled shotgun, which was resting on a blood-soaked shoulder. The head was all but gone. Only the lower jaw remained intact. The remains of his brains and skull were splattered across the rear wall in a funnel shape. Globules of pink matter dripped from the rafters above him. As he looked around, it was what covered the walls beneath the viscera that gripped Stirling's attention.

'He's blown his own head off,' an FET officer said quietly.

'You think so?' Stirling nodded and decided not to comment on his powers of observation. There was a reason why some officers became detectives and others kicked down doors. While the ruined body was hypnotising to look at, the images, maps, and newspaper cuttings that covered every spare inch of wall were totally mesmerising. He stepped around the corpse and studied the images. Each headline made his heart beat faster. Barton had made a collage of articles from all over the globe, murders, kidnaps, rapes, and child abductions from every corner of the world.

There was a desk pressed to the far wall and above it was an enlarged map of the North-West of England and North Wales. Dozens of coloured pins adorned the map, some solitary and others in clusters. It was the cluster of pins that covered Crosby Beach, which fascinated him the most. There was a circle drawn in red marker pen and Stirling immediately identified it as where he was standing, Barton's house. The pins seemed to radiate out from there.

The newspaper cuttings around the left of the map were all about the hunt for Simon Barton. Post-it notes were stuck over each article with an illegible scrawl written on each. To the right were articles relating to the Butcher murders. 'Another Victim of the Butcher of Crosby Beach Located', each headline was painfully familiar. Stirling had mixed feelings about that case. He had met his wife during it, and she had been kidnapped and nearly died at the hands of Brendon Ryder, The Butcher. During the investigation, the DI had lost an eye and her confidence. It was all behind them now but seeing the headlines made him feel uneasy. Stirling studied the notes and checked them against the pins. It appeared at first glance that each Post-it note had a coordinate scrawled on the top right-hand corner. Each coordinate related to a pin on the map.

Stirling looked at the papers on the desk and sifted through the top sheets with a gloved hand. One of them was a list of local farms, local parks, woods, nature reserves, and graveyards. He was familiar with the area and the list seemed to run in order of their proximity to his house. Each one had a tick on one side and a cross on the other. He placed the list back on top of a stack of Ordinance Survey maps and an orienteering compass.

'Have you seen this?' an officer asked disturbing his thoughts. Stirling turned and walked over to him. One section of wall was covered in blood and brains. The paper cuttings beneath the gore were a collage of Peter Barton's arrest, trial, and incarceration. 'Evil Uncle, Peter Barton Refuses to Give Up the Body of his Nephew.' Stirling read the headline several times. He walked slowly around the cellar and glanced at each map and each cutting before taking one last look at the reeking corpse.

'My DI is going to love this,' he grumbled as he climbed back up the steps.

CHAPTER 25

Annie Jones shivered as she walked along the path to Barton's house. Autumn was quickly giving way to winter at an increasing rate of knots and the nighttime temperatures were plummeting rapidly. Every light in the house was on as CSI teams searched the scene. She reached the door and noticed the splintered frame. A white-clad figure walked up the stairs to the first floor and another disappeared through a door beneath them. Stirling appeared from a room to her left, his bulk filled the doorway. He grunted hello and sheepishly handed her a forensic suit.

'What the hell happened?' Annie asked as she removed her coat. Stirling noticed that her prosthetic eye didn't narrow as much as her real one when she was annoyed.

'We knocked on the door, he locked himself in the cellar and blew his head off with a shotgun.' Stirling shrugged. 'There's not much more to it.'

'There was no dialogue at all between you?'

'None, guv.'

'Who knocked on the door?'

'I did.'

'So, it's your fault,' she said dryly.

'Completely.'

'Good,' she said zipping up her suit. 'I'm glad that's sorted. Now where is this map that I need to see?'

'Maps plural, guv,' Stirling corrected her. 'Lots and lots of maps. Let's start in here.' He turned and walked into the living room. The plasma television was still on. 'He was watching BBC one.'

'So, he probably saw the appeal.'

'Probably,' Stirling grumbled. 'It would explain his decision to eat his gun. He was sitting here when we arrived,' he said,' he said pointing to a well-worn armchair. 'We're guessing that he was using his laptop to print off information about the murders. It was found underneath the table; the screen was cracked but it was still switched on. He had a wireless printer on the dining table over there and there are a couple of articles printed off in the print tray,' Stirling said walking around the armchair. 'There's an empty bottle of scotch on the floor so he may have been intoxicated. Take a look over here.' Stirling pointed to the wall above the dining table. It was covered in Ordinance Survey maps, which were overlapping to make one huge map of the Northern Hemisphere. There were crosses and circles marked all over them.

Surrounding the map were press cuttings from a myriad of publications. The table was stacked with newspapers and articles printed from the Internet. Some of the papers were yellowed with age and some looked unread. A pair of reading glasses and a biro sat next to a packet of cigars and an overflowing ashtray. 'It looks as if Barton spent a lot of time sifting through newspaper cuttings.'

'London, Paris, Talin, Prague, Amsterdam,' Annie said as she studied the markings on the maps. Her eye crossed the Atlantic. 'San Francisco, Flagstaff, Phoenix. Have we found a passport?'

'Not yet, guv.'

'When we do, we need to see if he travelled to these places.' Annie scanned the wall and frowned. 'There's seems to be a newspaper clipping relating to murders in each city.' She looked at Stirling and shrugged. 'What was he doing?'

'He was collecting.' Stirling shrugged. He picked up a yellowed newspaper. 'Some of this stuff goes back ten years or more. We would need months to analyse this and make any sense of it.'

'It might be more obvious than you think,' Annie said. She didn't think that it was obvious, but she had to be positive. 'Has he left any journals, diaries, or anything personal that might explain what he was doing?'

'Nothing yet, guv,' Stirling shook his head. 'There are some hand-written lists downstairs.'

'He certainly put a lot of time and effort into it.'

'Wait until you see the cellar.' Stirling said. 'I've got some ideas, but I'd like you to see it first.' He turned and walked towards the door. Annie lingered a moment and pictured Barton reading the articles and mapping them. An article from San Francisco caught her eye. Several words had been highlighted in yellow marker. Similar words were highlighted on another article from Bakersfield. 'That's a long way from home.' She muttered. A tingle ran down her spine as she read on. 'What were you up to, Barton?' she whispered to herself as she turned to follow her sergeant. She noticed an old upright piano on the opposite wall. It reminded her of her childhood. Her mother had paid a small fortune to a local piano tutor to teach her to play. She remembered taking a cardboard stencil home to help her practice. It sat on top of the keys as an idiot's guide to the chords. It was money wasted. Chopsticks was as far as her talent stretched.

The rest of the living room was a mishmash of furniture spanning four decades. The sofa was an imitation Chesterfield from the 70s. Annie's Grandma Jones had one similar. She only removed the plastic wrapping when guests came, quickly recovering it as soon as they left.

She remembered her granddad rolling his eyes to the heavens every time she did it. 'The bloody thing is meant to be sat on!' he would complain.

The dining table and chair, singular, were MFI flat pack from the late 80s but the television, laptop, and printer were new models. Expensive top of the line stuff. It reminded her of furnished rented accommodation rather than someone's home.

Stirling was in the hallway waiting patiently for her to catch-up. 'We lost his heat signature here, which led us to the cupboard under the staircase. It is well hidden and not on the plans. We wouldn't have found it during a normal search.' He pointed to the splintered wood around the hatch. 'It took us a while to break in because the access hatch was fastened from underneath. There was no way that we could have stopped him.'

'That makes sense.' Annie nodded. 'Alec has acquired copies of the original case files and he said that once the original warrant was issued, it took the arresting team two weeks to locate Barton. They searched this place from top to bottom three times. He must have been hiding down there when they came for him.'

'Where did they make the arrest in the end?'

'He was in his car near a local nature reserve.'

'He has lists of similar places downstairs,' Stirling raised his eyebrows. 'You'll see what I mean when we get down there.'

Annie ducked into the cupboard and cautiously navigated the steps. She wrinkled her nose as the smell of death reached her. The corpse was gone but the body fluids that had leaked from it were still present. The remnants of Barton's head and its contents were darkening as they congealed on the walls and ceiling. 'Barton was a busy boy,' she said as the scale of his research became apparent. 'The New York Times, Chicago Tribune, San Francisco Post, The Prague Post, L'Echo de Paris, Het Parool from Amsterdam and some that I've never heard of,' Annie said as she studied the clippings on the walls. Some clippings were covered by three or more others that related to the same story. They were stapled at the top so the observer could lift each one to read the one behind. As she moved along the wall, she looked at the collection of British headlines that covered Barton's arrest. 'The headlines about him being convicted are all page one news but he only made page five when he was released.'

'I think that this is where he started his collection,' Stirling said from the opposite end of the cellar. He stood in front of the desk. 'I think that this is his first map,' he said pointing to the wall. 'This is his house circled here and then he has marked concentric circles that get wider as the distance increases.'

Annie stood next to him and soaked up as much detail as she could at a glance. She could have been looking at a search pattern from one of their own investigations. 'So, he starts off with his home as the epicentre of what exactly?'

'Look at this,' Stirling picked up the list that he had found earlier. 'Local parks, playing fields, streams, woods, farms, even slag heaps from some of the old coalmines.'

'Hunting grounds or dumping grounds?'

'Dumping grounds. That's what I think.'

Annie spotted the cluster of pins at Crosby Beach. It made her stomach knot and she felt a little nauseous. The headlines about the Butcher murders screamed at her from the wall. 'Why the fascination with Brendon Ryder?' she swallowed hard as she spoke. 'Why the fascination with any of this?' she gestured around the room. Murders across Europe and America occupied every inch. 'From the first look at things, he's posted notes on each case.'

'He has,' Stirling agreed. 'Most of them have a map coordinate noted in the corner. Look at this list though, he's crossed off the entire list of local areas,' Stirling said studying the list. 'It goes as far east as Snowdonia and Anglesey and as far north as Cumbria and the Lake District. I think he was looking for the best place to dispose of Simon Barton. Somewhere during the process, he has developed an affinity to other killers and began tracking them.'

Annie held her chin between her finger and thumb and looked over the list. 'This list has been compiled by an organised and intelligent mind.' She shook her head in disagreement. 'It is so thorough that it could have been put together by a detective from our team searching for a victim's remains. This is exactly what we would have done,' she said pausing to think. 'My question is, was he trying to rule out the obvious dumpsites where he knew that the police would look or was he tracking something else?'

Stirling frowned and looked at the map. 'Tracking what?'

'I don't know.' Annie shrugged. 'We need a list of where the original searches were made by the investigation team and in what order they were carried out. I've got a hunch that they'll correspond closely with his list.'

'Do you think that he was just following where the investigation was focused?'

'Let's say he held the boy down here,' Annie said looking around. 'He could have held him for weeks before he killed him. What would you do if you were a suspect?'

'I would follow the investigation and try to second guess where they wouldn't look.' He pointed to the mountainous areas of Snowdonia and The Lakes. 'If you had the time and the strength to dismember a body and then took it into these areas, the pieces would never be found.'

'Why go that far away?' Annie mused. 'There are thousands of rivers and ponds, quarries and beaches between here and the mountains.'

'Agreed, but if he was under the spotlight, he may have felt pressured to dump the body somewhere that no one was looking for him.' Stirling pointed to the county boundary lines. 'He would have known from the reaction of the residents and his family that they would never stop looking for Simon. As the main suspect it would follow him for the rest of his life like a dark cloud hanging over his head. The only way that he could ever get any peace of mind,' he tapped the map with his finger, 'take the body over the borders where the murder wouldn't be as much as a blip on the radar of a different force.'

Annie listened but she wasn't feeling Stirling's theory. It was solid thinking, but she didn't think that he was being open-minded enough. She stepped back from the map to look at it in its entirety. The area that it represented was vast. 'No one could begin to search an area this wide. Simon Barton might as well be buried on the moon.' She sighed. The newspaper headlines caught her eye again. 'Simon went missing during the height of our investigation into the Crosby Beach murders, right?' she asked herself. 'Did Barton feel that he had some kind of connection to Brendon Ryder or was it something else completely?'

'I don't follow.'

Annie pointed to the area of Crosby Beach. 'If he was following the case as it unfolded, then maybe he was trying to offer the investigation a different suspect.'

'You've lost me, guv.'

'What if he was innocent?'

'My gut says he wasn't'

'Ignore your gut for a minute,' Annie gestured at the map. 'What if his alibi is genuine and he didn't abduct him?' She looked at Stirling and turned her palms upwards. 'What if he thought Simon was taken by a killer like Brendon Ryder or a local paedophile?' Stirling's face was a picture of confusion. 'What if Barton wasn't looking for a dumpsite to use himself and he was in fact, looking for where Simon's body had been dumped?'

CHAPTER 26

When Annie stepped out of the lift at MIT, Alec waved at her from his office. His face was flushed red and she could see Kathy Brooks standing behind him. She felt a jolt of adrenalin surging through her. Forensic results were such a rush. Finding trace evidence was exciting enough but finally receiving the true interpretation of their relevance to a case was another thing totally. It was like the green light at the start of a race. The wait between finding trace and receiving the results was a tortured limbo. Theories were useful but concrete evidence was like gold dust. She headed for his office without stopping to speak to anyone. Her detectives were busy, each engrossed in their role in the investigation. When she stepped into the office, Kathy looked drawn and tired.

'I believe my team are going to be busy at the Barton residence.' Kathy smiled thinly. 'What happened?'

Annie shrugged off her coat and smoothed her trousers as she sat down. She took a deep breath and smiled. 'Peter Barton locked himself in his cellar and blew his head off.' Annie sighed. 'There's no question whether the arresting team influenced his actions or not. He was on his way into the cellar when they knocked on the door. From the evidence we found, he was immersed in some kind of depressive obsession with unsolved murders.' She looked at Alec. 'We think the Crimewatch appeal and a bottle of scotch might have pushed him over the edge.'

'You said he was tracking unsolved murder cases?' Alec prompted. The lines on his face deepened.

'Hundreds of them going back ten years or more.' Annie nodded. 'He seemed to be looking for something. There were detailed search patterns, maps marked with the coordinates of murders and abductions and press cuttings from all over Europe and the States.'

'A troubled mind?' Kathy said folding her arms. 'Guilt maybe?'

'I'm not so sure.' Annie shook her head and looked at the floor. There was so much to take in and make sense of that it made her head hurt. 'Simon Barton was abducted at the height of Brendon Ryder's reign and Barton was tracking the case in detail along with others,' Annie explained. 'He was the main suspect in his nephew's abduction, and I think that Barton was desperate to find another one.' She sighed. 'We checked his car on the way out. The boot was full of search equipment.'

'What do you mean, equipment?' Alec frowned.

'He had four metal detectors, spades, a pick-axe, trowels and wellington boots,' she explained. 'It could be that he had a legitimate hobby treasure hunting, but I've got a hunch from the markings on his maps that he was looking for Simon Barton's body.' Alec blew air through his front teeth making a quiet whistling sound and made a steeple with his fingers beneath his chin. Kathy looked disturbed by the thought. 'We'll have to sift through the mountains of data that he collected to have any idea of what was going on in his head.' She shrugged. 'Worst case scenario is that he was an innocent man desperate to clear his name but couldn't take the scrutiny anymore, or best case is he was a murdering paedophile drowning in guilt. Whatever it is, the result is unchangeable.' She stood up and leaned against the wall. 'I can't allow this to bog down the investigation. All I need to know for now is if Barton had anything to do with this case.'

'I agree,' Alec said. 'If we find anything relating to the original investigation into Simon Barton, then we pass the information back to Halewood.' He sat back in his chair and nodded to Kathy. 'Let's not get sidetracked. We need to hear what you have got.'

'I thought that you would never ask,' she tutted sarcastically. 'This might cheer you up a bit.' She said holding up a file to Annie.

'Please give me some answers.' Annie sighed and sat down. 'I need to put some of the pieces together before I go mad.'

'Where to begin,' Kathy opened the file and flicked through the top pages. 'Our initial thoughts at the first scene were correct. The evidence that we managed to bag before the explosion was damning.' She looked at Annie, 'the entire scene was bleached and wiped down. There were no DNA deposits except the trace fluids. We found epithelial cells that belong to the victim, mixed with spermatozoa and spermicidal gel.'

'Which means?' Alec asked.

'Jackie Webb was raped by a male who used a condom and she was raped by a male that didn't wear one.'

'Two perpetrators?' Annie asked.

'Not necessarily,' Kathy shook her head. 'It could be the same man.'

'It doesn't make sense.' Annie sighed. 'Why clean the scene and then leave DNA.' She shrugged and crossed her legs. 'I don't get it. He was so careful to remove evidence.'

'Maybe he was counting on the fact that all the evidence would be incinerated in the explosion.' Alec shrugged. 'It was pure chance that bagged evidence was removed when it was, isn't it?'

'Definitely,' Kathy agreed. 'If it wasn't for the fact that we were sure the firemen would ask us to leave, the evidence would have stayed with me until we had finished.'

'He didn't count on us having the chance to analyse anything!' Alec scoffed. 'Everyone makes mistakes,' he added. 'Maybe he was preoccupied with building his incendiary device and was convinced that it would destroy everything and overlooked any other scenario?'

'I'm inclined to agree,' Kathy said. She paused for a moment. 'The good news is the initial genetic markers match your suspect, Tod Harris. I'll need another twenty-four hours to get an exact genetic match but the odds of it being anyone else at the moment are in the millions.'

'Fantastic!' Alec said.

'That is great news,' Annie agreed. 'What about Jayne Windsor?' Annie sat forward excitedly. Butterflies were swarming in her stomach.

'The second scene keeps giving. We found a rubber mask in the trash,' Kathy handed them a photograph. The mask was a demented looking old man with a bald head and white tufts of hair over the ears. 'The sweat and saliva gave us DNA, which matches Harris. We also have a perfect thumbprint on the mirror in the bathroom that also belongs to him.' She lifted another sheet. 'I ran a sample of urine from Jayne Windsor's bladder. It tested positive for Rohypnol breakdown. The drug itself was gone but cells that it leaves behind prove that it was in her system.' She shook her head and raised her finger, 'We haven't recovered the knife that he used to remove the head yet.' She shrugged. 'He must have taken it with him. The final nail in his coffin is the seminal trace inside Jayne matches the first samples.' Kathy smiled and raised her eyebrows. 'Tod Harris is your man.'

'We've got him,' Alec clapped his hands together. 'We need to know where we are on tracing his whereabouts.'

Annie nodded and stood up. 'Thank you, Kathy,' she said squeezing her arm. She walked out of the office, a woman on a mission. Stirling had returned to the office and was stood talking to Google and his team. 'The DNA matches Tod Harris,' Annie announced to the entire office. A cheer went up and muted expletives were exchanged. 'Do we know where he is yet?'

'We know that he took an Easy Jet flight from the Midlands to Alicante and we've found a T Harris booked into the Hotel Lavante in the Old Town area,' Google said removing his glasses, 'I'm waiting for the local Guardia to call me back.' He held up his finger and sat back in his chair. 'We could have a break here, guv.'

'Go on!' Annie said frustrated.

'The locals have a male English tourist in hospital,' he paused. 'He was stabbed during a foiled robbery. The ID that he has on him names him as, Tod Harris. They're waiting for confirmation from the officers at the hospital that he is the same man from the hotel. Once they have it, they'll place him under arrest and hold him there until we can raise a warrant to extradite him.'

'Bloody fantastic!' Annie punched the air. 'Becky, where are we on warrants for Harris?'

'The judge had to amend it because he is abroad, guv,' she replied, 'A courier is bringing the new one over now. It should be here in the next half an hour.'

'Good work, Becky,' Annie said smiling. 'Google,' she said thoughtfully. 'Have you got any more on translating the text?'

'More of the same, guv. Nothing new.'

'I want Tod Harris's home searched tonight then everyone is to go home and get a good night's sleep. When you're fresh tomorrow, we're back at it, everyone. Well done,' Annie said enthusiastically. 'The DNA is a huge breakthrough, but it doesn't mean that we can ease off. If we don't get a confession, we'll need a cast iron case to make sure this bastard goes down.'

'Guv.' The team replied in unison.

CHAPTER 27

'Mrs Harris?' Annie said showing her badge. The lady that opened the door peered at her through a three-inch gap between the UPVC door and the frame. A chain lock dangled loosely between them. 'I'm Detective Inspector Jones and I have a warrant to search the premises. Open the door please.'

'Is this about Tod?' her voice was reedy and timid.

'It is,' Annie replied assertively. 'Open the door, Mrs Harris.'

'What has he done now?'

'Open the door and we can discuss it.'

The chain rattled and the door opened. Mrs Harris was a little over five feet tall and her dark hair was styled in a short tight perm. Her face was a map of deep creases; the skin looked to have the texture of putty. She hadn't put her false teeth in, and her lips curled into her mouth giving her a reptilian appearance. Annie put her in her mid-fifties, but the odours of cigarettes and alcohol explained why she looked ten years older.

'What has he done?' Mrs Harris tutted. 'Has he been chasing women again? I've warned him a thousand times. I told him after the last time that if he did it again, he was on his own. I didn't bring him up like that. His father will be spinning in his grave.' She stood back and allowed Annie inside. It was a large dwelling built in the thirties with high ceilings and ornate plaster covings. Polish and air freshener mingled with the smell of stale cigarette smoke. 'Come on in and make sure they all wipe their feet. It's a full-time job keeping this place clean, but I do my best.'

Annie half listened and half organised the search team as they entered. Mrs Harris rattled on oblivious to the number of detectives that walked by her. She had seen it all before. That much was obvious to Annie. 'We'll be searching the entire property, Mrs Harris,' Annie handed her the warrant, but she didn't read it. She shrugged and folded it in half with yellowed fingers. 'There's a garage at the bottom of the driveway,' Annie said. 'Do you have the keys?'

'No,' Mrs Harris bit her bottom lip. Her face darkened. 'Tod has the only key although he doesn't have a car for more than five minutes. I can't keep up with him and his cars.' She said as if in conversation with a friend. 'He changes them as often as he changes his socks.' Stirling walked past and headed upstairs. 'About once a month.' Mrs Harris looked him up and down and the gravity of the situation hit her. 'Oh, Tod,' she mumbled. 'What have you done now?' She lit a cigarette with trembling hands and inhaled deeply, closing her eyes as the soothing smoke worked its magic. She exhaled and looked Annie in the eyes. 'Has he hurt another woman?'

'Yes.' Annie kept her answer short. 'When was the last time that you saw him?'

'Tuesday or Wednesday, I think.' She frowned. 'He rushed in early in the morning, like a baby elephant. Woke me up.' She rolled her eyes. 'I must have gone back to sleep, eventually. I heard a car horn outside and the last time I saw him, he was getting into a taxi.' She shrugged. 'He didn't even say goodbye. I knew he was up to something. Haven't heard from him since.'

'He's in Spain.'

'Benidorm?'

'Yes.' Annie nodded. 'Has he been there before?'

'Every time he does something wrong. That boy has been trouble since he was old enough to walk. He was born bad.' She smiled sadly. 'That might sound harsh coming from his mother but it's the truth,' she sucked hard on her smoke and sighed. 'To look at him, you wouldn't think he was such a loser. Such a handsome boy.' Mrs Harris wiped a tear from the corner of one eye. 'We used to go there on our family holidays. I think he grew attached to the place. He's been there a couple of times a year for as long as I can remember. He's always travelling somewhere.'

'I see.' Annie gestured to a uniformed WPC. 'Take Mrs Harris into the living room until we're done please.' Her shoulders hunched and she seemed to shrink as the policewoman led her away. Annie could hear her muttering beneath her breath. She felt for her. It was one thing to watch her son fail in life but another all together to witness him becoming a monster. There was no need to inflict more pain with the details yet. She would find out soon enough.

Annie climbed the stairs and looked around. The house had four bedrooms and was furnished well. The carpets were thick and the wallpaper expensive and tastefully matched. Her ornaments were dated and tacky but there wasn't a speck of dust to be seen. Annie could hear most of the activity coming from the room at the end of the landing. She glanced into each bedroom as she passed. Every bed was made up with pastel coloured bedding and satin valance sheets. She reached Tod's room and paused. From the doorway, the bedroom looked like it belonged to a teenage boy. Posters covered the walls; some pop divas and others super models. The constant theme was their state of undress and the suggestive poise. Tod Harris had an eye for beautiful women. Stirling turned as she stepped inside the room.

'We've got a laptop and a couple of butterfly knives,' Stirling said gruffly. 'And four 100 mil bottles of a clear odourless liquid in his bedside cabinet.'

'Rohypnol?'

'That's my guess.' He nodded. 'They're bagged and on the way to the lab. The rest of the room seems pretty bland so far.' He walked to the bedroom window and looked outside. 'Mrs Harris keeps the house in good shape. I don't think that he would keep anything incriminating in his room.'

'The garage?' Annie said standing next to him at the window. They could see Bomb Squad officers inspecting the garage door. 'Let's go and see if they're ready.'

They walked down the stairs and along the hallway. All the pictures that Annie saw were of Mr Harris and Tod when he was a child. A few were of all three together. It was as if nothing worth capturing had happened since he was young. Tod looked sullen but normal. He only smiled in a few of them. It was hard to imagine that kid growing up to be a rapist. A murderer. A beast that could remove the lower half of a woman's face and carve intricate text into her flesh with a metal hook while she screamed for mercy. A monster.

The kitchen was a bright open plan space with a sloping glass roof and windows on three sides. A hybrid of kitchen and conservatory. There was a centre island with a deep porcelain sink built into wooden worktops. Black marble tiles glistened like mirrors on the floor. It was a blend of vintage and modern styles. Annie glanced around and shook her head. 'Tod Harris had a good start in life.' She commented. 'I feel for his mother.'

'I'm sick of hearing that a 'difficult childhood' was to blame,' Stirling took her point. 'My dad kicked the crap out of my mother; therefore, I can't be responsible for anything that I do as an adult.' He snorted. 'Psychobabble bullshit!'

'Bullshit indeed,' Annie agreed. The back doors were open, and a cold breeze flowed in. Annie shivered as she walked outside. Icy fingers touched her scalp and face looking for a way inside. The wind seemed to claw at her clothes. 'It's getting cold at night now.'

'It is,' Stirling agreed. 'We could do with a quick trip to Benidorm, guv. Warm up for a few days.'

'Few days?' Annie scoffed. 'We'll be lucky if Alec pays for a taxi from the airport let alone accommodation.'

'I won't pack my swimmers then.'

Annie grimaced. 'You in swimmers?' she shook her head. 'Twilight zone material.' Annie followed the path, which led to the driveway. Low hedges lined the drive and the garage was set back 20 metres at the rear of the house. Stirling trudged behind her. Three officers were struggling to lift the door.

'There was a new padlock fastening the door to an anchor bolt,' the lieutenant said as they approached. 'We've cut the power supply to the garage and we can't see any evidence of a device on the door.' He gestured to his men and as they lifted the up-and-over, the metal groaned in protest.

Annie looked at Stirling disappointedly. She had hoped that Jackie Webb's Mercedes would be parked inside. There was no vehicle inside at all. The concrete floor was spotted with oil stains and the left-hand wall was lined with shelves. Four plastic fuel containers stood in a line against the right-hand wall. They exchanged concerned glances as they stepped inside. The lieutenant walked over to them and studied the wall and the space around them.

'They're empty.' He smiled. He looked at the shelf above and noticed a thick plastic bag. 'Ball bearings,' he said pointing to the bag. 'And four new 'All Ride' twelve-volt water heaters, still in their boxes.'

'Like the incendiary device?'

'The same.'

A rush of adrenalin coursed through Annie's veins. Her heart rate increased. More evidence to bury Tod Harris with. She scanned the shelves to the right. Peg boards held an assortment of power tools. Hammer drill, sander, grinder, jigsaw, circular saw, blow torch. To her left, a full set of two headed spanners were laid out symmetrically in a line. Thirty of them at least. Plastic tubs filled with screws, tacks, and washers of various sizes were stored neatly next to a comprehensive set of screwdrivers and pliers. Everything was equidistant from the next, the product of a tidy mind or even a sufferer of OCD. It was a DIY fan's heaven on earth, yet the tools were pristine and unused.

'Everything is covered in a thin layer of dust,' Annie said wiping her finger across the handle of a wrench. A clean stripe appeared. 'Nothing on this side has been touched for a long time.'

'Tod Harris doesn't strike me as the, 'do it yourself' type,' Stirling agreed. 'But look here.' He added. A pick and shovel stood against the back wall. The blade was coated with soil and sand and a dark substance. 'We had better get these tested.' He peered along the shelves on the rear wall. His height enabled him to see without craning his neck. 'There's nothing here, guv but I want to know where he's been digging.'

'Me too,' Annie said. 'Get the team to check the gardens.'

'Guv.'

Stirling left Annie in the garage. She walked along each wall, studying every inch from floor to ceiling. Everything was old except for the petrol containers, ball bearings, and water heaters. They were nails in Harris's coffin. She wasn't sure why, but she felt deflated. Annie sighed and walked outside. She took a Maglite from her jacket and joined the others. They were walking in crisscross patterns, searching the borders, lawn and hedges. Annie took her torch and shone it at the base of the garage. There was a narrow gap between the concrete base and the lawn. She walked slowly, scanning the area carefully. Looking for any breaks in the soil. At the end of the garage, she squeezed into a gap between the wall and the garden fence. The ground space had been covered in shingle to discourage weeds. Digging there would have been impossible. The space was too narrow and the floor too hard for a spade. She shimmied along, her back against the fence panels until she reached the other side. The fence continued for another few metres before it formed a right angle where it joined the fence that bordered the street. She shone the torch along the fence and under the hedges, but she couldn't see anything untoward. Crouching, she searched the corner where the fences met. The ground was untouched. She sighed and walked back to the garage wall, sweeping her torch across the ground.

Nothing.

She looked to her right and aimed the torch at the fence. The hedges had been replaced by rose bushes and she swept the beam along them. They had been planted using a tape measure, exactly the same distance between them. The tools in the garage belonged to the same person that planted those roses. Nothing looked out of place. Frustrated, she walked on until she had reached the end of the garage wall.

'Anything?' Stirling called.

'Nothing.'

Annie looked back where she had walked and folded her arms against the cold. The line of roses caught her eye again. She thought about the tools inside the garage. 'Look for anything that doesn't look symmetrical,' Annie said. 'This garden has been planted by someone with OCD.'

'Guv!' a voice called from the side of the house.

'What is it?'

'There's a shed here, guv.'

Annie shrugged and they walked over to it. Overhanging tree branches had hidden it from view. It was a wooden construction topped with green roofing felt. The roof slanted left to right so that the rain could run off. 'What do you think?' Annie asked.

'The ball bearings and heater coils we found are for making motion triggered devices,' the lieutenant said matter-of-factly. 'Once they're set, you can't disarm them from outside. We're safe but we'll take the hinges off the door to be on the safe side.' He smiled and gestured to his men. They removed the screws from the hinges in seconds and lifted the door off. It remained attached to the shed only by the shiny silver padlock and clasp beneath the handle. They swept torches around the frame and checked the floor inside. 'You're clear, Inspector.'

'Thanks,' Annie said. Stepping through the door, her senses began to bristle. Tod Harris used this space to hide his perversions from his mother. She could sense it immediately. The presence of evil lurked in the darkness. The shed was long and narrow. Three metres wide by six metres long. In the shadows, she could make out an armchair, a coffee table, and a television. A row of three metal filing cabinets stood against the back wall. Lights flickered on and she blinked to avoid the glare. Three lanterns hung from the ceiling and a bright table lamp glowed on the coffee table.

'LED, lights. Battery powered,' Stirling grunted. He pointed to a switch just inside the door. 'This is a proper little man cave,' he said,' he said gesturing to a glass-fronted beer fridge that stood next to the armchair. It was half filled with bottles of Carlsberg. An Xbox sat next to the television, the controller on the arm of the chair. At first glance, it appeared innocent enough.

Annie walked to the television and looked at it. It was a flat screen Samsung portable with a built in DVD player. The cabling behind it looked complicated and she involuntarily stepped back. 'He's wired the television and the fridge to a truck battery and then he has a camping inverter to convert the twelve volts to two hundred and forty for his Xbox,' the lieutenant sensed her fear. 'It's geeky but it won't explode.'

'Must be a man thing.' Annie shrugged. Three empty beer bottles stood next to the television. She picked up a DVD storage wallet and slid out one of the disks. It was marked with only the manufacturers' brand. 'Can we bag these please.' She switched on the television and pressed play on the DVD player. 'Let's see what he was watching last.' Jackie Webb's image appeared on the screen. Mascara had run down her face in blackened streaks. Her eyelids were glued open, giving her a mad staring look. Her eyes were glassy like a dead fish. The lower half of her face was missing, and the exposed muscle, cartilage, and bone glistened. The wounds were fresh. 'Jesus Christ!' Annie hissed. 'He sat here drinking beer and watched this. The sick bastard.' She turned it off quickly, but the images were emblazoned on her brain. Taking the disk from the player, she looked at Stirling and held it up. 'Get this to the team,' she said quietly. 'This is the smoking gun. We'll nail this bastard now.'

'He's going down, guv. Scumbag.' Stirling nodded still staring at the blank screen. He was rattled too. Not so much by the images but by their situ. It took a special kind of disturbed psyche to relax and drink beer while watching that; someone ice cold and detached from any human empathy.

Annie felt sick inside. The evidence was rock solid, yet she still felt unsettled. Breathing deeply, she turned and walked to the chair. On the floor was a waste paper basket, half-full of used tissues. She grimaced and shook her head. An empty box of Kleenex sat next to the bin, 'Man Size Tissues' screamed from the logo. 'When he wasn't playing on his Xbox, he was playing with himself,' she said with a sigh. 'Sometimes I have to wonder what planet some people are from.'

'Guv,' Stirling said. He was holding a thick lever-arch file open. Inside, Annie could see clear plastic sleeves and coloured material. 'Underwear, guv.' He raised his eyebrows. Annie walked next to him so that she could see the contents. 'Jayne Windsor,' Stirling said pointing to a Polaroid, which had been inserted into the sleeve with a pair of black cotton panties. The picture showed the woman's face. She looked peacefully asleep on a pillow. Stirling turned the page and looked at Annie. 'Jackie Webb. The bastard keeps their underwear.' He scowled. His face was purple with anger. A Polaroid image of Jackie showed a similar pose. 'He hasn't got a leg to stand on, guv,' Stirling growled. He turned the page and the image of another sleeping woman was inserted next to her underwear. The next page was the same, different face, different panties but the same. As was the next. And the next. And the next.

Stirling turned the sleeves sixteen times until he stopped. 'For God's sake!' he whispered. Annie put her hand to her mouth. 'This bastard needs hanging,' he hissed. Instead of panties, the sleeve held a small pair of Y-fronts. He turned the page to find the Polaroid but there wasn't one. Behind it was another pair of underwear. SpongeBob Square pants boxer shorts. Next to them was the image of a young boy sleeping. 'How old is he?'

'Nine maybe ten?'

'I don't recognise any of their faces,' Stirling said. His fingers were trembling as he flicked back through the file.

'Nor me,' Annie said quietly. 'We need to cross reference their faces against sexual assault complaints.' She paused. 'You have to wonder how many of them know that they were assaulted. Get this to the team ASAP. I want to know who each and every one of these people are.'

'I'll get on it now.' He turned to the other detectives. 'Bag everything and move it out of here. Are the CSI unit here?'

'Yes, Sarge.'

'Tell them that the stuff we found in the garage, the DVD and the file need to be transported now,' he spoke slowly to keep anger from his voice. 'Anything else we find is a bonus. They can send the van back for the rest later.'

Annie walked deeper into the shed and tried to shift the images from her mind. Jackie Webb, her face wet and glistening like fresh meat. Jayne Windsor sleeping peacefully, completely unaware of what was to come. Her decapitated head on the dressing table, money shoved into her mouth. The images flashed by like a carousel of the damned. She faced the filing cabinets and took a deep breath. The contents could be totally unrelated to their case. They knew that he worked online. It could be his records but somehow, Annie didn't think that it was.

'I'll take the left-hand side,' Stirling's gruff voice made her jump. She was lost in her thoughts. She looked confused. 'Are you okay, guv?'

'I'm fine.'

'If it helps, it knocks me sick too.' Stirling smiled thinly.

'It just makes me feel sad,' she said walking to the filing cabinet on the right. 'Sad and incredibly angry.' She breathed deeply and opened the top drawer. It clattered against its rollers and dropped at an angle.

Empty.

Stirling opened the left-hand side. He looked at her and shook his head. Annie opened the remaining two drawers quickly.

Empty.

Stirling followed suit with the same result. 'They've been cleared out.'

'What about the middle cabinet?'

Annie bit her lip and opened the top drawer.

Empty.

She bent slightly to open the middle drawer.

Empty.

'We're not going to find anything more damming than we have already,' Annie muttered as she opened the final drawer. It clattered to a stop and something rattled loudly against the metal. She frowned and stared inside. 'Bloody hell!' she gasped. 'I'll take that back,' she said as she stared at an evil-looking hunting knife. One side of the blade was razor sharp and caked in dried blood; the serrated edge on the other side had pieces of flesh wedged between the teeth. The smell of decomposition drifted up to her like a familiar but unwanted guest.

CHAPTER 28

36 Hours Later

'Interview with Tod Harris,' Annie began, 'present DI Annie Jones, your names for the record please,' she prompted.

'DS Stirling.'

'Kate Bartlet, defence lawyer for Tod Harris.' She paused and nudged him. 'Say your name for the tape, Tod.'

Tod Harris coughed nervously. 'Tod, Tod Harris,' he stuttered. The cramped interview room made him feel claustrophobic. He looked decidedly pale for a man who had been in the sun. The pain from his stab wound had become a dull ache, gnawing at him. The painkillers took the edge off but little more. 'Can I just say for the record that I'm in severe pain following a mugging. I have nine stitches in my back and I'm not happy about being dragged from Spain in handcuffs without any explanation.' He glared at Annie. 'They refused to talk to me all the way back.'

'We charged you before we left,' Annie interrupted him. 'That was explanation enough until you had legal representation with you.'

'I can't remember anything. I was under anaesthetic,' he protested. 'I didn't have a Scooby Doo what was going on.' He had decided that he was going to aggressively deny everything. He had made his mind up before the Guardia officers had even arrived at his hospital bed. Attack was the best form of defence. It had worked with his previous rape charge so he didn't see why it wouldn't work this time. 'I'll be claiming for a flight back to Spain when this farce is over and seeking compensation too.' He snapped arrogantly. Inside, he didn't feel anywhere near as confident as the man he was trying to portray. 'This is bullshit.' Kate Bartlet nudged him again and threw him a scolding glance. 'What is your problem?' he snapped at his brief. 'You're supposed to be on my side. This is bullshit and you know, it is!'

'Let's just listen to what the detectives have to say, Tod.'

'It will be bollocks!'

'Have you finished?' Stirling growled. Tod nodded and sat back in his chair. He winked at Stirling and smiled sarcastically. The bolts that fastened his chair to the floor denied it any lateral movement making it uncomfortable to sit on even for short periods of time. He shifted his weight but couldn't find any relief from the pain in his back. 'Are you ready to begin?'

'As ready as I can be.' Tod grinned. 'I can't smile wide enough I'm so happy to be here.' He stopped smiling and frowned. 'Get on with it and get me out of this dump.'

'I would get used to your surroundings, Tod.' Stirling glanced at Annie and a silent communication past between them. 'You could be here a while.' They shared an understanding that their suspect had no idea how much evidence they had against him.

'Can you tell us what you do for a living,' Annie asked casually.

Tod seemed to relax a little. 'I'm self-employed as a copy writer.' He smiled. 'I write content for company websites. Mostly in the gaming industry.'

'And you live with your mother at 42 Princess Drive, Liverpool, right?'

'At the moment. I travel a lot, so my flat was always left empty.' He shrugged and blushed a little. 'She's not been well, so I moved back to help out.'

'Admirable,' Annie smiled thinly. 'I'm sure she's very grateful.'

'She is actually.' Tod's face turned dark with anger.

'I don't doubt it,' Annie replied flatly. 'I'm sure she's ever so proud that her son is on the sex offender's register.' His eyes narrowed and he had to restrain himself from responding aggressively. Annie gauged his reaction. He was highly strung and that would work in her favour. 'Do you recognise this woman?' Annie asked pushing a photograph of Jayne Windsor across the table.

Tod glanced at it and shrugged. 'I don't think so.'

Lie, she thought. She noticed that he twitched slightly when he lied. It was subtle but it was there. A movement of the shoulders, only slight but perceptible to the experienced eye. 'You don't remember meeting her at a nightclub?' Annie pushed an image from the nightclub to him. 'This is you with her in Flatfoot Sam's, isn't it?'

'I don't think so.' Tod flushed. 'The image isn't very clear. It might be.'

'It is you, Tod, isn't it?' Annie pressed. He shrugged nonchalantly but didn't answer. She pointed to the image and looked him in the eye. 'That is you with Jayne Windsor, isn't it, Tod.'

'It could be I suppose.'

'Do you remember talking to her there?'

'No.'

Annie saw the twitch again. 'Are you sure?' she pushed another picture towards him. 'This is an hour later. Same club, same girl. This is you with her.'

'I don't remember her.' Twitch.

'Funnily enough, there are quite a few photos of you with her. You don't leave her side except to go to the bar.' Stirling added nudging the picture closer again. 'She was a Special Constable. A serving police officer. Did you know that?'

'Interesting.' Tod shrugged. 'And I should be bothered why?' he asked sarcastically.

'Oh, you should be very bothered,' Stirling smiled coldly. The urge to break his jaw was intense. 'She must have told you that she was a police officer?'

'Like I said, I don't remember talking to her.'

'Look again.'

He looked at the picture and shook his head. 'I talk to a lot of women in nightclubs,' Tod sneered but the way his Adam's apple bobbed up and down told Annie that he was worried. His throat was dry, a classic symptom of lying and he couldn't meet her gaze. Annie knew that he was lying through his teeth. 'I meet women online and I meet women in town.' He smiled at Annie. 'Lots and lots of women.' He shrugged. 'I can't be expected to remember them all, can I?'

'Must be a nightmare for you but I'm surprised you can't remember her.' She lifted the photo in front of his face. 'Are you sure that you don't, really?' Annie frowned. She pushed another photo to him. 'Well let me help you to remember.' Annie lifted her index finger and feigned helpfulness. 'You may have a lot of girlfriends but you gave this one,' she pointed the photograph, 'her name is Jayne Windsor, a lift home in her own car the same night as these pictures were taken.' She paused for effect. 'Remember her now?' Tod glanced at the photograph. He flushed red and swallowed hard. 'This is you leaving the club with her, you see?' Annie looked him in the eye. He couldn't look back at her. She placed another photograph in front of him. 'And this is you bundling her into the front seat of her car, see?' Annie stared into his eyes. 'Do you remember her now?'

'Can't say that I remember her clearly.' Tod shook his head. 'I may have taken her to her car but that's just the type of guy that I am.' He appeared almost genuine. 'If I can help someone, I will.'

'You like to help people?' Annie asked smiling. She held up another photograph. 'Well, this is a picture of you 'helping' her friend, Jackie Webb, from the stairwell of the car park into the back of the car.' Annie turned to Stirling and showed him the picture. 'He does like to 'help' doesn't he, Sergeant?'

'Clearly.'

'I'm surprised that you don't recall 'helping' two women back to their car?' Tod's face darkened at their sarcasm. 'Anything coming back to you yet?' He folded his arms and tilted his head to one side. A narrow smile touched his lips. 'What is so amusing?' Annie asked.

'You are. I'm enjoying watching you sweating your pretty little head.' He grinned. 'You're quite attractive considering.'

'Tod!' Kate Bartlet said shocked. It was obvious that he was referring to Annie's false eye. 'I don't think that's helpful. Just answer the Inspector's questions.'

'Oops, sore subject.' Tod shrugged. 'I was just passing a compliment, that's all.'

'I'm glad that you feel comfortable enough to make light of the situation, but this is very serious.' She paused and tapped the photo. Annie felt anger rising inside her. She swallowed and returned her focus to the pictures. 'If you think it's funny so far, then you'll find this hilarious,' Annie looked directly at him. 'This is you with both Jayne Windsor and Jackie Webb.' His eyes flicked to the photo. He swallowed hard again. 'You're on camera getting into the car and driving them away,' Annie smiled coldly. 'See how funny that is?'

'I think he's lost his sense of humour,' Stirling added.

'As much as I enjoy the cut and thrust of mental jousting, Tod.' Annie shrugged. 'But I think we've messed about enough now, don't you?' She smiled coldly. 'I'll ask you once more. Do you recognise them now?'

Tod sat in silence for a few moments. His eyes were fixed on the photographs, but Annie couldn't work out what was going through his mind. Suddenly, he looked up, smirked, and held up his index finger. 'You know what, now that I've seen their pictures properly, it's all coming back to me.' He nodded thoughtfully and rubbed his chin.

'Tod, your acting is forced and unconvincing,' Stirling said gruffly. 'It is also very annoying so pack it in and get on with it!'

'Can you throw your gorilla a banana or something please, Inspector, he's becoming aggressive,' Tod sneered and looked at Stirling. 'Calm down King Kong, who rattled your cage?' Tod smirked again. Stirling looked ready to explode. 'Okay, Inspector.' Tod held up his hands. 'So, you have pictures of me in their car.' He shrugged nonchalantly and looked down at his fingernails. 'So, I drove them home, so what?' Tod shrugged. 'They were as drunk as skunks. I was helping them out that's all. Like I said, I love helping. It's just part of who I am.'

'Where did you drive them to?'

Tod frowned. 'Wherever home was. I can't remember. I took them home and called a cab.'

'That was very good of you,' Annie smiled thinly. 'You're a real model citizen.'

'I try my best.'

'So, to summarise, you left the nightclub with Jayne?' Annie tapped the photograph.

'It looks like I did.' Tod shrugged. 'Like I said before, I can't really remember much about it.'

'Tell me, how did Jackie Webb get from the club into the car park stairwell?' Annie frowned. 'She didn't leave the club with you, did she?'

'I have no idea.' He sighed.

'You see I'm puzzled,' Annie looked at the photographs again. 'Were you with a friend that night?' Annie raised her eyebrows. 'Could he have escorted her to the car park?'

'I was alone.' Twitch.

'Then how did she get there?'

'We're going around in circles here.' Tod rolled his eyes skyward. 'I've told you that I don't remember anything. If it's such a big deal, why don't you ask her?'

'Because she's dead, Tod.' Annie snapped and watched his reaction. His expression didn't change but his eyes darted around the room. Annie pointed to the photographs again. 'They are both dead,' she said flatly. 'But then you know that already, don't you?' Annie was quite surprised when the colour drained from his face.

'How would I know that?' Tod looked genuinely shocked. He shuffled uncomfortably in his chair. 'I don't know anything about them being dead, honestly.' His eyes looked frightened but there was no sincerity in his voice. He looked from Annie to Stirling. 'You dragged me all the way from Spain for this?' He scoffed nervously. 'Is that what this is all about?'

Annie swallowed her anger once more and ignored his sarcasm. 'Tell me, did you target them before you went to the club or did you pick them at random once you were inside?'

'What drugs are you taking?' Tod snapped. 'Targeting?' he shook his head and frowned. 'I don't know what you mean.'

'You know exactly what I mean, Tod.' Annie smiled thinly. 'How did you choose who to target?'

'Listen to me and listen really well,' he leaned forward and glared at Annie, 'are you listening properly?' he paused. 'I don't have a fucking clue what you're talking about.' His face reddened angrily and the muscles at the edge of his mouth twitched slightly. His eyes were cold and piercing. Annie could sense the violence inside him. 'I repeat for those who are hard of hearing, I haven't got a clue what this about.'

'Mr Harris is struggling to understand what this is about,' Annie said to Stirling.

Stirling shook his head and smiled. 'It is not rocket science, is it?'

'Nope it is not. In fact, it's quite simple,' Annie said tight lipped. 'It's about the kidnap, rape, and murder of two women, Tod.' She pointed to the photos. 'The two women that you drove home from the nightclub,' she tapped the pictures again. 'These two women here, Jayne Windsor and Jackie Webb. Raped and murdered.' She sat back and shrugged. 'Do you understand what we're talking about now?'

'What?' he asked incredulously. 'Rape and murder?' he left his mouth open and stared at Annie. 'Are you crazy?' Tod held up his hands in surrender and shook his head. 'Look here,' he croaked and tapped the photos. His voice was shaking, the arrogance gone. 'Listen to me, they were so drunk that they couldn't stand up,' Tod stammered. 'I drove them home and that's it. I don't know anything about them dying.'

'Jayne Windsor didn't drink.'

'So what?' He shrugged and blushed again. Annie could see the cogs turning in his mind. 'She might have dropped something in the club.'

'She was a serving police officer. She didn't do drugs.'

'And you're all angels I suppose?'

'They were drugged,' Annie snapped. 'You drugged them. It's on the CCTV from the club.'

'You're mistaken.'

'No.' Annie put three photographs down. 'This is you giving Jayne drinks. Spiked drinks.'

'No chance. I don't need to drug women to get them into bed.'

'Really?' Annie frowned. 'We've had a good look through your computer and your DVD collection, Tod,' she shook her head. 'You have a lot of images and videos of women being raped, don't you?'

Tod grinned nervously and looked at his brief. She shifted uncomfortably in her chair and nodded. 'It's not a crime. I like watching porn,' he said flatly. 'You know, handcuffs and the like. You have handcuffs don't you, Inspector?' He winked. 'Don't tell me you've never used them in your spare time, eh?' He laughed. 'She's blushing. I bet you have!' He looked around nervously. 'Tell me, Inspector.' He frowned thoughtfully. 'When you fuck do your boyfriends ask you to turn the lights off?' His eyes glared at Annie. In that moment, she knew he could kill without conscience. 'You know the glass eye and the scar must put some guys off.'

'That's enough.' Stirling leaned towards him and glowered at him. Tod blushed and looked away. 'Do you know that our computer techs are able to retrieve everything that you've ever looked at, downloaded, purchased, stored on a memory stick or even deleted?' he paused for effect. 'And I mean everything. You may think data has gone from your computer, but it hasn't.' Tod stopped smiling and frowned. Stirling pushed a printout of an online invoice across the table. 'You deleted this from your history, but we found it.' Tod swallowed hard. 'You purchased roofies online two months ago. A lot of it.' Tod bit his bottom lip and glanced at the invoice. 'You know what roofies are, don't you Tod?' Stirling sat back and tapped the invoice. 'Rohypnol. The 'date rape' drug. The same drug used on Jayne Windsor, the woman in that photograph.'

'I've never seen that before.'

'Jayne Windsor wasn't drunk, you drugged her.'

'You're mistaken.'

Stirling held up an evidence bag. 'We found three bottles of it in your bedside cabinet.'

'What?' Tod looked at his brief angrily. 'What is this?'

'You heard me,' Stirling said smiling. 'Rohypnol, which was found in your bedroom.'

'In my bedroom?' Tod frowned and looked at his brief again. 'Are you listening to this?' She nodded and blushed but didn't say anything. 'They've been to my mum's? Can't you object or something?'

'We're not in court, Tod,' she muttered.

'Not yet anyway,' Stirling added with a sarcastic grin.

Tod looked furious. 'You can't do that,' he pointed his finger at Stirling. 'You've been to my mum's house and searched it, bastards!'

'Yes.'

'You can't, can they?' Tod looked at his brief and she nodded her head. She whispered in his ear. He looked rattled but listened to her advice. 'I'm saying nothing more, fuck you!'

'That won't help you,' Annie said.

'No comment.' He grinned and raised his middle finger to her. He felt his heart pounding in his chest. Tod shifted; his hands were clasped tightly together beneath the table. His knuckles were white, and his palms were sweating. He licked his lips, but his mouth was bone dry.

'Tod.' Annie sat back and folded her arms. 'Do you have any idea how much trouble you are in?'

'No comment.'

'We found your DVD collection in your mum's shed.'

'No comment.' The colour drained from his face again. His eyes dropped to the table. He shifted his weight uncomfortably.

Annie placed two more photos on the table. The colour drained from Tod's face and his jaw clenched. She could see the vein pulsing in his forehead. His eyes narrowed as he stared at one and then the other. 'What the hell is this?' Tod asked in a whisper. He looked at Bartlet angrily. 'What the hell is that?'

'It's a picture of your shed,' Stirling said. 'You know, it's where you sit and drink beer and watch DVD's.'

'No comment.'

'Do you recognise this?'

Tod's face showed fear and something else. He looked genuinely sickened. 'What the hell is that?' he muttered. Sweat formed on his brow. 'That is sick.'

'That is Jackie Webb with no face left,' Stirling tapped the photo.

'Oh my God!' Tod looked at his brief. 'I've never seen that before, honestly!'

Kate Bartlet looked like she was going to vomit. 'Don't say anything else.'

'You have never seen that before?' Stirling frowned.

'Never.'

'Tod, say nothing more,' Bartlet said again.

'You should recognise her like this.' Stirling pushed the photograph closer to him. 'She stars in the DVD that we took from your player, you know, the last DVD that you watched before you ran off to Spain.'

'No comment.'

'You drank beer and masturbated in your armchair,' Annie added with a sour grin. 'The waste bin was full of stained tissues.'

'I haven't got a clue what you're talking about,' Tod stared at the picture of Jackie Webb's body incredulously. 'I've never seen this before and I certainly had nothing to do with that!'

'The DNA on the tissues we found is yours, Tod,' Annie said dryly. 'Your semen is all over them.'

'No comment. That's sick!'

'It is sick.' Annie nodded. 'But masturbating over it's sicker still, don't you think?'

'I've never seen that before,' Tod stressed. Rivulets of sweat trickled down his forehead.

'Tod,' Bartlet said angrily. 'My advice is to say nothing more!'

'I didn't do that,' Tod replied in a whisper.

'Are you denying being in the shed?' Annie asked calmly. 'Your DNA is on the tissues and it's on the beer bottles too.' She paused. Tod blushed bright red. 'You sat in that armchair and masturbated in front of the television. Didn't you?'

'No comment.'

'This is the DVD that you were watching,' she pointed to several stills from the recording. 'It shows Jackie Webb, her face missing and then it shows the headless body of Jayne Windsor.'

'Headless?' he muttered. 'Jesus! No comment.'

'Both women are on that DVD.' She tilted her head and looked at his eyes. They were full of fear. 'The game is over, Tod.' He sat forward and shook his head. His face was pale, and his bottom lip quivered. 'What happened, Tod?' Annie spoke calmly. 'Raping women wasn't enough anymore?' she paused. 'Did you need something more extreme to get it up?'

'Screw you!' Tod snapped. 'What is going on here?' His face had a confused expression across it. Annie watched his reactions with interest. 'What the hell are they playing at here?' He looked at Bartlet again, but she looked equally shocked by the images. 'This is a stitch up. Do something!' he leaned towards Annie. 'I don't know what you're talking about! Can you hear me?'

'I can hear you well enough but you're lying.'

'I'm not lying!'

'Are you denying sitting in that chair before you left for Spain?'

'No,' he said flustered. 'But I've never seen that DVD.' He swallowed hard. 'I was watching porn, not that!'

'How did it get into your player?'

'It must have been planted.'

'That's difficult to believe, Tod.'

'I didn't kill anyone.'

Annie ignored him. 'You admit that you drove them home that night though?'

'No comment,' he snapped.

'You've already admitted that, Einstein,' Annie said flatly. 'You drugged them in the club, drove them home, and raped them.' She looked into his eyes and paused. He hesitated as if he was going to confess but then he seemed to calm himself. Annie continued. 'And then you tortured them to death and mutilated their bodies.' Annie placed a series of crime scene images in front of Tod. He sat back in his chair as if trying to get away from them. She paused to let the images take effect. The pictures were difficult to look at. 'We found this Cyrillic script intricately carved into the skin of Jackie Webb.' She watched his reaction. 'This is especially interesting. It must have taken hours.' Annie looked Bartlet in the eyes. 'We can tell that she was alive during the entire process. Like something from a horror movie, don't you think?'

'That's sick.' Tod stammered. 'I wouldn't do that. I couldn't do that. This is mental!' He turned to his brief, his eyes watery and pleading. 'Do something, please! They are trying to frame me!'

'Calm down, Tod,' Bartlet said irritably. The photographs had rattled her too. 'Say nothing else. Do you understand?' Tod took a deep breath and nodded. He closed his eyes and sat back as far as his wound would allow.

Annie placed three pictures of the intricate carvings on the victim's skin onto the table. Tod shook his head in disbelief. His brief looked like she was about to pass out. She swallowed hard and looked at the ceiling. 'Nasty, isn't it?'

'I need to talk to my client alone,' Bartlet said quietly.

'I didn't do that,' Tod shook his head. He looked at his brief for help. 'Tell them that I didn't do this!' he turned to Annie. 'I didn't kill anyone!'

'Really?' Annie asked sarcastically. 'How do you explain the DVD at your mother's house?'

Tod shrugged and shook his head. His pallor was grey, and his lower lip trembled. He looked to Bartlet for advice. She shook her head. 'No comment.' This time his voice was little more than a whisper.

'Kidnap, rape, murder,' Annie smiled thinly. 'If you add to that the fact that you deliberately tried to murder and maim the responders, you're looking at three life sentences back to back.'

'I don't know what you're talking about. I didn't try to murder anyone.'

'Tod, don't say anymore,' Bartlet advised him again. 'I must insist on a break.'

'Shut up! I want to know what you mean about the responders,' he said impatiently. 'What are you talking about?'

'The incendiary device that you rigged up in the attic?' Annie said placing a picture of the burnt-out shell that was Jayne Windsor's home. Tod looked at it and looked at the ceiling.

'Incendiary device?' Tod shook his head in disbelief. It was the image of a burned-out shell that he had seen in the newspapers. 'This is going from the sublime to the fucking ridiculous. I didn't kill anyone, and I didn't build any bomb.'

Annie placed another photo on the table. 'We found this equipment in your mum's garage.' She paused as he looked at the picture. His eyes widened. 'It's the same as the material used to set fire to Jayne Windsor's house.' She put more pictures taken in the garage in front of him and watched his face. 'Ball bearings, water heaters, petrol cans.' There was another painful pause. 'It destroyed most of the evidence at the first scene, but we still managed to get these pictures.'

'I didn't make any device,' he hissed angrily. 'For God's sake, you have to believe me.'

'I told you that our tech guys are thorough. You'll see what I mean here, Tod.' Stirling put two pieces of A4 on the table. 'This was taken from your laptop's deleted history,' he paused to let it sink in. 'You searched and browsed three different sites for instructions on how to build an incendiary device.'

Tod shook his head. 'I looked, that's all. A friend asked me to. I didn't do anything about it. I was just looking!'

'A friend?'

'Yes.'

'Which friend?'

Tod hesitated. 'I don't remember.'

'The same friend that was with you at the nightclub?'

'I told you that I was on my own!'

'Of course, you were.' Annie smiled. 'Do you think a jury will believe you?'

'Am I fucking invisible!' Kate Bartlet snapped. Annie was taken aback by her outburst. 'Firstly, if you don't want to heed my advice then I can't help you,' she said angrily to Tod, 'and second, I'm demanding a legal break to discuss the situation with my client.'

'How can I say nothing when they're trying to pin this on me?' Tod pointed to the photos. 'This is madness, I didn't do that!' Tod argued. He looked at Kate Bartlet, but she couldn't meet his gaze. His voice became louder and more urgent. 'I'm telling all three of you and anyone else that's listening, I didn't do this!'

'I really need to speak to my client,' Bartlet murmured. 'Don't say anything more, Tod. You're making things worse!'

'Worse?' he moaned. 'How can it be worse?'

'Trust me; it can get much worse if you don't listen to me.'

'But I didn't do this!'

'The evidence says that you did.' Stirling said gruffly.

'I really need to speak to my client.'

'And I really need to know what the hell these idiots are talking about,' Tod snapped. 'I want to hear what they've got to say.' He glared at the detectives. 'I didn't do this.'

'The evidence is irrefutable.'

'Bullshit!' Tod shook his head. 'What evidence?'

'We have seminal DNA inside both victims,' Stirling said gruffly with a thin smile. Harris looked like he had been kicked in the face. 'It's yours, Tod.' Stirling shrugged. 'Listen hard. The CCTV footage proves that you drove them home. We can prove that you bought

Rohypnol from the Internet and the seminal DNA proves that you raped them.' He shrugged again. 'And the DVD at your mother's house seals the deal.'

'That is enough!' Bartlet slammed her hand on the desk.

'I'm not a killer.'

Stirling reached down and picked up a lever-arch file. He opened it and placed it on the table. 'How do you explain this?' Tod Harris didn't look confused anymore; he looked guilty. Stirling pointed to the open file and pushed it towards Bartlet. He turned several plastic sleeves that each displayed a pair of women's knickers. She looked at the underwear and the colour drained from her face again. 'This is quite a collection isn't it, Tod?' Stirling prompted him. His face flushed red and he closed his eyes. Guilt, embarrassment, fear. 'You seem to collect knickers, Tod. Did you take Jayne and Jackie's knickers and put them in your collection?'

'No comment,' Tod mumbled. His mind had gone blank, all the bravado gone. 'That's not mine.'

'Are you telling us that you've never seen this collection of underwear?'

'No comment.'

'Which is it, Tod?' Annie smiled thinly. 'It's not yours so you haven't seen this before or no comment?'

Tod glanced at Bartlet and she shook her head. 'You asked me how this could get worse, well this is worse, much worse,' she said harshly. 'You shouldn't say anymore.'

Tod sighed and looked at Annie. He looked broken. 'No comment.'

'But you just said that this isn't yours?' Annie frowned. She turned to Stirling. 'He did just say that that wasn't his, didn't he?'

'He did.'

'I thought so,' Annie turned back to Tod. 'Your fingerprints are all over this, Tod, every page.'

Silence.

'You lied to us.'

Silence.

'This is yours, isn't it?'

'No comment.'

'Your mother was very upset about the search,' Annie said. 'She was asking a lot of questions during the search.' She paused. The mention of his mother had visibly upset him. 'Unfortunately, she saw some of the evidence being removed. It was very upsetting for her.'

Tod's eyes seemed to glaze over. 'She saw this collection, imagine what she was thinking. She was even more upset when we recovered the bloody knife.'

'What knife?' he snapped. He sat bolt upright; his eyes wide like a startled deer.

'This is ridiculous, Tod,' Bartlet spoke. 'I'm advising you to say nothing more! I want a break.'

'Shut up,' Tod said to her angrily. 'I don't want a fucking break!' Stirling smiled. 'I don't know anything about a knife so what are you talking about?'

Annie pushed the image of a bloodstained knife in front of Bartlet. 'We conducted a search of your client's home,' she tapped the photo. 'The knife that was used to cut off Jayne Windsor's head was found in a filing cabinet in your mother's shed. It's covered in her blood.'

Tod looked at the ceiling and gritted his teeth. Annie could see that he was fighting to control his emotions. He was going into meltdown. His breathing was erratic as he spoke. 'There is no way that you found that knife in my mother's shed,' Tod said angrily. He tried to stand up, but he was chained to an anchor between his feet and it clattered against the table. The sudden movement made Annie move back in her seat. His face was like thunder. 'That knife has been planted. Will you please listen to what I'm saying? I did not do any of that!'

His sudden lunge frightened her. Annie tried not to look as flustered as she felt. She felt the tiny muscles around her prosthetic eye twitching. The memories of losing it were still fresh in her mind. She cleared her throat and placed three more crime scene images on the table. 'The evidence clearly says that you did it.'

'No way.' He shook his head and a tear escaped from the corner of one eye. 'I didn't do this to them.'

'So you keep on saying. I'm ready to listen to your explanation.' Annie shrugged. 'If you didn't do this, explain how your DNA was at both scenes?'

'For the last time I'm advising you to say nothing more until we've spoken in private, Tod,' Bartlet snapped. 'The evidence that you were there is irrefutable, Tod.' She turned to Annie. 'I really must insist that we break while I speak to my client.'

'Shut up,' Tod turned on her. 'I'm telling you that I didn't do that. I didn't kill anyone and if you don't believe me then get out and I'll find another lawyer!' He looked at Annie and shook his head. 'I can see how this looks but I didn't kill anyone.'

'Then this is your opportunity to explain your side of the story,' Annie pointed to the photographs. 'You see even though they're dead, your victims have already told us their side through the evidence and at this moment in time, everything is pointing to you.' She sat back and smiled thinly.

The brief stood up. 'I can see that the evidence is overwhelming, Inspector, and my client hasn't been a hundred per cent forthcoming with me,' Bartlet said assertively. She had had enough. 'At this point, I think it only right and proper for you to give me ten minutes alone with my client whether he wants it or not. I must insist!'

Annie looked at Stirling and raised her eyebrows. He grunted and stood up. 'You've got five minutes. Unless we hear something, mind-blowing, then we're going to charge him with what we have.' Bartlet nodded and turned to Tod, her face a mixture of fear and anger. 'DI Jones and DS Stirling are leaving the room for a five-minute recess.'

Annie and Stirling stepped out of the room and a uniformed officer stepped in to guard Harris, closing the door behind him. Annie looked at her watch and leaned her back against the wall. Alec spotted them and waved. 'Why have you stopped?' He had a look of concern on his face. 'What's happened?'

'Bartlet wants ten minutes with him alone,' Annie said. 'Harris hasn't been totally honest with her.'

'She looked like she was going to throw up when she saw the crime scene pics,' Stirling added.

'No surprises there,' Alec said running his hands through his sandy hair. He held up a thin file. 'Becky has been busy with the financials on Barton. We've cross referenced the phone records and found some very interesting connections.'

'I'm listening,' Annie said calmly. Although she wanted to hear the news, deep inside she was concerned that it might muddy the waters.

'Barton called Jackie Webb over a dozen times in the months leading up to Simon Barton's abduction,' he paused to let the facts sink in. 'The calls stopped while he was being investigated but then there's another clutch of calls before the appeal hearing.'

Annie sighed and folded her arms. 'Sounds like he was a customer of hers. What do the financials tell us?'

'Becky has found this,' Alec said holding up the file again. 'Jackie Webb had a savings account with an online bank. A week after the appeal hearing, one hundred thousand pounds was paid into it from a firm of solicitors in Manchester. We contacted them and the money was part of the estate of 'Graham' Barton.'

'Barton's stepfather?' Stirling frowned.

'Yes.' Alec nodded. 'Jackie transferred half of the money to another firm of solicitors in Liverpool that were dealing with the conveyance of a property for Jayne Windsor.'

'Bloody hell.' Annie sighed. 'So, they were bribed.'

'It looks like it. I can't see any other reason behind it.' Alec agreed. 'The money trail is damaging to Peter Barton's alibi and it gives him motive. They could have asked for more money or threatened to change their statements,' he mused. 'Barton had a motive to shut them up, permanently.'

'This doesn't change where we are at with Harris,' Stirling pointed out. 'The evidence is overwhelming.'

'It doesn't change anything, but we should listen to what he has to say,' Annie said frowning. 'Did you see his face when I showed him the crime scene photos?'

'He looked scared.'

'He looked genuinely shocked.'

'Maybe he was,' Stirling grunted, 'but there's nothing that he can say that can explain away the DNA and the DVD. That's without the knife! He's as guilty as sin. Anything that he says to us in there from now on will be fabricated to dilute responsibility.'

'No doubt but what could he dilute it with?' Alec raised his eyebrows and pointed to the file. 'Peter Barton.'

'An accomplice.' Stirling grunted.

'My thoughts exactly.' Annie began. Her sentence was interrupted when the interview room door opened.

Kate Bartlet poked her head around the door. 'We're ready, Inspector,' she said meekly. Annie could tell that her stomach wasn't in the fight. She doubted that she would see the case through to court. Some defence lawyers could defend the devil himself but Bartlet wasn't one of them. The detectives took their seats and studied their prime suspect. He was looking at the floor and biting his lip. Although she couldn't see his legs, Annie could feel them trembling beneath the desk.

'Interview resumed, DI Jones and DS Stirling have returned. Same persons present,' Annie said staring at Tod. 'Do you want to explain your side of the story, Tod?'

He sighed and rolled his eyes. 'I admit that I had sex with both women,' he mumbled. 'But I didn't kill anyone.'

'Is that the best that you can do?'

'It's the truth.'

'Fine,' Annie smiled thinly. 'Then we'll charge you with both murders.'

'Just a minute, Inspector. Tell them what you told me,' Bartlet said coldly. 'It's your only chance.'

'Five seconds, Tod and we're out of here,' Annie snapped.

'Wait a minute!' he turned to his brief, but she didn't offer any more advice. 'Useless bitch!' he whined. 'Okay, okay! I was working with someone else.' He sighed. 'We drugged them, but I had nothing to do with killing them,' he said pointing to the photographs. 'He must have done that later. He's a weirdo, a proper nutcase!' Tod shook his head as he rambled. 'I'm sorry that I got involved with him. He scares the crap out of me. If he knew that I was talking to you like this, I'd probably end up like them.' He looked from the detectives to his brief and back again. Their baffled expressions told him that he wasn't doing himself any favours. 'I had sex with them. I took those pictures of them in bed and I took their underwear and that's it,' he emphasised *that's it*.

'What is this man's name?'

'I don't know.'

'You don't know?'

'No!'

'Charge him.'

'Wait, wait, okay!' Tod went very pale. 'He threatened to visit my mother if I said anything. His name is Rob something.'

Annie shook her head in frustration. 'Okay,' she took a deep breath. 'Take me back to the beginning,' Annie said. 'You said that you were 'working' with someone called Rob. What did you mean 'working'?'

Tod shrugged and shifted awkwardly. The chains on his wrists rattled beneath the table. 'I mean that we were a team.' He blushed. 'We planned to take two women back to their place and, you know,' he gestured with his head.

'No, I don't know,' Annie said flatly. 'Enlighten me.'

'We planned to take two women back from the club and have sex with them.' He shrugged, 'and then swap them over so we both had a go with each.'

'You drugged them?'

'Yes.'

'How did you pick which women you attacked?'

'He picked them.' Tod shrugged. 'He always picked them.'

'Randomly?'

'Sometimes.'

'I'm asking about this time.' Annie pushed the photos closer still. 'Jackie Webb and Jayne Windsor. Were they picked at random?'

No.' Tod shook his head. 'He knew their names.'

'How did he know them?'

'I don't know.'

Annie shook her head and looked at Kate Bartlet. She couldn't hold Annie's gaze for more than a moment. 'So, you admit to drugging Jayne Windsor and Jackie Webb, taking them back to Jayne Windsor's house and raping both women?' Tod tilted his head sideways and nodded. 'I need it for the tape please.'

'Yes.'

'Yes what?'

'Yes!' Tod snapped. 'I drugged them and raped them.' He took a deep breath to calm his nerves. 'When I left that house, they were alive. I swear they were alive.' His eyes darted from Annie to Stirling. 'You have to believe me.'

Annie steepled her hands and thought about her next words. 'So, you're telling me that you last saw the women at Jayne Windsor's house?'

'Yes.'

'Jayne Windsor was found in Jackie Webb's flat with her head cut off,' Stirling interrupted him. 'Are you telling us that you had nothing to do with that?'

'Yes!' he stressed. 'I don't even know where you're talking about. I've never been to her house. I certainly didn't cut anyone's bloody head off for God's sake!' His eyes darted from one detective to the other. 'I've slipped roofies to a few women,' he said gesturing to the file. 'But I'm not a killer.' He looked at them open-mouthed. 'I couldn't do that!'

Stirling sat back and sighed loudly. 'This is getting boring,' he growled. He tapped the photos as he spoke. 'You have a DVD of the dead women in your possession.' He paused and pointed to the image of the jawless woman. 'Jackie Webb. After she was dead, Tod!' he picked up the image again. Tod looked flummoxed. 'Explain that.'

Silence.

Stirling continued. 'The knife that cut off Jayne Windsor's head was found in your mother's shed,' he paused to gauge the response.

Silence.

'Your thumbprint was on the mirror in Jackie's bedroom, at the house you say that you have never been to,' he paused again.

Silence.

'Your DNA was inside her at that house.'

Silence.

'Yet you were never there?'

'Yes. He's framing me.' Tod looked down and tears ran from his eyes. 'I had nothing to do with killing them.'

'So, your accomplice did all this once you had left?' Stirling pressed him. 'He's trying to set you up and all you can give us is that his name is Rob 'something'.'

'You need to explain that, Tod,' Annie added. 'We need his name and we need it now!'

'Rob Derry,' Tod sat back and sighed heavily, his head in his hands. 'Rob Derry is his name.' he closed his eyes and Annie thought he looked almost relieved. 'That's who must have killed them. He did all this.' He nodded his head frantically. 'I helped get them back to their house, I admit that.' He looked at the detectives, his eyes pleading. 'I had sex with them while they were drugged but that's all I did. When I left, Rob Derry was still busy. He had dropped a Viagra tablet. There was no talking to him, he's nuts. I said that we should go but he wanted to stay.' He squeezed his eyes closed. 'The last time that I saw him, he was still with those women and they were alive.'

'Rob Derry?' Annie wrote the name down. She looked at Stirling and grimaced. 'Where did you meet this Rob Derry?' she smiled sourly. 'If we run his name, is he going to come up or is he another figment of your imagination?'

'You'll find him,' Tod said aggressively. 'He's got form I'm telling you. He must have a record. He's a nutcase!'

'So you've said,' Annie said sarcastically. 'Where did you meet him?'

'In a club.'

'Which club?'

'The State,' Tod answered reluctantly. 'I had just spiked a girl's drink and it turned out that he was watching every move that I made.' Tod sounded almost offended. 'He knew what I was up to. He came over to me and made it very clear that if I didn't invite him along with the girl, he would call the police. That was it. That was how we met.'

'So, you took this girl where?' Annie said angrily.

'To a crappy hotel on the docks.'

'When was this?'

'A few years ago.'

'Her name?'

'Claire something.'

'Then what?'

'He had pictures of me,' Tod looked ashamed. 'He said he would show my mother and if that didn't work, he would hurt her.' He shook his head and sighed. 'We met up every now and then and went for a few drinks. One thing led to another and we worked as a team. I didn't want to go out as often as he did, but he wouldn't take no for an answer. He's a psycho. I was terrified of him.'

'You obviously had a lot in common,' Stirling said. 'Where does this scumbag live?'

'Formby somewhere.' Tod shrugged. 'I never went there. I didn't want anything to do with his private life like where he lived. He's a very scary man.'

'But you chose to hunt and drug women with him to rape them.' Annie scoffed. 'I would say you're two peas from the same pod.'

'I can see how it looks.' Tod sighed. 'You have to believe me. I didn't kill anyone.'

'I don't have to believe anything,' Annie said slowly. She pointed to the photographs again. 'I believe what the evidence says, and it tells me that you did kill these two women.'

'No, no, no!' Tod shook his head. 'Rob Derry did this.'

'Have you got a number for him?'

'No.'

'Why not?'

'He calls me from payphones, he doesn't use a mobile.'

'Do you have the number of the payphone?'

'Maybe, if I do it's in my mobile.'

'How old is this Robert Derry?'

'I don't know, fifties, maybe.' Tod shrugged. 'His name isn't Robert.'

'What is his name?' Annie tutted. 'You said he was called Rob.'

'Rob something.' He shrugged again. 'I can't remember. There's a double 'B' or a double 'R' in it somewhere but he shortens it to Rob. He used to go on about it being an unusual name. I didn't listen to him at times. Like I said, he was nuts.'

'We'll take a look, but I'm not convinced that he exists,' Annie said. 'Was he in the club with you that night?'

'I don't know to be honest.'

'You don't know?'

'He said that he would make sure that Jackie Webb was in the car park.' Tod shrugged. 'When I got there, she was in the stairwell.'

'How do you think she got there?'

'I didn't ask.'

'Where did you meet up?'

'I picked him up further up Brownlow Hill.'

Annie and Stirling exchanged glances. The CCTV from the wine bar on the hill showed the car stopping. 'You didn't see him in the club?'

'No.'

'Come on, Tod,' Stirling pushed. 'Why are you lying to us?'

'I'm not lying. I didn't see him in there. I was focused on getting Jayne out of the club, but I had no idea any of this was going to happen,' he pleaded. His eyes filled with tears again. 'He must have done all this and then planted evidence,' Tod said angrily. 'He's setting me up!'

Stirling shook his head. 'The evidence puts you at both scenes and you have the murder weapon and video evidence from the second scene at your home.'

'I wasn't there. I've told you!' He raised his voice. 'He must have broken in and planted the DVD in the player.' Tod looked at their faces in desperation. 'It's the only explanation.'

Stirling shook his head. 'And the prints on the knife?'

'I don't know.'

'Thumbprint?'

'I don't know.'

'Semen?'

'I don't know how my semen was at the second house!' Tod shouted in frustration.

'But you admitted having sex with them,' Annie pushed.

'I used a condom,' he said sarcastically. 'I always use one. I'm not stupid.'

Annie looked at Stirling and smiled. 'You're not stupid?' She sat back and folded her arms. Tod glared back at her. 'If you expect us to believe your story, you're beyond stupid, Tod.'

'My client is admitting to the rapes but he's denying murder, Inspector,' Bartlet interrupted.

'You have heard of the term 'concrete evidence'?' Annie sighed. 'We've got it and your client is going down.'

'I'm being set up! Rob Derry killed them.'

'You're throwing up shadows, nothing more.'

'I'm innocent!'

'Innocent?' Annie frowned and sat back. She folded her arms. 'Are you tripping?' she snapped. 'How many women have you slipped roofies to and raped, Tod?' Annie asked changing the direction of the attack.

'I don't know.'

'Oh, come on!'

'I don't know.'

'There are eighteen pairs of underwear in that file and we'll find out who they belong to.' She frowned, 'if it takes me the next ten years, we'll find them.' Tod looked angry and confused. The pain from his back was becoming unbearable. His hands were shaking visibly. Another tear trickled from the corner of one eye. 'You're a sick rapist, Tod.'

'I'm not a murderer. Those pictures are just twisted.'

'Drugging women for sex is about as twisted as you can get but I have to say that I was surprised by the young boys' underpants,' Annie flicked to the back of the file and placed it in front of Bartlet. She turned pale and threw Tod a glance that expressed her disgust for him. 'Raping adults is one thing but kids?'

'What?' Tod closed his eyes and then opened them again to look at the file. He blinked as if he was seeing something that he couldn't fathom. 'I've never seen those before in my life,' he snarled. 'You've planted them in there!' his face twisted in anger. 'Now that's just wrong!' he shifted awkwardly in his seat. 'I'm not a paedophile, young boys?' he asked incredulously. 'Never!'

'Explain it then, Tod.'

'I'm being set up, that's what it is,' he stammered. 'Rob Derry has set me up.'

'Why would he do that?'

'I don't know!'

'How would he know about your precious collection of underwear?' Stirling asked.

Tod thought for a few seconds, a look of confusion on his face, 'I honestly don't know.'

'Did you ever show him this file?'

'No.'

'Did you ever talk to him about it,' Stirling pressed, 'You know, bragging about your souvenirs?'

'No!'

Annie took a photograph of Peter Barton and placed it on the table. 'Do you know this man?'

Tod glanced at the picture and then leaned over to look closer. 'His face is familiar,' he muttered. Recognition sparked in his eyes. 'Wait a minute, I know him. Didn't he kill that kid from Halewood a few years back?'

'Yes, not far from your mother's house.' Annie nodded and took the picture away. 'Do you know him?'

'No. I know of him.' He insisted. 'He was all over the news. I've never met him.'

'You're sure that you don't know him?'

'I'm sure.'

'A few days ago, he blew his own brains out with a shotgun.'

'Good!' Tod snapped. 'He was a paedophile. Why would I give a toss about him?'

'Funny!' Stirling turned to Annie. 'We didn't find any kid's underwear at Barton's house, did we?' he held up the file again. 'We did find two pairs at your house. Who is the paedophile?'

'Bullshit!' Tod shouted. 'I've never seen those before today.' He turned to Bartlet. 'I'm being set up here. You can see that can't you?'

'We need to talk alone,' she answered flatly.

'I don't believe a word you're saying and neither does your brief,' Annie said thoughtfully. It was a long shot that Tod would identify Barton as the mysterious accomplice. Not that she believed for certain that there was one. 'You're a murderer, a rapist, and a paedophile. They'll love you in jail.'

'You can go and fuck yourself, you goggle-eyed freak.' He turned purple and snarled at Annie. 'This is a fix up. I'm not saying another word to you. Screw you, you bastards!'

Annie felt the sting of his insult but tried to push it from her mind. She needed to keep her head clear. She looked at Stirling and shrugged. 'Like I said.' He blushed.' She smiled coldly and picked up the file. 'I'll find out who every single one of those people are, starting with the young boys.' She paused for effect. 'Obviously we'll have to question those close to you first to see if the boys are related to you.' She paused for his reaction. His eyes widened. 'Are they nephews or neighbours' children?'

He looked stunned. 'No of course not,' his voice was a whisper. 'I don't know them.'

'We'll have to question everyone connected to you to track down who these boys are.' Annie sighed and shook her head. 'We'll have to start with your mother of course,' Annie looked him in the eyes. 'Imagine how she'll feel having to look at a little boy's underwear.' She paused again. Tod was shaking. 'Your poor old mother.' Annie sighed again. 'She'll be mortified won't she, Tod?' The reality of what his family would think of him hit home. His eyes widened in horror. As she watched his discomfort growing to epic proportions, Annie felt a surge of adrenalin. 'Goggle eyed freak,' am I? She thought.

'Don't do that!' he shouted. Spittle flew from his lips.

'We have to, Tod. Unless you want to tell us who they are?'

'I don't know!' his voice was panicked. 'Please don't show these to my mother,' he pleaded. 'Please!'

'Charge him,' she said standing up.

Tod Harris let out a wail of anguish. 'Fucking bitch!' It was animal like. He banged his forehead on the table, but nobody paid him any attention. There wasn't much sympathy in the room.

CHAPTER 29

Annie twisted the bottle and felt the top crack open. Ideally, she would have left the Merlot to breath for an hour or so but tonight the need to drink outweighed the need to improve the taste. She poured a third of the bottle into her glass and took a long sip, closing her eyes as she swallowed. She released a deep breath and felt the stress of the last week flowing out of her. Not all of it, just enough to feel normal for a few moments. She picked up a side plate that she had prepared. There was a selection of mixed cheeses, dark chocolate, and salted biscuits. She carried the wine in one hand and the plate in the other. Annie walked into the living room and put her supper down onto a low marble coffee table. As she sat down, the leather couch felt cool on her bare legs. Her dressing gown felt loose and comfortable. The towel around her head was warm and damp and her freshly washed hair smelled of apples. The television screen was blank, and the sound of Emile Sande drifted from her CD system. 'I'll be your clown, behind the glass.'

She slipped a piece of chocolate on top of a slice of cheese and put them into her mouth, leaning back into the cushioned leather; she closed her eyes and chewed slowly. The flavours complemented one another, and she wallowed in the taste explosion. It was a rare moment of personal pleasure. A stolen minute of selfishness, a snippet of peace and quiet in a life filled with horror and grief. She sat forward and washed it down with a mouthful of wine and opened her laptop.

She logged onto the city's missing person's site and narrowed her search to males under the age of eleven. A copy of the photograph found in Harris's souvenir file sat next to her computer. She sighed as the list of the missing filled three columns on the first page, which went back only three months. The faces on the page were a mixture of family photos and custody suite images. She resisted the urge to read each profile. If she started, she would be there all night. She scrolled back in time, six months, twelve months, two years, three years. Nothing. Bland pictures, blank faces, and a few lines of information was all that remained of them. Each page was just more of the same. The faces of the lost and the missing. Some would be alive, and some would be dead. Each one had a family somewhere, however distantly related they were. Each had a different story but the one thing that they had in common was that they had disappeared. Annie knew that they couldn't all be sleeping in cardboard boxes under railway arches and there weren't enough park benches on the planet to accommodate all the missing. 'Where are they all?'

An hour later her eyes were sore, and her head ached. She had munched her way through her supper and swallowed the last drop of wine. She was tired. Emile Sande had sung her album twice and was starting again for the third time. Annie stood up and towelled her hair. Once she would have done it in front of the mirror but not anymore. Mirrors were still not in favour. All bar one in the house had been replaced with modern black and white prints. She shook her hair loose and walked into the kitchen to recharge her glass. The white tiles felt cold beneath her bare feet. She tipped another third of the bottle into the glass unsure if she could stay awake long enough to finish it. Sleep was calling her, but she wanted to give it another half an hour at least before she gave up and climbed the stairs. She took a long sip of Merlot and headed back into the living room. She paused at the CD player and invited Adele to perform for a while. The melancholy in her voice took her away from the search for a moment. 'But I set fire to the rain, watched it pour as I touched your face. Well it burned as I cried, 'cause I heard it screaming out your name, your name,' Annie sang along with the track, her feet moving slowly to the beat. Her eyes closed and her hips swaying in time. She could have stayed there all night listening to her voice but she had work to do.

Annie sighed and slumped back down onto the couch. She sipped her wine and clicked onto the next page of lost children. She wondered if she would be as good at her job if she'd had children of her own. She doubted it. How could a mother sit and look through pages of faces without thinking about her own offspring? They were all someone's sons. Sometimes she wondered if the job had made her tough or if she was born cold. How else could she do her job without breaking, drowning beneath the sea of dross that she had to swim through every day? She slurped another mouthful of Merlot and clicked to another page. She swallowed the wine with a gulp and sat up straight. The shape of the eyes was the same. The nose and mouth were identical. The boy in the picture was looking right back at her. Annie clicked on his tab and read the information. The date of his disappearance rang alarm bells in her mind. She reached for her mobile and dialled.

'Annie?' Alec answered. 'I thought I told you to get some sleep.'

'Sorry it's so late, guv,' Annie said excitedly. 'The boy in the photograph is James Goodwin, aged ten. Reported missing from a care home in Childwall the same day that Simon Barton was abducted. He was from a travelling community, in and out of the care system for years and a serial run away.'

'Any indication that his disappearance is connected to the Barton kid?'

'I'm looking at the missing persons website, guv,' she shook her head and sipped more wine. 'There are hardly any details. We need to speak to DI Haig at Halewood to see if there was any link. Barton was from a good family, decent school, nice home so I can see why his case attracted the news and Goodwin's didn't.' She sipped the wine again. 'Care home runaways are a dozen a day. The fact is, Tod Harris has his picture and his underwear in his collection, and he has never been recovered.'

'God almighty.' Alec sighed. 'We should do the world a favour and string him up from the bars in his cell.'

'By the bollocks!'

'Language, Inspector,' Alec joked.

'I'll call Haig first thing in the morning, guv.'

'Good work, Annie.'

'Thanks.'

'Get some sleep. That's an order.'

'One more glass of wine and I'll sleep.'

'Have two just to be sure.' Alec smiled. 'Goodnight, Annie.' Alec hung up. Annie looked at James Goodwin's face once more and then turned off her laptop. Enough was enough for one night. She sat back and closed her eyes, emptying the wine glass as she did so. Adele was mourning the loss of yet another boyfriend, but she was adamant that one day she would find someone just like him. 'Don't forget me, I pray,' she crooned. Annie wondered if James Goodwin had been forgotten and if he had, by whom.

CHAPTER 30

Kathy Brooks was wrapping up her autopsy. It was about as straightforward as it could be. The cause of death didn't need to be explored blindly. The lack of facial features and skull above the bottom jaw made it simple. Massive head trauma caused by a twelve-bore shotgun being placed into the mouth and discharged. That would do it every time. The internal organs had shown signs of alcohol abuse and the lungs were stained and blackened by smoking, but he would have lived for decades. The death was a clear suicide.

Still, procedures had to be followed. Weights and measurements were recorded. Incisions made, the organs removed, and weighed. Blood samples were drawn for analysis and fingerprints were taken to be crosschecked. It should have been a simple one. She had an indication of who the victim was, and the cause of death was obvious. Peter Barton was already in the system. He had done time. Checking her findings was the last part of the procedure.

****

'James Goodwin, aged ten,' Annie explained. 'He went missing from a care home in Childwall the same day that Simon Barton disappeared.'

'Simon Barton is ancient history for heaven's sake. Why are you asking me about this?' DI Haig said yawning. He took a swig of coffee and rubbed his eyes with the back of his hands. 'It's seven thirty in the morning. I'm still at home.'

'I'm sorry,' Annie said sarcastically. 'If you can tell me what time detectives clock on for work at Halewood, I'll call back when you're officially working.'

'Ouch!' Haig said embarrassed. 'No need for that kind of attitude,' he said,' he said defensively. 'I'm sorry if I seem a little groggy but it's early, I've had a very long week and you're asking me about a case from years ago.'

'Apologies if I'm intruding while you're at home.' Annie sighed. 'I'm asking you about a missing child on your patch. Do you remember him or do I need to go to my DS for permission to access your records?' There was an awkward silence. 'Obviously it would be easier for us if you can tell me what you can remember. If you can't I'll have to apply for access. You know what a pain in the arse that can be.'

'Wait a minute,' Haig flapped. There was no wriggling away from the MIT detective. She had a reputation as a ball breaker. He really did not need a historic case scrutinised by the brass. 'What was the kid's name again?'

'James Goodwin, aged ten.' Annie sighed. 'He went missing from a care home in Childwall on the same day as Simon Barton.'

'I remember now,' Haig said taking another slurp of coffee. 'He was a gypsy, wasn't he?'

'He was from a family of travellers,' Annie corrected him. 'There's nothing to say they were gypsies.'

'It amounts to the same thing,' Haig said flippantly. 'They flit about from one place to the next leaving a trail of bin bags behind them. We had a nightmare tracking down his family and when we did, no one would talk to us. They don't want to help themselves never mind the police.'

'Whatever you think of travellers shouldn't matter when one of their children goes missing should it?' Annie asked. 'He was ten years old and he was reported missing the same day as Simon Barton.' She paused. 'Surely that was significant to the investigation?'

'Not at the time,' Haig argued. 'When he actually went missing is subjective.'

'What do you mean?'

'Social Services don't always report missing kids at the exact moment they realise that they can't account for one,' she heard him slurping. He yawned loudly again. 'They tend to report them when they're absolutely certain that they can't be found. In this case, we felt that they were unsure when the boy had gone missing. He could have been missing days before they actually made his disappearance official.'

'But the date of the report is the same as Simon Barton's.'

'I'm aware of that,' Haig said irritably. 'But that doesn't necessarily mean that that was when he actually went missing.' He stressed his point. ', they could have been days apart. I wouldn't let Social Services look after my cat.'

'Are you saying that there was an issue with the details in their report?'

'There's always an issue with them,' Haig sounded frustrated. 'Look, he was a runaway. Social Services had a file on him as long as my arm. He would frequently runaway and each time he did, they found him back with the travellers. They would remove him back into care and he would run away again. The kid was like a ping-pong ball bouncing all over the place.'

'Why did they keep taking him into care?'

'The father was in jail and the mother was an alcoholic. She beat him and her other six kids black and blue. The siblings were in care all over the country.'

'Did his name crop up relating to the Barton investigation?' Annie pressed him.

'No, there was no reason to connect them. We dismissed it as soon as we had his file.'

'Was there any connection between them at all no matter how tenuous?' Annie felt that he was holding something back.

'Tenuous!' he scoffed. 'I don't know why you're fishing for something that isn't there.' He sighed. 'If I remember rightly, I think that they played in the same leisure centre football club, but Goodwin was just there to keep him off the streets. He never made any of the teams and he only turned up for practice sessions for a few weeks.'

'And that didn't strike you as a possible connection?'

'No,' Haig insisted. 'That centre has hundreds of members from five-year olds up to the senior teams.' She could hear anger creeping into his tone. 'It is a big sports social club with tennis, badminton, a swimming pool, basketball, you name it and they play it there.' He sounded exasperated. 'Football is just one of the sports they teach and there is a team for each year group. The seniors had a spell in the Conference League for a while. It's a coincidence that they were in the same club. They may never have met.'

'But on the flip side, they could have,' Annie countered. 'Please answer me honestly now,' she said flatly. 'Did you investigate any link into their disappearances at the time?'

'I know how to investigate, Inspector,' Haig snapped. 'And can I remind you that we're the same rank.' He took a deep breath. 'Look, I don't want to fall out with you here, but they lived in different worlds. We explored every possibility to find Simon Barton and there was no tangible connection to the Godwin boy.'

'Goodwin,' Annie corrected him annoyed.

'What?'

'His surname was Goodwin.'

'Whatever.' He sighed. 'I really need to get to the station so are we done here?'

'No, we're bloody well not done here, Inspector!' Annie said sternly. 'Listen to me and listen hard.' She paused. 'If anyone looked at this as a cold case, they would discover that they played in the same football club, went missing on the same day and neither of them ever turned up, coincidence?' Annie said calmly. 'I would say that that's slightly more than a coincidence and your investigation looks flawed.'

'I disagree.'

Annie took a moment to allow her anger to settle. 'Did you ever follow up with Social Services to see if he ever found his way back to the travellers?'

'I don't see that as our remit.' Haig yawned. 'We're detectives not social workers.'

'So, we don't know if this kid is alive or not.'

'We handed his file back to Social Services. His and a lot of others,' Haig said impatiently. 'You're chasing a ghost. How the hell can we keep tabs on every runaway?'

'Because that's our job.' Annie sighed. 'A couple of phone calls could have sufficed.'

'I had other priorities. Our investigation was thorough and conclusive.'

'Other priorities, really?' Annie sighed.

'Look, Inspector,' he snapped. 'The Barton case was dissected by the review team, both before and after the appeal.'

'Maybe it was but did you make it clear that James Goodwin disappeared on the same day?'

'No, as I explained, I didn't know for certain that he did!'

'In that case, I'll make it my priority to find out.' She paused, 'I'll need everything that you have on the Simon Barton case and I want it at MIT before noon today.'

'You have no authority to insist on such a thing,' Haig replied sourly.

'I'm the lead detective on the Major Investigation Team, which pretty much means that I can ask for whatever I want if it's connected to one of my cases,' Annie said calmly. 'If you really want me to go over your head for this, I'm quite prepared to do that.'

'Are you kidding me?' Haig said aghast. He was annoyed but he knew that she was right. The brass would back her to the hilt. They may have been the same rank, but she was his senior when push came to shove. She was earmarked for the upper echelon of the force while he worked in the outback. There was only one winner. He bit his tongue and sighed. 'Do you have any idea how much information that is? That could take me days.'

'Lunchtime today, DI Haig or Detective Superintendent Ramsay will be crawling up your arse with a big torch. He is overseeing this case with a microscope and we'll see if he thinks your investigation was thorough and conclusive, shall we?'

'I'm happy with the way we handled the investigation.' Haig sounded anything but happy.

'Good. Then you won't have any problem sending the files over, will you?'

'No.'

'You can start by sending everything related to James Goodwin first,' Annie said. 'Any problem with that?'

'None at all. It will be there this morning.' Haig hung up.

****

'We'll find you, kiddo, one way or the other.' Annie looked at the picture of James Goodwin and then closed the file. She dialled Alec.

'Annie,' Alec answered. 'Any joy on tracing this Rob Derry?'

'Nothing, guv. We're using names that can be shortened to Rob. There are over sixty people on the electoral roll with that name.' Annie sighed. 'It's a work in progress but so far we can't find anyone that fits the bill. I think it's an alias, guv.'

'He's hardly likely to use his real name, is he?'

'Tod Harris does.'

'Fair enough.' Alec smiled, 'although he isn't the sharpest tool in the box, is he?'

'No,' Annie had to agree, 'I've just spoken to the DI at Halewood.'

'What did you find out?'

'That DI 'vague' lives up to his title,' Annie said sarcastically. 'The boys were members of the same leisure centre football club although Haig insisted that Goodwin only attended practice sessions for a few weeks and there was no connection found between their disappearances.'

'And you disagree with him?'

'I can't look past the obvious, guv.' Annie shrugged and thought about her words. 'I don't think the idea that they could have been connected was explored properly.' She explained. 'There was a solid connection between Peter Barton and our victims,' she began. 'We have established that as a fact. Now our main suspect is found in possession of a photograph and underwear belonging to a young boy that went missing on the same day as Simon Barton did. The boy that Peter Barton was convicted of abducting. Can that be a coincidence?' Annie paused. She waited for Alec to comment but he didn't. She knew that he wanted to hear what she thought before he would give his opinion. 'If Tod Harris took those boys, then he has a motive to remove Barton's alibi. Barton took the fall for it. Okay, he was released on appeal, but the case remains closed, which says it all to me. He's still guilty in the eyes of the law and in everybody else's opinion too, he's a child killer that got away.'

'Hence he shot himself?'

'Imagine yourself in his shoes, innocent of child murder but no one believes you.'

'Difficult.'

'Difficult is an understatement,' Annie said thoughtfully. 'Wrongly accused and then your alibis are murdered. It may have sent him over the edge.'

'What about the money, Annie?' Alec played devil's advocate.

'That I'm not sure about. Maybe it was a gift.'

'A hundred thousand pound thank you for the alibi?'

'Maybe.'

'Where are we on proving this one way or the other?'

'DI Vague is sending over the case files for the Barton and Goodwin investigations. I really need the DNA on the second pair of underpants to come back as a match to Simon Barton then we're in business.'

'That would help matters considerably.'

'Kathy said we'd have results later today.'

'Good,' Alec said. 'Let me know when you have them.'

'Will do.' Annie hung up. A knock on her door made her look up. 'Come in.' Google poked his head around the door. 'Morning,' Annie smiled. 'Please give me some good news.'

'I have news,' Google waved a handful of papers, 'I'll let you decide if it's good or not. Have you got ten minutes?'

'Of course, come in,' Annie gestured to the chair. 'What have you got?'

Google put two photographs onto Annie's desk. One was Jackie Webb's body from the front, the second her back. The carvings in her skin had turned black and scabbed. Annie looked at them and shuddered. She thought about a tattoo that she'd had done a few years before. A blue rose on her shoulder blade. The outline had hurt her to the point of tears. She could only imagine how much Jackie must have suffered as the killer carved the text into her skin. 'We're done translating, guv,' he said taking a seat. 'I have to be honest, some of this still has me baffled and I struggled with this bit for a while,' he said smiling. He waved his finger at the photos, 'especially the numbers and sequences. But once we translated all the text, we matched it up with the numbers and suddenly some of it makes sense.'

'Okay, what does it mean?' Annie asked frowning.

'Our killer is quite the criminal historian, guv,' Google said excitedly. 'See here, 71-73-3.'

'Yes.'

'On its own it meant nothing to me but then we translated the text below and it reads, Rochester, New York, and below that, the Alphabet Killer.'

'Go on,' Annie prompted him.

'The Alphabet Killer murders happened between 1971 and 1973 and there were three victims, 71-73-3. No one was ever convicted of the murders.'

'Why carve that into Jackie Webb?'

'That's just the start,' Google held up his hand. 'See here, 76-77-4, the Oakland Child Killer, Michigan.' He looked at Annie to see if she was following him. 'Four children were murdered between 1976 and 1977, again unsolved. He carves the date of their activity and the number of victims.'

'Okay.' Annie nodded thoughtfully. 'But what is the point?'

'I can have a guess,' Google said removing his glasses. 'See here, five victims in Nevada were officially accredited to the Zodiac Killer between 1960 and the early 70s but our killer carved 60-72-37, next to his name. He replaced 5 with 37.' He put his glasses back on and pointed to the photo. 'I considered this and although police records show five victims, some experts put his body count much higher, some as high as thirty-seven.' He pointed to the number. 'The dates and the number of victims, again all unsolved.'

'Okay.' Annie looked intrigued. She could see the pattern but not the message. 'I'm keeping up so far, but I don't know where we're going with this.'

'Bear with me, 88-89-9, the New Bedford Highway killer, Massachusetts. The dates and the number of victims again.' He shrugged. '86-91-10, the Hwaseong serial murders in South Korea,' he carried on, '85-87-13, The Stoneman murders, Calcutta, India.' He looked at her and pushed his glasses to the bridge of his nose. 'Each time the killer has carved the dates and number of victims of unsolved serial murders from across the world. The key point is that they were all unsolved.'

'Am I missing the point here?'

'The odd one out is this one,' Google raised his finger again. 'It is much different to the others, 05-OG-22 td.'

'That is different.' Annie commented on the letters where the date should have been. 'Twenty-two victims?'

'Twenty-two, td,' Google emphasised.

'Where does he say that these murders were?'

'This was written below 'the Butcher of Crosby Beach'.' He sat back and shook his head. 'He was building up to this. I think the letters O and G mean, ongoing,' he explained.

'And TD?'

'To date.'

'Twenty-two victims?' Annie stood up and walked to the window. 'That's many more than we thought although we guessed that there would be more. Brendon Ryder had been at it for years.' Peter Barton's home was full of newspaper reports from all over the world and they found several books about serial killers. He had also followed the Crosby Beach murders closely. The analysis of Tod Harris's laptop searches had showed that he frequently searched online for images of murder victims, autopsies, and worse. 'This is very good work, Google,' Annie said looking out across the river. The sun was rising but it radiated little warmth. 'Tod Harris is a dangerous schizophrenic, I'm convinced that he is completely unhinged from reality,' Annie said thoughtfully. 'What do you think he's trying to say?'

'I think that he's taunting us with unsolved serial killers and telling us that he thinks the Butcher is still at large and that there are far more victims than we thought.' He frowned and checked his sheet. 'Twenty-two 'to date' in fact, which implies that there'll be more to come.' He shrugged. 'I think he's trying to claim that he is either responsible for the Butcher's victims or that he knows who is and that he intends to keep on killing.' He coughed into his fist. 'Again, that's just my opinion of course.'

'That would explain some of it.' Annie nodded and frowned. 'Why imply that he is the Butcher when there can be no credibility applied to it?' Annie turned and leaned against the glass. 'It isn't like we didn't catch the killer.' She shrugged. 'Brendon Ryder is dust.'

'In my opinion,' Google rubbed his chin and lowered his voice. 'He's a raving lunatic. We shouldn't try to find sense and logic in a damaged mind.'

'Maybe.' Annie smiled.

'For some serial killers that I've read about, it's all about becoming notorious.' Google sat back. 'But the most dangerous killers in my opinion, have no desire to be caught. They are totally focused on remaining at liberty to continue their lives as normally as possible so that they can kill when the urge takes them. I don't think that we know half of what the most intelligent killers have done purely and simply because they're clever,' he paused. 'If they change their victim's profiles, their hunting zones, and their MO, we'd never connect their victims especially in places like the US, Russia, and Asia.'

'And that's if they choose to leave the bodies for us to find,' Annie agreed. 'But Tod Harris.' She paused and shook her head, 'part of him wanted to create a sterile crime scene but the other side wanted us to connect the dots and work it out.'

'I think that he simply unravelled, guv.' Google pointed to the photographs. 'As you said, he was unhinged anyway but something switched off in his mind and he lost control. Hence leaving the scenes compromised. Reading all this script, I genuinely think he has tipped over the edge.'

'I agree,' Annie said. 'Good work, Google.' She smiled. 'I want you to share these pictures with Interpol. Let's see if there are any similar cases out there.'

'Will do, guv.' Google smiled and stood up. He picked up the photographs and then stopped in the doorway. 'There are more number sequences, guv but we're still working on them,' he paused. 'Do you mind if I get some of the team to start working on the books and computers taken from Harris's home, guv?'

'No.' She frowned. 'Do you think that he's kept the reference material for the script?'

He nodded and smiled wryly.

'Carry on with it,' she said with a grin. She sat back in her chair and closed her eyes. They had Tod Harris, hook, line, and sinker. That was a definite but there were too many unanswered questions left to put the case in the hands of the Crown Prosecution Service yet. She had to investigate Harris's claims that a man called Rob Derry existed and she had to look at the abductions of Simon Barton and James Goodwin. Her thoughts were disturbed by the phone ringing. 'DI Jones,' she answered.

'Annie,' the familiar voice of Kathy Brooks said. 'We've got a problem with the Peter Barton autopsy.'

'What kind of problem?' Annie asked confused.

'The worst kind,' Kathy replied flatly. 'The body in my lab is not Peter Barton and I don't believe it was a suicide.'

Emilia Harris sat on her son's bed and touched the duvet with the fingers of her right hand. Her mind went back to a time when she would sit on the edge of his bed and watch her little boy sleeping. She would stroke his hair and listen to his breathing and wonder what life had in store for him. Would he be a lawyer or a doctor? He was intelligent enough for sure. There was a sparkle in his eyes that captivated people and his smile was angelic. He had all the gifts that a child could need. What went wrong? Another tear leaked from her reddened eyes onto the moist scrunched up tissue that she held tightly in her hand. She had changed the sheets just in case Tod came home although she knew deep down that he wouldn't. Not this time. She'd felt angry at first, not with Tod, with the police. They were picking on him because of the other girls. Young girls nowadays asked for it, going out half-dressed and falling over drunk. Was it any surprise that young men got the wrong signals? Tod had misread the moment. Well, he had unfortunately misread several moments. He'd made mistakes, sure, but he couldn't have done what they were accusing him off. Murder? Rape? Since the police arrested him, she had been on an emotional elevator ride that only went down. She had been bouncing from one emotion to another and just when she thought that she couldn't go any lower, the elevator went down to another level, and another, and another. She hadn't stopped crying for days. She felt that nothing else could hurt her more than this. The police were so cold and callous. They had trawled through every inch of the house and garden as if she didn't live there. It was as if she was invisible. Men and women in white paper suits walked past her as if she didn't exist. When they did look at her, their eyes were full of disapproval and accusations. She'd been confined to her living room for most of the day. When she had asked a question, they'd spoken to her as if she was a nuisance. A nuisance in her own home. Her son was being accused of some terrible crimes.

Rape?

Murder?

Little boys?

When they'd shown her the picture of the young boy, she couldn't understand what they were saying. Was the boy a relation or a neighbour's child? And then they asked her if she recognised some underwear. Once she realised the implications, her stomach turned. She had not been able to answer their questions after that. Her head felt like it was filled with cotton wool. She had felt numb inside. They were convinced that Tod was a rapist, a murderer. That was bad enough but little boys? She could never live that down as long as she lived. She had given birth to a monster. That innocent little boy had grown up to be evil. She wondered if she should have seen it in him, could she have stopped it somehow. Her little boy that she cherished so much had gone and that's what hurt so much. The child was gone, replaced by a sickening monster. Her flesh and blood.

Emilia sobbed and lay down, her head on her son's pillow. The smell of him was still there beneath the freshness of the fabric conditioner. She closed her eyes and pulled her knees to her chest as her tears trickled down her cheeks onto the cotton. For the first time since her husband, Ben had died, she was glad that he was dead. If he had been alive the shock would have killed him anyway. The shock and the shame of it all. The neighbours were avoiding her already, pretending that they hadn't seen her. One of them had crossed the road when she saw her coming. What would it be like after a trial? Especially when it came out about the boys. It would be a hundred times worse, a thousand times worse, maybe even a million times worse. She didn't think that she would be strong enough to cope with it all. Was any mother strong enough to sit in a courtroom and listen to the details of what their own flesh and blood had done with their hands? Hands that were once so tiny, sticky hands that helped him to crawl and then pull himself up when he began to walk. Hands that were covered in paint and glue and jelly and blancmange. Hands that were once tender and loving. The same hands that he had used to butcher other human beings, women, children. She felt as if her heart was being ripped out of her chest and crushed by the hands of an invisible giant. She closed her eyes tightly and her chest heaved as she tried to breathe through the tears. She felt like she wanted to die.

The doorbell rang and was followed immediately by a loud knock. Emilia sat upright and wiped her eyes. She straightened her blouse and blew her nose before walking out of the room closing the door behind her. The caller knocked again, louder this time. 'Coming!' she shouted. She could see the shadow of the person at the door. They rang the doorbell again. 'I'm coming!' she shouted. 'I haven't got a jetpack strapped to my backside,' she muttered beneath her breath. From the stairs, she could see that the silhouette behind the door belonged to a male. She reached the door and checked her appearance in the mirror on the wall. Her eyes were puffy, and it was obvious that she'd been crying. She took a deep breath and slid the chain into the lock before twisting the handle and opening it.

'Mrs Harris?' the man asked. His thick curly hair and stubble were greying.

'Yes.'

'Police, Mrs Harris,' the man said. He flashed his identity card. 'I've got a few questions that I need to ask you.'

'More questions?' Emilia mumbled. She took the chain from the lock and opened the door fully. 'How can there be more questions? It's Tod you need to be asking not me. I'm sick of the whole thing.'

'I won't keep you long, Mrs Harris,' he said smiling. He tucked his hands into the pockets of his long raincoat. 'It is very important.'

'You'd better come in then,' she said stepping back to allow him in. 'You look like Columbo in that coat,' she said without thinking. 'Might be a bit before your time but he wore a raincoat like that.' She smiled nervously. 'Do you remember him?'

'Yes, I do.' He nodded but didn't return her smile. 'This is very important.'

'Come into the living room. Sit down. Do you want a cup of tea?' she gestured to the settee.

'No. I'm fine thanks.' He smiled thinly and sat down. 'There are some very difficult questions that I need to ask you about Tod, Mrs Harris,' he gestured for her to sit in the chair. She straightened her floral-patterned skirt and sat down opposite him. She eyed a packet of cigarettes on her coffee table but resisted the urge to light one. Her twenty a day habit had ballooned into a forty a day habit. He sensed her discomfort. 'Smoke if you like. I don't mind.' He smiled thinly. Emilia shrugged and reached for the packet. She lit one up and inhaled deeply. 'Did Tod ever mention a friend of his to you, a man by the name of Rob Derry?'

'Rob Derry?' she inhaled again. Her eyes narrowed in thought. 'I don't think so. He never talked to me about his friends.' She sighed and took another drag, 'in fact, he never really talked to me at all except when he needed something.'

'You're sure about that?'

'Yes.'

'Did he tell you that he was going out at weekends and drugging women so that he could rape them?'

'Of course not,' she inhaled and scowled. 'What do you think I am?'

'You tell me,' he said quietly.

'If I had known,' she shook her head but didn't finish her sentence.

'What?'

'I'm sorry,' Emilia stuttered.

'If you had known what he was doing, you would have done what?'

'I don't know,' she said in a whisper. 'I don't know what I would have done.'

'Did he ever bring women back here?' he asked. 'You know, girlfriends.'

'No.'

'Never'

'No.'

'What about when he was a younger man?'

'No, never.' Her eyes glazed over as she thought back. Why had he never brought his girlfriends home?

'What about young boys?'

'What?'

'Did he ever bring young boys back here?' He shrugged. 'Maybe to play on his computer games in the shed?'

'I know what you're implying,' she said angrily. 'Don't be disgusting.' Emilia shook her head. Her hands were shaking as she stubbed out her cigarette and lit another one immediately.

'You have a very tidy house, Mrs Harris,' he sat forward and steepled his hands beneath his chin. 'Did you ever look through his personal stuff?'

'No,' she said quietly. Her face changed colour.

'Never.' He smiled. 'I can't believe that you were never tempted to take a little peek in his drawers, maybe?' She didn't answer but her face reddened. 'Did you look at his laptop to see what he'd been watching?'

'I did no such thing!' she snapped.

'Oh, come on.' He sighed. 'You knew that he was a little pervert and yet you didn't ever look through his things?' He shrugged. 'I don't believe you.'

'How dare you,' she said in a whisper.

'How dare I what?' he snapped. His eyes were wide, angry, and accusing. 'Tod is a disgusting human being and you knew it, didn't you?' a tear trickled from her eye. She feared him. 'Didn't you?' he whispered. 'He'd been charged before. You knew what he was.'

'I wasn't sure,' she cried. 'I didn't want to believe it.' She blew her nose again. 'You don't when it's your own. He was such a gentle child.'

'I know this will be very painful for you, Mrs Harris,' he said calmly. 'Now, answer me honestly this time,' he lifted one hand to calm her. 'Did you ever go through his things?'

'Yes.' She nodded and sniffled. 'I wanted to know if he was misbehaving, that's all.'

'What did you find?'

'Nothing,' she shook her head. 'He kept his private things in the shed or the garage. There was never anything in his room. He hid his things from me.'

'Okay,' he paused for a second, 'I'll ask you again. Did he ever mention, Rob Derry?'

'No.'

'You're sure?' The policeman took a small hatchet from his raincoat and placed it on the table between them. Emilia's eyes focused on the weapon. 'What is that?' she asked confused, her voice a little shaky.

'It's an axe, Mrs Harris,' he said placing a roll of duct tape next to it. 'This is very strong tape.' He stood up and walked to the window. He closed the curtains with one sweep and turned to face her. 'And these are pliers.'

As he approached her, Emilia wanted to scream. She opened her mouth but only cigarette smoke came out.

CHAPTER 32

Alec stood next to Annie and waited for Kathy to finish washing her hands. He felt like a naughty schoolboy waiting for the headmaster to acknowledge his presence outside his study. The anticipation was worse than the actual event. He shifted his weight from one foot to the other and checked the time. Kathy finished washing her hands and dried them before snapping on a pair of surgical gloves.

'Right, where do I start?' Kathy said without any pleasantries. She stood to the right of a stainless-steel post-mortem slab and removed the sheet that was covering the body beneath it. She positioned a light above so that they could see the body in more detail. 'The fingerprints taken from him do not belong to Peter Barton.' She looked at Annie, 'and the blood type doesn't match either. My initial thoughts were suicide for obvious reasons,' she explained pointing to the bloody remains of the head. 'But I noticed ligature marks on the wrists here,' she pointed to deep red welts in the skin, 'he'd been restrained for a period, I can't be sure how long for but there is some atrophy of the muscles and dehydration of the skin. Days rather than weeks at a guess.' She put her hands on her hips and tilted her head. 'There is no gunshot residue on his hands,' she raised her eyebrows as she spoke. 'I think that the gun was forced into his mouth and discharged while his hands were tied behind him. Then he was untied and positioned to look like he had taken his own life.' She shrugged. 'Your detectives had no way of knowing this until the post-mortem was performed.'

'Bloody hell.' Annie sighed. 'We need to go back to his house with fresh eyes.'

'They had to break into the basement after they heard the gunshot?' Alec frowned. 'That's right, isn't it?'

'Yes.' Annie nodded. 'There must be another way out of that cellar.'

'Do we know who this is?' Alec turned back to Kathy.

'We're running his prints and DNA through the system.' Kathy said picking up a sheet of paper. 'On the plus side, the epithelial cells from the underwear you gave me,' she raised her eyebrows. 'Belong to Simon Barton.' She handed the sheet to Annie. 'We got the match through from the lab a few minutes ago.'

Annie and Alec exchanged glances. 'The bastard took those boys, guv.' She shook her head. 'Tod Harris must be connected to Simon Barton. There's no other explanation. I'll take a team back to Barton's house this morning.'

'Make sure that Jim Stirling is with you,' Alec suggested. 'He was the first officer at the scene after all. I'll put an APB out on Barton, but he could be anywhere by now. Do you think that Peter Barton is also Rob Derry?'

'Harris denied that when we showed him his picture. I don't know what to think,' Annie said pointing to the faceless corpse. 'This could be Rob Derry for all we know.'

'Kathy,' Alec said. 'I don't care how much it costs; I want these results rushed through.'

'I'll call as soon as I have something.' She nodded and walked to her desk. 'I have three different forensic companies drafted in on this. We should have something later today.'

CHAPTER 33

Google and his team of three detectives were almost hidden by the stacks of books and piles of papers that they'd accumulated during their research. Translating the script was slow and painstaking but it was doable. The sequences of numbers were virtually impossible to analyse. They were blindly running searches to try to identify them. The possibilities were infinite, and it was a painfully slow process of elimination. Detective Constable Gwen Evans was working on two specific sequences that she had translated from Jackie Webb's left thigh. 'I think that we could have something here,' Gwen said as she typed on her laptop. 'One digit followed by three letters and then three more digits.' She looked over her screen as she spoke. Goggle frowned and ruffled his hair. 'These two sequences match the format of Californian vehicle registration plates.'

He hammered commands into his keyboard. 'You're right, they do,' Google said checking it online. 'I want you to check number and letter formats for every state in the USA,' he said to the others, 'in fact, check Europe too.'

'What are the sequences that you have there, Gwen?'

'6DZG271 and 6RVG290,' Gwen answered.

'San Francisco area plates,' Google said. 'You're spot on.' He took his glasses off and sat back to clean them with his tie. 'I think that you should make a few calls, Gwen,' he said pushing them back onto his nose. His eyes looked magnified and he blinked rapidly. 'See if we can't work with the San Francisco PD to identify whether these are actually registration plates in use and if they are, can we work out their significance to us.'

****

Annie and Stirling ducked underneath the yellow crime scene tape and walked up the path towards the Barton residence. The sun was a yellow glow behind thick white clouds that were tinged grey at the edges. A sharp breeze blew all the warmth away and made the tape flap about wildly. 'Okay, what did we miss first time around?' Annie said as they climbed the step to the front door. The frame was still splintered. 'You knocked on the door and then forced entry.'

'Right, units entered front and rear and his heat signature disappeared beneath the staircase, which meant that he must have headed downstairs into the cellar. We heard the gunshot and we turned the power back on. Then we found the hatch.'

They walked down the hallway to the staircase. The cupboard door was open, and the hatch cover had been removed. 'You forced the hatch and climbed down the stairs,' Annie said stepping inside. She headed down the creaky wooden stairs and then paused at the bottom. The cellar was oblong in shape and looked bigger now that the maps and press cuttings had been removed from the walls. Stirling stood behind her and looked around. 'The body was in the middle of the room,' Annie said stepping to the middle. 'He couldn't go up, which means that he either went down or he went through the walls.'

Stirling walked around the room and knocked on the walls. 'Nothing but bricks,' he muttered. He desperately wanted to find an answer. Although nobody had pointed the finger of blame at him, he felt professional guilt. Discovering that they'd been duped in a manner seldom encountered by many detectives was painfully embarrassing despite the unusual circumstances. 'These walls are solid.'

'Then we look at the floor,' Annie said. The floor covering gave the impression that it was tiled. 'You start at that side and I'll work this side. We'll meet at the other end. This is linoleum over levelled concrete, right?'

'Yes,' Stirling agreed. 'It's screed. Usually just a thin layer of concrete laid wet to get a flat surface beneath laminate or tiles or this stuff. It looks like tiles but its warmer and a tenth of the cost to lay.'

Annie scanned the edges of the floor where they met the walls.

Nothing.

The symmetrical pattern made her eyes wander. It was difficult to focus on it. She skirted the staircase and bent low to check the area where it joined the cellar floor. It was dirty and covered in dust but there was nothing unusual. 'Unless Barton was a magician, there has to be another way out of here.'

Stirling had reached the far end and he picked up the desk that was pressed against the wall. He dumped it down near the opposite wall. He rapped at the bricks where it had stood.

Solid.

Annie followed the skirting board line and met him where the desk had been. She squatted and ran her fingers across the linoleum. 'Look here,' she said pointing to four small holes where the desk had been. The edges of the holes were raised slightly. 'Are they screw holes?'

Stirling knelt and ran his hand across the floor. 'There's more screw holes here?' He stood up and picked up the desk again, putting it back where he had moved it from. The legs were made from box metal with stabilising bars between them and they covered the screw holes completely. They looked at each other and Stirling flipped the desk upside down. The stabilising bars had been drilled. 'These holes line up with the holes in the floor.' He frowned. 'So, the desk was screwed to the floor?'

'Yes, but from underneath.' Annie pointed to the legs. 'The screw holes are only underneath these bars. Put it back where it was,' she said deep in thought. Stirling flipped it over and put it back where he'd found it. He slid it to line up with the holes in the floor. 'There,' she said. 'Now if there were screws attached from underneath, we'd be able to lift the desk and pull up the floor,' she shook her head. 'Then if you climbed down and removed the screws from below, if someone moved the desk they wouldn't realise.'

'The linoleum would remain in place.' Stirling nodded. 'He could have stayed down there until he was sure that we were gone and then resurfaced and left at his leisure. I'll get this floor lifted.'

****

'I've spoken to a sergeant at the San Francisco Metro Division's traffic unit.' Gwen rolled her eyes skywards. 'I had to repeat everything that I said at least four times. Can you believe that they can't understand what we're saying?' she shook her head. 'We invented the bloody language… they misspell everything at every opportunity and then they wonder why they can't understand what we're saying!'

Google smiled and shook his head. 'But you're Welsh, Gwen,' he pointed out. 'I can't always understand what you're saying and as for spelling, your lot can't talk!'

'Charming.' She shrugged.

'What did you find out?'

'Ah, now that's the interesting thing,' she raised her index finger. 'Both plates do in fact exist and they belong to what he called, an RV rental company,'

'Recreational Vehicles.' Google nodded wisely and looked around the team.

Gwen raised her eyebrows. 'I think everyone knows what RV stands for.' He blushed a little. 'When I told him why we we're investigating these plates, he said that he would contact them today and ask some questions and that he would also contact their Investigations Department and ask one of their Captains to call and talk to us. He said that he would get back to me later today.'

****

With the linoleum cut away, they could see an access hatch. The lid had been set into a metal frame where it was flush with the concrete. 'You're safe to lift it,' the Bomb Squad officer said chirpily. 'Give me a minute; you can see what is below.' He mumbled to himself as he inserted tungsten hooks into the screw holes and lifted the lid. He shone a torch into the void. 'A proper little hideaway.'

Annie and Stirling looked inside. There was a cot bed covered with a sleeping bag, a torch, and a large water bottle. 'He lifted the desk and the linoleum and hatch were lifted with it,' Annie said. 'Then he pulls the hatch down and the weight of the desk pushes everything back into place.'

'Then he unscrews the desk from underneath and if we had moved it, there would have been nothing obvious to make us think there was another way out.' Stirling felt better about the situation now that they had an explanation. 'Not that we were looking for anyone else.'

'So, who did he shoot?' Annie sighed.

'Someone that he was holding captive.' Stirling shrugged. 'But who was he and why did he shoot him?'

****

'I'm looking to speak to Detective Evans?' Gwen heard an American accent when she answered her phone. Her pulse quickened.

'Speaking.' She smiled at the sound of the voice. 'Who am I speaking to?'

'This is Sergeant Kowalski from the Metro Investigations Division,' he introduced himself. 'My captain asked me to give you a call regarding a couple of vehicle plates that you're looking at.' Gwen smiled at his pronunciation of vehicle, 'vi-hi-cal'. 'We had it handed to us from traffic.'

'Firstly, thanks very much for taking the time to call me back,' Gwen said. 'What time is it there?'

'What?'

'The time,' Gwen repeated. 'How far behind us are you?'

'Er, I'm not sure,' Kowalski said confused. 'It's five after ten here.'

'Eight hours,' Gwen commented. 'Tell me did the traffic department explain what it was all about?'

'They did but I don't understand it all,' Kowalski replied. 'All I was told was that you guys are working a double murder and there could be more victims, so we thought it was worth a look.' He paused. 'I thought it was going to be a bug hunt but we're glad that you contacted us.'

'You are?' Gwen couldn't help but sound surprised.

'Sure. We traced those plates to a company that works out of the bay area; they rent out trucks and RV's. It's kinda quiet here now in the winter so both vehicles were in their pound.' He paused as if he was checking something. Gwen could hear papers being rustled. 'The owner is a very helpful lady and she let us take a look inside both vehicles. Now we didn't know what we were looking for, so we took CSI with us and one of our crime scene guys sprayed a little Luminol around and guess what?'

'What?' Gwen said hanging on every word.

'The place lit up like Epcot on the fourth!'

'Blood trace?'

'Yep, lots of it,' he said. 'We have both vehicles being pulled in as we speak. Our CSI will take them to pieces.'

'That's great,' Gwen commented. 'And you'll keep us in the loop with any results?'

'Of course.'

'Thanks very much for the help.'

'No problem but now you can help us a little,' Kowalski lowered his voice. 'My captain wants to know where all this blood came from.'

****

As they walked back to the car, Annie checked her phone for messages. Nothing. They seemed to be constantly waiting for forensic results before they could slot the next piece into place. Each time that they did, they didn't appear to move any closer to the conclusion. Each piece to the puzzle raised more questions than answers. 'What are you thinking, guv?' Stirling asked blowing into his spade-like hands.

'I'm thinking that I should be winding this investigation down but instead we're still chasing shadows.' She shook her head. 'Tod Harris butchered two women and we've locked him up for it.' She shrugged her shoulders. 'So why do I feel so crappy about it?'

'If it had been Barton that had blown his brains out like we thought at first, we'd be laughing,' Stirling said opening the car with the remote. 'Do you think Barton is Tod Harris's accomplice?'

'I don't know.' Annie shook her head. 'Are we sure that he had an accomplice?'

'There's no forensic evidence to say that he did but,' Stirling didn't finish the sentence.

'There's a connection between Barton and the victims so it goes without saying that there's a connection between him and Harris.'

'Barton was the number one suspect for Simon Barton's abduction and now we know that Harris had the boy's underwear in his trophy collection. Coincidence?'

'I can't swallow coincidences,' Annie grumbled. She opened the passenger door and climbed in. 'If he did take the kid then they're working together. If Barton didn't take the kid and was innocent, then why blow a man's brains out in his cellar?'

'Peter Barton is a very clever man who has used every grain of his police training to throw us off the scent. Sorry, guv, I need to get this.' Stirling looked at his phone. 'DS Stirling.'

'Sergeant,' a familiar voice said. 'This is Coco from Flatfoot Sam's.'

'Hello,' Stirling frowned and climbed into the driver's seat and put the call on speaker. 'How can I help?'

'I was chatting to some of my men last night about your investigation,' he paused. Stirling remained silent and looked at Annie. 'You know that we couldn't find any camera record of Jackie Webb leaving the club.'

'Yes.'

'Well, one of my men remembers a woman being outside of the fire exit next to the Ladies toilets.'

'Go on.'

'Obviously, when he saw that the exit was opened, he went to investigate,' Coco explained. 'He said that there was a woman outside, and she was drunk as a skunk, falling all over the place.'

'Jackie Webb?'

'He said she was a blond.'

'Okay, then what?'

'He remembers that there was a guy holding her up and when he challenged him, he showed him a badge,' he paused. 'A detective's badge. He said that he would make sure that she got home safely so he closed the door and never thought about it again.'

'There's no cameras on that exit?'

'It covers the entrance to the toilets but there's a support column blocking the view of the exit.'

'Is it alarmed?'

'As soon as he told me, we checked the door. The sensor had been cut and bypassed. We didn't even notice until now.'

'Did he give you a description of the man?'

'Thirty to fifty, wearing a hat. About six feet tall. That's all he could remember. Like I said, once he saw the badge, he didn't give it a second thought.'

'Doesn't sound like Tod Harris,' Stirling offered.

'I thought that too,' Coco agreed. 'I showed him a picture online, but he couldn't be sure.'

Annie made a hand gesture as if she was holding a pen. 'We'll need him to sit down with one of our sketch artists. When is he working again?'

'He'll be in tonight at about nine.'

'Thanks for calling,' Stirling said. 'I owe you one.'

'No problem. You're welcome.'

The call ended and Stirling sat back and raised his eyebrows in surprise. 'Rob Derry?'

'I'm not convinced.' Annie sighed. She let out a deep breath and looked out of the window. 'So, Tod Harris might be telling the truth about an accomplice.'

'To a degree,' Stirling agreed. 'The evidence still says that he raped and killed them. It makes no difference if there was someone else involved, he's bang to rights.'

'Agreed.' Annie nodded. 'The existence of an accomplice may throw some seed of doubt to a jury, but the forensic evidence would overwhelm that.'

'But regardless, now we know that we're looking for another killer,' Stirling said starting the engine. 'Peter Barton.'

'And he's out there with a head start. What is he trying to achieve?' Annie felt her phone vibrate before the ringtone kicked in. 'DI Jones,' she answered. The number calling was from a switchboard.

'It's Becky, guv,' her DC sounded stressed.

'Becky, what's up?'

'We've just had a call from uniform at Halewood,' she babbled. 'Emilia Harris was found hanging from her stairs.'

'When did this happen?'

'Twenty minutes ago, guv. Her sister called around to see her and noticed that all the curtains were closed. When she couldn't get an answer, she called 999. The responding officers said that there's a note in a sealed envelope addressed to you.'

'We're at the Barton property,' Annie said holding two fingers to her forehead. She rubbed at her temples to sooth the dull ache that was developing. 'We're not far away, ten minutes at the most. Thanks, Becky.'

'Guv.'

Stirling looked at her and waited for her to compose herself. She took a deep breath before she spoke. 'Emilia Harris has strung herself up from the banister.' Annie sighed. 'We'll have to notify Harris via his brief. I'm not sure that a warped bastard like Tod Harris will give a monkey's!'

'I wouldn't put a rope around my neck for him even if he was my son,' Stirling said, anger in his voice. 'Poor woman. It must have been too much for her.'

'She's left a note.' Stirling looked at her and waited for more. 'Apparently, it's addressed to me.'

They drove through the suburban streets in silence, each consumed by their own thoughts. Murder was never just about the victim. There were always many victims. Husbands, wives, mothers, fathers, grandparents, siblings, uncles, aunties, nieces and nephews, friends, work colleagues, schoolmates, and even neighbours were often distressed by the victim's death. Grief rolled out like a ripple in a pond washing over those close to the epicentre. People expected this to happen without giving much thought to those close to the perpetrators. Their grief was equally as devastating but gained far less empathy from onlookers.

'I was talking to a relative of Brendon Ryder at court not long ago,' Stirling broke the silence. 'His mother rarely leaves the grounds of her house nowadays.' He tilted his head and glanced at Annie. 'Imagine being known as the mother of the Butcher of Crosby Beach. She's a prisoner in her own home.' As they pulled up at the Harris home, a mortuary van arrived. Stirling opened his door. 'I'm chalking Mrs Harris as another victim for Tod, the little shit. She's as much a victim as Jackie Webb and Jayne Windsor.' He climbed out and slammed the door with the force of a hurricane.

Annie grimaced and opened her own door. 'Are you sure that's closed?'

'Sorry, guv. Heavy handed.'

'Do you think so?'

Stirling shoved his hands deep into his leather jacket and walked towards the front door. He nodded to the uniformed officer that was guarding the house. 'It won't be long before the Press arrives,' Stirling said. 'Can you tape off the driveway so they can't get near.'

'Sarge.' He stepped away from the door to allow them access.

They climbed into forensic suits and placed plastic overshoes on and then stepped inside. The smell of pine air freshener mingled with urine and excrement. Annie closed the door behind them to stop any prying telephoto lenses from snapping images of the body. Emilia Harris was dangling from a blue rope. It was thin but looked strong. Her neck was snapped, and her head lolled onto her left shoulder. The mouth was wide open, and the blackened tongue hung over her bottom lip. 'The rope has cut deep into the flesh,' Annie observed. 'Washing line cord maybe?'

Stirling nodded in agreement. 'There's haemorrhaging to the whites of the eyes.' He looked up at the staircase to where the cord had been anchored. 'She must have climbed over the banister and then dropped.'

Annie walked into the living room and looked around. On the coffee table a sealed envelope stood leaning against a book. It was addressed in blue ink to DI Jones. Annie picked it up with a gloved hand and opened the gummed flap making sure that she didn't rip the envelope. She slid out the letter and unfolded it carefully. Stirling stood behind her, looking over her shoulder. She read from the tear stained notepaper.

Inspector, I'm afraid that I'm not strong enough to cope with things. My son is an abomination and the fact that he came from my body is something that I can't live with. I found this book in the spare room. It was hidden. I think it might help you with your investigation. I truly hope that it does. I want to apologise to the families of the people that my son has hurt as I'm certain that he won't. His dreadful acts lie too heavy on my heart for me to stay in this world any longer.

Emilia Harris

Annie looked at Stirling as she folded the letter and placed it back into the envelope. She put it onto the coffee table and picked up the book. 'Harry Potter?' Annie said confused. The hardback had a thick plastic protector around it. She opened the cover and read the stamps inside. 'Halewood library,' she pointed to the most recent date, 'Call them and find out who borrowed this book last.'

'That's four years ago.' Stirling nodded and took out his phone. He dialled directory enquiries to get the number. Annie turned the book in her hand and noticed that a marker had been placed about halfway through the book. She opened the pages at the marker and a Polaroid fell out facedown onto the floor. Stirling frowned as he spoke on his phone. Annie picked up the photograph and studied the image. At the forefront there were two shadows on a sandy beach. Sand dunes rose in the centre ground. The background was blurred and out of focus, but it showed thick evergreen woodland that gave way to a row of houses in the far distance. She recognised the area and she felt her heart quicken. A sinking feeling of dread crept up her spine like icy fingers.

'You're not going to believe this, guv,' Stirling muttered as he neared and looked at the photograph in her hand.

'Nothing would surprise me right now.' Annie couldn't take her eyes from the picture.

'The last person to borrow the book was Simon Barton.'

'Oh, no,' Annie said beneath her breath. Her stomach twisted. A gut-wrenching ache gripped her insides. 'Do you recognise this?'

'Crosby Beach,' Stirling said. Their eyes met for a moment; the significance of the place not lost on either. He pointed to the shadows on the sand. 'The sun is behind him. This is the photographer and this,' he paused.

Annie looked at him and nodded. 'It's one of the Iron Men.'

'We're going to need the dogs again,' Stirling muttered as he began to dial again. 'We'll lose the light in a few hours; I'll book them for first light tomorrow.' Annie nodded although she still couldn't take her gaze from the Polaroid.

CHAPTER 34

The sun was hidden behind thick grey clouds as Stirling walked along the sand. The Iron Men stood stoic as the tide swept in over them, driven by a strong wind. Seagulls combed the sandbanks for titbits and stranded jellyfish. Their efforts were becoming more frantic as the sea claimed their feeding grounds. He could hear the dogs from the K-9 unit coming closer. 'We'll get them to sweep from the dunes over there, to the tree line first,' Stirling said studying a copy of the Polaroid.

'Good,' Alec said pulling his coat tightly around him. He eyed the eerie Iron Man that stood silently between himself and Stirling. Cockles and barnacles encrusted the metal from the chest down. They were standing on the exact spot that the photograph had been taken. 'How many uniformed officers have we drafted in?'

'Fourteen men, guv. I didn't want to go overboard,' he waved to the dog handler as he spoke. 'It's been four years. There won't be anything left on the surface but if we find anything, we'll need them.'

'Where's the DI?'

'She's walking the tree line already, guv.'

Alec nodded and looked along the beach. Only the bleak statues closest to the shore were visible now, their brethren in varying stages of submergence. He turned his back to the biting wind and walked towards the dunes. The memories of the Butcher investigation drifted back to him. The case had been a web of murder, lies, and unresolved puzzles. Brendon Ryder had kidnapped, raped, and murdered at will before taking Stirling's pregnant girlfriend hostage, being shot dead in the process. His stepfather, a major player in the UK drug world had been murdered in Amsterdam. His demise had left a rift in the underworld that had been filled quickly by young wannabies who fought each other brutally to fill the void and claim the millions at stake. The death toll was still rising, a legacy of the Ryder family. Was Tod Harris a fan of the Butcher, a Brendon Ryder groupie or was he just another sexual predator? 'You could drive yourself mad trying to work it out, Alec,' he whispered to himself. He pulled his sleeves over his hands to keep the wind from them and headed inshore.

Alec reached the path that led between the dunes towards the trees. One of the dog handlers waved to him from a steep sandy incline. Alec stopped for a moment unsure if it was a greeting or a signal that he had found something. The dog was still on the move sniffing excitedly, innocently unaware of the gruesome nature of his job. 'I hope we're wrong this time,'

Annie's voice disturbed his thoughts. She was wrapped up tightly in a thick black bubble jacket. 'Although it would be nice to give their families some closure.'

'Sadly, I think you're right, Annie.' Alec smiled thinly. 'Emilia Harris must have thought the same.' Annie looked out to sea. The huge offshore windfarm looked alien yet fascinating against the darkening clouds. Alec could see that she was troubled. 'What's on your mind?'

'I don't know really,' she wiped a tear from her good eye. The wind was making it weep. 'I couldn't sleep last night. I was mulling things over in my mind.'

'Sounds familiar.'

'Perks of the job, eh?'

'Oh, yes.' Alec smiled. 'It's up there with alcoholism, depression, drug addiction, and divorce. Anyway?'

'I had to wonder at how Emilia Harris put two and two together when she found the book.'

Alec nodded and shrugged. 'We had questioned her about the missing boys.' He shrugged. 'Finding a children's novel might have been enough for her to join the dots.'

'Maybe.' Annie seemed to dismiss her concern. Her mobile rang and she smiled thoughtfully at Alec before answering. 'DI Jones.'

'Annie, it's Kathy.'

'Hey,' Annie said. 'It's windy here so you'll have to speak up.'

'I heard that you were back at Crosby Beach,' Kathy spoke softly. 'I don't envy you.'

'Thanks,' Annie said. 'Have you got something for me?'

'Yes. The fingerprints are back on our John Doe.'

'Who is he?'

'His name is Brian Taylor.'

'Have you passed this on to MIT?'

'Becky has the details,' Kathy explained. 'She said she would run a detailed search and call you straightaway. I'll leave you to it, good luck.'

'Thanks.'

'Progress?' Alec asked. He checked his own screen for messages, but he had no signal.

'Let me make a call and then I'll know more,' Annie held up her hand. She dialled Becky's direct line.

'DC Sebastian.'

'Becky, it's Annie.'

'I was about to call you, guv.' Becky said. 'Brian Taylor, thirty-five years old, unemployed, son of Charlotte Taylor, who lives next door to Emilia Harris's sister.'

'Next door to Simon Barton?'

'Yes.'

'What have we got on him?'

'He's on the sex offenders register.'

'For?'

'Possession of indecent images.'

'Was he spoken to during the Barton investigation?'

'No, guv. He lived in London at the time, but I'll keep digging.'

'Thanks, Becky.' Annie ended the call. She turned to Alec. 'Peter Barton shot a man called Brian Taylor. His mother lived next door to his aunt and he's on the register.'

'So, Peter Barton was questioning him about Simon?' Alec raised his eyebrows. 'Maybe Barton was innocent after all.'

'Maybe he was but he isn't now, is he?' Annie blinked to move sand from her eye. The wind was whipping the grains into tiny stinging projectiles.

'Guv!'

Alec turned towards the trees. Stirling waved a hand calling them over. Next to him one of the search dogs was sat down wagging his tail and a few metres away, the second dog was doing the same thing. 'Jesus,' Alec whispered into the breeze.

CHAPTER 35

Tod Harris stared at his feet as he walked into the interview room wearing standard prison jeans and a pale-blue canvas shirt, escorted by two burly prison officers. His hands were cuffed behind his back until he reached the table. The guards restrained his arms while they fastened the cuffs to the anchor beneath the table and he sat hunched in a chair. His eyes were red and puffy, dark circles and heavy bruising had spread beneath them. Wads of cotton wool protruded from his nostrils; congealed blood had soaked through them. He didn't look up at any point. There wasn't an ounce of arrogance about his demeanour; he looked shattered and broken. The sound of slamming doors and angry voices drifted through from the prison.

Stirling squeezed his wide frame into the chair opposite him and handed a thick file to Annie. 'DI Jones.' Annie nodded to the brief across the table. 'This is DS Stirling.' She smiled. 'Kate Bartlett didn't have the stomach for it then?'

'She's doing more magistrate cases nowadays,' the brief lied. His bald head reflected the glare of the lights and tiny beads of perspiration formed on his mottled pink dome. 'I'm Ken Graff,' he said with a nervous nod. 'I'll be representing Mr Harris from now on.' He placed his hands on the table and smiled thinly. 'My client is very upset at the moment. His mother's death has been very traumatic for him.'

'Traumatic?' Stirling muttered. He glanced at Annie. 'Have you seen the crime scene photographs?'

Graff blushed and nodded. He cleared his throat nervously. 'I need you to keep in mind that his mental and physical condition is fragile at best.' He took off his glasses. 'How can we help?'

'Do you recognise this picture, Tod?' Annie asked. She slid a Polaroid towards him. Tod's eyes didn't move from the floor. Annie noticed an egg-shaped swelling on his temple. 'Your mother found it inside a book at her home not long before she took her own life.' Tod looked up momentarily with blank eyes and then looked away again. 'She left me this note,' she continued. His eyes flickered up for a second. 'Would you like to read it?'

Silence.

'Tod?'

Graff looked at his client. 'I don't think my client is in any fit state to continue, Inspector.' He sat back and sighed. 'You can see from his face that he's been attacked and injured.'

'Has he made a complaint against anyone?'

'No.' Graff sighed. 'He claims that he fell in the showers, but I would have thought that it's obvious that he's been attacked by another inmate.'

'That happens a lot in here.' Stirling shrugged. 'Especially to rapists and paedophiles,' an icy smile crossed his lips. 'Only another fifty years or so to go, Tod.' Tod seemed to sink in on himself. His eyes remained fixed to the floor. 'Karma is a bitch, isn't it?'

'I don't think that's helpful,' Graff said calmly.

'I don't really care what you think,' Stirling said flatly. Graff looked insulted and shook his head, but he chose not to counter the remark. 'In fact, I couldn't care any less.'

'Charming.'

'Have you ever seen this book, Tod?' Annie asked. Tod looked at the book and shook his head imperceptibly. 'Tod?'

'I don't think that you're going to get anywhere here, Inspector,' Graff said gruffly. His jowls wobbled as he spoke. 'He's practically catatonic.' He took a silk handkerchief from his pocket and wiped the sweat from his brow. 'He's clearly traumatised by his mother's suicide.'

'She didn't kill herself,' Tod murmured. He looked at Annie for a second. 'She wouldn't kill herself.'

'What did you say?' Annie asked surprised.

'She didn't kill herself. I told you that he would visit her.'

'Rob Derry?' Annie rolled her eyes at the ceiling.

'I told you, but you wouldn't listen. He got to her!'

'What makes you think that?'

'She hated suicides.'

'People crack beneath the strain sometimes.'

'She was a Catholic.'

'Read the note, Tod,' Stirling said pushing a copy across the table. 'What you did is enough to test anyone's faith no matter how strong it is.'

Tod glanced at the note scared to read what was in it. He shook his head. 'No.'

'In the note she says that she found this book hidden in her house.' She paused. 'Did you hide it from her, Tod?' Annie pointed to it. 'And this Polaroid was inside it.' Tod looked blankly at them both, no expression on his face. His reaction was zombie-like. 'The book was borrowed from a library by Simon Barton three days before he disappeared.' She placed a picture of the young boy onto the table. 'It was four years ago.' She looked at his eyes. 'Do you recognise him?'

'Yes.' Tod whispered.

'You do?'

'From the television.'

'The television.' Annie sighed. 'Did you see this boy in real life?'

'No.'

'Are you sure?'

'Positive.'

'I'm confused, Tod. You had his underwear in your collection.' Tod looked straight at her but again, his face showed no reaction. 'You had his underwear and James Goodwin's too.'

No reaction.

'If you didn't meet them, how did you get their underwear, Tod?' He looked up for a second. 'Explain it to me.'

Nothing.

'We searched the area in the photograph with dogs this morning and found the bodies of two young boys.' His face reddened slightly. His eyes darted to the picture momentarily. 'We think the bodies belong to Simon Barton and James Goodwin and we think that you abducted and killed them.'

Silence.

'Are you insinuating that my client is involved in their murder or are you asking him if he is?' Graff cleared his throat and shifted his considerable bulk uncomfortably in his chair.

'Insinuating?' Annie frowned. She looked at Stirling. 'No, I'm not insinuating. That would imply that I'm not absolutely convinced that he is involved, which isn't the case. We're here to charge him.'

'I see,' Graff raised his eyebrows. A sheen of perspiration formed on his forehead. 'That was unexpected.'

'You're not surprised though are you, Tod?' Stirling prodded.

'Anything to say, Tod?' Tod's eyes were blank like a shark's. He looked at the book and the photograph and a tear leaked from the corner of his eye. The emotion took Annie by surprise; even Stirling looked surprised. He began to shiver and shake, and saliva dribbled from his chin as he cried hysterically. Annie frowned at Stirling and they waited several minutes for his tears to subside.

'I'm sorry about those boys,' Tod said in a hoarse whisper. 'I would never hurt a child.' He put his face in hands and sobbed uncontrollably. Annie looked at Stirling and frowned again. His reaction was completely unexpected. They allowed him some time to regain his composure. 'I've never seen these boys in real life, and I didn't hurt them,' he sobbed. Tod looked at Annie, his eyes pleaded. 'I'm being set up, honestly. If that really is their underwear, then it was planted in my file. Rob Derry is setting me up.'

'Why would he?'

'I don't know for sure,' he shifted nervously. 'How could I be sure?'

'But the rest of the collection in your file was yours, wasn't it?'

'Yes.'

'So, someone is going to a great deal of trouble to set you up and they killed those two little boys?'

'Yes.'

'How did they get Simon Barton's library book into your mother's house where your mother would find it?'

Tod looked thoughtful. His eyes were glued to the book. 'I really don't know. I've never seen it before today.'

'But your mother found it.'

'I don't think she did. I had nothing to do with those boys so how could I have that book?'

'I don't believe you and I don't think your mother believed you either,' Annie sat back as she spoke. 'I think she found it and realised that it had some significance and it pushed her over the edge.'

'Her death is obviously weighing heavily on you, Tod,' Stirling said. 'Why don't you get it all off your chest and tell us what happened?'

'Please believe me,' Tod pleaded with Stirling. 'She didn't kill herself and I didn't kill those boys.'

'So you said.'

'She didn't,' his voice was a whisper.

'Can you see what all the evidence says to us, Tod?'

'Yes.'

'Help me to help you. Tell the truth.'

Tod looked at Graff and then back to Annie. 'I've told you what happened.' He shrugged. 'I drugged the women and had sex with them, but I didn't kill them. I'm innocent.'

'You're deluded, Tod. You think that you're innocent and that you had sex with them?' Stirling grumbled. 'You raped them repeatedly.'

'Whatever. I didn't kill them.' Tod shrugged and stared at the Polaroid.

'You raped them and then you tortured them and then you murdered them.' Stirling tapped on the desk with his knuckles. 'You did the same with the boys.'

'No, I didn't.' His lip trembled. 'He's setting me up and there's nothing that I can say to make you see the truth. He's planted everything that you need to pin the murders on me.' He looked from Annie to Stirling, his voice calm and cold. 'I drug women and take them home for sex. You can think what you like about that, but I didn't kill anyone.'

'You told us that you raped the women and then you left.' Annie changed tack. Tod nodded. 'Then Rob Derry stayed at the house, carved the women up, killed Jackie Webb, moved Jayne Windsor to the second scene and then killed her and removed her head and he did all of this on his own?'

'Yes.' Tod tilted his head slightly towards Stirling. There was a glint in his eyes that Annie couldn't fathom. One minute he appeared almost dumb, the next there was an intelligent glimmer behind them. 'He must have broken into my mum's garage and the shed and planted all your evidence when I was in Benidorm. He's very clever.' He eyed the detectives to gauge their reaction to his version of events. 'You have to admire him, don't you? He has got all of you fooled. Can't you see that he's setting me up?'

'You're trying to tell us that Derry planted your DNA, planted Simon's library book in your home and then picked the locks on the garage and your shed to plant the other evidence?' Tod shrugged and nodded. 'Is Rob Derry some kind of Ninja?' Stirling scoffed. 'Explain how your thumbprint ended up on the mirror at the second scene if you were never there?'

'He planted it.' Tod shrugged. 'I've seen that done on one of the Jason Bourne films. They set him up by planting his thumbprint.' He looked at Annie. 'You know that it's possible to do that kind of thing, don't you?'

'You're not Jason Bourne, Tod and this isn't Hollywood,' Annie said calmly. She placed her palms on the table and leaned forward. 'We're not buying any of this, Tod. There are two little boys that you left rotting on Crosby Beach and I need to tell their families how they ended up there,' Annie snapped. She took a breath and sat back. 'Have a little respect for them.' She paused. 'Do you want to tell me about what happened to the boys?'

Tod rolled his eyes to the ceiling and let out a long sigh. He clenched his teeth together. 'Okay,' he grimaced. 'Enough of the games. I can't win anyway.' He smiled. 'I did it,' Tod said hoarsely. 'That's what you want to hear isn't it?'

'Mr Harris.' Graff nearly choked the words. 'I must insist that you take this seriously.'

'I'm serious,' Tod said flatly. 'I did it.'

Annie looked at Stirling and frowned. 'You did what, Tod?' she asked. She leaned towards him. 'What did you do?'

'All of it and more,' he whispered. 'I did it all by myself. I can't help myself.'

'Mr Harris, do not say anything more!'

'I did all of it,' he said ignoring his brief. 'I have no control over my urges. I'm sick and there is no cure. I'm a monster.' He squeezed his eyes closed tightly. Tears ran freely down his face and dripped from his chin. 'I killed those women,' he swallowed hard. 'And I killed those boys and buried them in the sand. I'm guilty. I killed all of them.' He began to shake, and his lips quivered. 'You can see from the evidence that I'm guilty, can't you?'

'It is conclusive.'

'There you go then,' Tod said quietly. 'I can't make you see that there are any other possibilities. I'm obviously guilty?'

'You're confessing?' Annie frowned.

'Yes, I did it all.' Tod shrugged.

'Mr Harris is clearly unhinged,' Graff protested. 'I'm going to apply for a court order to have him examined.'

'I'm sick but I'm not unhinged,' Tod said. 'I killed those boys and I killed those women.' He looked Annie squarely in the eyes.

'You did it?'

'Yes.' He shook his head and smiled. I also bombed the London underground in 2007, invaded Poland in 39, brought down both Malaysian airliners and invented the HIV virus.' He grinned like a lunatic. 'Draw up a statement of any unsolved murders that you have on the books and I'll sign it.' He wiped his eyes on his sleeve. 'Now if there's anything else you want me to confess to, it will have to wait. I'm tired. I want to go back to my cell. Guards!'

'We need to clarify what you've just said,' she held up her hand to halt the prison guards. 'Are you confessing, Tod, or is this just another delaying tactic?'

'No,' he recanted and smiled. 'I didn't kill anyone. I'm just sick of listening to your bullshit, I'm sick of this idiot that's supposed to be defending me, I'm sick of your gorilla growling at me in fact I'm sick of it all.' He shrugged. 'I'm telling you that I didn't kill anyone. He did it and he is setting me up.'

'Rob Derry is responsible for all this?' Annie sighed.

'R.O.B.D.E.R.R.Y, Rob Derry!' Tod shouted. 'You're not listening to me.' He turned to Graff. 'I don't feel well enough to talk anymore. Get them to take me back to my cell!'

'I need to ask you some more questions,' Annie tried to stop him. She placed pictures of Brian Taylor and Peter Barton onto the table. 'Is one of these men Rob Derry?'

Tod's eyes focused on the pictures. Annie saw something flicker in his eyes, but she wasn't sure what it was. He looked up at her and then looked back. He shook his head, a thin smile on his lips. 'He killed my mum as a warning to me. I have other family. You don't know who he is yet do you?' he stared at the pictures. 'Both of those men are guilty of things far worse than I could ever do. Good luck working it out, Inspector because I'm not saying anything else,' Tod said flatly. 'You want a confession?' he asked tight lipped. 'Go and fuck yourself. I'll never sign anything because I didn't do it. You can do whatever you want to me but I'm innocent.' He turned to the prison officers who looked unsure what to do. 'I feel unwell; take me back to my cell.'

'Fine,' Annie said annoyed. 'Charge him,' she said to Stirling. Stirling began to charge him formally as the prison officers stepped forward and transferred his cuffs so that his arms were behind his back.

He glanced at Annie as they led him out his eyes dead and accusing. 'He'll come for you, Annie Jones,' he sneered. 'He's going to spend days on you.' He smiled crookedly and then began to sob like a child.

CHAPTER 36

Gwen waited for the clock to tick onto four o'clock before she dialled, the eight-hour time difference top of mind.

'Kowalski,' the American detective answered.

'It's DC Evans speaking, we spoke about the registration plates,' she rambled as she introduced herself. 'From the UK.'

'You didn't need to tell me where you're from I don't get many callers with accents like yours.' He sounded amused. 'I'm a detective you know, I would have worked it out eventually.'

'Sorry,' Gwen said embarrassed. 'It's been a long day already.'

'Please don't be sorry,' Kowalski said politely. 'Okay, you want an update, right?'

'Yes please.'

'We've been busy here, so I hope you have a pen ready.'

'Of course, I do,' Gwen said sifting through a raft of papers to find one. Her fingers clutched a silver Parker and she selected a sheet of A4 that didn't have much written on it.

'You set?'

'I'm set.' Gwen smiled.

'Okay, CSI found blood trace inside both RVs.' He sounded like he was reading. 'We have blood trace in one, which is unusable and two blood types in the other vehicle. The killer cleaned up pretty good so some of the DNA is degraded so don't hold your breath on getting anything solid from the blood.'

'When can we get the results?'

'We have a two-month backlog for testing here.'

'Two months?'

'Two months for murder cases, nine months for rape kits.' He sounded proud of the delays. 'Crazy shit, isn't it?'

'Crazy shit indeed.' Gwen shook her head. 'I'll never complain about our forensics again. So, you can't tell me anything for two months?'

'I didn't say that,' he corrected her. 'We got plenty to be looking at.' He laughed. 'We lifted two partial prints from one of the RV's and we got matches to both. It won't mean anything to you, but it gives us something to follow up on although I don't hold out much hope of identifying any potential victims.'

'I don't follow,' Gwen said.

192

'The prints matched to a Rosa Martinez and Maria Hernandez,' he explained. 'Both women are in the system for solicitation and minor drugs charges.' He paused. 'Now I don't know how it works over there but here we process them and spit them back out as fast as we can. So, we have files on them and not much more.'

'I still don't follow,' Gwen said confused. 'Are they missing?'

'That depends on your definition of missing.' Kowalski sighed. Gwen rolled her eyes and listened. 'The prints that we found match up to their rap-sheets, right?'

'Right.'

'That's where Rosa Martinez and Maria Hernandez cease to exist. We don't have any tax returns, medical insurance, driving licenses, or dental records to follow.'

'They're illegals?'

'Them and a few million others just like them.'

'So, they gave false addresses?'

Kowalski scoffed. 'We don't even know if they gave their real names. All we know is that something bad happened in those RV's but we're not even going to begin looking for women who never existed.' He sighed. 'I hope I'm not coming over as an asshole but that's the reality here. Until DNA comes in, we're batting blind.'

'I understand.' Gwen felt deflated. She felt sad too. She tossed the pen back onto the desk.

'That's the bad news,' Kowalski chirped. 'Do you want the good news?'

'Yes please,' Gwen said routing for the pen again. 'I would love to hear the good news.'

'We asked the RV company to run their records for those two vehicles, looking for customers from the UK who hired them in the last three years.'

'And?'

'Only one British customer has ever returned to rent another RV from them. He rented them two years apart. The guy paid the rental and the insurance with a platinum card in the name of Robden Derry.'

'Can you spell that for me?'

'Sure, Robert, Ocean, Boy, David, Edward, Nora, Robden,' he paused. 'You got the second name as, Derry okay?'

Gwen frowned at the use of a different phonetic alphabet. If they didn't spell things the same way, why would they use the same phonetic alphabet? She asked herself. 'Derry?'

'You got it?'

'I have, thank you very much.'

'The name mean anything to you guys?'

'Let's say it's been mentioned by one of our suspects.'

'Is he in the tombs?'

'Pardon?'

'Has he been charged?' Kowalski chuckled.

'Yes, he has.'

'Can you keep me posted?' he sounded concerned. 'My captain is gonna need to close off this case if we get a DNA match. You know how it is, right?' He laughed sourly. 'Figures and targets. If we don't hit them, the captain kicks us in the ass.'

'Figures and targets,' Gwen smiled. 'I get it. I'll keep you up to speed as soon as we have anything solid.'

'Cool.' He paused. 'You guys are working in Liverpool, England, right?'

'Right.'

'I looked it up,' he said. 'The Beatles, right?'

'Oh, yes,' Gwen said smiling. 'The Beatles.'

'John Lennon, right?'

'Yes, John Lennon,' she said flatly.

'Cool! I heard they named the airport after him.'

'They did,' Gwen said chirpily. 'Do you know why?'

'Because he's from the city, I guess?'

'No, it's because it's the first place that he went to when he made some money, to get a flight out of the city!'

'Really?'

'No, it's a joke,' Gwen said but Kowalski remained silent. 'Thanks again for your help.'

'Welcome,' he said a little confused. 'The Beatles, cool!'

'Yes, cool. Bye now, thanks again, I'll be in touch,' she said hanging up. 'We all walk around Liverpool with bowl haircuts singing 'Love me do',' she muttered beneath her breath. 'Not.'

The MIT office descended into a hushed silence. The crime scene photographs from the beach recovery flicked across the screens. Annie was leaning against a desk clicking the remote to move the images on. Bodies in the sand, déjà vu, she thought. 'Kathy Brooks is positive that the bodies belong to young males around the age of Simon Barton and James Goodwin,' she stood up and composed herself. 'Their hair colour matches but that's all she can say for certain.' Her heart was pounding in her chest and she could feel her blood rushing through her ears. Anger boiled just below the surface. 'First impressions from the decomp are that they've been in the sand for several years so we can assume that they were buried not long after they disappeared.' She paused. The room remained silent. 'You can see that breathing tubes were inserted into the nostrils and taped to the forehead,' Annie paused. The images were a cruel reminder of Brendon Ryder's victims. 'They were buried alive in a similar manner to the Butcher's victims.'

'The killer made them look like prawns,' Stirling said shaking his head. 'Just like the Butcher did.'

'How far away from the Butcher's victims were they buried?'

'About three miles along the sand,' Annie answered. 'That's why they weren't found during the initial searches four years ago.'

'What we need to clarify is if their burial is similar to or the same as the Butcher's victims?' Alec mused. 'I mean they look the same, but are they?'

'We won't know until she's extracted the bodies completely and got them to the lab. For now, we have to think it's similar rather than the same.'

'Tod Harris has their underwear in his collection,' Stirling added. 'He is denying killing Jackie Webb, Jayne Windsor or the boys,' he added looking around the room. 'The evidence against him is conclusive. We think he buried the boys in a copycat fashion hoping that their disappearance wouldn't be linked to him.'

'If they'd been found, he wanted us to assume that they were victims of the Butcher.' Annie nodded.

'We'll know soon enough, until then what else have we got?' Alec nodded for them to move on.

'Google, can you brief the team on the link to the case in America, please,' Annie gestured to him. She clicked the remote and an image of the number plates appeared on the screen.

Google stood up and referred to his notes. 'We translated part of the text that was carved into Jackie Webb but it made no sense to us. We ran the format and identified that this sequence of numbers and letters matched up with a popular format of Californian vehicle registration plates.' He smiled proudly.

'Why would he do that?'

'We have to assume that Harris was leaving us clues to follow. He wanted us to know about his other victims. He's bragging about it to us.' Google frowned. 'I'm of the opinion that Harris is a narcissist who craves attention and wanted us to catch him.' He looked around the gathering. A few nodding heads agreed with him. 'Gwen followed up on the plates with the San Francisco PD, so she's best placed to bring you up to speed about what they found.' He pointed to Gwen and she stood up.

'Firstly, we had to confirm that the sequences were registration plates that actually existed and if they were still in existence. The San Francisco traffic division confirmed that these plates were assigned to two vehicles registered to a business in the city and they passed us over to the Metro division.' She paused to take a breath. 'The Metro Investigations Department traced the plates to a company in the bay area of San Francisco and because of the nature of our investigation, they decided to take a look at them. Their CSI's found blood trace and two partial prints that belonged to a couple of illegals, Maria Hernandez and Rose Martinez.' Images of the women appeared on the screen. 'They were in the system for soliciting and minor drug possession.' She paused and looked at her notes. 'This is where it gets complicated.' She shrugged. 'They can't tell us if these women are missing because, they never existed. They used false ID's and their addresses didn't check out.' Murmurs drifted around the room. 'I don't think that Metro will find the real identity of the women. It's a dead end.' Disappointed faces looked on. 'The good news is they traced the man who rented both vehicles, two years apart, Rob Derry.' An image of a platinum credit card appeared on the screen. 'You can see from the card that he used his full name, Robden Derry. There are no records of flights being booked in that name and no British passport exists in that name either.' Gwen paused. 'This is all we have. It's a prepaid card that was loaded with cash at a post office in the Knightsbridge area of London, so we think he took a flight from either Heathrow or Gatwick under a different alias. The Met looked into the address where the card was originally registered and it's a car park.' Gwen shrugged. 'We have a two-month wait on the DNA results from Metro before they can try to trace the victims.' She shrugged and nodded to Google. 'We know that Rose and Maria were hurt in that campervan, but I don't think they'll find them.'

'Thanks, Gwen.' Google took the reins. 'Once we had confirmed that Harris had given us the license plate numbers involved in his crimes, we applied the sequences to some of the other parts of the text.' He pushed his glasses against his nose with his index finger. 'We're currently following up on three more plates, one in Flagstaff, Arizona, and two more in Spain. Bearing in mind that we arrested Harris in Benidorm, we could be onto something.' He smiled. 'We have identified the card that he used, we're hoping that he used it before so that we can track where he has been. We should be able to trace the vehicles quite easily as long as they're still on the road. The Spanish traffic division are running the plates.' He paused. 'We've acquired a warrant for the platinum card records,' he held up his finger and took a breath, 'if he was stupid enough to use the same card each time that he travelled abroad then we should have something solid to work on. We'll know later on tomorrow.' He smiled at Annie signalling that he was done.

'Thanks, Google, good work.' Annie gestured to Becky. 'Becky, could you bring us up to date on Peter Barton and Brian Taylor.'

'Guv,' she stood up and Annie noticed the male detectives giving her the once over. Some were more discreet than others. 'We knew that Peter Barton had served in the force, but we didn't have much detail on him,' Becky began nervously. 'His personnel records have been redacted but I did a little digging and it turns out that he was an analyst for the Met. He left under a cloud, but his file isn't clear why.' She held up a sheet of paper with Barton's image on the top left-hand corner. 'I have a copy of his appeal and it looks like he found something that he shouldn't have on a senior officer's computer.' Murmurs rippled through the detectives. 'It looks like he was forced out because two months after his termination, he made a claim for unfair dismissal and he won.' She paused. 'He refused the offer of reinstatement and sought compensation. He was awarded two hundred and fifty thousand pounds and forced to sign a confidentiality clause.' Murmurs rippled again.

'That kind of money will buy you a decent alibi.' Stirling muttered.

Becky grinned and carried on. 'The search of his house has revealed a vast amount of what can only be called research.' She shrugged and smiled nervously. 'Press cuttings from across the world, maps, crime scene photographs, autopsy reports, the list goes on. We'll be collating it all but without his input it's hard to know what his focus was on. The information he has is too broad for us to pinpoint what he was doing.' She nodded to Annie who switched the image on the screen to a map of the Crosby Beach area. 'He had a considerable amount of material revolving around the Butcher murders especially about where the burial sites were located.' All eyes were riveted to the screen. 'We found spades and metal detectors during the search of his vehicle, which leads us to think that he was either burying something or looking for something.' She shrugged. 'We know that Simon Barton was taken during the height of the Butcher investigation and now we know that James Goodwin was taken at the same time.' She paused for breath. 'Peter Barton was arrested and convicted of Simon's kidnap but was released on appeal when Jackie Webb stepped forward with an alibi supported by Jayne Windsor's uncertain testimony. We also know that they received a significant amount of money from Peter Barton's inheritance fund. Financially he was in a strong position.' Annie changed the image once again. 'We have to surmise that Peter Barton was holding Brian Taylor in his cellar before he killed him with a shotgun.' She picked up another file and Taylor's image appeared on the screen. 'Barton had a stack of old cuttings about Taylor's arrest and trial. He was following his conviction in fine detail and with good reason.' She shook her head. 'An initial search of Taylor's flat has turned up a substantial amount of child porn. We're still going through his laptop and a more detailed sweep of the flat will be made tomorrow. Peter Barton could have discovered Taylor's record, connected him to his aunt next door and decided that he could have abducted Simon. All he had was a hunch, so he decided to interrogate him himself.' She shrugged. 'There's a possibility that Peter Barton was searching for Simon's abductor.'

'On the flipside, what if Barton did take his nephew and Taylor knew about it? He could be systematically silencing his alibis, all the loose ends and other possible suspects?' Alec said.

'We have to consider all the options, guv.' Becky blushed. 'It may well be that Barton knows Harris. He could be the mysterious Rob Derry,' she gestured to Annie that her summary was complete.

'Thanks, Becky,' Annie said changing the image again. 'Harris has always claimed that his accomplice is called Rob Derry,' Annie said. She pointed to the credit card. 'He claims that he is only guilty of rape and that Rob Derry is the murderer and that he has planted all the evidence to set him up.' Sarcastic laughter and derogatory comments rippled between the detectives. 'He also told us that Derry's first name is not Robert and that it's an unusual name with a double letter somewhere. We know from the credit card that his full name is, Robden. Unusual name, isn't it?' There were confused glances exchanged. 'If you add a double 'N', we get the spelling 'Robdenn'.' She walked closer to the screen and pointed to the name again. 'Robdenn Derry is an anagram.' Some of the detectives could see it immediately but some were lost. 'Shuffle the letters and you get, Brendon Ryder.' She sighed. 'The Butcher of Crosby Beach.' Annie looked around and let the information sink in. 'Brendon Ryder was riddled with nine-millimetre bullets and cremated four years ago.' There was silence across the office. 'Tod Harris is mimicking Ryder. Look at the location where he buried the boys and the manner that he buried them. I think Tod Harris did all this and he is trying to take the piss out of us by inventing his imaginary friend, Rob Derry.'

'Is it possible that Ryder had an accomplice?' Gwen asked.

'Anything is possible although it's not probable,' Annie replied.

'Harris had Simon Barton's library book and the Polaroid stashed at his mother's home. Could he be linked to Brendon Ryder?' Gwen said.

'I think it's more likely that he was imitating him,' Stirling said. 'Trying to pass the murders onto Ryder by burying them on the beach.'

'As much as it pains me to do so, we may need to speak to Ryder's relatives just in case,' Alec said shaking his head. 'We would have to tread very carefully talking to that family, but I think that I should go and speak to Laura Ryder,' he rubbed the dimple on his chin. 'I'm sure if I make an appointment, she'll speak to me. She may recognise Barton or Harris and if she doesn't then we can put the idea to bed.'

'Thanks, guv,' Annie said thoughtfully. 'Here is what we need so that we can clarify things,' Annie held up her hand to stop any more questions. 'First, we cross-check Tod Harris and Peter Barton's travel movements for the past five years or so. Once we have forensic results from Kathy on the bodies, we'll know if they were victims of Harris or someone else.'

'Agreed,' Alec said. 'Brendon Ryder is toast and Harris is banged up in jail.' Alec shrugged. 'So, our priority is that we need to find Peter Barton.'

CHAPTER 38

Becky Sebastian was tired. Working long hours was nothing new to her but this case had sapped her energy more than any other. The level of depravity that she had witnessed had drained her mentally and physically. It was always harder when the victims were women and children. She hadn't seen her mother and father for nearly three weeks. Her sister had recently had twins and she desperately wanted to see more of them. Cases like this were a reminder of how much she missed her family. The job demanded huge sacrifices not least to her personal life. Her last boyfriend had lasted a month. There simply wasn't time to balance her career and life.

When Annie had finally told her to go home, her adrenalin levels crashed, and fatigue caught up with her quickly. The office was emptying out and a handful of detectives that were scheduled on the nightshift were mulling around and catching up on the day's progress. She tidied her desk as best as she could to accommodate the influx and looked for her mobile phone. She remembered moving all her things before the briefing and she looked around the nearby desks before spotting them. She picked up her Blackberry and her keys, dropping them into her bag. Her chair had been moved too. She had hung her coat on the back of it earlier. 'For God's sake!' she muttered as she spotted it across the room. 'Why can't people put things back where they found them?' She put on her coat, said her goodbyes, and headed to the lift alone. The journey to the car park was swift and when the doors opened, the breeze that blew in off the river was refreshingly cool. As she walked from the lift, her movement triggered the sensors and huge spotlights illuminated the secure parking area.

Her Suzuki was parked fifty metres away from the lift doors and she weaved between the dozen or so remaining vehicles to reach it. Using the remote, she opened the doors as she approached the car and the lights flashed twice. The interior lights came on automatically and she opened the driver's door and climbed in. The engine fired up on the first turn and Ed Sheeran began singing on the radio. She was a big fan, but she turned it down a little, tiredness made the music sound too loud. The engine purred as she engaged first gear and headed towards the gates. A uniformed officer waved a gloved hand as the gates slid open enough to let her pass. She steered her car through them and then waited at the junction to allow a bus to go by, but it was closely followed by a wave of black cabs. She slipped the vehicle into neutral while she waited for them to go past. The traffic on the dock road was heavy for that time of night and she guessed that a concert at the Echo Arena had just finished. Thousands of people would be trying to leave the area at the same time. There was a continuous stream of traffic blocking her exit. She had to wait for the lights to change before she could move and then she pulled across the road and headed towards the city centre. It wasn't her usual way home, but she thought that because of the concert traffic, it would be quicker.

She pulled up at the next set of traffic lights and a motorcyclist stopped between her and the car in the next lane. She envied his ability to slip between the heavy traffic unhindered. If she had gone to work on her motorbike, it would have knocked half an hour off her journey home, but she only used it in the summer. A second later, the heavens opened and hailstones the size of marbles began to bounce off her car and she changed her mind about being on her motorbike. Despite the traffic, the car was definitely the preferred mode of transport especially as the hailstorm became more intense.

She watched as the hailstones hit the road and then bounced up to waist height before settling on the ground. The world turned white in minutes. As the traffic lights changed, she could feel the ice crunching beneath the wheels, and she could hear tyres squealing behind her as some of the rear wheel drive vehicles struggled to find purchase on the ice-covered Tarmac. The traffic crawled until she reached the junction for Duke Street, where she waited in the filter lane until she could turn into it safely. The traffic thinned significantly, and she accelerated through the gears as fast as she dared. The icy downpour had made drivers cautious. Vehicle headlights were dazzling, and their brake lights were blindingly red and blurred. Her eyes were sore and felt gritty. She noticed that the motorcyclist was now a few cars in front, and he was taking it easy too. It was difficult for four wheels to grip. Staying upright on two wheels would be almost impossible. She thought that if he had any sense, he would park up and wait for the storm to pass.

She opened the window an inch to clear the mist from the windscreen and the salt air rushed in. The urge to curl up into her bed was overwhelming. She needed sleep. It wasn't far to where she lived, just a mile or two away from the river behind the Anglican Cathedral, which loomed to her left. Its monstrous gothic silhouette was framed by the dull glow of yellow street lights behind it. She glanced at it quickly, unwilling to take her eyes from the road but unable not to look at it either. She thought that it was imposing and impressive in daylight but at night, it was dramatic. It was hard not to stare at it in awe.

She focused her attention on the road ahead of her. The traffic was thinning but the ice was not. The motorcyclist was weaving between the central reservation and the curb trying to avoid manhole covers and white lines, which had been turned into lethal hazards by the ice. Becky slowed down as the cars ahead of her braked and she was dazzled by a set of headlights reflecting in the rear-view mirror. She swore beneath her breath as the vehicle came dangerously close to the rear of her car.

****

Annie looked out of the office window and watched the Ferris wheel turning slowly. At that time of night, it would usually be closed but the operators had kept it open to tempt the hundreds of people that were flooding out of the Echo Arena on foot. Some were heading into the bars at the Albert Docks; many more crossed the busy dock road heading into the city's restaurants and clubs. Crossing four lanes of traffic in a hailstorm was a lottery and she smiled as she watched cars crawling along to avoid flattening a pedestrian on one of the zebra crossings. Braking distances were difficult to judge on the ice. Some vehicles crawled and the more reckless drivers fishtailed on the ice. She checked her watch and yawned. It was time to try to get some sleep. The traffic was ridiculous, so she decided not to drive home. A couple of hours in one of the station's cots would have to do.

She checked the desk for her mobile, but she couldn't see it among the files and papers. Lifting everything up, she checked again and then despite having checked twice, she looked a third time with the same result. Annie remembered putting her phone into her bag earlier, but she was sure that she had used it since. She searched inside from right to left and then repeated the process left to right, again with the same result. She tutted and tipped the contents of her handbag onto her desk and then one by one she put them all back into it. No phone. She looked around her office once more before opening the door into the MIT office. 'Has anyone seen my Blackberry?' she shouted across the office. Blank faces told her that the answer was no.

****

The cars in front picked up speed and she breathed a sigh of relief as she accelerated to catch-up with them. Her delight was short lived as three sets of brake lights illuminated simultaneously. The motorcyclist indicated left to let a Ford go past and it accelerated away throwing jets of dirty slush into the air behind it. The car in front of her followed suit splashing more dirty water onto her windscreen. Becky switched the windscreen wipers to full speed, but they struggled to clear the salty slush from the glass. She almost didn't see the motorbike swerve back to the centre of the road and she had to brake sharply causing her car to skid. She steered into the skid and managed to bring it under control, but her heart was in her mouth.

Becky swore as the motorcyclist slowed to a complete halt. Aware that he was holding up the traffic, he steered the bike to the pavement so that the vehicles behind him could pass. She guessed that he had decided to wait until the hail had melted. It wasn't below freezing, and it wouldn't be long before the ice turned to water. Familiar with motorbikes, she knew that it was the sensible option without a doubt. As she overtook him, she thought about the last time she had been out on her motorcycle. The sun had been shining, the roads were clear, and the fish and chips at the end of the ride had made the journey perfect. She longed for the summer months and light nights to return.

Becky yawned and rubbed her eyes. The road ahead was clear as she accelerated up the hill away from the river. She put some distance between herself and the vehicle behind although the headlights still dazzled her in the mirror. As the city turned into the suburbs, the streets changed from tall Victorian terraces to rows of rundown shops and boarded up pubs. The hail had turned to drizzle, and the traffic had dissipated making the drive towards Calderstones Park easier. She stopped at a set of traffic lights; the vehicle behind encroached too close to her bumper again. Normally the infringement wouldn't be so annoying but with a headache and tired eyes, it was infuriating. She swore beneath her breath as she waited for the lights to turn green. A single headlight flashed in her wing mirror and a motorbike pulled alongside her. She glanced sideways. The rider's leathers matched the fairings of the bike. She wasn't sure if it was the same motorbike as she had seen earlier or not. She was tired.

The lights turned green and the motorcycle sped away with a roar. Its acceleration was impressive. Becky pushed her Suzuki through the gears as she circumvented the tree-lined park roads. The wipers squeaked annoyingly, and the heater was making her drowsier. When she pulled up outside her house, the rain had stopped. She had never been so pleased to see the semidetached. Turning through her gateposts, she parked the vehicle underneath a carport that was attached to the side of her house. The security light above her kitchen door didn't switch on as it usually did. She made a mental note to replace the halogen bulb in the morning. Becky turned off the engine and the lights and closed her tired eyes for a second.

CHAPTER 39

Jose Peres grabbed his flashlight from the passenger foot well and tested the batteries by switching it on and off a couple of times. The beam shone through the open driver's window making a big circle of light on the crumbling whitewashed wall of an abandoned compound. He climbed out of the Guardia Civil vehicle, checked that his pistol was loaded and used the torch to illuminate the immediate area. The concrete forecourt was cracked and broken, and weeds had taken hold where the slab was compromised. Six concrete posts bordered the plot; the thick metal security chains that were once slung between them had long since been weighed in at the scrapyard. A low wall surrounded a rectangular area the size of a football field, which was now overgrown with cacti and nettles. The whitewashed plaster was pockmarked and discoloured by the harsh Mediterranean sun that had sapped every drop of moisture from the weathered paint making it flake and peel. Jose could still make out the faded name of the business. Excavadora.

Years earlier, the owner of 'Excavadora' had rented heavy plant vehicles to the construction industry making millions during the hotel building boom. Later it branched out into renting cars, campers and even motorboats to tourists before going bust when the recession hit and construction ground to a halt. The building that had stood there had been demolished so that the plot could be sold on to developers. Only a concrete floor plan remained. The compound behind it was cluttered with the rusting hulks of abandoned vehicles. Jose had driven by the site every day for over a decade. He remembered it in its heyday especially the speedboats that had sat gleaming on the forecourt. Every time he passed, he used to think, 'one day I'm going to buy one of those boats'. He never did but that was the way life worked. When the business folded, anything of value was repossessed and sold to clear the debts but the vehicles that needed repairs were left to rot. Other vehicles were owned by companies that had themselves gone bust in the crash and they too were left to turn into corroding carcasses. The landowners were too stingy to pay to have the vehicles removed, choosing to leave the task to whoever bought the plot. No one ever had.

Earlier that day, a call had come through from detectives in England, who were working on a double murder case and they were reaching out for information on Spanish number plates that may be linked to their killer. One of the vehicles was found in the north of the country and one was last registered as being owned by Excavadora, but it hadn't been insured for eight years. Jose guessed that it might have been left to rot and had made an offer to check out the plate the next time he passed the site. Although it was a sticky humid night and the sea breeze was warm, he felt a shiver run down his spine as he entered the compound.

CHAPTER 40

Becky opened her eyes and let out a deep breath. Fatigue was slowing her movement and the thought of stepping out of her nice warm car into the cold wet night didn't appeal. She steeled herself to the task at hand using the lure of her cosy bed as her motivation. She grabbed her handbag from the passenger seat and opened her door before climbing out. An icy cold drop of water fell from the carport and landed on the nape of her neck. She shivered as it trickled down her exposed skin and she pulled her coat tightly to her. She closed the door and locked it with the remote. The wind blew noisily, and she tucked her hands into her pockets as she walked around the car to the back door of her home. She cursed the security light for not working. Finding the right key for the lock would be fun in the pitch-darkness. She reached into her handbag for her Blackberry and used the screen light to illuminate the bunch of keys in her hand. As her tired eyes focused on them, she heard a shuffle behind her.

She turned quickly and stared into the shadows. Her eyes were adjusting quickly but she could only see blurred shapes beyond the carport. Dark shadows loomed against an even darker backdrop. The trees creaked in the wind; bare spindly branches tapped against the roof beams of the carport. Twigs trembled like skeletal fingers reaching out to grab her, but she couldn't see what had made the noise. Her eyes narrowed as she looked towards the road. The street lights twinkled through the trees casting moving shadows onto her driveway and the sound of traffic drifted to her from the distance. A scratching sound from above made her jump. She took a sharp intake of breath and looked upwards.

Tree branches tapped against the carport. Tap, tap, tap. Was that what she had heard? It had sounded more like a dull splash. Maybe a footstep on the wet concrete. She slipped the keys between her knuckles to act as an improvised knuckleduster and walked to the front of the car. She peered around it.

Nothing.

The branches scratched against the Perspex roof to the rear. Another one closer tapped again. Tap, tap, tap. She stepped out of the carport and walked level with the front of the house. Staring into the blackness, she couldn't see anything to worry about. She heard a splash to her left beneath the trees and held her breath to listen harder. Splash, splash, splash. The wind blew again, and the splashing noises increased in frequency. She smiled in the darkness and listened to the rain dripping from the trees into puddles below. It was an orchestra of drips and drops, some close to her and some further away in the bushes.

Becky shook her head and sighed. It was late. She was tired and the case had made her jumpy. She looked around 90 degrees but couldn't see anything to be concerned about. A cold blast of wind cut through her clothes and chilled her to the bone. The need to get inside increased in intensity. Satisfied that all she could hear was the rain finding its way to earth, she walked back into the carport to the back door. She looked down at the keys again and switched on the Blackberry screen to help her to find the right one. She fumbled through them until she saw the familiar markings on the key. She clutched it between her fingers and thumb and lifted it to the keyhole. As she inserted the key into the door, she felt a blow to her neck and fifty thousand volts surged through her nervous system shutting her brain down in an instant.

****

Jose Peres walked slowly through the compound using the flashlight to guide him. He had called home to his wife, said goodnight to his three little girls and promised to bring home some Chinese takeaway. Both he and his wife needed to lose a few kilos, but the truth was that they loved eating. Jose heard his stomach rumble as he picked his way through the spiked vegetation. Some of the cacti had grown taller than he was. Their shapes cast shadows on the orange dirt making them look like deformed humans. A rusting hulk loomed to his left, the remains of an earth moving truck. The windscreen was encrusted with salt and sand and the peeling green paint had faded in patches. He aimed the torch along its shape from top to bottom. The huge tyres were white with dust and flat against the dirt. The rubber was warped and degraded by time; wire protruded through the tyre walls. Its number plate was corroded but readable. Jose checked it but it wasn't the one that he was looking for. He thought about what to eat from the Chinese and moved on deeper into the compound.

A few yards further on to his left, there were three small saloon cars parked in a row. When they'd left the production line, they had been crystal white but now they appeared to be rusty orange. Auto scavengers had all but stripped them of anything that could be removed. The wheels, tyres, bonnet, seats, and engines had all been salvaged. Only the rusting carcasses remained. The corroded registration plates were in sequence with each other but didn't resemble the one in his notebook. He began to think that he was wasting his time but moved on regardless. The torchlight picked up a larger vehicle a few yards on. It was a transit type vehicle, but its state of decay made it difficult to identify which manufacturer had made it.

Jose shone the light across it. The windscreen was cracked, and the wipers had been pulled forward. All four tyres were flat to the floor and weeds had grown through holes in the rusty sills. He walked closer and aimed the torch at the front grill. The number plate was missing. Jose sighed and walked around to the driver's door and shone the torch inside. The stereo had been ripped out at some point and a thick thistle was growing from the handbrake rubber. The seats had been removed and the bulkhead had been marked with black aerosol paint. Painted skull and crossbones grinned at him. He walked around the back and tugged at the rear doors, opening them with a loud squeal. A rat scurried from beneath the van and ran across his feet startling him. He jumped back and nearly dropped the torch. He cursed beneath his breath and felt sweat forming on his back. His shirt was beginning to stick to him.

Catching his breath, he scanned the light inside. There was an old sleeping bag and some blankets laid out on the floor and some old colouring books were stacked in the corner nearest to the door. He stepped closer and inspected them smiling as he recognised the characters on the front cover. His children loved to colour, and it was a cheap way of keeping them quiet for a few hours. The covers were spotted with mould and the pages were curled at the corners. He poked at the sleeping bag and blankets with his torch. They had been well used at one time, but they were caked in dust. If a vagrant had used it for shelter, they'd moved on a long time ago. He slammed the door closed and shone the beam around the compound. To his left, he could make out an agricultural tractor, but he could see no point in looking at it. Looming against the night sky behind the tractor was the remains of a JCB digger, its arm was extended at right angles to the ground and the rear wheels were missing. It reminded him of a huge child's toy that had been discarded by its owner in favour of something shiny and new. To his right a hundred metres away, the beam picked out a bulky rectangular vehicle that he couldn't identify immediately. Cacti and vegetation made it difficult to make out what it was from a distance, so he decided to take a closer look.

Jose picked his way across the weed strewn compound until he reached the vehicle. It was an odd shape but as he neared, he understood why he had been confused. It was a pick-up truck that had been converted into a campervan. The living area bolted to the back looked out of place. Although it was factory built, the camping quarters looked far too big for the vehicle which carried it. He approached it from the front and shone the torch onto the number plate. It was rusty but he could read it. He took out his notebook and compared them and shook his head in disbelief. After checking it a second time, he was happy with himself. He chuckled quietly in the breeze. The registration number matched.

Jose felt a warm sense of satisfaction. His hunch had been correct but now he had two choices, take a look inside or hand the information directly to the detective ministerial department. He didn't think that they would have the time or the inclination to investigate on behalf of the British unless there was something of substance to report. They were always snowed under with domestic crimes and they resented the influx of foreign criminals that had chosen to escape arrest in their own countries by moving to the 'Costa Del Crime'.

They would roll their eyes and laugh at him if he went to them with what little he had. It was blindingly obvious that the camper hadn't moved for years. What could possibly be gleaned from sending a crime team in to look at it? His inspector would give him an earful about the financial crisis, shrinking budgets, and redundancies. If he had to listen to him ranting about it one more time, he would shoot him. That would save the department a hefty salary. It didn't take him long to make up his mind. He was pleased with himself for at least making the effort and decided to take a look inside. If he didn't take a look, he would be asked why not? If he did take a look and he found anything of substance, they would ask him why he had not come to them sooner and compromised a crime scene. He was damned if he did and damned if he didn't. At the end of the day, he had taken the initiative to come and follow up on the lead and now that his hunch had paid off, he wanted to look inside.

Despite his curiosity and excitement, he suddenly felt nervous. As he stepped closer to the camper, his hand went to the butt of his automatic instinctively. It wasn't often the he felt the need to use his weapon. Often, it was there to deter rather than destroy. He wasn't sure why he felt uneasy, but the fact was that he did. Alone in this vehicle graveyard, he felt exposed and vulnerable. It was an irrational fear, but it was real, nonetheless. The British were investigating a double murderer but the fact that they were expanding the investigation meant that they suspected that their suspect had killed abroad too. Did they think that he had killed here in Benidorm? Jose didn't know the answer, but he could hazard an educated guess. He wiped perspiration from his brow and looked up at the star filled sky. Looking at the night sky away from the light pollution of the giant resort below, helped him to put things into perspective. The murderer was in custody in the UK. He was just following up on a number plate that might be linked to their case. That was all. Nothing more. Nothing less. He tried to convince himself that in this situation his caution was unnatural and unnecessary. His gut told him to proceed with care, but his head told him that this was merely a fishing trip on behalf of the British. If his head was correct, then why should he suddenly feel so nervous?

He took a deep breath and calmed his nerves. His hands felt sweaty on the torch. He changed hands and wiped them on his trousers before moving around to the side of the camper. The bonnet was up, and the engine had been removed. A fat prickly pear cactus was growing in its compartment. The wipers had been ripped off, but the windows were intact. He scraped the sand from the windscreen with the side of his hand and peered into the driver's cab. The floor was littered with empty coffee cups and Coke cans, hamburger wrappers, and crisp packets. There was no way that the company would have parked up a vehicle in that state.

The litter had been left by someone that had entered the campervan since the business failed. Kids? Maybe but it was more likely to have been a vagrant. He walked around to the back of the camper and the vegetation became thicker making his progress slower. Thistles poked through the material of his trousers scratching his shins. He used his torch to avoid being punctured by the marauding cacti. They seemed to be the dominant plant in nature's fight to regain lost ground. He picked his steps carefully as he turned towards the back of the camper. The door was raised a few feet from the rear bumper at an awkward height. He reached up and pulled at the handle, but it was fastened tight. Jose aimed the torch at the handle. The lock was rusted and pitted with corrosion, but the keyhole was shiny silver. Someone had opened the lock recently. His concerns turned to fear in an instant.

Jose took out his pistol and stepped back. He used the butt of the gun as a hammer to crack the handle casing. It disintegrated beneath the blows, but the lock remained intact. He pulled hard and the camper swayed slightly but the door wouldn't open. Pointing his pistol at the door, he fired a single shot through the lock and then slid the gun back into its holster. Because of the awkward height, opening the door, holding the torch, and aiming the gun simultaneously was impossible. He kept his right hand on the gun and tugged at the handle stepping back quickly as the door creaked open. The smell of must and mould and something much more sinister drifted out as if it had been waiting an age for the door to be opened so that it could escape. The smell of human decay was instantly recognisable. The sweat began to pour from his head in rivulets as Jose pulled his weapon, held his breath, and looked inside.

****

Becky felt like she had been hit by a bus. Her neck was bruised, the muscles taut like wire. She felt that moving her head in any direction might make them snap. Her head felt like her brains had turned to sludge. The floor that she was lying on was cold, metallic. She could feel the vibration of an engine and she had the sense of movement. Her arms and legs were dead, and they ached from her fingers to her toes. Pins and needles had seeped through every muscle. It took long seconds for the seriousness of her predicament to sink in. She remembered driving home. She remembered the storm and she remembered arriving at her house. Then she remembered the feeling of being hit by a bus. The space between then and now was blank.

The fog in her mind began to clear. She had been zapped by something but what and more to the point, why and by whom? An electric shock? Maybe a taser or maybe a cattle prod. What and why and whom? Was it a random attack or was it something to do with a case she had worked on? She had been involved in locking up some very dangerous people. The who and why would have to wait. She needed to break free and she needed to do it quickly. She struggled to move her legs, but her ankles were stuck together painfully. She tried to straighten her legs to aid her circulation; pins and needles cramped her muscles. Her arms were tied behind her back and moving them sent white-hot pain through her shoulders. She opened her eyes and tried to look around without moving her head. The van was cluttered with stuff, but she couldn't make out what. Metal rattled against metal. Each time she so much as flinched, pain shot up her spine to her brain. The sound of music drifted to her from the driver's cab, although it was muffled, it was loud. It was loud enough to mask the screams of a woman in the back of a moving van. She had to think straight. She had been abducted. She was in the back of a white van, at least it was white inside and she was tied up. She was separated from the driver by a metal bulkhead and even if she could break free, there were no glass windows that she could break.

Becky tried to slow her breathing down as she worked out her options. Whoever had abducted her was taking her somewhere that she didn't want to be. Removing a victim from their home to a second location served only one purpose and that was to take them somewhere that the abductor wouldn't be disturbed. If this was a hit by a drug cartel, then she would already be dead. Abductions usually followed a certain series of actions. Once a victim was taken to a second location, bad things followed. If she allowed that to happen and they reached their destination, then the chances were that she would never see her family again. She had to remove her bindings without the driver hearing her and if she died trying then she was okay with that because she would probably die anyway. She wasn't going to lie there and wait for her abductor to decide what happened. No chance.

She wriggled her knees and hips and tried to reach the side of the van. The pain in her shoulders was unbearable. She felt the wall of the van with her fingertips. The panels were flat and smooth but the upright struts that strengthened the body were rough around the welds. If she could sit up, she may be able to grind her bindings against the sharp edges. Becky held her breath and brought her knees up to her chest. She twisted her waist and tried to sit up. She almost made it too, but the van jolted, and she fell back down onto her side. The pain from her neck and shoulders peaked and then subsided. Her breath was coming in short sharp blasts. She waited for the pain to go off a little before trying again. Becky leaned onto her knees as far as she could and then lunged all her weight upwards from the shoulder. The momentum carried her into an upright position, and she used her feet to shuffle backwards until her back was pressed against the panels. She had to shift her weight to the left to position her bindings against the metal struts. She listened intently to see if the driver had heard her moving. Nothing changed. The van maintained its speed and the music maintained its volume. Her wrists felt sticky and the hairs on her skin were ripped out whenever she moved; she guessed it was masking tape that held her. She began to slide her wrists up and down against a strut. The muscles in her shoulders screamed at her and cramps ran down her triceps and forearms into her hands and fingertips. It was agony but she felt the tough sticky fibres ripping slightly. Every movement, no matter how slight, brought another wave of pain but each vertical stroke of her body split a few more strands. She felt her flesh tear on the metal and blood trickled down her wrist, but she had to fight through the pain to survive. There was no other choice.

****

At first glance, Jose wasn't sure what he was looking at. The floor of the camper was knee deep with fast food wrappers. A double bed was covered with old clothes and a knitted blanket. He made out a shape beneath the bedding. Jose gripped his pistol tightly and aimed at the figure in the bed. The torchlight illuminated the shape. Sitting up against a pillow was a skeleton, the ribcage bones were brown with age, but slivers of rotted flesh still clung to them in places. The skull wasn't attached but he didn't have to look far to find it. As he scanned the torch to his left, he saw that it had been placed on a dressing table in front of a mirror, which was daubed with some words that he didn't recognise. The writing was smeared on the glass with a black substance, which he assumed was congealed blood. The stench of decomposition became stronger as he stepped closer to the vehicle. Scanning the interior again, he realised that the headless skeleton had been poised as if it was reading in bed; a book lay open in the bony hands. He shook his head and relaxed a little. It was gruesome find but the dead were harmless.

The British detectives had done a good job. Their killer had obviously been to Benidorm and he hadn't come for a holiday. He had come to Jose's city to ply his evil trade and he was mocking the police. He was a devout Catholic and he thought that posing the victim was hideous. It was sacrilege; no respect for the victim in life and even less in death. Jose made the sign of the cross on his chest and took the crucifix that he wore around his neck between his finger and thumb and placed it to his lips. He shone the torch at the floor and saw two metal steps, which made it easier to climb into the campervan. He put his left foot onto the step and used the doorframe to pull himself inside. The vehicle rocked with his weight and he heard the rusty suspension springs creaking. As he looked around a sense of dread filled him. Whatever evil had dwelled there had left its presence. In the enclosed space, he could feel the desperation that the victim must have felt. It pervaded the very air that he was breathing. The torchlight picked out stainless-steel tools on the dressing table. A scalpel, hooks, picks, and bone saws glinted in the torchlight. They were caked in dried blood from a long time ago, years he guessed. He tried to ignore the skull's reflection in the mirror. Its ceaseless grin made his hands tremble. A glass container caught his eye and he picked up a large jar that was next to the skull and held the torch to it. The liquid inside was brown like vinegar and the contents were floating freely. He shook it to get a better view and an eye floated against the glass. It stared accusingly at him. Behind it was a lump of furred pinkish flesh, which was unmistakably a tongue. Jose slammed the jar down in a panic and backed away from it as if the contents would jump out and attack him. He tripped over a discarded can and nearly lost his footing. Jose swore beneath his breath and staggered to one side of the camper, as far from the jar as he could. He leaned against the wall and wiped sweat from his eyes with the back of his hand. His weight caused the balance of the vehicle to shift. The camper creaked and tilted to one side. He heard a metallic 'click' and then a metallic rolling noise from above the cab and deep inside the living space he saw a green LED light switch on.

****

Becky felt the tape cracking above her wrist, but she still couldn't move her hands. She took a few deep breaths to calm her nerves. Sweat trickled from her temples as she began to rub the bindings once more. The rough metal was grating against her skin and she felt blood running from her right wrist across her palm and down her fingers. It was acting as an unwanted lubricant, but she ignored the dull pain and carried on. Another strand cracked and split spurring her on. She closed her eyes and took her mind to another place as she continued to grind her arms against the metal. There was a ripping sound as a layer was cut, then another snap as the layer beneath was severed. She flexed her muscles painfully and she could twist her arms an inch. She gritted her teeth and increased the speed and the pressure. The weld ripped through the tape and her flesh with equal disdain. Tears formed in her eyes and she gave one last Goliath effort. She closed her eyes again and felt the salty liquid running down her cheeks as she pumped her arms against the metal struts relentlessly. Another crack. Another strand split. Another crack and the next layer of tape gave way. She felt it ripping and tearing. Her wrists could move and rotate and then with a last snapping noise, her hands were free.

Becky felt the blood returning into her shoulders and arms as she brought them in front of her. She rubbed her wrists and clasped her fingers together to aid the circulation. Adrenalin coursed through her veins and she felt a surge of energy pulsing through her muscles. She had to control her breathing again and take stock of what she needed to do next. Tugging at the tape around her ankles, she quickly realised that undoing it would waste valuable minutes. She looked around at the contents of the van. There was something bulky in the corner to her left and the dark circular window at the centre told her that it was a washing machine. She reached out to her right and grabbed at a strip of angled metal that was rattling against the floor. It looked like a piece of shelving of some kind. Maybe the van belonged to an odd job man or a scrap dealer, not that it mattered but her inquisitive detective's brain was working overtime.

She slipped the angle iron beneath the tape and used it in a sawing action. The tape ripped easily and within thirty seconds, her legs were free. She felt like screaming with frustrated delight, but her dilemma wasn't over just yet. Becky searched for her handbag even though it was highly unlikely that her kidnapper would have put it in the back of the van with her. She cursed as she remembered that her mobile had been in her hand when she was zapped. As she felt around, there was no sign of her bag.

She crawled towards the back doors on her hands and knees and stumbled into a cardboard box. She searched inside and felt crockery. Cups and plates and a couple of old vases. 'Brick-a-brack is just what I need,' she murmured to herself. She had to keep her spirits high. 'Maybe he's taking me to a car boot sale.' She pulled the box out of the way and scrambled to the doors. Grabbing the internal handle, she twisted with all her might, but it wouldn't budge. She was locked inside.

Becky felt her way along the side of the van and fumbled around at the contents. She felt an old golf bag with a couple of clubs in it. The side pocket held four golf balls and some tees. Next to it was an ironing board and a basket full of material. She couldn't see exactly what it was but guessed it was curtains. It seemed to be a random load from a house clearance or something similar. There was no sign of her handbag.

Her heart sank but she searched on and when she couldn't find anything to help her open the doors, she went through her coat pockets as an afterthought. When her hand touched the familiar shape of her Blackberry, she could have cried. Her breath stuck in her chest as she took it out and looked at it. Could it be her phone? Would her kidnapper have been so stupid? She was scared that it might be a mirage or that it might turn out to be a bar of chocolate or something equally useless. She was convinced it was a Blackberry and when she took it out, she knew that it was. She clicked on the light and her eyes could hardly make sense of it until she noticed the screensaver. It wasn't her Blackberry. She was as confused as she was pleased. Her head couldn't compute what had happened. It was a Blackberry, but it wasn't hers.

Becky frowned and scrolled through the numbers and quickly realised that she had picked up the DI's phone by mistake. Her own phone was in her hand when the kidnapper struck. She must have picked up the DI's phone and put it into her coat pocket as she had left work. If ever there was a mistake to make, it was that one. She continued to scroll down until she recognised the number for the MIT office. She closed her eyes and said a silent prayer of thanks as she pressed dial.

****

Jose was rattled to the core by his discovery. He felt ice cold to his bones as he looked from the severed eyeball to the green light. He was confused and frightened by his discovery but not by the light. Bespoke campervans would have been manufactured by skilled coach-fitters. It would be full of appliances and gadgets to make a camping trip as homely as possible. The light didn't concern him as much as the contents of the jar had. He picked up the torch and turned it towards the source of the light. He could see there was an inverter and some wires. He followed the wires, which ran into three green plastic containers. Jose recognised them as five-gallon petrol canisters. He frowned and wondered why anyone would wire them to an inverter but before he could fathom it out; the heater coils reached ignition temperature and the fuel exploded. He tried to scream but as he opened his mouth the flames scorched the soft flesh of his trachea and lungs silencing him. The inferno engulfed him in a millisecond. As his flesh blistered and sizzled, he felt evil touch his soul.

****

'Major Investigation Team, DS Stirling speaking.'

'Sarge, I'm in trouble.' Becky whispered. 'I've been kidnapped!' she said feeling very frightened and a little bit stupid. She didn't feel as if she had said it in the right way but then how should she have said it? In the end, she had just blurted out. 'Can you hear me, Sarge?'

'Is that you, Becky?' Jim Stirling said yawning. He rubbed his eyes and sat back in the chair confused by what she had said.

'Yes, it's me!' she whispered. 'I've been kidnapped, Sarge.' Her voice cracked with emotion. 'I'm not joking around, I'm serious. I was zapped with something, a Taser I think, maybe a cattle prod but the bastard got me from behind.' She began to ramble. Just knowing that her sergeant was on the end of the call made her feel better. It gave her hope. 'I thought that I heard something behind me but when I looked around, I couldn't see anyone.'

'Slow down, Becky.' Stirling sat forward and frowned. He waved a hand at Annie and summoned her over. Sensing that something was happening, some of the other detectives followed her and listened in. 'Where are you, Becky?'

'I don't know. All I know is that I'm in the back of a van,' she said meekly. 'God, I feel so bloody stupid!'

'What's going on?' Annie asked. She could tell by the expression on Stirling's face that something untoward was happening.

'It's Becky, guv,' he covered the mouthpiece. 'She says that she's been kidnapped.' Stirling pointed to another handset and gestured for her to pick it up and Press the party line.

Annie heard it click and connect. 'The DI is on the line, Becky,' he said calmly. 'Now take a deep breath, calm down, and tell us exactly what has happened.'

Becky closed her eyes and took a breath. She released it slowly and explained in a whisper. 'I drove home and when I was putting the key in the door, someone whacked me from behind.' She paused. 'He Tasered me I think.'

'Jesus,' Annie said. She was concerned and equally confused. 'Where are you calling from?'

'Your mobile, guv,' she said embarrassed. 'I must have picked it up from the desk by mistake. Sorry, guv.'

'Don't be sorry. Annie shook her head. Putting her hand over the mouthpiece, she turned to one of her team. 'Get a trace on my phone now!' he turned and ran to his desk. 'Where are you now, Becky?'

'I'm in the back of a white van. At least it's white inside but I've no idea what make or model it is.'

'Did you see your attacker?'

'No,' Becky said frustrated. 'I felt a whack from behind and the next thing I know I was tied up in the back of this van.'

'You've broken free?'

'Yes, guv.'

'Good girl,' Annie said shaking her fist. 'Are you hurt?'

'A few cuts and bruises but I'm okay.'

'That's good. Have you got any idea how long you have been in there?'

'Not really,' Becky thought out loud. 'I reckon it took me twenty minutes to cut the tape off.'

'Was the van travelling the entire time?'

'Yes.'

Annie covered the mouthpiece again. 'Forty-mile radius to begin with.' Her detectives nodded. 'Okay,' Annie said thoughtfully. 'Becky, is there anything that you can use as a weapon?'

'I've got a piece of angled iron in my hand,' Becky gripped it tightly. 'I used it to cut my feet free. It's heavy enough to do some damage.'

'Good. Keep hold of it. Can you tell if you're in the city or moving away from it?' Annie asked.

'I don't really know.'

'Is the van travelling at a constant speed or is it stop starting?'

'Constant.'

'Hold on there, Becky,' Annie said. She turned to look at Stirling. 'Let's check how long it will take to get the trace on my phone immediately.' She paused, 'and get an alert to traffic on the main motorways out of the city, M62, M6, M56, M57, and get armed response here and in all the surrounding counties on standby.'

'Guv,' Stirling said calling over another detective who was listening. 'And get a list of all vans that have been stolen in the last week. Let's start with white vans for now.'

'Yes, Sarge.'

'Becky,' Stirling spoke slowly, 'is there anything in the back of the van?'

'Yes,' she muttered looking around. 'There's a washing machine and some metal bars, some golf clubs, and boxes full of crap. I didn't want to move around too much in case he hears me.'

'Have you checked the doors?'

'Of course, I have,' Becky said frustrated. 'I'm not stupid.'

'I know you're not, Becky but I need to ask. We need to understand everything that's happening to help you, okay,' Stirling calmed her. 'I want you to find something hard enough to jimmy the bottom of the doors, okay?' A beep interrupted the line. 'What was that?'

'The battery,' Annie said. 'My phone was nearly dead. I meant to charge it. How many bars have you got, Becky?'

Becky felt a lump in her throat as she looked at the screen. 'Less than two.'

'We've got at least fifteen minutes, Becky,' Annie said. 'That's more than enough time for us to find out where you are, okay?'

'Okay. Are you running a trace?'

'Yes,' Annie said. 'We'll have a lock on it before the battery runs out.'

'Okay.'

'Becky,' Stirling said, 'you said there were metal bars in the van?'

'Yes. I think they're old railings or something.'

'Good. Grab one and stand near the back doors.'

'Okay,' Becky gasped. She crawled to the bars that she had felt earlier and picked them up to gauge their weight and density. One of them was heavier than the others. She picked it up and shuffled towards the doors. 'Okay, I'm at the doors.'

'Good,' Stirling said. 'The door with the handle on is the weak point. Try to slide the metal between the bottom of the door and the van. I want you to bend the corner open if you can.'

'I'll try,' Becky whispered. 'I'll have to put the phone down a minute, okay?'

'Okay. I need you to force the bar in as far as you can and the pull back as hard as you can.'

Becky hesitated before putting the phone down. She didn't want to stop talking but she knew that she had to. Kneeling close to the door, she placed the bar at the bottom of the door and pressed her weight on it. The door moved a few millimetres from the van but not enough to wedge the metal between them. She wiggled it and tried again but it wouldn't budge. 'Shit!' she hissed and picked up the Blackberry. 'I can't get it in, I feel so bloody useless,' she said close to tears.

Annie sensed the panic in her voice. 'Take a breath, Becky. Jim seems to forget that we're not all built like a brick outhouse.' She smiled and felt Becky relax a little. 'Put your foot against the bottom of the door and try again. Take your time.'

'Okay.' Becky sounded determined. She placed the phone on the floor and put her foot against the corner of the door. She could see light between the narrowest of gaps and she forced the bar a couple inches into it. Becky pulled back with all her strength and the corner of the door buckled an inch. Fresh air streamed into the van and she could hear traffic. She forced the bar even further into the gap and then she pulled backwards using all her weight to jimmy the door. The gap widened to six inches and she pulled again. Her hands slipped off the bar and she fell backwards clattering into the box of plates. The metal bar sprang back against the door with an almighty clang.

The van slowed immediately. Becky held her breath. She heard him turn the music down as the vehicle slowed to a steady pace. She felt the van move across a lane and prayed that he didn't pull over and stop. She could hear her own breathing and the blood pounding through her head was deafening. She lay perfectly still, frozen in fear. The driver had slowed down, but the van was still moving. Becky felt for the Blackberry blindly but all she touched was cold metal. She reached further to her right and her fingers brushed against the phone. She felt the van accelerate again and the driver turned the music up to its previous volume.

Becky breathed a sigh of relief and put the phone to her ear. 'Guv,' she whispered. She waited for a reply. 'Sarge, are you there?' Nothing. 'Guv!' she whispered louder. Nothing. 'Sarge, can you hear me?' She looked at the screen and her breath stuck in her throat. She felt tears forming in her eyes. 'Oh no!' It was cracked from one side to the other. The keyboard was crushed, and an impression of a shoeprint was stamped across it. The only sign of life was a dull green glow from behind the fractured screen. 'Oh, no!' Becky hissed. Her heart felt like it would punch its way through her chest. She felt that she was about to vomit. 'Oh, God no!' Her mind was racing as she thought about what she had done. She thought that the phone trace might have been completed but it was just as likely that it hadn't. She wondered if the sim was still traceable even after a donkey had cracked the screen. She felt useless and helpless in equal measures. A twist of fate had given her a lifeline, which she would be eternally grateful for. Squashing it wasn't in the plan. She covered her eyes with her hands and stifled a sob. 'Get a grip, Rebecca,' she whispered to herself. She couldn't afford to break now. She had to be strong. 'Pull yourself together and do something.'

Becky thought back to the phone call. Jim Stirling wanted her to bend the bottom of the door. He hadn't said why precisely but she had to assume that it was to make it stand out from all the other vans on the motorway. She had to attract attention to the van. She wasn't sure if the buckled door would work quickly enough. She knew that the DI would have alerted the traffic division, but no one had a clue which motorway she was on or in which direction she was being taken. She might not even be on a motorway; there were plenty of dual carriageways encircling the city. She could be on any number or them. The sergeant wanted her to attract attention to the van and that's what she intended to do.

CHAPTER 41

Becky reached behind her and grabbed the golf bag. She put her hand into the pocket and took out the three golf balls. Crawling back to the door, she leaned towards the gap and dropped one of the balls through it. She didn't see it hit the Tarmac, but she knew that it would bounce across carriageways causing havoc with oncoming vehicles. She listened for a reaction, but none came. Becky dropped the other two onto the road and waited. She heard a horn blaring and lights flashed but the van maintained its speed.

Becky reached into the bag and grabbed the clubs. She didn't know much about golf, but she recognised them as irons. She took one and slid it through the gap. She heard it clatter on the road followed quickly by a series of horns blasting. Her heart began to beat faster. She could see lights flashing off the bumper; the traffic behind was reacting angrily. Angry isn't enough, she thought. She needed them to be so livid that they picked up their telephones and called the police. Becky reached for a second golf club and she slid it through the gap and let it go. It clattered from the back of the van and was greeted by more horn blasts. When she dropped the third club, the reaction intensified further. This time the drivers behind seemed incensed. The horn blasts were continuous. She clapped her hands together in joy and looked around for another potential missile to launch through the gap.

When the van slowed quickly and veered to the left, her delight waned to be replaced with fear. 'Shit, shit, shit!' she shouted as the vehicle slowed to half its speed. The music was silenced, and she felt a layer of perspiration form on her chest and back. She gripped the piece of angle iron in her right hand and sat down behind the door. She closed her eyes and took a breath and steeled herself for the fight that would come. When her kidnapper opened the back doors, she would pounce like a scorched wild cat. She swallowed hard and realised how thirsty she was. She thought about what she would give for a drink of ice-cold water. She thought it was odd to feel so relaxed and yet be totally ready to fight to the death. Maybe she was resigned to her fate? If her attacker had a firearm, she would probably die. She knew that he had a Taser or similar but that didn't matter right now. The angle iron was heavy, and it was sharp at one end. She was trained in unarmed combat by the police. Her Krav Maga lessons drifted through her mind in a blur. Strike for the weak areas, the eyes, throat, and testicles. She would do that with every ounce of strength in her body until her breath stopped coming. She wouldn't let him take her life cheaply.

Suddenly, the van picked up speed quickly. She was thrown backwards and had to hold on tight. She heard horns blasting violently, long sustained blaring from three or four different vehicles. The van swerved and increased speed again. He was panicking. Becky squeezed the metal bar with both hands, closed her eyes and listened to what was happening outside. She could hear the tyres on the road. She could hear rainwater splashing beneath the van as it accelerated to full speed.

Becky decided to maintain the pressure. She grabbed the basket of curtains and scrambled to the back doors again. She screwed up the top piece of material. It felt like a curtain. She fed it through the gap inch by inch and let it flap wildly in the slipstream. She heard horns blasting in response as it was ripped from her grasp. The next piece felt like a cotton bed sheet. It fell through the gap with ease and she felt it billowing to full width before she let it go. Lights flashed and the van swerved violently to the left. Becky stumbled backwards and landed on her elbows with a sickening thud. 'Bastard!' she shouted at the top of her voice. She struggled to her feet and banged her fists on the bulkhead. 'You have no idea how much shit you're in!' she hammered her fists against the cold metal. The driver chose not to reply but he responded by swerving sharply to the left. Becky was thrown against the side of the van cracking her head against the washing machine. 'Fuck you!' she screamed. She felt the van lurch forward again as the driver pushed the engine to the limits. Warm blood trickled down the side of her face. She touched a deep gash on her forehead and felt tears of frustration filling her eyes. 'Fuck you, fuck you, fuck you,' she shouted as she slammed her fists against the metal. 'There is no way I'm giving up,' she whispered in the dark.

Becky crawled to the ironing board and picked it up with both hands. She staggered to the back doors once more and tried to force it through the gap. It disappeared halfway and then jammed. She picked up the metal bar and used it as a hammer, striking the top of the board as hard as she could. Each blow forced it another few inches. She hit it again and it slipped out further. The sound of metal scraping against the road filled her ears. The high-pitched squealing was deafening. Sparks flew in an arc as the board grated against the Tarmac and then it was ripped free by the immense friction as it clattered away from the back of the van. Becky clapped her hands in glee, but the van maintained its speed.

'Tell me someone has called the police,' she muttered in the darkness. The driver showed no sign of stopping and he was sticking to his route. She could tell from the speed of the van that they were on a main artery. He hadn't turned off because he had somewhere to go. 'I can't sit around here and wait to see what happens,' she whispered to herself. The darkness and exhaust fumes were making her claustrophobic. She looked around and focused on the washing machine. Becky cleared the clutter from the back doors and then made her way to the corner. The machine was held in place with luggage straps and she fumbled with the clips and wrestled it free. It slid easily along the floor runners and Becky pushed it halfway across the van. She stopped, placed both hands flat against the top of the machine and braced herself. 'On three, Becky,' she geed herself up. 'One, two, three!'

Becky drove hard with her legs and pushed the washing machine as fast as she could along the floor runners. It slammed into the back doors with a deafening clang, the vibrations jolted painfully up her arms. The doors buckled at the bottom but held firm. She dragged the machine back and positioned herself for another attack. The machine hurtled towards the doors again and impacted with a deafening crunch. The left-hand door burst open and flapped loosely in the slipstream. 'Get in there, you beauty!' Becky screamed. She pushed the washing machine another half a metre and watched as it bounced down the carriageway, shattering into a dozen chunks of scrap.

There were three lanes, a motorway. The traffic behind was staying a safe distance away, avoiding the missiles that were falling from the van. The drivers were using one lane as far away from the rogue vehicle as they possible could. Becky felt a huge sense of relief. She took a deep breath of fresh air and sat down near the open door and screwed up the curtains one at a time. She tossed them out and watched them billowing like kites and then drop onto the motorway.

She could hear the angry motorists venting their spleen on their horns and then she heard the most beautiful sound that she had ever listened to. Sirens in the near distance, first one and then another and then there were so many that she could no longer distinguish how many there were. When the blue lights came into view, she allowed the tears to flow freely.

CHAPTER 42

Peter Barton swore loudly as he looked in the wing mirrors and saw four sets flashing blue lights gaining on him. He knew that taking one of the MIT officers was a dangerous play, but it had been a balanced decision. It wasn't done on a whim. He planned everything down to the minor details. He picked Becky because she was petite. Some of the MIT detectives were real bruisers. He didn't need a fighter. Over the years since he had been ejected from the police, every time he tried to pre-empt what they would do, he'd been correct and reacted accordingly. Killing Brian Taylor could have been avoided but he hadn't anticipated them knocking on his door so soon. It was down to his foresight and planning that he had avoided escape on that occasion.

This time he had underestimated the concussive power of the Taser. He had also underestimated the determination of the detective that he had kidnapped. How they'd identified the van wasn't beyond him. His captive had somehow managed to bombard the trailing traffic with junk. He had anticipated them catching him but not this early; not until he was ready. His plan was in the toilet and while he worked out what to do, there was a good chance that he could be shot in the process.

His attention was taken by lights in the sky. They swooped over the motorway from his left to his right and a spotlight that hung beneath the chopper blinded him. The arrival of the force helicopter was the final act of the play. It was impossible to outrun it on the roads and on-board heatseeking technology made it impossible to hide from it on foot even in the dark. He shook his head and bit his bottom lip as he searched desperately for a way to control an impossible situation.

A mobile ringing disturbed his thoughts. He grabbed the detective's handbag from the passenger seat and looked inside. Her Blackberry was flashing, and the screen read 'DI Jones calling'. From his research, he knew that she was poised to head up Merseyside's MIT when the aging detective superintendent took retirement. He weighed up his options and took it from the bag and then checked the wing mirrors again. The blue lights behind him had formed a rolling roadblock across the motorway. As the helicopter swung back overhead, he answered the phone. Talking could give him the time that he needed.

'Inspector,' he answered. He steered the van into the centre lane and kept one eye on each wing mirror. The interceptors didn't seem to be ready to make a move yet. He noticed a sign going by in a blur.

'Peter Barton,' Annie said calmly.

'It is.'

'I need you to pull over onto the hard shoulder so that we can get my detective to a hospital and then you can tell me what this is all about. There's nowhere for you to go.'

'Okay,' he said. 'But we talk first. I'm all too familiar with how the police negotiate once you're in a cell. It becomes a little one sided. I don't want a repeat of the last time that I was questioned. I want to help you and you need to negotiate.'

'There's nothing to negotiate about but I'll listen to what you have to say.' Annie kept her cool. 'Make it quick.'

'I killed Brian Taylor.'

'I know you did.'

'But do you know why?'

'We have a good idea.'

'I need to hear what you think happened.'

'What I think doesn't matter.'

'It does to me. Humour me.'

'He used to visit a relative that lived next door to your nephew,' Annie paused, 'he has a conviction for kiddy porn and you think that he had something to do with Simon's abduction.'

'I don't think anything, Inspector,' Barton said calmly. 'I know that he took him.'

'How do you know for sure?'

'I just do.'

'Okay, why kidnap my detective?'

'I took your detective because I wanted to sit down opposite one of you without handcuffs on and explain everything. I just wanted to put over my side of the story. I was going to let her go as soon as I'd explained everything.'

'You tasered a detective because you wanted a chat?' Annie asked incredulously. 'Why not pick up the telephone?'

'I needed to communicate how vital my information is. The situation was too urgent for a phone call. No one would believe me.'

'You have created a dangerous situation. You could have killed her and got yourself shot to boot.'

'Hindsight is a great gift, Inspector.' He sighed. 'But how else could I get you lot to listen to me.'

'If I'm honest, I can think of a dozen preferable ways.'

'I can't change what I've done.' He paused. 'How did you track the van so quickly?'

'A six iron through the windscreen of an unmarked interceptor.' Annie smiled to herself. 'It grabbed their attention.'

'Your detective is very resourceful.'

'Her name is Rebecca Sebastian and she's incredibly bright.' Annie humanised his captive. What do you want, Peter?'

'I need you to listen to me.'

'I'm listening.'

'I know that bastard Taylor took Simon. I spent years as a pariah of the worse kind because of that scum.' He sounded angry. 'I lost years of my life as a child killer. Can you imagine what that was like?'

'Not really but this isn't helping.'

'This is not about me being railroaded into a prison cell. It's about Simon. I didn't touch him.'

'We know that you didn't.'

'You say that now, but your attitude will change as soon as I'm locked up. It always does.'

Annie didn't want to get involved in an argument. 'Okay, Brian Taylor kidnapped Simon. I believe you. Now pull over and we can sort this out before you get hurt.'

'Don't patronise me,' he snapped. 'You see this is exactly why I took your officer. I have to make someone listen to me and take me seriously.'

'I can see your point of view, Peter but you need to stop now. The Armed Response Units will drop you the first chance they get.'

'You think that you can see my point of view?' He sighed. 'Your head is so far up your own arse that you can't see what's staring you in the face.'

Annie bit her lip. 'What can't I see, Peter?'

'You're dismissing me as if what I have to say isn't important, that's why I'm in this mess in the first place.'

'I'm agreeing with you, Peter. We know you didn't abduct Simon.'

He paused before speaking. 'But you don't know everything.'

'What don't we know?'

'Who is behind all this.'

'If you know then I'm all ears.'

'Brian was too scared to talk at first, but he did eventually.'

'A shotgun in the mouth will loosen most tongues,' Annie said sarcastically. 'What did he tell you?'

'He admitted taking Simon.'

'Did you record his confession?'

'You're patronising me again, Inspector. We both know that a recording of a suspect under duress cannot be used in evidence.'

'I'm not interested in what happens in a courtroom. I'm interested in what he had to say.'

'He confessed.'

'Okay, so I have to take your word for it. What else did he say?'

'He told me that your number one suspect, Tod Harris was involved too.' He waited for Annie to react, but she remained silent. 'And he said that he had proof that Harris was involved.'

'What proof?'

'He said that Harris had kept Simon's library book.' Annie paused to think. There was no way that Barton could know that without inside knowledge. No one outside of the MIT knew about the book or the Polaroid. 'That book proves that he took Simon and that's all I wanted to do. I just wanted justice for Simon and to clear my name finally.'

'The book did cement things for us.'

'You're not kidding it did,' Barton scoffed. 'I've been looking for something, anything to prove to you that I didn't take him. When he told me about the book, I knew that I could finally get some justice for Simon.'

'How did you know that we knew about the book?'

'I don't remember,' Barton stammered. He realised that he had said too much. 'All that matters is that you have it.'

'Harris's mother left it for us with her suicide note.'

'She knew what that animal, Harris had done.'

'She probably did.' Annie sighed. Suddenly the integrity of the library book was shattered. Barton could have given it to Harris's mother. She couldn't air her thoughts just yet though. 'You have achieved what you set out to do, Peter,' she said calmly. 'Now pull over and let's bring this to a close.'

'Bring it to a close.' he laughed. His laughter confused her. 'You really don't have a clue what I'm talking about do you?'

'Obviously not,' she replied curtly. 'Enlighten me.'

'Do you know what connects Harris to Taylor?'

'Apart from being sick paedophiles?'

'Apart from that,' he said frustrated. Another signpost flew past. This one registered in his mind.

'No, I don't know what the connection is.' Annie hoped that he did despite his method of gleaning the information.

'They both have convictions going back years.'

'We know.'

'Do you?'

'This game is boring me, Peter.' Annie sighed. She was happy letting him talk as he continued to drive. His fuel supply was burning down and all the motorway exits had been blocked. Sooner or later, the van would stop of its own accord. 'If you have something that we don't, please share it.'

'I'm boring you?' He snorted. 'If you lot did your jobs properly, we wouldn't be having this conversation. Boring!'

'Are you going to tell me or not?'

'Did you go right back to their young offender files?'

'Of course, we did. They were sealed but we had a judge release them to us.'

'And you didn't find any connections?' he sounded smug.

'No,' Annie said confidently although he had planted a seed of doubt that they'd missed something. 'They had no joint convictions.'

'Did you look past their convictions, Inspector?'

The seed of doubt germinated. 'Obviously their records are still being analysed.' She said defensively. 'The case is still ongoing.'

'That could take your lot weeks!' He laughed. 'I'll save you some money.'

'Please do,' Annie was curious. He had been a police analyst after all.

'As teenagers, they were both represented by the same solicitor,' he paused for reaction. Annie felt the skin on her neck glow and tingle. 'Have a guess at his name, Inspector.'

'I can't do that,' she said. Suggesting a name to him would cause problems later. 'You know I can't.'

'I'll put you out of your misery,' he shouted. 'Geoff Ryder.' He waited for a reply. 'Ring any bells, Inspector?' he chuckled but there was no mirth in his tone. 'Brendon Ryder's uncle! Coincidence?' he waited again. 'Nothing to say, Inspector?'

'I'm thinking,' Annie said flatly.

'Get your people to check.'

'I will.'

'He's behind the entire thing,' he said quietly. 'He planned Simon's abduction. He is responsible for what happened to me, but do you know what is worse, much worse?'

'Go on,' Annie said. If his information was correct, it changed a myriad of things past and present.

'I've been following murders all over the world and I've been trying to track him and Tod Harris as much as I could. It was difficult but not impossible.' He paused to think about his next words. 'It doesn't make much difference what happens to me now, but I'm convinced that you shot the wrong member of the Ryder family.'

'I get the picture,' Annie said calmly. She could see how engrossed in his search for answers he had become. It was all consuming to the point where he was blinded by the most dubious connections. Now wasn't the time to enter into debate with him. 'I can give you my word that we'll look into everything that you have to say but you have to pull over right now and let us get Becky out of the van. You're running out of time, Peter.' He remained quiet. 'If you stop of your own accord, it will look better later on.'

'In court?'

'There's nothing else to be gained. You've made your point, now stop the van.'

'I can't go back to jail, Inspector.'

'Who knows what will happen?' Annie lied. 'There are extenuating circumstances surrounding everything you have done. Don't make things any worse and you have a chance.'

'I don't think so. I'm screwed.'

'Maybe not. But if you don't stop the van, you'll never know, will you?'

There was silence on the line for long minutes. Annie had to let him think about what he was going to do. 'Inspector.'

'I'm here.'

'I slipped up, didn't I?'

'What, generally or are you relating to something specific like kidnapping a detective?' she joked although there was no malice in her jibe.

'Funny,' he appreciated the humour. 'You know that I went to see Harris's mother, don't you?'

'I worked it out.'

'I knew that she had to know something. When Taylor told me that Harris had kept the library book, I knew it.'

'You were right.'

'I pretended to be a detective and I frightened her into telling me about the book.' He paused as he thought about what he had done. The old lady had been terrified. 'I know what you're thinking but I didn't take the book there and plant it. She showed it to me, and I begged her to show it to you. I didn't think that she would top herself.'

'Okay. I believe that,' Annie lied again.

'And I didn't kill her.'

'She committed suicide.'

'But now that I've admitted talking to her, they'll re-examine the scene and the body, won't they?'

'You know that they will.'

'I need you to believe that I didn't kill her.'

'What I believe is irrelevant. It's what the evidence proves that matters. If you're telling the truth, you've got nothing to worry about have you?' There was another uncomfortable silence. Annie could almost hear the cogs of his mind turning. She almost understood the turmoil that he was going through.

'Inspector.'

'Yes.'

'Tell your people that I'm pulling over.'

'Okay. Do it slowly. When you've stopped, turn off the engine and throw the keys out of the window. Then listen to the armed officers and do everything that they say, okay?'

'Make sure you look through my work, Inspector.'

'We will.'

'Geoff Ryder is a killer.'

'I'll look at everything you have said.'

'Harris is a puppet.'

'Concentrate on doing what the officers tell you or they will shoot you, understand?'

'Goodbye, Inspector.' Annie heard the line disconnect and the hairs on the back of her hands stood on end.

CHAPTER 43

Peter Barton checked the wing mirrors. The convoy of police interceptors had grown in numbers. He recognised that the traffic police had dropped back to allow the armed units to take pole position. They were poised to surround him the moment he stopped the vehicle. The motorway began to climb a long incline and as he drove beneath an overhead gantry of signs, he knew that they were nearly there. He switched on the hazard lights and put his right hand out of the driver's window and waved it to signal that he was slowing down. Two vehicles moved forward taking up positions on either side of the back of the van. The officers inside were only metres away from him. Their faces were expressions of pure hate. To them, he was a convicted child killer and could be involved in the slaying of one of their own. He knew that they would drop him at the blink of an eye. The engine laboured as the slope increased in gradient and he dropped it into third gear. His headlights picked out a motorway sign to his left that welcomed him to Preston.

The timing couldn't have been better. As the van reached the brow of the hill, that rolled steeply down into the Ribble Valley, Peter floored the accelerator. The van set off like a rocket completely wrong-footing the police drivers. Peter gritted his teeth as the accelerator needle climbed over sixty. A swarm of blue lights swerved left and right trying to overtake him, but he narrowed the gap on the left-hand side. Peter pulled the van across the left-hand lane onto the hard shoulder showering the vehicles behind with grit and glass. Four interceptors used the empty lanes and screamed past him to his right and the helicopter dropped as low as it dared dazzling him with its spotlight. Barton waited for the gap in the crash barrier. He knew it was there as he had used it before. It was where he had planned to leave the motorway anyway. The police used the lay-by as a speed trap on a regular basis and he prayed that there wasn't an interceptor parked there now. Long seconds went by as he shielded his eyes from the blinding spotlight. A voice bellowed instructions at him from a loud hailer. 'Pull over now!' He ignored the orders and struggled to keep the vehicle on an even keel as he waited for the gap to appear. 'Pull over now!' An interceptor roared past him on the right and lurched across the lanes into his path. Its brake lights dazzled him as it tried to slow him down. Suddenly he saw the gap in the barriers and wrenched the steering wheel to the left on full lock. He closed his eyes, gritted his teeth, and waited for the impact.

Becky was flung sideways as the vehicle veered sharply. The van was travelling at ridiculous speed tilted sharply to one side. She felt her ribs crack as she bounced off the metal and tumbled over and over before slamming into the bulkhead. She felt her shoulder pop from its socket, and she screamed as the red-hot pain engulfed her nervous system. The breath was knocked from her lungs and she struggled to suck air into them. She gasped desperately trying to drag air into her chest and panic gripped her as the overwhelming sensation of suffocating swamped her. Tears streamed from her eyes and mingled with the blood from her head. She felt like a marble in a jam jar as the van hit something hard and she was launched violently into the air again. Her fingers clutched at fresh air as she grabbed desperately at the side of the van to steady herself, but she was tossed into the void before crashing down with a sickening thud.

Peter dragged the steering wheel hard left. The van careered over the lay-by and hit the kerb, catapulting it upwards over a grass embankment. The front wheels span uselessly in the air as the van was launched over the embankment and into the steep gorge. Becky had the sensation of weightlessness as the vehicle cleared the grassy bank and plunged headlong into the black fast-flowing waters of the River Ribble.

CHAPTER 44

The van was almost vertical when it hit the water. He had the sense to release the steering wheel, which stopped his wrist from being snapped on impact. The splashing sound was deafening, and the windscreen was thumped out of the rubbers. It cracked into pieces allowing the icy water to flood into the cab. Peter Barton held his breath as the water gushed in. The freezing river numbed his limbs in seconds. The water level rose quickly, engulfing him and he reached blindly for the seat belt release. The impact felt like hitting a brick wall at forty miles an hour and the combination of the cold water and whiplash had stunned him. The belt had bruised his ribs and winded him. His fingers fumbled with the clasp, clawing, scratching, and pressing anything in the hope that it was the release button. The van spiralled deeper and he could feel the current carrying the vehicle along with ease. Its size was insignificant in comparison to the power of the river.

When the van hit the river, Becky was catapulted the full length of the van. She hit the bulkhead with bone breaking force. Her skull cracked against the metal splitting her scalp from her forehead back to her crown. Blood gushed from the deep gash and blinding white pain flashed through her brain. The pain in her shoulder was unbearable; each movement sent another wave of mind-bending agony to her already stunned nervous system. She could feel her body shutting down, her brain refusing to take any more pain. Her senses were fading. She was confused when she heard the deafening splash and the sound of water gushing into the cab and only when the icy liquid hit her did, she realise that the vehicle was beginning to submerge.

The water was black and freezing. Peter Barton was completely submerged, and his lungs were screaming for oxygen. The urge to breathe out and suck in the icy liquid was overwhelming. He scrabbled with the belt and tugged desperately at the clip. His brain told him to slow down, stop panicking or he would die. He followed the line of the fastener with his fingertips and finally felt the release button click and the seat belt fell away. The van sank lower as he fumbled with the door handle, but it wouldn't budge. He slammed his weight against it time after time, but it wouldn't open. He kicked out with his feet against the bulkhead trying to dislodge the glass from the broken windscreen. The cracks gave way and it disintegrated without too much effort; he found himself swimming down through the windscreen into the river. The weight of the sinking van pushed him down deeper still. He grabbed at the wing mirror to right himself, flapped his arms, and kicked for the surface. His lungs threatened to defy his brain and breathe in.

Becky felt her senses returning as the icy water revived her. It flooded into the rear of the van; the pressure pinned her to the bulkhead. She struggled for air and tried to stand but the water made her spin and somersault. She was racked with pain and the blow to her head had disorientated her. The bitter cold sapped every ounce of energy from her limbs. The sensation of floating in a vortex increased her panic. She wasn't sure which way she was facing. Becky stopped thrashing for a moment, and she felt the water lift her towards the open door. She paddled aimlessly with her good arm desperately trying to keep her head above the deluge. As the water level evened out, the pressure lessened. Her head bobbed above the water and she sucked in air noisily. She was free of the van and she could see dozens of blue lights flashing at the top of the riverbank. The sound of the helicopter whirred above her. Torchlight pierced the darkness, sweeping across the river from one side to the other. She wanted to shout for help, but her muscles were frozen by pain and the cold. Sheer exhaustion pulled at her consciousness. Giving up and letting sleep take her would be so easy. Relax, Rebecca, close your eyes and let go, it won't hurt anymore.

Peter Barton broke the surface and gasped for air. He clung to the back door of the van, which was now just below the surface. He coughed to clear his airways and looked around. The van had drifted a hundred metres from where it entered the water and the current was taking it further down river. Torchlight from the riverbank swept across him. The police were in pursuit on foot, but they were struggling to keep up through the undergrowth. The van had floated to the centre of the river, but he could feel the water dragging it down into the depths. He needed to get to the far bank. He took a breath and readied himself to push off when he heard gurgling and a splash.

Barton turned back to the van and watched as the detective floated to the surface, coughing and spluttering. Her head was tilted to the sky, her mouth open, and her face was covered in blood; she appeared to make no effort to swim or tread water. Shouts from the riverbank shook him into action. The helicopter swooped over the river illuminating the scene with its spotlight. He was about to swim for freedom when the detective sunk beneath the water. Barton waited a moment. Surely, she would come back to the surface. He felt the van sink away from him and watched as bubbles floated to the surface at the point Rebecca Sebastian had been. The water was inky black. He shook his head and cursed himself as he dived beneath the water to find her.

Becky felt herself sinking into the darkness, but it didn't matter. The pain, which tortured her body was fading. She was floating into a blackness that she had never seen before, darker than dark, colder than ice but welcoming all the same. There was no energy left inside her. The will to survive had been knocked from her. She had been rendered weary and helpless by the struggle. Her lungs gave out and released her last breath and she heard the bubbles racing skyward. Peace seeped through her veins.

Barton dived and found nothing. His hands reached blindly in the inky water. He resurfaced and gasped for air before diving down once more. His fingers touched her hair and he dived deeper still. Her arms were floating limply above her and he grabbed at them trying to get a grip on her. He reached beneath her arms and stopped her from sinking any further. As the current clawed at them, he kicked towards the dazzling spotlight above. As they broke the surface, he gasped for air. His face was numb, and his teeth chattered uncontrollably. 'Breathe,' he whispered but there was no response. He wrapped his arms tightly around her chest and jerked hard. She rasped air into her lungs and spluttered but her body was still limp. There was no way that she could make it to safety alone. 'Just keep breathing,' he gasped as he turned onto his back and kicked for the riverbank.

CHAPTER 45

Annie slept fitfully; her dreams haunted by images of the dead. The sounds of the police headquarters coming to life drifted to her. Voices and laughter, doors slamming and footsteps on the stairs. She pulled the coat that warmed her over her head and tried to vanquish her sleep demons. Her body was exhausted, but her brain was still racing. It wouldn't allow her any peace as it constantly searched for answers. She checked her watch. It was five thirty. She had been resting for two hours. Her mind begged for more time to recover. She pulled her knees to her chest and drifted back into her troubled slumber.

'Guv,' she heard a second later. 'Wake up, guv.' She felt a hand nudging her shoulder.

She peered out of her makeshift blanket and the light made her squint. Stirling stood next to the cot. 'Not what I want to see when I first open my eyes in the morning,' she moaned. 'Tell me you've brought coffee,' she said looking at her watch. It was just turned nine. 'Shit!' she sat up with a start. 'Why didn't someone wake me up sooner?'

'The super said to let you sleep,' Stirling said. 'You must have needed it, guv. Coffee and bacon sandwiches are on the way. I'll see you in the office when you're ready.' He turned to walk away.

'Any news on Becky?' Annie stood up and stretched. Guilt gripped her. How could she have slept so long when one of her detectives was fighting for her life in intensive care?

'There were complications apparently,' Stirling grimaced. 'She was taken by air ambulance to the specialist neurology unit.'

They've finished with her in surgery but she's in an induced coma because of the swelling on her brain.'

'And Barton?'

'No sign of him yet. The armed unit inspector reckons he's probably drowned. They say that he dragged Becky to the riverbank. Saved her life by all accounts but he went back into the water when the armed unit approached.' Annie looked thoughtful. There was a deep conflict between being grateful to Barton for rescuing Becky and wanting to shoot him for taking her in the first instance. Stirling could see her struggling. 'Take your time, I'll see you upstairs, guv.'

'Yes,' Annie said flustered. 'Sorry, I'm still groggy. I'll get a quick wash and follow you.' Stirling smiled and nodded. Annie sighed and thought about the day ahead. Whatever happened, it would be a long one. She picked up her coat and bag and headed for the washrooms. The thought of hot coffee and food spurred her on. She couldn't remember the last time that she had eaten.

Alec looked out of the window and watched the choppy waters of the river rush past to the sea. Early morning rush hour was in full flow and the streets below were busy. Their case was running wild and galloping in one direction and then another. The involvement of foreign police departments had both helped and hindered the investigation but now their involvement had been escalated to the upper echelons of government. Things would get worse before they got better. The fact that Tod Harris was already in custody was the only thing that was keeping the pressure at bay. The kidnap of Rebecca Sebastian had hit the team hard. The only upside was that it was another force that was responsible for allowing Peter Barton to avoid capture. There was a Detective Superintendent in the Lancashire Constabulary that would have a bad day today. Alec felt for him, but it was all part of the job. A knock on the door disturbed his thoughts. 'Come in,' he called.

Annie poked her head around the door. He restrained from telling her how rough she looked. There would be no thanks for honesty in this case. 'You want to see us, guv?'

'Yes please,' Alec replied and returned to his desk.

Annie opened the door fully and stepped inside carrying three cups in one hand, Stirling was close behind. He carried a tray with a jug of coffee and a plate of bacon sandwiches.

'Coffee, guv?' Stirling grunted with a smile.

'Definitely.' Alec smiled. 'How are you feeling?' he asked Annie.

'Better for some sleep, thanks.'

'Good.' Alec nodded. 'We have some very important news from our friends in Benidorm.'

'About the number plates?' Annie asked surprised.

'Yes.' Alec nodded. 'They traced the second plate to an abandoned hire business on the outskirts of the resort. Apparently, when the business folded, there were several vehicles left to rot. One of them was the vehicle that we are looking for.' Alec paused while Stirling handed him a mug of coffee.

'That's great news, isn't it?' Annie was confused by Alec's demeanour. He didn't appear enthusiastic about the discovery at all. 'Why do I get the feeling that this isn't good news?'

Alec sighed and sipped his brew. 'A Guardia officer went to investigate last night. From what they can gather, he found the number plate. It was on a campervan and for some reason he entered the vehicle.' Annie felt her nerves jangle. She guessed what was coming although she hoped that she was wrong. 'They don't know what he found because the vehicle exploded.' Alec shrugged. 'First impressions are that it was an incendiary device.'

'Is he dead?' Stirling asked.

'Yes. Jose Peres, twelve years on the job, father of three.' Alec read from his notes.

'Oh, dear God. Annie shook her head. 'We warned them that there could be booby-traps when we sent the communiqué.' She was flabbergasted. 'Why on earth did they send an officer alone and why wasn't he warned?'

'Their top brass is playing it down by claiming it was a translation issue.'

'What is the Spanish for 'complete fuckup'?' Annie scoffed. 'The poor man and what about his family? I bet his wife will feel much better knowing it was a translation issue.'

'I wonder what he found,' Stirling added as he bit into his sandwich. 'There were no devices planted in San Francisco.' He shrugged as he chewed. 'If his previous MO is applied then there was a victim in that campervan. We won't know until forensics come in and that could be a while.'

'How much credence are you giving to what Barton had to say?' Alec raised his eyebrows.

'I honestly don't know.' Annie sighed. She looked at the bacon sandwich in her hand and forced herself to bite it. Her appetite had vanished after hearing the news from Spain. 'Barton implicated Geoff Ryder as being behind all of this. Can you believe that?'

'We all met him a few times.' Alec shook his head. 'He always seemed to be the most balanced member of the Ryder family to me. What do you think?'

'He came across as a clever man to me.' Stirling nodded.

'It seems ludicrous to me,' Annie agreed. 'He said that both Harris and Taylor were represented by Ryder as young offenders,' Annie turned back to Alec. 'If he's telling the truth, we need to speak to Geoff.'

'Even if he is right, he could be leading us up the garden path,' Alec said. 'Let's take it at face value and unless we find a solid link between Geoff and this case, we leave him alone. The family will crucify us in a libel court. Barton's accusations have no standing with me, I'm afraid.'

'Has he flipped?' Stirling asked. 'We know he had a hard time in jail and I can understand him being pissed off but kidnapping Taylor, torturing him and then blowing his brains out is a little over the top,' he said sarcastically. 'His visit to persuade Emilia Harris to tell us what she knew doesn't help us either. He openly admitted that he frightened her into turning over information. That library book is key to Simon's kidnap but now we don't know if

Harris had it hidden, or Barton gave it to her.' He shrugged. 'Then he kidnaps a detective. He has lost the plot if you ask me. The sooner he's behind bars, the safer we'll all be.'

'It's complicated enough without Barton being involved. All we can do is check up on what he's saying.' She paused in frustration 'His stunt with Becky throws what little credibility he had down the toilet. How can we take him seriously?'

'We can't.' Alec shook his head. 'He murdered Brian Taylor in cold blood. We can't use him as a source. Whatever he says, we need to find evidence to back it up.'

'When are you planning to talk to Laura Ryder, guv?'

'I said that I would be at her house at eleven,' Alec said looking at the clock. 'Now that's a conversation I'm not looking forward to.'

'It will be a tough one.' Annie nodded in agreement. 'How do you feel about me coming along, you know, the woman's touch?'

'Good idea.' Alec nodded.

'Do we mention Geoff?'

'We can ask how he is and when she last saw him and go with the flow.'

'Agreed.'

'While you're there,' Stirling added, 'I'll chase up all the information that we're waiting on. If we can nail down the recent travel movements for Harris and Barton, at least we'll know which avenue is a dead end.'

'Good,' Annie agreed. 'Schedule a syndicate meeting for three o'clock this afternoon and if you hear anything from the hospital on Becky, call me.'

CHAPTER 46

Tod Harris woke with a start. His cell door was rattling loudly, the metallic booming echoed across the upper landing of the prison. 'Fucking nonce!' a voice hollered through the door. 'You won't be locked in forever and when you come out, we'll be waiting for you!' Another series of kicks rattled the door in its frame and then he heard footsteps running away. The banging and shouting roused the other inmates and they joined in with the abuse. The upper landing exploded with noise first, but the two tiers below followed quickly. Threats and vile names bounced off the thick prison walls. Each one made him shrink further beneath his rough blanket. He felt like a rabbit in its warren, the dogs at the entrance waiting to rip him to pieces. There was nowhere to run and nowhere to hide. He had already been attacked in the washroom. His nose was still painfully sore and the bruising beneath his eyes had surfaced. The guards despised him as much as the inmates did. He couldn't expect any protection from them. In fact, he was convinced that they would turn a blind eye each time he was jumped. There was no light at the end of this tunnel. When he heard keys rattle in the lock, his heart pounded in his chest. He was frozen in fear when the door creaked open.

'Visit, Harris,' the prison officer growled. 'Get yourself ready sharpish!'

'Who is it?' Tod asked confused. 'I'm not expecting anyone.'

'Do I look like your private secretary?' the guard snapped. 'Move it or I'll drag you down there in your birthday suit.' Tod pulled his clothes on quickly and slipped his feet into his trainers. He walked onto the landing with trepidation. The caterwauling reached fever pitch. Three landings full of inmates went berserk, kicking their doors, banging cups against the metal and screaming abuse. 'Sounds like you're popular, Harris,' the officer sneered. 'Mind you, if you will go around raping women and killing kids then you get what you deserve in here. Can't say it would bother me if they skin you alive to be honest.' He carried on chirpily. 'I've seen a few nonce attacks in my time,' he grimaced and sucked air between his teeth, 'they're never pleasant I can tell you. One bloke had his balls ripped off. Can you believe that?' he turned to Tod. 'Literally ripped them off with their bare hands.' Tod walked in front of him, head bowed, and shoulders hunched. He was trying hard not to listen. 'Funny thing was that we only found one of them. I never worked that out. Amazing really. Did it with their bare hands,' he repeated. 'Makes your eyes water just thinking about it, doesn't it?' Tod wanted to be sick. The hate from the inmates was palpable. He reached the stairs and took them two steps at a time but there was no escaping the deafening assault.

When they reached the bottom landing, the officer led him through a series of four gates; each one was opened and locked tightly behind him. The screaming abuse became muffled, but it hadn't abated. The prison population wanted his blood as retribution for his alleged crimes and it was only a matter of time before they had their opportunity. He found it bizarre that convicted criminals could sit in judgment over him. How dare they? He was surrounded by scum, who felt justified enough to hand out their own brand of justice. 'Fuck them,' he thought.

'Come on, over here,' the officer ordered. They reached the visiting area and he was taken into an anteroom used for sensitive visits such as marriage breakups or the communication of a death in the family. 'Best to keep you out of the way.'

Tod stepped into the room and nodded a silent hello to his brief, Ken Graff. The guard handcuffed him to the table and took his position behind him. 'What is all this about?' Tod asked. 'Are the police coming?'

'They won't talk to you again unless you have something new to say.' He gestured to his briefcase. 'There have been some developments. I see it as an opportunity,' Graff smiled and cleaned his glasses. He shuffled his papers and put them back on. 'You, my boy, are looking at a full life term with no chance of parole.' He looked over his lenses like a wise old professor. 'You understand the enormity of the evidence against you, don't you?'

'I understand the enormity of how much I'm being butt fucked by Rob Derry,' Tod protested. He sat sulkily in his chair and frowned like a petulant child. 'I know that no one believes me but what can I do?'

'You can start by not bullshitting me,' Graff snapped. 'I'm on your side although lord only knows why I agreed to replace that spineless bitch, Bartlet. She should be struck off.' He spat as he spoke. 'I won't beat around the bush. The police have seen through your 'Rob Derry' game and let me tell you that it's just another link in the chains that they're going to fasten you with for the remainder of your days. I was very embarrassed when they told me. I should have seen it straight away.'

'What Rob Derry game?' Tod frowned. 'I have no idea what you're talking about.'

'They found a prepaid visa card used by this 'Rob Derry' on a trip abroad. It looks like they think that he's killed abroad,' Graff removed his glasses and looked sternly at Tod. 'It is in the name of Robdenn Derry, which I'm reliably told is an anagram of, Brendon Ryder!' He watched Tod's facial expression for his reaction. Tod frowned; deep creases rippled on his forehead. Far too many for a man his age, Graff noticed. If he was faking confusion, then he was doing a great job. He looked baffled and there was no response. 'Has the cat got your tongue? You know who Brendon Ryder is don't you?'

'Of course, I do.'

'You didn't think that the police would see through it?' Graff snorted. 'You may think that it was very clever, but it hasn't helped your case at all.'

'Is it just a coincidence?' Tod shook his head and bit his bottom lip. 'I didn't realise that. Are they taking the piss?' he asked quietly. 'Rob Derry isn't his real name?'

'No.' Graff wasn't sure who was taking piss, Tod or the police. 'They are not and what's more, I agree with them that you made it up to throw them off the scent.'

'I wouldn't think of something like that. I'm really not that clever.'

'The police think that you did.' He sat back and waited for a reaction. 'Do you know anything about his activity abroad?'

'No. Of course I don't.'

'Have you been to Spain with him?'

'No.'

'They will find out and if we get blindsided in court, you're screwed.'

'I don't know anything about it.'

'You can appreciate that it doesn't look good, does it?'

'It's coincidence.'

'I don't believe that it is.'

'So, you believe them over your client?'

'What I believe isn't the issue, Tod. We have to look at what we think a jury will believe.' He shrugged. 'Put yourself in my position.' Graff shrugged and tapped the file. 'If you were on the jury and heard all this, what would you think?'

Tod sat forward, his lips thin and pale, his eyes piercing and accusing. The bruising beneath them made him look much older. 'I would think that Rob Derry made up his alias to trick me and the police.' He banged his fist on the table angrily. 'I've been sitting here since day one protesting my innocence in these murders.' He tilted his head and stared at Graff. 'I admitted the rapes and I've explained that I'm being set up by Rob Derry or whatever the mad bastard is really called, and no one is listening to me. Now they've worked out the bastard has been tricking me by using the name of a serial killer and that's my fault?'

'I'm not saying it's your fault. I'm saying it's difficult to explain it away.'

'This just further strengthens their resolve that I'm a murdering lunatic, doesn't it?'

'Yes.'

'So where is this opportunity that you're talking about?' Tod asked exasperated. 'I can't see it.'

Graff shuffled uncomfortably. 'The police are desperate to find this 'Rob Derry' character, whoever he may be. If you can identify him then we may be able to shift the burden of guilt onto him.' Graff frowned. 'It is your only chance. I can't see any other way out, Tod.'

Tod sighed and looked at the ceiling. He shook his head. 'Surely if they catch him, he'll blame me for everything?' He sighed. 'The evidence is already there. They'll bury me no matter what I do.'

Graff took a photograph from his file and placed it on the table. 'The police showed you this picture before, didn't they?'

Tod nodded.

'This man kidnapped a police officer last night.' He looked Tod in the eyes. 'Between you and I, do you recognise him?'

Tod nodded. 'He killed that kid a few years back.'

'Let me enlighten you,' Graff shook his head. 'He was sent to prison for kidnapping his nephew, Simon Barton.' Graff placed another photo down. 'Do you recognise the boy?'

Tod sighed and nodded his head. 'Of course, I do. That is the kid that they're accusing me of killing.'

'Exactly, now hold that thought.' Graff raised his hand. 'His uncle's name is Peter Barton. He was once a policeman, an analyst, I believe, so he's a very resourceful man.' Tod shifted his gaze from one picture to another. 'He was released on appeal although his alibi was dubious.' Graff sat back and folded his arms. 'He kidnapped a man called Brian Taylor, who he suspected of taking Simon. He tied him up in his cellar and questioned him for days. When the police arrived at his house to question him, he blew his brains out.'

Tod frowned. His eyes lit up with realisation. 'And then suddenly the kid's underwear and library book turn up at my mum's house?'

'That would appear to be the case.'

'He's evil. I told them all along that he was. He killed my mum.' Tod looked at the photographs. His mind was racing. 'Did he kill the cop that he took?'

'She's in intensive care.'

'And he killed the Taylor guy?'

'Yes, blew his brains all over the ceiling with a shotgun.'

'I told them he was a lunatic.' Tod sat back and shook his head. 'I'm terrified of him. That's why I didn't say anything when they showed me the photograph. He is a psychopath. I thought he would kill me and all my family if I said anything.'

'What do you mean?' Graff half smiled.

'That is Rob Derry or whatever his real name is.'

Graff nodded and wiped sweat from his forehead. 'You know that holding this back hasn't helped you at all?'

'I was scared.'

'That's understandable,' Graff said gravely. 'Identifying him will help our case.' He paused and thought about his next words. 'I want to get some things straight in my mind.'

'Like what?'

'If you want me to help you, I need you to answer me honestly, okay?'

'Okay.'

'You admit being at the first scene but when you left the house, both women were alive and unhurt?'

'Yes, absolutely. I've been saying this from day one.'

'How do you explain your semen being at the second scene?' Graff asked gruffly. He twiddled his pen between finger and thumb.

'Rob Derry planted it. I mean him, whoever he is' Tod tapped the photograph.

'Peter Barton.'

'Yes. Barton must have kept the condoms that I used.'

'Feasible, I suppose. Didn't you throw them away?'

Tod sat forward and steepled his fingers. 'Whenever we were in someone's house, we used one bag for any rubbish and we always disposed of it away from the scene. We never flushed anything because it can be retrieved.' Tod lowered his voice. 'He taught me that. Police training, I bet?' He shook his head. 'I think the bastard kept the condoms to set me up.'

'Okay that may throw up a shadow of doubt but what about the thumbprint?'

Tod held up his finger eager to answer. 'He told me that they can pick up fingerprints using superglue, right.' He paused and looked over his shoulder at the prison officer. 'It makes a raised imprint and once they have the raised print, it can be used to make a false print. Do you think that's true?'

'I don't know the science behind it, but we can check it out. It makes sense on the face of it.' Graff nodded and made notes. 'I'm trying to eliminate all the evidence that puts you at the second scene,' he paused. 'How do you explain the knife and the DVD at your home?'

'Barton broke in and planted them.' Tod shrugged. 'If he was a policeman then he could break in without leaving any sign, couldn't he?'

'Probably.' Graff ticked his list. 'The ball bearings and petrol canisters?'

'He planted them all when I was in Benidorm.' Tod paused. 'And the underwear, all of it!' Tod filled up with tears. 'He told me to leave the country for a few days, so I did. I thought it was just to avoid getting pulled but looking back, he knew what he was going to do didn't he?'

'That is what we're going to pitch to the police. He has the knowledge to carry out all of this and his recent spate of criminal behaviour shows that he is more than capable of organising a set-up.'

'He is capable of anything. He said that he would kill my mum and he did!'

'Okay, Tod.' Graff packed his papers away. 'I'll get this information to the DI immediately. This changes your position dramatically. I think the police will have a lot of questions for you and my advice is to tell them everything that you can. The more you can put onto Peter Barton, the better for you, understand?'

'Yes,' Tod said meekly. 'He'll have me killed … I know he will. He's a psycho.'

'You'll be safe here, Tod. I'll speak to the governor personally and make sure that they protect you.' Graff looked at the prison officer. 'If there's so much as a hair on his head ruffled before his court case, I'll bring personal lawsuits against any officer on duty. I suggest you spread that among your colleagues.' Graff nodded his head and his jowls wobbled. The prison officer scowled and his face reddened. 'Now please escort my client back to his cell. I'll be in touch very soon, Tod.'

'Thanks,' Tod said. He breathed a massive sigh of relief. 'Thank God someone believes me at last.' Graff picked up his briefcase and headed for the door. 'There's a chance, although it's slim, that we could get all but the rape charges dropped,' Graff said as he opened the door. A tear ran from Tod's eye and Graff smiled thinly. He was unsure if he was fighting for justice or not.

CHAPTER 47

Alec pulled up to an ornate set of wrought iron gates that were designed with security in mind rather than decoration. High walls ran in both directions as far as the eye could see. He wound down his window and pressed a buzzer for the intercom.

'Drive up Alec,' the familiar voice of Laura Ryder greeted them. He turned to Annie and smiled as the gates parted slowly.

'CCTV,' Alec commented. 'The place is still like a fortress.'

'I can't blame her considering who her husband was.'

'True.'

'I always felt sorry for her,' Annie said looking out of the window. 'Poor woman lost everyone she loved.'

'She doesn't sound worried to see us,' Alec said.

'Why would she be?'

'Her late husband being a drug dealer, her son being a serial killer?'

'Hardly her fault, though is it?'

'If the police had shot my son dead, I would be concerned if they came knocking on my door even if it is four years later.'

'I wouldn't.' Annie shook her head. 'I would assume it was a follow up or something new had come up.'

'Must be a woman thing.' Alec laughed. 'Or maybe the job makes me paranoid.'

They relaxed a little as they drove up the long crescent-shaped driveway towards the house. A brand-new Porsche was parked in front of the double garage. The private plate read LT1. Annie frowned and looked at Alec. He shrugged and raised his eyebrows. 'She changed her name?' Annie asked.

'Maybe,' Alec said bringing the car to stop at the front door. 'She might have remarried.'

Laura opened the front door and smiled at them. She held out her hand. 'You look well, Annie,' she said looking at her prosthetic eye. 'You've healed well; you look as beautiful as ever.'

'Thank you.' Annie blushed. She had to admire how straightforward she was. There were no false graces about her. 'You haven't aged at all.' Annie returned a compliment.

'Well, I could tell you that I don't smoke or drink and that I make my own smoothies and bathe in vitamin C but that would be bollocks.' She winked at Alec. 'Botox every six months!'

'You do look well,' Alec said taking her hand. 'Maybe I should try some.'

'It is good, Alec, but it can't produce miracles.' She winked again. Annie smiled and Alec nudged her with his elbow. 'Come in. Can I get you a drink?' she asked. She led them into a huge L-shaped living room. Panoramic windows gave a view of the expansive grounds.

'I'm fine thank you,' Alec declined.

'Not for me.' Annie shook her head. 'We really don't want to take up much of your time.'

'I presume that you haven't come to sell me a ticket to the policeman's Christmas ball so what can I do for you?'

'We found two more bodies on Crosby Beach,' Alec got straight to the point. 'Two young boys.'

'Boys?' Laura looked confused. 'Oh dear,' Laura said quietly. 'I'm not sure how I can help.'

'Do you recognise either of these men?' Annie handed her two photographs.

Laura studied them and shook her head. 'No., should I?'

'We wondered if either of them were friends of Brendon.'

'No. I don't think so but then I didn't know all his friends.' She paused. 'In fact, I didn't know much about him at all did I?'

'It was a long shot, but we had to ask, sorry to drag the whole thing up for you again,' Alec apologised.

'Don't apologise you have a job to do. Brendon was a sick man and he paid for it with his life She smiled thinly. 'The rest of us have to get on with it. Especially me!'

'I noticed the plates on your car,' Annie changed the subject tactfully. 'Did you change your name?'

'Always the detective, Annie. There's no getting anything by you is there!' She held up her ring finger. 'And it's not what you think either. I took my maiden name Thomas back.' She shrugged. 'I've lost two husbands and a son to the Ryder name, enough is enough. I wanted a clean break, a new start.'

'I don't blame you,' Annie said looking around. There were no pictures of any of the family anywhere. 'It's the least you deserve.' She paused and smiled. 'Do you see much of Geoff at all?'

'Geoff?' Laura looked surprised. 'I haven't seen him for about three and a half years.' Her face seemed blank, from the look in her eyes, she had drifted off somewhere else. 'We fell out not long after the funeral.'

'Do you mind if I ask why?'

'Do you mind if I ask why you want to know?' There was an edge to her voice now.

'We want to ask him about these men.' Annie lifted the photos. 'We checked his old address, but he doesn't own the property anymore.'

'He sold that place years ago.'

'His office told us that he was on extended leave.'

'He's a wealthy man. Why go to work when you don't need to?'

'What happened between you?'

'He made a move on me.' She rolled her eyes. 'He took my need to lean on him the wrong way and he took the rejection very badly. He walked out and I haven't heard from him since.'

'Do you know where we could find him?'

'No but I can tell you that he was always talking about travelling. I heard that he wanted to relocate.'

'Do you know where?' Alec asked.

'I believe he bought a villa in Spain somewhere and he planned to drive across the continent and maybe explore the Far East, but I haven't heard anything since.'

'Do you know where in Spain?'

'Not a clue. He may be back I really don't know and to be honest, I don't care. If I never see another Ryder in my life it will be too soon.'

Alec nodded and rubbed the dimple in his chin. 'I understand, Laura, thanks for speaking to us.'

'You're welcome.' She smiled although there was no warmth in it. 'I'll show you out.' Annie felt awkward as they walked back to front door. They hadn't been there long, but they'd already outstayed their welcome. The warmth that she had had in her eyes when they arrived was gone. She opened the front door and looked down at the floor as they walked past her.

'Thanks again and good luck,' Annie turned as she stepped outside, but Laura had already closed the door behind them. Annie felt a little saddened by it. They climbed into the car in silence and Alec drove them along the driveway. The gates opened automatically and then closed behind them. Alec let out a sigh. 'Well that went well.' Alec broke the silence. 'Ryder has a villa in Spain?'

'I heard that.'

'Thoughts?'

'I'll reserve judgment until we have all the travel movement information.'

'She wasn't very forthcoming, was she?'

'We got answers, what more could we ask from a widow whose only son was shot dead because he was a serial killer?' Annie felt drained by the experience. 'She tried her best to be normal with us but when it comes to the Ryders, she doesn't have anything left to give.'

'Can you get that while I'm driving?' Alec's mobile phone rang, and he passed it to Annie to answer it.

'DS Ramsay's phone,' Annie answered. She listened intently and frowned. 'When was this?' she asked with a sigh. She rubbed at her temples with her fingers and thumb and closed her eyes. 'Thanks, we'll be in touch to arrange an interview.' She hung up and looked at Alec with a blank expression.

'What is it?' Alec asked.

'Tod Harris has identified Peter Barton as his accomplice.'

'Out of the blue?'

'Seems that way.'

'What do you think?' Alec looked at her face. 'I know.' He nodded wisely. 'You're deferring judgment until all the facts are in, right?'

'Damn right,' Annie said in a whisper.

CHAPTER 48

Peter Barton reached up and dragged a tyre from a shelf. It was old and well-worn, but he didn't like throwing things away. He dumped it onto a workbench and turned it with his hands. The inside was bone dry and flaking. He checked over the items on the bench. Fishhooks, superglue, firelighters, and cling-film. He picked up one of the display fireworks that he had bought online and placed it on a plastic sheet next to the tyre. The label read 'Armageddon'. Peter took a craft knife and sliced through the side of it. He held an empty soup tin beneath it and dark granules trickled out making a small pyramid in the bottom of the can. He moved the firework to one side and then took a box of matches from the bench. He struck one and watched it flare and then burn. The smell of sulphur drifted to him. It reminded him of his childhood. He dropped the match into the can and stepped back. A plume of blue flame shot skywards with a whoosh. He smiled and nodded. It would do the job.

He looked at the television screen across the room and saw another image of himself on Sky News. It seemed that he was the story of the day. The kidnapping of a police officer was big news and the Press had linked it to the murder of Brian Taylor. Sources within the police had confirmed that he was a person of interest and was considered to be dangerous. The broadcast warned the public not to approach him but to contact the police immediately. There was no way that he could go out in public. His features were too distinctive. He would be recognised. He walked over to his kitchenette and switched on the kettle although he felt a burning desire to drink something more potent than coffee. Getting smashed wouldn't help. Relaxing would have to wait until he had finished his preparations.

He had rented a small workshop unit years earlier and it had been his safe house on numerous occasions. He always felt anonymous there. Since the recession, the remote industrial estate that it was situated on was only partially occupied. His unit was big enough to park his vehicles inside and small enough to heat easily and keep comfortable. It was a home from home and had everything that he needed, water, power, and a partitioned office that he had converted into a cosy living space. He had his bed, television, toilet, hot water, and a small kitchen. His refrigerator was as tall as he was, half fridge, half freezer, and it was packed and well organised. The workshop was fully fitted with everything that he needed, and he had stocked it well over the years. He didn't need to go out until he was ready.

Peter watched the kettle boil and poured the water over two spoonfuls of coffee. He carried his drink to a washbasin and placed it onto a shelf above it. The mirror above the sink reflected a man with shoulder length greying hair that curled out around the ears. His eyebrows had a mind of their own and seemed to grow at an abnormal rate. He bared his teeth and put his tongue out, turning his head from side to side. The police wanted the man in the mirror, and he didn't feel as anxious about it as he should. Murderer. The title didn't offend him. He felt numb inside. The years had destroyed his faith in humanity especially his own. He wasn't sure if he had human emotions anymore or if he ever had. Maybe he didn't deserve to be living freely among other human beings. More to the point, he didn't want to be among them. If they caught him, they would lock him up with the other animals but that didn't matter to him either because he would take his own life before he had to spend another hour in prison. He looked at the rack of shotguns in the mirror behind him. They would be key players in his future however short it was.

He picked up a box of 'Just for Men' and read the instructions. Opening the box, he took out a plastic tray and placed it on the basin. There were two tubes inside, and he took the first one between his finger and thumb and squeezed the dark gooey contents of a tube along it. The second tube was a white paste and he mixed them together with a plastic paddle. The substance turned black and the smell of ammonia drifted to him. He smeared the black paste into his eyebrows making sure that they were completely covered and then he used the remainder on his facial hair. He smiled and thought of the video game character Mario. The bristles began to darken immediately. He switched on the hot tap and let the water flow before picking up a pair of scissors. Peter took a thick chunk of hair and began to chop at it. As the basin filled with greying curls, he swapped the scissors for a razorblade and shaved the remainder to the scalp. With each smooth stroke, the man in the mirror began to change appearance.

CHAPTER 49

'Are we all here?' Annie asked. She looked at the clock, which showed ten past three. 'I want to get the syndicate meeting underway. Are you ready, Jim?'

'Yes, guv.'

'Kathy Brooks is on her way over,' Alec said. 'She's stuck in traffic.'

'We need to get on,' Annie said irritably. She turned on the screens in readiness. 'She can join us when she's ready. Right, everyone!' The office fell silent and all faces turned to her. 'I'll begin with some news from Harris's brief.' The screens displayed custody suite photographs of Tod Harris and Peter Barton. 'Tod Harris has had an epiphany and claims that Barton is our elusive Rob Derry.' Whispers rippled through the detectives. She nodded in acknowledgement of their reaction. 'Some of you will be saying 'I told you so' but don't get too carried away. Unless we have evidence to back up his information, his claims are worthless.' She paused and looked at the faces in the room. 'Personally, I think Harris is trying to deflect blame. He's clutching at straws. Pictures of Barton are on every news broadcast so I'm confident that we'll pick him up soon.'

Alec held up his hand to interrupt. 'The DS in charge of the search for Barton told me that they found an inflatable rib at the mouth of the River Ribble. It was floating freely in the bay and the engine was still warm. They think that Barton had it tied up somewhere near where he entered the water. Some fishermen recalled seeing the rib tied up in that area a few times last week. Barton may have been planning his escape. It would explain the lack of a body or footprints on either bank.' Alec explained. 'Lancashire have set up a systematic search of the area south of the Ribble. They're combing the rural areas with the force helicopter and conducting house to house. If he's hiding, they'll find him, if he's running, the public will find him.'

Annie wasn't convinced but she kept her opinion to herself. 'Jim?' she prompted the big sergeant.

He rubbed his bristly jaw with a gnarled hand. 'We ran checks on Taylor and Harris and Barton was correct in saying that they were both represented by Geoff Ryder as juveniles.' He tilted his head and looked around. 'We have a connection between the three men which, we hadn't seen previously. When we examined their travel movements, we discovered that Geoff Ryder left the country two days after Simon Barton disappeared.' Silence greeted the news. 'There are no records of him returning but if he was on the run, he wouldn't use his own passport to come back.'

250

'Where did he go, Sarge?'

'We don't know but he sailed from Dover to Calais with his car and no passengers. We're still waiting on the ship's foot passenger list in case one of them booked on.'

'Laura Ryder told us that she thinks Ryder bought a villa in Spain but we're still tracking it down.' Alec added.

'Spain links Harris and Ryder. If Ryder is involved, we'll know soon enough. There are no records of Peter Barton leaving the country at all.' Stirling shrugged. There was a disappointed silence. 'We know he's shrewd so he may have travelled under an alias. He's not off the hook just yet.' He stepped to the screen and pointed at Harris. 'Tod Harris has travelled to Spain three or four times a year every year for the last six years. There's no record of him travelling to the States but,' Stirling paused, 'there were large cash withdrawals made from his bank accounts in the weeks before the RV's were rented in San Francisco.'

The lift doors opened, and Kathy Brooks stepped out. She looked cold, wet, and flustered. 'I'm sorry I'm late,' she reddened as she struggled out of her coat. 'I do have something for you that's worth waiting for.'

Annie felt her stomach lurch. She looked at Alec and he nodded to her. They were of the same mind that the forensics would answer their questions. They usually did. 'We're about out of new updates anyway,' Annie said. 'What have you found?'

Kathy hung her coat on a chair and stood next to Alec. She took a deep breath before she spoke. 'The bodies that we recovered from Crosby Beach were not buried by Brendon Ryder.' She looked at Annie. There was an audible sigh of relief around the room. 'Some of the details that we kept from the public were not replicated. There were similarities but, in my opinion, it was a copycat.' She paused.

'So, Harris is in the frame,' Stirling said nodding.

'Better than that.' Kathy smiled thinly. 'We found a hair stuck in the glue that was used to fix the breathing tubes into the nostrils.' She paused. There wasn't a sound in the room. Annie felt her breath stuck in her chest. Come on, come on, come on! Her mind screamed. 'The DNA matches Tod Harris.'

'Yes!' Annie punched the air. Cheers and shouts and several profanities came from the gathering. 'He can't slither his way out of that the fucking snake!' she said looking at Alec.

'He won't be able to slither out of a few things,' Kathy said over the noise. The celebrations stopped dead as all eyes turned to her again. 'I was contacted by the lab in San Francisco. They asked me to share our samples for cross referencing.' The tension in the room was electric. 'They found Harris's DNA inside one of the mattresses.'

'So, he was there but as it stands, the Metro PD doesn't have any victims,' Annie said smiling. 'If they can prove that by finding bodies, that bastard is nailed good and proper.'

'I think it's academic, Annie but what we need to know for sure is was he alone?' Alec interrupted.

'I can't tell you that for sure I'm afraid but there's something else,' she said stopping him from changing the subject. 'The bodies on the beach are not who you think they are.' She paused and the room fell silent again. 'The boys we extracted from the sand are brothers. We identified sibling DNA.' Annie and Alec exchanged confused glances. 'I don't know if this is good news or bad but neither of the boys is Simon Barton. They're James Goodwin and his brother.'

CHAPTER 50

Peter Barton finished grinding the welds. The petrol tank that he was working on lifted apart into two sections and he laid them side by side on the workbench. He took his 12-gauge Mossberg from the gun rack and placed it next to the tank. He measured it and cursed under his breath. It was ten inches too long. Marking the barrels, he fastened the shotgun into a vice and tightened the handle to hold it securely. The grinder whirred and a shower of sparks exploded from the diamond tipped disk as it cut through the gun. After a minute of ear-splitting whining the unwanted section of barrel clanged on the concrete floor. He unfastened the vice and measured the size again. The Mossberg would fit snugly. He could fit a plastic sleeve to hold the weapon and keep the tank sealed and re-weld the edges so that he could slide the shotgun from beneath the Jeep when the time came to use it.

His attention turned to the tyre. The inner rim bristled with large fishhooks that he had straightened and melted into the rubber. The lethal barbs glinted in the lights. Peter slipped on a thick pair of welding gloves and picked it up wincing at the weight. It was packed and wrapped but the contents made it much heavier than he had imagined. He carried it to the Jeep and opened the rear passenger door. The back seat had been removed and he lifted the tyre into the well beneath it. He tried to slot the back seat back into place above it and smiled when it clipped in without a struggle. There were a couple more things to load and then he would be ready.

CHAPTER 51

Tod Harris trotted into the interview room as fast as the prison officers would allow. He looked energised and excited and eager to sit down with the detectives. Ken Graff walked in behind Tod and the officers; his face was stern. He barely acknowledged Tod as he sat down. 'Morning, Detectives,' he said opening his briefcase. 'I trust we're here to discuss reducing the charges against my client?' he asked in a matter of fact manner. 'Have you made any progress finding Peter Barton?'

Annie looked at Stirling and raised her eyebrows in surprise. Stirling shook his head in disbelief. Annie ignored the question and put a photo of Geoff Ryder onto the table. 'Do you remember being represented by this man when you were a juvenile?' she asked sharply. Tod flinched visibly; the wind taken from his sails in an instant. His demeanour changed from light to dark. 'His name is Geoff Ryder. Do you remember him?' Tod turned pale and sat back. His eyes didn't move from the photograph. 'Do you remember him, Tod?'

'I remember him.' Tod nodded slowly. 'He was a nasty man.'

'He travelled to Spain two days after Simon Barton went missing,' Annie added. His reaction was strange. He seemed confused but almost amused. 'Do you know anything about that?'

'No.' His face remained unmoved, but his eyes smiled. 'Why are you asking me about him?'

'Because he represented you and this man, Brian Taylor around the same time. Do you remember Brain Taylor?'

'No.' Tod looked disinterested. His mind was somewhere else. He was nervous and fidgeting. 'I've never met the man.'

'I'll tell you about him, shall I?' Annie pressed on. 'Peter Barton shot and killed Brian Taylor because he thought that he was involved in Simon Barton's abduction,' Annie put another photo down. Tod stared blankly at the image. 'Both you and Taylor were represented by Geoff Ryder, which is an unusual coincidence. What do think about that?'

'Ask Barton,' Tod sneered. 'He pulled the trigger.'

'Brian Taylor told Barton that you had Simon's library book. He said that you had kept it as a souvenir.' She paused and lowered her tone, 'you kept it as trophy. We know you like to keep trophies, don't we?'

'I kept women's knickers. Nothing else.' He snapped. 'I've told you that I didn't touch those kids.'

'But the book ended up at your home. So did his underpants.' Annie pushed. 'I don't think that you have explained that satisfactorily.'

'Nothing to do with me. Barton planted them while I was in Benidorm.'

'I'm not buying that,' Annie sat back and folded her arms.

'I thought you said that you would get these charges dropped. You said we could answer everything but the rape charges.' Tod shook his head and turned to Graff. 'Why is she still banging on about these kids?'

Graff shuffled his papers and blushed. 'My client has offered his defence on this matter. This Peter Barton chap is an ex-intelligence office from the Met and as such, he is forensically aware and more than capable of planting evidence. Tod is the victim of an elaborate set-up.'

'Elaborate?' Stirling scoffed. 'He's delusional and if you have told him there's any chance of convincing a jury otherwise, then you're delusional too.'

'Find Barton,' Tod snapped. 'I'm sick of this. How many times can I answer the same questions?'

'We're determined to find Simon and we think that you know where he's buried.' Annie changed tack.

"Find Simon', did you say?' Graff looked confused and removed his glasses. 'I thought that you had found him.'

'We thought that we had too. We thought he was buried on Crosby Beach, but it turns out the he isn't one of the bodies that we discovered.'

'Really?' Tod smiled sarcastically. 'You must be very disappointed. I suppose you'll be pinning their murders on me regardless. So, I have a library book and you don't have a body?'

'You think this is a game?'

'Life is all a game.' Tod sighed. 'You win some and you lose some.'

'Are you winning, Tod?'

'Do I look like I'm winning,' he said pointing to the bruises around his eyes. 'I don't mind losing when we're playing on an even pitch but I'm being fucked over here.'

'Have you ever been to America?' Annie changed tack.

'No, why?' He looked confused.

'Just a question,' Annie smiled thinly. 'Did you travel to Benidorm with Geoff Ryder?'

'Never.'

'Did you ever meet up with him there?'

'Never.' Twitch.

'Did you know that he had a villa there?'

'No.'

'Can I ask why you're questioning my client about Geoff Ryder?' Graff interrupted.

'He left the country two days after Simon Barton vanished and his body isn't buried with James Goodwin,' Annie said sternly. 'The other victim is James's brother.'

'I still do not see the connection to my client and Geoff Ryder.'

'We received information from a good source that Ryder may have orchestrated things.'

'A good source?' Tod snorted.

'Would this source be Barton?' Graff raised his eyebrows in surprise. 'Are the MIT using wanted murderers as informants now, Inspector?'

'We need to investigate every avenue.' Annie blushed a little. 'We wanted to give Tod the opportunity to come clean and allow us to find Simon and let his family have some closure and lay him to rest and if Ryder was involved, then we need to investigate that too.' She paused. 'Tod may not have been 'in charge' of the situation.'

Tod smiled sourly. 'You're on a fishing trip,' he scoffed. 'I didn't kill any kids. Peter Barton is your psycho, not me. Are you deaf?'

'I can't accept your version, Tod. We have new evidence that you were involved.'

'Bullshit!'

'What type of evidence?' Graff asked angrily.

'The best kind, DNA,' Annie said with a narrow smile.

'You can't be serious.' Tod looked like he had been smacked in the face. 'That is not possible.'

'We can prove you were involved in burying James Goodwin and his brother.'

Tod smiled nervously and shook his head. He giggled and then he laughed hysterically. Annie and Stirling swapped glances and waited patiently for his laughter to subside. When he finally stopped, he wiped tears from his eyes and sighed. 'That's the funniest thing I've heard in a long time.' He shrugged and turned to Graff. 'Is there anything that I haven't done?' he chuckled. 'I can't take anything they say seriously anymore. You don't listen, do you?'

'Clearly not.' Graff shifted uncomfortably. He coughed to clear his throat. 'Have you anything more than circumstantial evidence for accusing my client of this murder too?'

'Yes.' Tod sighed. 'More bullshit is what they have!'

'Not at all,' Annie said flatly. 'We found a hair in James Goodwin's nasal passage.' She placed a picture of the corpse onto the table. 'You can see from this picture that the breathing tubes were still attached inside his nose. I'm afraid a hair was stuck in the adhesive that you used.' Tod flushed red and he swallowed hard. His eyes darted from the photo to Annie. 'The hair was yours, Tod. The DNA matches completely.' She tapped the photo. 'You prepared this young boy to be buried alive in the sand.'

'I didn't!' Tod shouted. 'I drugged a few women and raped them. The rest of this shit is just sick, and I had nothing to do with it!'

'For God's sake.' Graff shook his head and looked angrily at Tod. He picked up his notes from their previous meeting and ripped them in half. 'I'm lost for words,' he muttered.

'What is wrong with you?' Tod snapped at his brief. 'It's just another part of the set-up by Peter Barton.' His eyes filled with tears. 'I don't believe this is happening to me.' His bottom lip quivered. 'What can I do to make you believe me that he's setting me up?' He tried to stand up, but the chains held him. The prison officers stepped forward and pressed him back into his seat. 'Get your hands off me!' he whined. Annie gestured for the guards to release their grip. Reluctantly, they stepped back. 'Listen to me.' He tried to calm himself and lowered his voice. 'Inspector, I know you're an intelligent woman and I know that you must despise me for what I did to those women.' He looked at her, his eyes pleading like a puppy. 'It was wrong, and I deserve to go to jail for what I did to them, but I did not kill anyone. Not those women and not those two boys. Honestly, I don't know anything about it.' He tried to smile. Another tear broke free. 'What can I say that will make you consider that what I'm saying could be true?'

'Nothing,' Annie said coldly.

'Then there's no point in me saying anything else is there?' Tod looked desperate. 'What is the point if you won't consider the possibilities?' He looked from Stirling to Annie. 'What is the point?'

'You could tell us where Simon is and if Geoff Ryder is involved in anyway.'

He sat back and folded his arms. 'I would have to be involved to be able to tell you who was involved, Inspector.' He shrugged.

'Was Ryder involved?'

'No comment,' Tod said slowly. 'There is no point in us talking again until you have interviewed Peter Barton and I can't see that happening anytime soon. I won't say another word. Take me back to my cell please, officer.'

'We won't be coming back, Tod,' Annie snapped. 'We have enough to proceed.'

'Proceed away, Inspector.' He smiled. His face appeared to relax. 'The game is over anyway,' he chuckled. Tears streamed down his cheeks yet there was a twisted smile on his face. The prison officers held his arms and led him to the gate. As they turned the key, Tod turned. 'Hey, Inspector.' He looked at Annie. His eyes bored into her. 'I take back what I said. I've never met Peter Barton,' he sniggered. 'Geoff Ryder is Rob Derry.'

'Oh, really?' Annie said with mock interest. She twisted the pen in her hand and looked at Stirling. He shook his head and made a circular motion with his index finger near his temple.

'Cuckoo!' Stirling whistled.

'So, Peter Barton isn't Derry anymore?' Annie sighed.

'I lied.'

'You lie all the time.'

'Not this time.'

'Why would we listen to a word you say?'

'You don't listen to a word I say. You never have.' He turned away but paused again. 'Do you know what he always said to me when we were partying with a drugged woman?'

'Partying?' Annie raised her eyebrows. 'The term is rape.'

'Call it what you like.' He shrugged. 'Do you know what he used to say?'

'No.'

'He used to say, "Tod, we like women and we're bad men, for drugging them but do you have any regrets or remorse the next day? Do you ever feel guilty?".' he paused and smiled. 'He would ask me, "when you look in the mirror, what looks back at you?".'

Annie realised the significance immediately. She frowned as she mulled it over. 'Did Geoff Ryder really say that to you, Tod or was it Rob Derry, or Peter Barton or maybe it was the tooth fairy?' she grimaced. 'Or more likely, is it what you ask yourself when you're alone at night?'

'What looks back at you, Annie?' Tod said flatly. His eyes seemed to glaze over. 'I bet you don't like mirrors much, do you?'

'I like them just fine,' Annie lied.

CHAPTER 52

Peter Barton studied the map and sipped his coffee. The drive to the south coast had been simple and the ferry voyage to Bilbao was uneventful. The search of the Jeep by customs officers had been cursory at best and his forged documents were good enough not to attract a second glance. The change in his appearance was drastic enough for him to go unrecognised. The drive across Spain to Benidorm had been relaxing. The weather had improved as his journey progressed and although the winter months were nearing, the sky was blue, and the sun had warmth in its rays. The roads through the resort were busy and the many zebra crossings bustled with tourists wearing shorts and sunglasses while the Spanish were wrapped up in jeans and winter coats. He travelled up the quieter roads that led out of the resort for an hour before he found the villa on a quiet back road in a wooded area high in the hills. It was the perfect place to retire from the rat race; it was also the perfect place to hide.

He watched the villa from the woods but there was no sign of life at first. When he saw a plume of white smoke climbing skyward, he walked deeper into the trees so that he could get a view of the rear garden. A high fence blocked his view, but he could smell wood burning on the breeze. He could see a low double garage tucked away at the corner of the property and he edged carefully towards it. The closer he was, the more the wall obscured his view. He scanned the trees and found a sycamore that looked climbable. Shinning up a few metres, he could see a Mercedes with UK plates was parked on the driveway at the rear of the bungalow. It looked unused and was covered with a thin film of sand and dust. As night descended, he went back to the Jeep to prepare.

****

Tod Harris closed his eyes and let the hot water wash away the tension in his neck. The sound of gushing water echoed through the empty washroom. He soaped himself with shower gel and then rubbed it into his thick black hair. The bubbles ran down the lines of his torso and legs before forming a soapy white puddle beneath his feet. He could hear the prison officers that were protecting him chatting at the door of the showers. The water soothed his shattered nerves although he knew that the relief wouldn't be permanent. It was just a few minutes of peace from the world of anguish that he found himself in. The water stopped without warning and he cursed as the cold air touched his skin.

'Time's up, Harris!' one of the officers shouted. 'Move yourself!'

'Fuck you,' he whispered to himself. Shower time was never long enough. He could have stayed there all day. The thought of being banged up in his tiny cell again was depressing. It was oppressive. The walls seemed to close in on him at night, crushing him and suffocating his very soul. At night, sleep evaded him. His nights were haunted by the faces of his victims. They drifted to him hour after hour sometimes alone and other times in groups. Their eyes accused him; their sobbing echoed in his mind. He would awake soaked in sweat time after time. They taunted him night and day, always there in the back of his mind. It was a constant struggle to keep the images suppressed. He chased them from his thoughts and picked up his towel and began to rub himself dry.

As he dressed, he weighed his position in his mind. His situation was dire and claiming that he was being set up was futile. They weren't listening. He couldn't see any way out. They would give him life in prison without any chance of being considered for parole but how long would it be? Thirty years? Forty years or maybe even more. The jury would convict him on the strength of the evidence before them and the judge would crucify him. Rape was bad enough but what had been done to the police officer and her friend was far worse. The man that committed those atrocities was a monster. 'You're a monster, Tod. You did it,' the voices whispered. Despite his denials of guilt, they wouldn't give him any peace.

If there was a death penalty it would have been applied but that wasn't an option in the UK. Life in prison was probably worse. Minutes were hours, hours felt like days, weeks seemed like years. Being confined to a cell for the remainder of his days would be like hell on earth.

As for what had happened to the two boys, they would throw away the key. The system would look at the severity of the crime and they would section him as a dangerous psychopath that needed medical help rather than prison. Prison was all about rehabilitation. There was no rehabilitation for him, no regret, and no remorse. I have no regrets! They would send him to a secure mental unit. If they did, his tariff of incarceration would mean nothing. They could keep him captive until he turned grey and started dribbling in his chair. He didn't deserve that, no one did. Could he be blamed for what was inside him? He didn't think so. His urges were natural. He couldn't change them so how could they blame him. Man is born with desires. His sexuality couldn't be altered with a pill. His desires drove him to distraction. How could they punish him for acting upon them? They were in the wrong not him. His persecution was an injustice. He had to think of a way to escape or he wouldn't survive a year. The thought of growing old behind bars sickened him. He couldn't endure the monotony.

Tod tried to push such thoughts from his mind. He pulled on his underwear, fastened his trousers, and slipped on his shoes and socks as quickly as he could. Being naked in the prison showers made him feel at his most vulnerable. He rubbed his armpits with the towel and reached for his prison issue denim shirt. As he fastened the buttons, he heard the wing alarm blaring. Somewhere on one of the landings, an officer had been attacked.

****

Peter Barton approached the rear of the bungalow and crouched down behind the shrubbery. He looked through the patio windows and saw the figure of a man inside. The man looked fragile; his shoulders stooped by age. Barton began to think that he had made a mistake until the man turned and approached the window. His facial features were dark and drawn, his cheek bones sunken and his eyes had dark circles beneath them. Geoff Ryder had aged significantly in the years since he had emigrated but there was no doubt that it was him. He watched as Ryder put a mask over his nose and mouth and breathed deeply. A tube ran from the mask to an oxygen tank. It appeared he had been stricken by ill health. Barton felt no sympathy for the man no matter what illness had consumed him. He deserved no mercy and he would show him none.

He skirted the villa and approached a porch at the side of the house. The sliding doors were open at one end allowing the warm evening air to drift into the dwelling. He placed the tyre against the villa wall and checked the Mossberg. He clicked off the safety and slipped inside the door. Cooking odours drifted to him, onions and garlic mingled with roast chicken. He could hear a fire burning in another room, the wood spitting and crackling as the flames devoured it. The scent of smoke was faint and comforting. He raised the shotgun and looked around the room. The walls were lined, floor to ceiling with bookshelves, each crammed with books of every description. A single leather recliner was positioned at the far end to his right. Next to it was a side table with a cigar box and an onyx ashtray. He could sense the slightest whiff of stale tobacco drifting to him. A large teak globe stood to his left. The top was hinged and open to reveal a selection of crystal decanters that contained amber liquids of various shades. He envisaged Ryder sitting in the chair, reading a leather-bound novel while sipping an expensive brandy and chuffing a thick cigar. The abnormal pretending to be normal. The image made his blood boil.

Barton walked silently to an adjoining door and pressed his ear against the varnished wood. All he could hear was wood crackling on a fire and the muted tones of a television. He twisted the brass handle and pulled it open an inch. The window where he had seen Ryder was now empty. The oxygen mask was left hanging from the back of an armchair. He opened the door wide enough to step through and then swept the room with the gun raised. There was no sign of Ryder. The fire was burning in a wide brick-built fireplace that reached the ceiling. A slate mantelpiece was fixed at head height and was adorned with silver candlesticks and equestrian brasses. Fixed to the wall above was a huge mantrap. It seemed odd that such a device should be considered as an ornament. He moved quietly through the room; his heart thumped in his chest. A widescreen television showed Sky News from back home. It stopped him in his tracks. He was still the hot topic of the week. A noise from the next room made his breath stick in his chest. He froze and waited.

****

Tod grabbed his wash bag and walked quickly to the entrance of the washrooms. He swore beneath his breath when he saw that the guards were gone. He caught sight of them running down the metal steps to the landing below. Shouts and screams echoed across the wing and the ear-piercing alarm was relentless. He stepped out of the washroom onto the landing and peered over the metal railings. The landings below were like a scene from a horror movie. On the ground floor, two prison officers were being subjected to a brutal beating. A dozen inmates surrounded their thrashing bodies, kicking, punching, and beating them with pool cues. With the absence of the guards, many inmates took the opportunity to settle old scores. Prisoners battled with each other on every landing. Homemade shivs of every description were being used with deadly effect. Tod could see blood splatter up the walls of the landing below him. The prison officers tried helplessly to stem the violence, but they were hopelessly outnumbered. Tod watched as the four officers that remained standing waded into the group that was attacking their two injured colleagues. Blows rained down on them in a sustained attack but they managed to drag their workmates along the floor to the wing's entrance gates where fellow officers with riot shields, unlocked them and dragged them all out of harm's way. They forced the gates closed and locked them. Until an armoured Tornado Riot Squad could be deployed, the wing and its inmates would be left to their own devices.

****

Barton tiptoed across terracotta tiles to an open doorway that led to a hallway. At the opposite end of the hall was the front door. He could see three doorways to his left and two to his right. They were all closed. A pan rattled and then clattered on to tiles. He jumped and squeezed the gun tightly. He heard Geoff Ryder cursing and mumbling to himself and then he heard plates being stacked. The smell of cooking became stronger. Barton walked along the hallway to the front door and locked it from the inside; sliding heavy bolts into place at the top and bottom. There may be others in the villa, and he couldn't afford to make any mistakes. He intended to perform a brief search of each room before neutralising Ryder himself. Once he had him contained, he could concentrate on what he had come for without the chance of being disturbed. He turned away from the front door and crept down the hall. He opened the first door and looked inside. It was a double bedroom, tastefully furnished but unused. The windows were blocked on the outside by ornate wooden shutters. He closed the door silently and moved to the next one.

The door creaked open and he froze to the spot. He listened intently for any warning that Ryder had heard him. All he could hear was the blood pounding in his ears. He waited for his pulse to settle and stepped inside. It was the master bedroom. Ryder's bed was beyond king-size and the headboard looked like it weighed a ton. It appeared to be crafted from a single piece of oak that had been carved into a frieze of Dante's Inferno. Each intricate detail had been hand-painted and lacquered. It was as disturbing as it was impressive. The thick quilt was covered in a dark Paisley print so fine that he could hardly distinguish the details. He took one step inside and felt his boots sink into a thick wool carpet. Each wall held an oversized hellish oil painting of Dante's ilk. The powerful aroma of patchouli oil saturated the air in the room. Its sickly-sweet smell reminded him of the leather jacket clad bikers that he hung with in his teens. He took one last glimpse of the hideous carving above the bed and then retreated into the hallway, closing the bedroom door behind him. He listened to make sure that Ryder was still distracted and stepped across the hallway to the next room. When he touched the handle, the metal was as cold as ice. A shiver ran down his spine as he twisted it and pushed it open.

****

Tod was transfixed by the violence below him. He watched as three inmates held another down and stabbed him repeatedly with sharpened objects. His white vest changed colour as deep red stains blossomed across his stomach and chest. His screams sent shivers through him. One of the attackers ran his shiv across his throat and a plume of arterial blood gushed skyward. All that blood! 'You did this to us, Tod.' I didn't kill anyone! Familiar faces flashed through his brain; their features twisted in agony. They picked the man up by his arms and legs and tossed him over the balcony onto the safety netting. He grabbed at the gushing rent in his throat desperate to stop his life force from leaving him, but the wound was too deep and the pressure too strong. Blood squirted between his fingers and his struggles weakened. His dispatch was met by a chorus of cheers from the inmates below. 'Nonce, nonce, nonce!'

The image of the twitching body on the net brought back memories. Warped and twisted memories that bubbled to the surface from the darkness of his mind. 'Remember us, Tod!' the voices whispered in his mind. 'Remember!' He closed his eyes and tried to compose himself. They were memories that belonged to another. They must be. Waves crashed on the eerie statues of the Iron Men as he dug in the sand. Memories of women lying naked, their eyes like those of stunned cattle waiting for the slaughter man to slit their throats. 'Remember us!'

His knees buckled and he grabbed at the rail to support himself. He stepped back from the edge as the image of two boys appeared in his mind. Their eyes, how could you look into their eyes? The images merged and he covered his ears to block out their screams. His heart thumped in his chest and sweat trickled from his forehead. The memories were so real, so sick, so evil. A darkness in him felt excited by them but another side felt weak and nauseous. He needed to escape from the violence below; the sight of blood made his mind play tricks on him. Tod took a breath and tried to banish the demons from his mind. He needed to reach his cell.

From the corner of his eye, he caught movement on his landing. A lone figure stood leaning against his cell door with his arms folded. The huge man glanced at the carnage below and then looked back at Tod and smiled. Tod instinctively moved back against the wall. He looked to his right and saw two more men staring at him. They had no interest in what was happening on the lower landings; they were totally focused on him. The first figure walked slowly along the metal grating towards him. His thick arms were covered in tattoos and he had swastikas on either side of his head, which was shaven. He grinned through a dark goatee. Tod recognised him as the man they called, Beast, the wing governor.

'Impressive, isn't it?' he said to the men on the opposite landing. They nodded silently and stared at Tod. 'Enjoying the show, Harris?' He smiled at Tod with crooked teeth but there was no friendliness in his smile. 'You should be impressed.' He gestured to the lower floors. 'All this is for your benefit, you fucking scumbag.' The smile twisted to a sneer. 'We don't want them sending you off to a nice secure mental hospital before we've had a chance to express our outrage at your hideous crimes, now do we, boys?' He grinned at the other men.

'We don't want that, Beast,' one of them sneered.

'Not until we've had a word,' the other added.

Tod could feel their hatred. He began to tremble with fear and his knees trembled again. He looked to his right and the two men moved along the walkway opposite towards him. Beast moved along the landing to his left and took a toothbrush handle from his pocket. He held it up and Tod could see razor blades glinting in the light. They were melted side by side into the plastic. He was trapped with less than twenty metres between him and the sinister inmates. Tod walked back to the railings and looked down. There was still some activity on the lower landings, but he quickly realised what they were doing. The prisoners were barricading the wing entrance gates with everything that they could rip loose. Mattresses, tables, chairs, and the pool table had been piled against the gates to prevent the guards returning in force. As he looked around the lower floors, it seemed to Tod that every inmate on the wing was looking up at him.

****

Peter Barton felt a rush of stale air hit him as he looked beyond the door. A staircase climbed to a loft room and the smell of unwashed humans wafted to him. The stench evoked fear and frustration inside him, deep rooted emotions from his past. Stale urine, sweat, vomit, and excrement. All the odours of his prison days. He felt gripped by a sense of foreboding and trepidation. Don't go up there, Peter. A voice whispered to him. Get Ryder first!

Common sense deserted him. He knew that he should wait. He also knew that if he had applied his common sense at any point since Simon went missing then things would be different. He wanted to see what Ryder had upstairs. His mind nagged him. No, you need to see. That's always been your problem, Peter, you don't think before you act. He climbed the first steps and pulled the door to behind him. As soon as it closed, he regretted his decision. The air was thick and cloying. Sweat trickled down his back and he felt wet and uncomfortable beneath the arms. He placed his feet close to the walls as he climbed. His progress was slow but silent. As he reached the top of the staircase, the stench intensified. Barton took a small torch from his pocket and switched it on. He aimed it at the roof and moved it from one side to the other. The rafters and tiles were bare. As he brought the beam lower, it settled on metal bars. He stepped closer and swept the beam along the bars. They are cells! Ryder has cells in his loft! He heard shuffling at the far end of the loft; shuffling and breathing. Then a whimper, like an injured cat. Chains clinked and rattled. Barton felt sick to his stomach as he crept forward. He drew level with the first cell and aimed the torchlight inside. A filthy mattress lay empty at the back of the cell. Handcuffs dangled loosely from the bars. An upturned water bowl designed for a dog was pressed against the bars. The door to the cage was ajar. He heard whimpering behind him and turned the torch towards it. The figure of a girl crouched in the corner, naked and trembling. A chain was anchored to the bars and padlocked into a metal necklace that was locked around her neck. Her long hair reached past her shoulders touching deep scars of various age. He could see her ribs protruding through skin. Her emaciated frame belonged to a holocaust survivor. She buried her face into the mattress and shivered with terror. Barton wanted to free her right there, but he knew that he couldn't. He tugged at the door, but heavy chains fastened it. The shotgun was capable of blasting the lock, but she still wouldn't be free. He needed the keys.

A shuffling sound made him turn around quickly. He aimed the torchlight at a second cage. He crept towards it with a morbid curiosity and a feeling of dread in his stomach. Another whimper from the shadows. Chains rattled and the floorboards creaked. He shone the beam at the source of the noise. The form of a young boy lay curled on the mattress in a foetal position. The disks of his spine protruded like the teeth on a cog. Scar tissue ran across his back from his shoulders down his buttocks to his thighs. His sandy blond hair was long and matted and hadn't been cut for an age. Barton felt his breath coming in short sharp blasts. His pulse was racing. The boy looked emaciated, his skin bruised and filthy. He could smell excrement from a plastic bucket at the rear of the cage. Barton winced when he saw a deep gash that ran from the boy's elbow to his shoulder. The congealed blood had not yet scabbed. Barton followed the wound with his torch and stopped at a blemish on the shoulder. Lights flashed in his mind. He recognised a pinkish birthmark on the boy's shoulder. It was shaped like the African continent. 'Simon!' he hissed. He had to see his face. The boy curled up tighter still. The chain around his neck clinked. 'Simon!' His anger coursed through his veins making his blood boil. He couldn't think straight. The urge to shout and call for help was overwhelming, but he couldn't. He had to tackle Ryder. He needed the keys and then he needed to take Simon back home where he belonged. 'Simon, it's me, Uncle Peter!' he hissed again. He shook the gate as hard as he dared. 'Simon!' He had to be sure that it was him. Could it be Simon? 'Simon!' He had to quell the urge to shout. 'Simon, it's Uncle Peter!' The boy stiffened and tilted his head. 'Simon!' The boy turned slowly and squinted at the light. Barton recognised his blue eyes although the life that used to shine in them was gone. There was a spark or recognition in them. Just a glint in his eye. 'Simon, it's me, Uncle Peter!' The boy cowered away from him; his face frozen in fear. 'Don't be afraid. I'm going to take you home,' he said in a whisper. The boy shook his head and shut his eyes tight. 'I'll get you out of here.' The boy began to shake uncontrollably and raised his index finger. 'Don't be afraid.'

Peter felt a heavy blow to the back of his head. A flash of blinding white light shot through his brain like a giant camera flash before the world went dark.

CHAPTER 53

There was an air of anticipation in the MIT office. Annie stood in front of the screens and an image of Benidorm and the surrounding area appeared. 'We know that Geoff Ryder bought a villa near Benidorm,' Annie added. 'The Guardia have been trying to trace, which properties are owned by Brits.'

'They've narrowed it down and this is their target. It's a villa purchased from a UK bank account.' Alec explained. 'It's somewhere here in the hills north of the resort in a forest reserve called Cocentaina.' He pointed to the aerial map of the area on one of the screens. 'It's a secluded property in a wooded area with no neighbours in the vicinity. The closest house is five kilometres away.'

'Our friends in Spain are in a spin because of the death of Officer Peres, their top brass is taking it very seriously. They're going to hit the villa with an armed unit and their Bomb Squad at dawn tomorrow.' Murmurs spread between the desks. 'If there's anyone home, they're in for a nasty shock.' She nodded at Alec. 'You said that we'll have someone on the ground, guv.'

'There's a DI Rind working on Organised Crime with Interpol. I've asked him to go along as our observer. He's meeting up with the Grupo de Acción Rápida tonight,' Alec said. 'There's nothing more that we can do from here regarding Geoff Ryder. Go home, get some sleep, and keep your mobiles on just in case.' Annie needed a decent night's sleep. They all did but she wasn't sure that sleep would come easily without the aid of a bottle of Merlot.

CHAPTER 54

Tod Harris edged along the wall with his back pressed to the bricks. Despite having just showered, his shirt was drenched with sweat. His mouth felt painfully dry and he couldn't swallow. He wanted to scream for help, but it was pointless. The guards were barricaded out. No one would hear him crying for help and if they did, they couldn't do anything. The sense of dread and helplessness was overwhelming. He could hardly draw his breath. Beast was only metres away. His steps were measured and purposely slow. He was toying with his prey, enjoying his fear. It's all about control, Tod. Like you did to so many of us, remember? He watched in horror as the landing filled with the other inmates. Each one carried a weapon, some sharp, some blunt and heavy. Their eyes were filled with loathing.

As they approached, his survival instincts kicked in. He did the only thing that he could do. He turned and ran into the washrooms. Running away sparked his stalkers into action. He could hear them running along the metal walkways, their heavy footsteps echoed through the wing. 'Kill, kill, kill, kill,' he heard them chanting. Tod bolted through the showers into the toilets. 'Nonce, nonce, nonce,' their voices boomed in unison. He lost his footing on the slippery tiles and fell hard onto his elbows. Tod tried to scramble to his feet as the inmates streamed through the shower room. He looked around in panic as if some imaginary door would appear and let him through, but none appeared. The walls were thick, and the windows were barred. There was nowhere to run; nowhere to hide. He ran for the toilet cubicles and skidded as he reached them. He was gasping for air as he slammed the door and put his weight behind it. Beast hit the door at full speed with his shoulder. The wood cracked and Tod was catapulted across the cubicle. His head met the bricks with an audible crack. A wicked gash opened on his forehead and blood poured into his eyes. He could smell its coppery tang and taste it at the back of his throat. His legs couldn't support him any longer. He fell onto the stainless-steel toilet pan, splitting his top lip and splintering his front teeth. As he tried to clear the blood and fractured teeth from his mouth, Beast grabbed his ankles and yanked him violently backwards from the cubicle. Rough hands grabbed at his clothes. They lifted him above their heads and carried him into the wider space of the shower room.

'Switch on the water,' Beast growled over the clamour. 'This could get messy, Harris,' he goaded. 'Drop him!' he ordered. Tod hit the tiles face up. The impact knocked the wind from him. Blood blocked his airways and choked him. He tried to scream but it came out as a gurgle. Blood and vomit spurted from his mouth and splattered onto the tiles. 'Hold him down,' Beast said gruffly. He held the razorblades in front of Tod's eyes and a smile touched his lips. 'You can watch yourself running down the drains piece by piece.'

Tod felt a warmth spreading through his pants as his bladder released its contents. He trembled uncontrollably, his vision blurred by blood and tears. He whimpered like so many had at his hands. 'Mum,' he whispered.

'She can't help you now,' Beast said slowly. He pulled his hair violently and looked into his eyes. 'This is going to hurt,' he whispered as the blades sliced through his lips. Tod prayed for unconsciousness to take him and spare him from the pain, but God wasn't listening.

****

Peter Barton felt his face being slapped. He opened his eyes and pain flashed in his brains. His head felt as if it was full of molten lead. He tried to focus on what was directly in front of him. His understanding of what had happened became crystal-clear when he realised that he was staring down the barrel of his own shotgun. Geoff Ryder gestured with his head. 'Get up,' he ordered. Ryder's breathing sounded laboured. 'Make a move and I'll blow your head off, clear?'

'Clear.' Barton nodded.

'Put your hands on your head and walk towards the stairs.' Ryder waved the gun. Barton glanced at Simon, but the boy was cowering in the corner of his cage. The girl followed his lead, her body racked with sobs. The sound was pitiful. 'Stop there,' he said sharply. Ryder kept the shotgun aimed at his head as he backed down the stairs. 'Walk very slowly. I really have no qualms about spreading your brains across the ceiling.'

Barton followed his orders. They progressed down the stairs and Ryder forced him into the living room. 'Lie down on the floor, face down, hands behind your head. Move and you're dead.'

Barton did as he was told. Ryder sat on the settee and kept the gun aimed at him while he reached for his oxygen mask. He placed it over his face and sucked in greedily. Barton clung to the thought that without the shotgun, he would be easy to overpower. He took one last deep lungful and put the mask down. 'Now then.' He aimed the shotgun at Barton's groin. 'Would you like to tell me why you're creeping around my home with a shotgun?'

'An ex-client of yours called Brian Taylor told me that you might be here. Do you remember him?'

Ryder looked thoughtful. 'Brian Taylor, Brian Taylor.' He frowned. 'Ah!' He nodded. 'I know exactly who you mean.' He eyed Barton with suspicion. 'I understand from the news that he is deceased?'

'Yes.'

'You killed him?'

'Yes.'

'Oh, my,' he lifted a hand. He looked impressed. 'You do look very different without hair. I never would have recognised you.' He paused thoughtfully. 'You shot him, right?'

'Yes.'

'Was this the gun you used on him?'

'No.'

'Shame.' He shook his head. 'I like a weapon that has history, don't you?' he watched Barton for a reaction. 'When a weapon has been used for its original purpose, they take on an entirely new character. They're no longer just a piece of steel. Do you understand that?'

'Yes.'

'I bet you do. You're a killer after all.'

'I am.'

'Poor Brian,' he said thoughtfully. 'I'm curious. Did he tell you anything else?'

'Yes.'

'Please expand. I get tired very quickly these days and my patience wears thin.' He picked up the mask and sucked deeply again. 'Emphysema,' he explained cordially. 'It's chronic. I've been a smoker all my life but not for much longer.' He smiled thinly. 'They say I have months.' He gestured with his hands. 'Anyway, you were telling me?'

'Taylor told me that a man called Tod Harris might have abducted Simon.'

'Tod Harris.' Ryder shook his head. He sucked oxygen and frowned. 'Slow down. You need to assume that I haven't been following the news from home for a long time. At least until Tod was arrested. That gained my interest. Explain it to me.'

'I was accused of kidnapping my nephew and sent to jail, but they released me on appeal.'

'I remember that.' Ryder seemed genuinely interested. 'What exactly came to light on appeal?'

'An alibi.'

'That will do it every time.' He paused and took another blast of oxygen. 'And as the 'falsely' accused uncle, you've taken it upon yourself to solve the mystery of your nephew's disappearance to keep you in the clear?'

'Something like that.'

'What made you focus on Brian Taylor?'

'His mother lived next door to Simon.'

'And?'

'He has a record for kiddie porn.'

'He was always a bad apple.' Ryder sighed. 'I knew him when he was a juvenile, but you know that already don't you?'

Barton nodded that he did. 'He pointed me at Harris as another possible suspect.'

'Did he indeed?' Geoff frowned. His breath quickened and he put the mask over his face. He breathed in and out for a full minute before he could continue. 'Taylor was a rogue, but Tod Harris was a different animal altogether. He had pure evil running through his veins.' He sucked oxygen again. 'Did he offer any proof that he wasn't lying?'

'He said that Harris had kept his library book.'

'And did you find this library book?'

'I knew where to look.'

'Of course, you did.'

'I showed it to his mother and explained a few things.'

'How did she take it?'

'She gave it to the police.'

'Did she now?' he paused and narrowed his eyes. 'And how did you persuade her to turn her son in?'

'It wasn't that difficult.'

'I'm sure.' Ryder stood up. 'And did you persuade her to testify?'

'She hung herself.'

'Did she? Very clever.' He put the gun to the back of Barton's head and patted him down. 'I think you're a very resourceful man.' He muttered as he searched his pockets. 'You shot Brian, persuaded Mrs Harris to turn in her own son and then kill herself. I need to be very careful around you. What have we got here?' He held up a bundle of cable ties. 'We might as well put these to good use,' he said fastening one of them to Barton's right wrist. 'I assume these were for my benefit.' He added as he slid the tie tightly around both wrists. His breathing was laboured again. 'What did you come here for, Mr Barton?' he asked. 'To kill me?'

'No,' Barton lied. 'To find out where Simon is buried. Harris is locked up but he's not talking. The police were looking for an accomplice called Rob Derry. Taylor indicated that you were pulling the strings. I didn't expect to find him here.'

'When he was young, Tod Harris always worked alone. Whatever he did, he did it by himself. As far as I'm concerned, his accomplice doesn't exist.' Ryder walked back to his chair and sat down heavily. He closed his eyes and breathed deeply. The air rasped in his lungs. 'Do you know why I left the UK in such a hurry?'

Barton contemplated his words carefully. He couldn't tell him what he really believed. 'No.'

'My health was already deteriorating. I could hardly walk up the stairs. Tod Harris became obsessed with my nephew, Brendon.' He looked at Barton for a reaction. 'You know who Brendon was?'

'Yes.' Barton nodded. 'But when I heard that the police were looking for an accomplice called Rob Derry, things fell into place. They were confusing before that.'

'Were they?' Ryder asked thoughtfully.

'I think that Harris invented a persona,' Barton paused. 'He began to call himself Robdenn Derry.' He looked at Ryder to see if he was following. 'It's an anagram.'

'I worked that out.'

'Of course, you did.'

'He thought that he had affinity with him?'

'Who knows what went through his mind.'

Ryder paused to breathe from the mask again. 'We are who we are, and we can't change that. I knew what he would become so I took the opportunity to leave. Harris was a nuisance, impatient, childish, a fucking idiot!' His chest heaved and he coughed. He put the oxygen over his face and sucked deeply. 'Tod Harris is a schizophrenic. He was obsessed with my family. I had him followed for a while; he spent a lot of time digging at his father's grave.' He paused. 'He was attracting attention. Attention that I didn't want to focus in my direction. I moved here for some peace.' He took another breath. 'It seems none of you can let me move on.' He pointed to the ceiling with the gun. 'Bringing the boy here was like handing a bag of crack to an addict. Then the girl!' He shook his head. 'I didn't know where they were from and I didn't ask. Maybe I should have.'

'And you just happened to have cages in your loft?'

'Oh, no,' Ryder shook his head. 'The previous owners were dog breeders. The cages were in the backyard. It didn't take long to rebuild them.' He sighed. 'You're sure that boy is your nephew?'

'Yes.'

'I didn't know.'

'I think you did.'

'I suspected.' He paused. He took another deep breath from the mask. 'Now what do we do, Peter?' Ryder closed his eyes again. 'This is all such a mess.'

'Leave the kids here with me and run,' Barton suggested. 'You could be across the border before anyone knows that we're here. Give us all a chance, you included.'

'Look at me.' Ryder sighed. 'Do I look like a man who could go on the run and start over somewhere new?' He shrugged. 'I can barely walk to the bathroom to wash myself.' He shook his head. 'I'm sorry, Peter,' he sounded sincere. 'Get up.' Barton stood up; his hands fastened awkwardly behind his head. 'Walk to the patio window.' Ryder slid the door open and stepped outside. The night air had a chill to it now. Barton stepped out and thought about running. He wouldn't get more than a few metres before the shotgun brought him down and he couldn't leave Simon in that cage. 'There's a spade over there,' Ryder gestured to a storage box. 'Lift your hands over your head carefully and pick it up. Try anything silly, I'll blow your head off.' Barton nodded and slid his hands above his head. Bringing them in front of him, the blood began to circulate again. 'Where is your vehicle?'

Barton picked up the spade from the box. 'Just off the road at the edge of the woods.'

Ryder gestured with the gun. Barton looked at a brick-built barbeque wide enough to hold a full hog roast. The chimney was almost as tall as the villa. 'I need you to dig a nice deep hole behind the barbeque.'

'Just the one?' Barton asked sarcastically. 'It won't be deep enough for three bodies.'

'Deep enough for one pile of ashes,' Ryder replied flatly.

'You're going to burn three bodies on your barbeque?' Barton shook his head. 'That will take time.'

'If I could dig a grave, those kids would have been dead years ago. So would you. Like I said earlier, I haven't got long left. It's not a permanent solution but it's permanent enough for my needs.' He waved the gun again. 'Now dig.'

Barton stabbed the blade into the ground and began to dig. Ryder looked weaker with every minute that went by. The topsoil was loose and broke up easily, but he took his time. He shovelled the dirt into a pile in silence until he was knee deep. Half an hour had gone by at least. He stopped and wiped sweat from his forehead. Ryder was leaning against the brick chimney and breathing heavily. 'You look like you need oxygen,' Barton said.

'I do.' He nodded slowly. 'This is where we have to part company, I'm afraid.' He waved the barrel of the gun. 'Get out of the hole.' Barton stepped up onto the patio. 'Around there near the barbeque.' He walked around the chimney. 'Put the spade on the ground and kneel down.' Barton bent down to put the spade on the floor and their eyes met for a moment. Ryder aimed the Mossberg at his head and pulled the trigger.

****

It was still dark when the Grupo de Acción Rápida crept into position. DI Rind was the fifth man in the entry team; behind him were two members of the Bomb Squad. They moved in silence, hugging the walls of the one storey villa. Guardia officers positioned themselves at the front door as the entry team went around to the rear. The windows were covered by ornamental shutters and Rind noticed that some of the hinges were coated in cobwebs. They hadn't been opened for a long time. Piles of decaying leaves had built up along the bottom of the walls and the grass was overgrown. As they reached the rear garden, they moved in tandem towards the back patio. Leaves and litter floated on top of a puddle of brown water.

The patio was twenty metres square, and the tiles ran from the glass sliding doors which, led from the house to the garden. A wide brick barbeque stood at one end; an upturned Y-shaped chimney reached as high as the roof. The entry team split into two and crouched either side of the doors. Rind heard a dull whirring sound as they drilled holes into the doorframes and inserted snake cameras. They scanned the frames for wires or switches and then checked the area around the doorways for devices. The team leader studied the screen once more and then signalled to move in. They dismantled the handles with drills and then forced the locks quietly with wrecking bars. The doors popped with the minimum of noise and the entry team moved inside in a practiced formation.

The patio doors led into a wide split-level living space that was furnished with expensive leather settees and goatskin rugs. The smell of must was overpowering. A thick layer of dust coated the terracotta tiles that covered the floors. The team leader pointed to the floor indicating that there was no sign of footsteps anywhere. Weapons raised, they peeled off into the hallway that serviced the bedrooms. When the hallway door was opened, the smell of human decomposition hit them like a brick. The first three-bedroom doors were wide open, and they moved from one room to the next without disturbing anything.

The last room was closed. They split either side of the door and the team leader signalled for the snake camera. He inserted it through a keyhole beneath the handle and twisted it. His face stiffened as he stood up and he twisted the handle and opened the door. Rind looked over his shoulder. The stench in the room was rank. He heard the entry team leader call the building clear and then they stepped into the bedroom. The stench intensified and his stomach turned. On the far wall, the decaying body of a man was crucified upside down. Nails pierced his ankles and wrists. Dried blood ran in blackened rivulets down the wall. The skin on his face was leathery and brown; his hair was long greying and weaved into dreadlocks. The blackened eye sockets were empty. His body was covered in text that Rind couldn't understand. The killer had carved words into every inch of the body bar the head. On the wall opposite the body was a full-length mirror, the words 'When you look in the mirror, what looks back at you?' were smeared onto the glass in blood. Rind took the photograph of Geoff

274

Ryder from his pocket and compared it to the leathery death mask of a black man. 'I think don't this is Mr Ryder, do you?' he muttered.

****

Peter Barton saw Ryder's trigger finger move but nothing happened. 'You left the safety on,' he said as he swung the spade in a wide arc. He hit Ryder with the flat of the blade above his ear and he collapsed into a heap on the patio. Barton was on him in a flash. He sat on top of his unconscious body and used the spade to split the cable ties. He picked up the shotgun and dragged Geoff Ryder into the villa by his ankles.

When Geoff Ryder came around, he was in excruciating pain. His shoulder, arms and chest felt crushed and his breathing was more difficult than usual. He could feel that one side of his face was broken and swollen. The pain brought him back to his senses quickly. He was tied into his leather reading chair, but he couldn't fathom why he was in so much pain. Looking down, he saw a tyre had been forced over his shoulders and was wedged around his chest. Sharp barbs had penetrated his flesh making it agony to move. Each breath meant that the weight forced the barbs deeper into his skin. The tyre was soaked, and his shirt felt wet. He could smell lighter fluid and it was powerful enough to make his eyes water. As his head cleared, he heard splashing behind him. 'What are you doing?' he croaked. 'Call the police. I'm ready to give myself up. You know that Brendon didn't kill all those women, don't you?'

No reply.

'Barton!' he gasped. 'You know that I did it, don't you?'

Splash, splash.

'Take your nephew and call the police!' he gasped desperately. 'I haven't killed since I moved here. You must know that.'

Silence.

'Barton!'

Silence.

'Get this fucking contraption off me!'

Silence.

'I need my oxygen.'

Silence.

He heard movement behind him and then the sound of a match striking. 'Barton!' Then the whoosh of an accelerant igniting. The flames rushed across the tiles to his chair. He felt the heat singeing the hairs on his legs first, then his trousers caught fire, blistering his skin. The flames spread rapidly up his body to the fuel-soaked tyre and the wrapping sizzled and the rubber crackled. Geoff Ryder was confused by panic when the gunpowder inside the tyre ignited. It burned white hot at a temperature so high that it melted through his flesh, muscles, and bones in seconds. When it reached critical temperature, packed so tightly in the tyre, it exploded and ripped him in half.

EPILOGUE

Annie looked at a butchered carcass on the stainless-steel slab. Alec and Stirling were opposite her. Kathy Brooks flicked through some crime scene images on her screen until she found the one that she wanted. 'Here is where the prison officers cut his body down when they finally regained control of the wing.' She pointed to the screen. 'Four inmates were killed during the riot.' She shook her head. 'I'm going to be here all night processing them. How long did the riot last for heaven's sake?'

'Sixteen hours,' Stirling said. 'The prisoners took down the barricade when they got hungry.'

'They certainly spent a long time on Harris,' Kathy said pointing to the corpse. Annie looked at Alec and closed her eyes to blot out the image, but it was already engrained on her mind. 'The attack took place in the shower room on the third landing and when they'd finished, they hung him from the top landing by his foot. The bruising around the ankle indicates that he was still alive, just.'

'Where is the rest of him?' Stirling asked coldly.

'We recovered his genitals from one of the drain traps but we're still looking for the rest. They probably flushed him down the toilets so that nothing could be sewn back on.' She shrugged. 'Once I've finished, I'll get a full report over to you.'

'Thanks, Kathy,' Annie said.

'Good news about Simon Barton,' Kathy said as she covered the mutilated corpse. 'It's not often we recover a missing person after so long. Who was the girl?'

'Marta Soreno,' Alec replied. She went missing from a school in Benidorm four years ago. Apparently, they're both doing well physically but they're not talking yet. Barton's parents flew out there yesterday.'

'We think that Harris was the abductor, or he certainly had a hand in taking him to Spain. He must have stayed in touch with Ryder over the years.'

'He got what was coming to him,' Stirling grunted.

'I hope you're going to keep that to yourself when the Press is around,' Alec said.

'Yes, guv.' Stirling mumbled.

'And Geoff Ryder had them in cages all that time?' Kathy asked incredulously.

'It would appear so.'

'The Spanish found his remains in a burnt-out villa about ten kilometres from the one they raided.' Annie sighed. 'They found the cages in the loft.'

'They raided the wrong address first,' Stirling scoffed. 'DI Rind thinks Ryder bought the villas that they raided but only used the surname 'Ryder' on the one that they raided first. They have no idea who the victim was there, but Harris's prints were found. They're searching the woods around it with cadaver dogs. A local postman said that he had never seen anyone coming or going but noticed a Jeep there every couple of months.'

'Geoff Ryder bought his other villa under an umbrella company, hence the mix up.' Alec added.

'Simon Barton says that his uncle took them from Ryder's villa but that's all he's saying. Peter Barton got to Ryder before we did.' Annie sighed again. 'The boy keeps on asking where his uncle has gone.'

'Any sign of him?'

'No. He called the Guardia to the villa, but he had gone when they arrived. He dropped the kids at the hospital, telephoned Simon's parents, and disappeared.'

'If he's got any sense, he won't resurface,' Stirling added. He looked at Alec and waited for a reprimand, but none came.

'Thanks again, Kathy.' Annie smiled.

'No problem.' She touched Annie's arm and walked away to carry on with her gruesome work.

Annie took off her gown and dropped it into a laundry bin. She couldn't wait to get out of the lab. They walked in silence along highly polished corridors for what seemed like an age until they reached the exit. An icy wind met them as they walked to Alec's car. Despite the cold, the fresh air was more than welcome although the stench of death lingered in her nostrils. 'I think I'm going to walk back, guv,' she said. 'I need to clear my head.'

'It might take more than a brisk walk to do that.' Alec smiled as he climbed into the vehicle. 'See you back at the office.' Stirling nodded and raised his hand before climbing into the passenger seat. She watched the car move to the exit and then it slipped into the traffic. She pulled her coat tightly around her and began the short walk to Canning Place where she caught her reflection in a shop window and stopped. 'When you look in the mirror, what looks back at you, Annie?' she heard Tod Harris's voice ask in her mind. 'I'm comfortable with what I see,' she whispered to herself. 'It will take time, but I'll get there.' Annie put her hands into her pockets and breathed in the sea air. As she walked through the busy streets, the breeze blew the shadows from her mind. She was thinking about visiting Becky in hospital, when her mobile rang. The screen showed a withheld number.

'DI Jones.' She frowned as she heard static on the line. The sound that comes with a call from abroad. 'Hello.'

'Hola, Inspector,' Peter Barton said gruffly.

'Barton?' Annie asked surprised.

'I'll make this quick,' he said calmly. 'I'm sick of law enforcement agencies not doing their jobs properly. You know how I've spent years tracking killers.'

'What are you talking about?'

'I know that you don't believe that Brendon Ryder was not the Butcher but that's all in the past anyway.' He sighed. 'Geoff Ryder told me that Tod Harris spent a lot of time at his father's grave. It didn't seem that important at the time, but I've had time to think. You might want to take a look there.'

'What do you think we'll find, Barton?' Annie shook her head angrily. 'And why would I listen to you anyway?'

'Because I worked out who the real Butcher of Crosby Beach was,' he said. 'As soon as Brendon Ryder was dead, you stopped looking and Geoff Ryder emigrated. Geoff was the Butcher. He set Brendon up.'

'I don't believe that,' Annie said although doubt had set in weeks before.

'He told me as much before he died,' Barton said frustrated. 'He fooled you, don't let Harris do the same. Do your job properly, Inspector, and nail Harris for everything that he's done!'

'Harris is dead,' Annie said flatly. She wasn't sure why she had divulged that fact, but it felt good to tell him. 'I know he took your nephew and I know he killed Jackie Webb and Jayne Windsor.'

'That's the tip of the iceberg.' Barton sighed. 'He kept Simon's library book. He kept trophies, Inspector, find them and you have a chance of putting some of his victims to rest.' The line clicked and Peter Barton was gone.

****

A stone angel looked on as Annie walked through the door of a forensic tent. A gust of wind followed her in and threatened to rip the material from its frame. Two white-clad figures were waist deep in the grave and the excavation was well underway. Annie felt a jolt of excitement as she spotted a row of plastic evidence bags to her left.

'Morning, guv,' one of the CSI acknowledged her.

Alec entered the tent a second later. 'How are you getting on?' he asked. 'Looks like you're fairly deep already.'

'Everything at the top was loose. The composition of the soil has changed now. Everything below here hasn't been disturbed for a very long time.' The CSI smiled. 'We've used ground penetrating radar to confirm that we've extracted everything that was buried here,' he pointed to the bags. 'It's quite a collection.'

'Thanks, good work,' Annie said distractedly. She bent down and studied the bags. Rings, watches, necklaces, she counted eight of them. She shook her head as she picked up a bag and read an inscription on the back of a silver locket. The words were in Spanish. Using her fingertips, she moved the rings beneath the plastic and saw a wedding band with a Russian inscription inside it. An elastic band held some old boarding cards and a bundle of blank passports. A larger bag had several envelopes containing photos, memory sticks, and SD cards. 'Can you get these straight to the lab as soon as possible please,' Annie said without looking through them. She had seen enough of Tod Harris's handiwork to last a lifetime.

'I'll send them straight away.'

'Thanks,' Annie said.

'Barton was right.' Alec sighed. 'Again.'

'Are we done, guv?' Annie replied curtly. She didn't want to give Barton any credit at all.

'I think so.' Alec nodded.

She turned and ducked out of the tent. The wind tugged at her coat and she pulled it tightly around her to keep the cold out.

'Do you wonder who they all were, guv?' Annie asked. 'All those rings and chains have their own story to tell, don't they?' They walked slowly through the graveyard and Annie contemplated how they could identify, which trophies belonged to which victims.

'I'm trying not to think about it, Annie.' Alec shook his head. 'Harris was infatuated with a monster to the point where he became one.' Alec had seen several. This monster was dead, and they would have to piece together where he had been and what he had done.

'You know when I think back to the mountain of research that we recovered from Barton's home, it makes me feel like we have our finger in the hole in the dyke, holding back the lake.' She shuddered. 'Harris is just one of hundreds of killers, who are active. Taking Harris down is just a drop in the ocean.'

'There could be thousands around the world, Annie,' Alec said grimly. 'We can only tackle what is in front of us and hope our colleagues abroad do likewise. It's not a job for the weak. Take comfort in the fact that we do it well.'

'Do we do it well enough?' she said beneath her breath. 'Sometimes, I have to wonder.' The wind gusted again, and a tear ran from her good eye. She wiped it away with the back of her hand and headed for her Audi with a knot in her stomach. She knew that it wouldn't be very long before the MIT had another killer to hunt.

'I need to take this,' Alec apologised. He answered his mobile and turned his back to the wind. 'Ramsay.' His face turned ashen as he listened. He nodded silently and turned to Annie. 'Simon Barton has started talking,' he said frowning. Annie felt a shiver as the wind blew through her again. 'We need to go and see him straight away.'

****

DC Hodge was losing the will to live as he pulled onto a rundown industrial estate near the mouth of the River Ribble. Most of the units looked closed or abandoned. The rain was hammering down almost horizontally off the estuary, carried in on a blustery wind from the north. He slowed down to encounter the first of a series of speed bumps and despite his careful approach, his head banged against the roof. There didn't seem to be any reception area for the site, so he took the left-hand fork and trundled over the speed ramps for a few hundred yards. The units on either side were locked up, many for sale or to let but he persevered until he reached a unit that was open for business. He checked the name of the business and pulled to a halt outside. Two elderly mechanics stopped working to see who their visitor was. Hodge thought they might be brothers. Their baldness was disguised by identical comb-over styles. It was hard to distinguish between them. Hodge sighed and opened the door, and then he took a deep breath and ran for it. He was drenched before he reached the shelter of the mechanics' workshop.

'Detective Constable Hodge,' he said shaking the rain from his leather jacket. 'I believe someone called the helpline yesterday?' The mechanics nodded in unison. 'Great. How can I help?'

'We saw the appeal in the local newspaper,' one brother said in a broad accent. He took a pouch of rolling tobacco from his filthy overalls and gripped a premade cigarette between oily fingers. 'You are looking for a man with curly grey hair. Something to do with a van, which crashed into the river a few miles down?'

'The newspaper said that the police found a rib adrift in the bay?' the other brother added.

'Yes.' Hodge nodded. 'Have you seen someone that fits the description?'

'Yep.' One brother said.

'Yep.' The second agreed.

'Could you tell me what you've seen?' Hodge encouraged them.

'Bottom unit on the left-hand side,' one brother said with a nod. 'The bloke who owns it has hair like that and he has a couple of inflatable boats in there.' He looked at his brother for support, but he was busy rolling another smoke. 'Funny thing is, I saw him leaving in a Jeep the other day. He had cut all his hair off. Shaved to the bone it was. I nearly didn't recognise him.'

'He told me, and I thought that was odd.' His brother chirped in.

'We both thought it was odd.'

'I mean, why shave all your hair off?'

'Especially in the winter.'

'That's odd.'

'We both think it's odd, so we called you.'

'When was it that you saw him?'

'Day before yesterday.'

'And you're sure it was the same man.'

'I'm sure.'

'Did you get the number plate?'

'No sorry, but it was a ninety-six Jeep Cherokee. Bottle green.'

'Do you see him there often?'

The brothers looked at each other and nodded. 'He's there a lot but at odd times. Never seen him with anyone else.'

'He's always alone.'

'Never waves hello, does he.'

'Never, miserable bastard.'

'I said there was something odd about him.'

'We both said he was not right. Odd, that's what we said.'

Hodge looked from one brother to the other and decided that they didn't get much opportunity to talk to people. 'Listen, I'm really grateful. I'm going to go and take a look around, thanks again.'

****

Simon Barton had a haunted look. His cheeks were sunken, and his skin was pale. His parents flanked him on a beige settee; their eyes darted from Alec to Annie as they walked in and sat down. The family liaison officer, who had called them, remained in the doorway.

'This is Detective Superintendent Ramsay, and this is Detective Annie Jones,' she introduced them. 'Simon, I want you to tell them what you told your mum this morning, okay?'

The teenager nodded almost imperceptibly. He looked to his parents for support and his father nodded and smiled at him. 'It's okay, Si,' he said squeezing his hand. 'Nothing can hurt you anymore.' Annie thought that he didn't look as confident as he sounded but who could blame him. His brother had abducted his child. An aura of guilt surrounded him.

Annie smiled at Simon. 'There's nothing to be worried about,' she assured them. 'We're here to listen to you.'

'Tell the detectives what you told me,' his mother said softly. Annie detected her voice breaking. The emotion was raw, and it was painful. Her eyes were watery but there was anger in them too. Intense anger.

'Take your time, Simon,' Alec encouraged him.

'Uncle Peter took me,' he swallowed hard. His eyes filled up and he buried his head into his mother's chest. Annie looked at Alec and frowned. They waited a few moments for the boy to settle.

'He can't hurt you now,' Annie soothed him. 'Can you tell me where he took you from?'

'I was at the park playing football,' he sniffed.

'Which park?'

'Woodend,' his father answered for him. 'It's just down the road.'

'I need to hear this from Simon.' Annie smiled. The father nodded and blushed. 'It's very important that I hear this in your own words, okay?'

'Yes.' Simon nodded.

'Tell me what happened in the park. Who were you with?'

'I was playing football with my friend James at first.'

'James Goodwin?' Annie glanced at Alec.

'Yes.'

'What happened?'

'We were playing football, then another boy turned up and James said it was his brother, Paul.'

'Had you met Paul before, Simon?'

'No. He lived somewhere else,' Simon mumbled. 'James said he had run away from a home.'

'He was in care like James,' Annie said smiling.

'We didn't know that he knew this boy,' his mother said apologetically. 'If we had known, we never would have let him mix with them.'

'It wasn't their fault,' the father snapped. 'You can't blame them just because they were in care.'

'I'm not blaming them.' She said very quietly. 'I'm blaming your brother.' She glared at him and Annie could feel the tension between them.

'That's why I didn't tell you that he was my friend,' Simon groaned. 'I'm sorry, mum.'

'You don't have to be sorry,' she held him tightly.

'Tell me what happened when Paul turned up, Simon.'

'He had some money and a bottle of beer.' Simon blushed. 'He gave us a sip, but I didn't like it much.' He paused as if he was worried about continuing. 'He said a man in the park had given him some money and the beer.'

'Then what?' Annie coaxed.

'Paul said that he could get some more from the man that he had met. He said that the man had a bottle of cider that we could have.' He seemed to be thinking about his words. 'I didn't want to go. I told James that he shouldn't go but they said that I was a big girl if I didn't.' He shook his head. 'I wouldn't go and so they walked off down the woodland trail. I played with the ball on my own for a bit but then I got bored of waiting for them.' He swallowed hard and looked at his father. 'I followed them, but I couldn't find them at first, so I turned back to come home.' He stopped and put his hands over his eyes. Tears leaked between his fingers and he leaned further into his mother. Annie waited for the moment to pass. 'Then I heard them shouting. Paul was swearing at someone. I ran through the bushes to see what was happening and I could see a man holding them around the neck. They couldn't get away.' The sobbing began again.

'I know how hard this is,' Annie said calmly. 'You're doing very well. Take your time.' She waited a minute. 'Did you recognise the man?'

'No,' Simon said wiping his nose.

'What happened next?'

'There was a van,' he said between the sobs. 'The man dragged them to the side door. I ran and shouted for him to stop but he wouldn't. Then the door slid open and Uncle Peter was inside the van!' Simon curled up, his knees against his chest. 'He saw me and chased me!' The boy became hysterical, his sobbing heartbreaking to listen to.

'Can we leave it there for now?' his father asked. Tears welled in his eyes. 'I don't think he's in any fit state to carry on.'

'Of course.' Annie nodded. 'Can I have a word with you alone, Dana?' Annie said softly to the family liaison officer. She turned to the parents and smiled. 'If he says anything new, please call me immediately.' They nodded and hugged their child. 'Thanks for your time. Good luck.'

'Thank you,' they said together.

284

'Good luck.' Alec smiled and followed Annie out of the room.

'Let's go to the car,' Annie said opening the front door. They walked down the path and climbed into her Audi. Annie felt shell shocked by what they'd heard. 'Did you hear the full version when he was speaking to his mother, Dana?'

'Yes.' Dana sighed. 'He said that they were tied up, gagged, and blindfolded. Apparently, there was a lot of arguing between the uncle and the other man because Simon was there.' She paused. 'He heard them talking about killing him. They were driven for a long time; Simon couldn't say how long and then they were separated. He was kept blindfolded, but he thinks that the uncle fed him a few times before he was moved.'

'Did he say if Barton hurt him?'

'He said he didn't, but he said that he could hear the other boys being hurt. He wouldn't expand. He just shut down when I asked him.'

'Did he say how he got to Ryder's villa?'

'No. He was drugged and woke up in a cage.' She shook her head. 'Ryder told him that he was looking after him for a friend.'

'Jesus!' Alec sighed. 'The poor kid.'

'He was lucky compared to what happened to Paul and James Goodwin.' Annie added. 'What did he say about when Barton turned up in Spain?'

'Not much. Barton told him to keep his mouth shut or he would come and find him. He's still traumatised.'

'The lying bastard did it all along!' Annie looked at Alec and banged the steering wheel with her fist. 'He's been playing games from day one and he's made fools of us.'

'How much of what Harris claimed is true?' Alec sighed. 'Was he telling the truth about Barton setting him up?' Annie didn't know the answer yet, but she felt sick inside.

****

Annie felt rough. The night before, it had taken three bottles of Shiraz to numb the feeling of being stupid and now she was suffering. It had been a pointless exercise. Today, she still felt stupid, but she felt ill too. The breeze on her skin was refreshing but it couldn't shift the cobwebs from inside her head. The police line was two hundred metres from the factory unit and as frustrating as it was, she had no desire to enter the building until the Bomb Squad were convinced that there were no more devices.

'You look rough,' Alec said as he approached. 'Did you go home and do what I did?'

'Looking at your eyes.' Annie nodded and smiled. 'I think that's a yes.'

'One bottle or two?'

'Three and a bit.'

'Fair play to you,' Alec tipped his fingers to his head in mock salute. 'Just a 'bit' more than I did.'

'Guv!' Stirling shouted them from the comms van. 'We're clear to go in.' Alec nodded and they walked through the cordon. Stirling joined them as they approached the unit and they were greeted by a Bomb Squad officer.

'You're clear now,' he said and gestured with a thumb up. 'The place was rigged to blow. Three different devices, one on the door, one in a side room and one attached to a refrigerator.'

'Sounds like we've hit the jackpot,' Stirling said as they stepped inside.

Annie pointed to the nearest vehicle. 'Jackie Webb's Mercedes.' She shook her head and kicked herself inside. The unit was L-shaped with a vaulted roof. There were three vehicles including the Merc and Annie walked around them. She looked into a small anteroom and cringed at the sight. Shackles hung from the wall and the floor was stained beneath them. Her imagination filled in the blanks as she moved on. She spotted a desk against the wall to her left. As she neared it, she saw a latex glove inside a clear plastic container. It was marked with 'Harris'. Next to it was a stack of sample sheets, each wrapped in plastic to preserve the imprints on them. A set of craft tools and a selection of adhesives were near them.

'Barton was crafting fingerprints,' Annie said loudly. She shook her head and felt her heart sink as she studied the desk. The Bomb Squad had left the drawers open after checking it over. Annie stared inside at velvet trays, which held gold and silver rings. Each one was labelled and dated. She let out a loud sigh as she thought about the trophies that they'd found in the grave. Barton had planted them and then played her to find them. He had manipulated her like a puppeteer with his hand up her backside. Her stomach knotted in anger.

'Annie,' Alec shouted. She shivered as she walked over to where he was stood. 'Take a look,' he said stepping back from the refrigerator. Annie looked at packets and sample jars and she leaned close enough to read the small labels. Head hair; blood; semen; skin; fingernails clippings; used condom; pubic hair.

'Harris's?' she asked herself in a whisper.

'Must be,' Alec answered quietly.

'Everything we had was there because he gave it to us.' She sighed.

'Not everything,' Alec patted her shoulder. 'Harris was a sick rapist. Barton spotted that and used it to his own advantage.'

'Just to prove how clever he could be?'

'More likely to torture Harris mentally.' Alec shrugged. 'And to prove to himself and us how evidence can be manipulated.'

'Think about it,' Stirling said looking over her shoulder. 'It's the ultimate nightmare for a criminal. Knowing the police have concrete evidence to nail you to a crime, yet you know that you didn't do it. Imagine how that would feel when they slammed the cell door closed.'

'Can't say I'll lose any sleep over it.' Annie nodded and shrugged. She couldn't disagree with him, but she had no sympathy for Harris. 'Justice comes in many forms. As long as it comes, I'm not too fussy how it happens.'

'I want to be there when Barton when gets his,' Stirling grumbled. 'The bastard has led us a merry dance indeed.'

'What I wouldn't give to see that happen,' Annie agreed although she doubted that she would.

****

He finished his whisky in one gulp and felt it burn his gullet as it went down. Calling it whisky was an affront to every malt on the planet. It was made locally and would have fit into the firewater category of spirits. He could feel his head spinning and the voices around him were becoming garbled echoes. Their black faces leered at him from the stools along the bar; huge smiles seemed to melt into one. They were friendly enough but there was a sense of danger beneath the smiles. Each time he wandered around the back to the ditch, which they called the toilet, he kept one hand on his knife. The roof of the bar was made from thatched reeds but there were no walls. He could hear the sea lapping at the shore but there were no lights on the beach. The sound of the waves was reassuring but he couldn't see it. Beyond the beach bar it was pitch-black. There were no lights on the narrow mud roads, which hugged the coast. He gripped the arms of the chair and pushed himself up. Dizziness rocked him again and he had to close his eyes until it faded.

'Are you leaving already?' The barman grinned. His white shirt was open to the chest, revealing a chiselled black chest. Dark sweat patches were spreading beneath his arms. 'Have another whisky!' The men at the bar jeered and encouraged him but he had had too much. Way too much. He knew that they didn't want him to leave because he had been buying all the drinks for the last few hours. They were less likely to mug him if he shared his wealth freely. Not that it was much money to him. They were poor locals. A round of drinks was a day's wages to them.

'I need to go,' he bumbled.

'Tomorrow, we see you?' the barman called.

'Yes, tomorrow.' His voice was thick and slurred. He staggered across the bar towards the Jeep. The door was unlocked, and he wrenched it open and climbed in. He knew that there would be no police around. When the sun went down, the Gambian police retreated to their stations in the towns. After dark, the streets were too dangerous, even for the police.

Barton fumbled for the keys and started the engine. He crunched the gearbox but eventually found first and the Jeep lurched forward into the night. 'Shit,' he mumbled when he realised that he couldn't see. 'Put your fucking lights on,' he mumbled to himself. The headlights flicked on and illuminated the road. Swarms of insects hurtled towards his windscreen and splattered on the glass. As long as he kept the sea on his left, he knew that he would eventually reach his hotel. It was a half hour trundle along the narrow-pitted roads, where he wouldn't be able to get out of third gear. Deep ruts had been carved into the red mud by passing traffic and tropical rainstorms. He couldn't stop the vehicle from lurching from one side to the other. The rocking sensation made him feel sick. He could feel the acidic whisky rising and he tasted thick yellow bile at the back of his throat. He retched and felt hot sticky vomit landing on his crotch. The smell reached him and made him vomit again. He felt the goo landing on his feet and dribbling between his toes. It made his flip-flops tacky and uncomfortable. His stomach retched again, and he heard the bile splatter in the foot well. He had no idea how many times he was sick. His focus was keeping the Jeep on the track. He had been driving for over forty minutes when he realised that he hadn't reached the hotel.

Barton pulled in and looked around. There was no sign of the coast, just jungle on either side of the road. He swore beneath his breath and found first gear again. He checked his watch but didn't know how long he had been driving for. The engine roared and the Jeep lurched forward at speed. He gripped the steering wheel tightly as he pushed the vehicle through the gears. The ruts became deeper and the Jeep bounced up and down violently as he encountered a series of potholes. Suddenly, the mud track ended, and he was faced with a wall of vegetation. The front wheel hit a large rock. He felt the vehicle veer to the right, and he yanked the wheel in the opposite direction. His momentum was too great, and he hit the trees at speed. The Jeep broke through the undergrowth and careered over the edge of a ravine. Barton was thrown about like a leaf in a wind tunnel as it tumbled and somersaulted down the rocks and through the tree canopy into the valley below. It didn't stop until it landed on its roof at the bottom.

When he came to, Barton was struggling to understand what had happened. The sun was up, and he could see himself in the rear-view mirror. When you look in the mirror, what looks back at you? He could see bone protruding from his left thigh and his right arm appeared to have three elbows, each bent in a different direction. His back was twisted at an acute angle and a piece of metal had punctured his torso from the kidney to his right hip. The whisky was masking some of the pain but not much. As his brain calculated the extent of his injuries, it suddenly realised the amount of agony he should be in and he was hit by a wall of pain. He opened his mouth and screamed but there was no one to hear him. All those years of hunting and killing his prey, flashed through his mind. He was too intelligent to be caught, too clever to die like this. He had spent months learning ancient scripts to make it possible for the police to track his murders abroad so that he could bask in the glow of his victims' agony. He wanted the credit for killing them but only when he was ready to claim it. His intelligence was supreme as was his addiction to pain. Other peoples' pain. But now he was wallowing in a sea of agony. His own. As the agony increased, so did his desperate attempts to escape the wreck. The more he moved, the more intense the pain became. At night, the insects and rodents came to feed. They didn't care that their meal was still twitching. His screams echoed off the walls of the ravine for three days before his heart finally gave up.

Printed in Great Britain
by Amazon

52599629R00173